In the Land of Silence

In the Land of Silence

Jesús Urzagasti

Translated from the Spanish by
Kay Pritchett

The University of Arkansas Press   Fayetteville   1994

We would like to acknowledge the role of Partners of America and James Whitehead in bringing this work to the English-speaking public.

First published by Hisbol in 1987
as *En el país del silencio*
Copyright 1987 by Jesús Urzagasti
Translation copyright 1994 by the Board of
Trustees of the University of Arkansas
All rights reserved
Manufactured in the United States of America
98 97 96 95 94   5 4 3 2 1

Designed by Gail Carter

⊗ The paper used in this publication meets the minimum requirements of the American National Standard for Permanence of paper for Printed Materials Z39. 48-1984.

Library of Congress Cataloging-in-Publication Data

Urzagasti, Jesús, 1941–
   [En el país del silencio. English]
   In the land of silence / by Jesús Urzagasti:
  translated from the Spanish by Kay Pritchett.
      p. cm.
   ISBN 1-55728-367-2 (alk. paper). —
   ISBN 1-55728-373-7 (pbk. : alk. paper)
   I. Pritchett, Kay, 1946–   . II. Title.
PQ7820.U7E513   1994   94-34498
863—dc20   CIP

To Boscaferro,
the constructor

Contents

Notebook Number 1

The Dead Man

The somnambulant Urundel *speaks.*   3

Jursafú

From the astral house of a Callawaya, I see the world full of hills and hollows.

7

The Other

In spite of my loneliness, I can remedy myself in dreams.   9

Jursafú

The only important news, the news of our own death, we'll never read in the newspaper.   11

The Other

Life said to me: I love you. Then I asked it for a mule and its foal.   13

Jursafú

I'm a dull, colorless translation of the beginning. But I presume, at any rate, to read that translation as if I were predicting my own outcome. The fruit is prefigured in the seed.   16

The Other

It would be beautiful if one didn't forget. But remembering is like cooking, and if you risk it, you may get blacker than an old pot.   22

Jursafú

Our fellow creature is like a mirror of our invulnerable country.

27

Notebook Number 2

The Other as the Dead Man Sees Him

All of these things lose importance and eventually become insignificant to those who obey a tradition, hold a patrimony, and, out of homage to the law, do not change it or ever question if such homage is due.

35

Jursafú as the Other Sees Him

Because he went away, he began to remember like a person who is awake but talked as if he were walking in his sleep. Because we must go away to become conscious of the language we speak, the language that redeems us.

47

The Dead Man as Jursafú Sees Him

In the Andean city, ocean of rock and transparency, the place where the dead and sages inhabit a world finished off in full splendor.

61

Notebook Number 3

Jursafú as the Dead Man Sees Him

One travels with what one is, unburdened of pointless weight. God grant that the trip enrich but not pervert you.

89

The Other as Jursafú Sees Him

Working is resting on oneself rather than upon the backs of others.

118

The Dead Man as the Other Sees Him

"We are the only examples of the impossible, and that is why love delights in torturing us," said a careworn man. Then Love said to the Devil, "Don't go easy on me because I'm not going to go easy on you."

141

Notebook Number 4

The Other and Jursafú
as the Dead Man Sees Them

You can see, I can hear; I speak, you listen; you dream, I remember; I write, you read; you sing, I'm the suffering for which you sing; I act, you are pure, trembling nostalgia. And that's the way it is and will be indefinitely, until we reach the place where destiny is taking us before hurling us off a cliff.   173

Jursafú and the Dead Man
as the Other Sees Them

God speaks to human beings by way of silence. Humans speak to God through the broad foreboding of death. A vast, cordial dialogue is appropriate to human beings. Also anger, which is common to beings that move from one place to another. It is impossible to imagine anger between immobile things such as trees and rocks. Could this be why people adore inanimate things even before God? Drawn by nostalgia for a world without hate, they sacrifice the White Llama of their tribe to obtain the hero, a god made to their own size and with whom they can communicate through mindful reverence.   241

The Other and the Dead Man
as Jursafú Sees Them

My head is a broad, stony ground; those who go away do not return, and those who are due to come do not arrive. That is why I am leaving: I do not pray to saints who perform no miracles.   306

Notebook Number 5

The Dead Man

The circle is mortal for the profane. But I march in, eyes closed and facing life.
     343

Translator's Introduction

Urzagasti's birthplace, Tarija, the smallest of Bolivia's nine states, is situated at the country's southern tip, bordering Argentina on the south and Paraguay on the east. Its mountainous western zone, famous for its fertile basins dotted with vineyards, olive groves, and fruit orchards, contains most of the state's largely indigenous population. Its eastern zone, by contrast, is a sparsely settled plain covered in scrub forest and dry savanna but where during the wetter months drainage from rain and snow attracts flocks of wading birds. Between this zone, which lies within the Gran Chaco, and the eastern range of the Andes, stretches a narrow band of forest from Santa Cruz southward into Argentina. These varied Tarijan landscapes with their equally diverse flora and fauna, together with La Paz and the mystical, wind-swept high plain, the Altiplano, provide the setting for Urzagasti's novel and represent, in geographical terms, the author's "land of silence."

An ability to perceive the primordial truths concealed in this native ambiance lies at the core of Urzagasti's talent as a narrator. A journalist, poet, and author of a short novel *Tirinea* (1969), with *En el país del silencio* (1987) he develops a mature style marked by a synthesis of poetic and novelistic techniques and a blending of the indigenous and European voices of his ancestral home. A thoroughly Bolivian persona emerges, one that Urzagasti splits into three: Jursafú, the Other, and the Dead Man. By portraying them as separate entities, he accentuates their interrelatedness, for one character cannot grow without the others nor can any one of them move toward an ultimate goal without the experience and knowledge of the other two.

Jursafú, who comes from a remote part of Tarija, leaves his native province to go to school. After attending college for a year, he drops out and goes to Europe. He returns to Bolivia to look for work in various towns and cities, and eventually, having failed to make a meaningful life for himself, returns to his primordial roots by seeking out a former lover, Orana. As he moves about from one place to another, he carries with him the silence and solitude of his youth.

Jursafú, the only visible one of the three, keeps constant company with the Other and the Dead Man. The Other, tied to the wisdom of Jursafú's indigenous heritage, signifies *otherness* in the sense of that which is not European. He also shows a special attachment to the dream world, the unconscious; speaking of dreams, he intimates, "Usually we must lie down to dream, in the definitive position, the one we die in, defenseless, a test of our faith in the invisible Other who saturates us with his symbols." The Dead Man, also of uncertain identity, appears to embody Jursafú's related-ness to death. Early in the novel Jursafú says, "I have seen death so often that I see myself as dead, still full of memories, and with my hand stretched out toward the unknown."

Like a circle, this amazing story begins and ends in the same place and on the same day. A day of violence in La Paz, December 31, 1980, is emblematic, even apocalyptic for Jursafú, who, roaming the streets, sorts through the events of his life. But with an eye to the future, he is keenly aware of the close of one decade and the beginning of another—the penultimate in the second millennium. His reminiscences transport us to a mysterious, sometimes treacherous world where astonishing truths are placed within our grasp. These humble revelations of a silent, unfamiliar land, fill us with wonderment for a country which, before we begin to read, may be little more to us than a lyrical sounding word, Bolivia.

K. P.

February 10, 1994

Notebook Number 1

The Dead Man

The somnambulant Urundel *speaks.*

At midnight on December 31, 1980, a man gave three soft but decisive knocks on a door illuminated by the moon. And the woman, lost in thought, heard the knocks and understood that the hour had come.

She hesitated for a long time, or so she thought. Actually, her indecision had lasted only an instant. She rose to her feet, governed by something that lay beyond her domain, beyond her daily concerns. She put on a thin nightgown and began to walk in the darkness, not knowing if she was moving in a dream or had begun to live out some frightening reality.

She slid back the bolt and opened the door halfway.

The man, who had lived some forty years on the earth, walked into the living room. The moon and the wind from the deserted streets entered with him; the wind bore a vegetable smell inhaled by the sleeping inhabitants of the town.

The woman came from a ruined land but went out with ageless beauty toward the tremulous night. Serenaded by the ambiguity of the hour, she tried to say something, but the man closed her lips with a passionate kiss, and once the shock had passed she responded with similar intensity. The manly breathing of her unexpected visitor hadn't changed.

The man pressed her against his body and, like an animal accustomed to danger, sensed her trembling. The visitor pulled her toward the door and felt in darkness for the bolt. She didn't pull away but turned the key three times in the lock. "So no one can get in," the man thought. "So he can never go away again," the woman decided.

"You were born to come to me, and I, to wait for you," she said, drawing pictures with her fingers on his broad shoulders.

The man breathed unsteadily in the night, like a fugitive or a redeemer. In spite of his tiredness, caused by the deserted roads, he arrived ready to traverse the ageless body of the woman; he warned her of his right to enter again the private universe and climbed upon her, pressing her against his sex and attending with studied slowness the rhythm of an imaginary rumba. She didn't feel alone anymore. She tried to follow the rhythm of the nostalgic dance and allowed herself finally to be carried where the visitor led, with intentions that could no longer be corrected and that she no longer wished to correct. Her desire had never died; perhaps she had been waiting for him all along, naked, a gift on illuminated ground.

The man kissed her passionately, his eyes open, watching the sleepy face of the woman, sensual beauty given up to the warmth of his mouth, lovely, naked breasts under the open gown. He slid along the silky garment, scratching the woman with his skin, holding her motionless and trembling, defenseless at the edge of an unforeseen land.

The man led her away and she allowed herself to be led. They walked arm in arm toward the bed which waited in silence, transformed into a landscape of trees and rivers melting into unfathomable light.

In darkness they continued searching until the intimacy of night began to glow, like a secret shared by the entire sleeping village: the phallus opened a passage through the soft brush of hair and penetrated the damp, throbbing vagina. The woman knew for sure that a treasure had been returned to her unsteady existence and sighed without a shadow of reproach. Her body was filled by a man who had despoiled her the instant she saw his brown face and found it beautiful, master of a terrestrial beauty very close to death.

The man mounted her and she became subdued. After a few intense moments, when silence—not words—was called for, the man's pressure and the woman's coy response, their bodies were transformed into docile, animal-like accomplices of a harmonious movement as if their rhythm might foretell either happiness or separation. He never stopped kissing her large breasts and penetrated softly, deeply, opening her completely with his powerful weapon, deaf to her pleading. In the intimate space of night glowing with stars of a forgotten sky, the woman recognized the power of the man who held her in his grasp. Her only outlet was a moan, muffled by the modesty of defeat; and she broke her decorum, convinced of approaching victory. Shocking the sleeping villagers, she lifted herself up by her companion's strong neck and kissing it, reached her first orgasm.

Attuned to the deserted roads, the nocturnal air inhaled by the sleeping villagers, the man with the unsteady breathing came and went with his untiring body covering the beautiful woman with movement that emerged from the light and returned to the shadows; he deserved to be in the light as he moved over her, without coming out of her burning body; he spent his strength, assailing her from the penumbra. They were immersed in a reality too familiar to be recalled. As if having lost his way in silky, luxuriant vegetation, the man pressed forward in search of a lost light, and the woman sought calm and refuge in the glow of her own astonishment. But passing through the penumbra, her silence turned to alarm, awaking the sleeping people of the village.

They had erased the final limits and had become a secret shared in darkness. Astride him, she offered him her breasts and, smiling, received the penis she knew well. Suddenly they decided to fight as if they were enemies, not letting up for a second, but then became reconciled to celebrate the triumph of their re-encounter or the jubilee of fitting one inside the other. They were panting like lost creatures on the dark limits of a new year, and the woman kissed him with unreined passion, as at the beginning of her life, when she handed herself without hesitation to a loving, coughing, consumptive stranger. The woman was from a ruined land but went out with ageless beauty, seeing her passionate visitor trembling and growing larger, like some sacred animal. Her eyes grew more beautiful with an approaching melancholy, and she began to look for honey in a desolate landscape, feeling the first spurt of semen and clenching the bristled locks of her lover's hair to keep from sliding into the abyss of her own being. Not slipping away, she closed her eyes and gave herself definitively to the man with the unsteady breathing, who had found in the woman's stone bed a tomb to take his rest. They lay holding each other like the perfect couple in the unequal geography of a vulnerable night, like warm lovers sleeping on the naked earth.

Along the deserted roads, dogs were barking; the dead whispered; shades passed inebriated with memories; the broad land throbbed, armored by the force of its mystery. Unexpectedly, the discordant sounds of silence came to a halt, astonished by voices of a happy time that miraculously came to life. When the woman was lightly sleeping, the man went away, walking—or believing that he walked—along a path through the middle of the awakened town, feeling his way along the route of eternity, like a trembling image of the collective memory. He went away as one goes from a dream, noiselessly, slipping into the crust of reality. After hearing brief, violent cross-fire, he could still see an explosion on the borderlands of his country.

His body breathed unsteadily for forty years and now is a cadaver among many. They have just died in an unequal battle and lie silent and irreconcilable in a ravine lost in the night near the bank of a blindly flowing river, at the edge of a sound so pleasant and soft that it appears to be the prelude to an unending dream rather than a nightmare.

The man came to the world to search for Orana amid brambles of loneliness. He was born in a remote area of Bolivia and arrived in La Paz some twenty years ago, laden with illusions, unaware that his dreams would be destroyed in the Andean capital. His story holds no interest except for the unmysterious solitude he carried with him and the terrestrial silence that was never hostile toward him.

In the distance the lights of miserable villages emerge, places he can no longer see. The sound of isolated gunfire increases with the anger of rebellion. To the rattle of machine-gun fire, the multitude responds with shotguns. The man believed that his reality was no longer clouded by anything. By breathing the most intense silence in the joyful land of human beings, he had come to know true life. "But dying isn't easy," he said. "In any language, no matter how superficial, it is difficult to grow weak, and even more so in a country such as this, which gathers up the sums of many human histories."

Watching the stars of a remote sky, he allowed the tension of midnight to retreat. A gentle rain seemed to fall, or perhaps it was only a warm breeze from the past, the immemorial dawn where blurred images of ghosts often appeared.

The man tossed in bed and his senses perceived the warmth of Orana's body, the lovely dark head of hair, and the unnameable face. The woman came from a world in ruins but miraculously emerged with ageless beauty in the resplendent land. Intense suffering, now far away, had heightened her beauty with muted signs of triumph.

Jursafú

From the astral house of a Callawaya, I see the world full of hills and hollows.

I have a premonition that someone is being tortured tonight, the last night of 1980, while sporadic bursts of gunfire alter the silence of Bolivia. For that particular person it is too late. I imagine him facing a wall and darkness, bidding farewell to the world he loved, where he wasn't strong enough to oppose the greatest outrage: oppression carried out in the name of the spirit. When I die my feeble wisdom will be truncated, my suffocation at the deaths of others, at the hoarse languor, will be resuscitated on every deserted street. La Paz is a city ruled by terror, but here lies my fate: to fight blindly with sterile destiny. Nonetheless, there is a light that does not belong to me, that is common property, like the air that one breathes only to put it back into circulation. Those who wish to keep what belongs to all people die. I don't want to die. But I've seen death so often that I see myself as dead, still full of memories, and with my hand stretched out toward the unknown. When I was a child, I saw an Indian put to death. I don't know if he was Guarani or Chaco since my memory deprives me of such exactness, though not of the man's image. He was a tall aborigine with a cleft chin; his was a beautiful destiny. He wouldn't have given up his hoe for anything in the world, and carrying it on his shoulder, he walked through the streets of his village, which for him was like the village each of us carries in our souls. Any fortuneteller might have known with a throw of the dice that this stranger would not last for long: he was a stranger in a land that had always been his, he had been shut out because he couldn't speak the patron's language. One afternoon the Indian killed the patron, for no good reason according to the victim's next of kin. Then, following his instinct, the Indian ran into the nearby forest. But Gabino Castillo, the dead man's only living relative, soon found him, and civil guards brought him back with a rope tied around his hands. Without saying a word, the Indian allowed them to tie him up, and, stunned, waited for the dead man's brother to fire a bullet into the back of his neck. The crime I saw avenged had been committed by a man who was silence and nothing more, from the top of his head to the bottoms of his feet. They performed a shameful thing in order to conquer one man's madness, a man who knew that he wouldn't be listened to and therefore chose to proceed on his own. But tonight he has been killed, and the matter has been put to rest. If thought is the supreme energy that leads us toward death, why must we kill him? This is what I ask myself as I walk along the road, vexed by memories of this indelible unreality, like so many fireflies buzzing around my head.

The Other

In spite of my loneliness, I can remedy myself in dreams.

Usually we must lie down to dream, in the definitive position, the one we die in, defenseless, a test of our faith in the invisible Other who saturates us with his symbols.

In this land, we all dream each other. For example, people who don't even know me have dreamed me; nor have I hung back, and I have allowed myself the luxury of dreaming people I've never seen and who serve no earthly purpose in my life. Maybe that's why I like to dream. It's a way to make friends with other people, and these circumstantial relationships depend to a certain extent on our own will, which is often proud. There are no hybrid roses in this business; I mean you can't predict ahead of time exactly what you're going to get. And if you end up with a dandelion, well, it's because there's no telling what the one in charge in that world holds in store for us. When you close your eyes, prepare to suffer the consequences.

I find dreaming to be quite pleasant, but that doesn't mean that I'm dependent on this worthiest of pastimes. In fact, for long intervals I don't dream at all; or the opposite, I dream quite a lot at certain times, vague dreams with no sudden jolts. It's not my other life; it's my real life. That's why they call me the Other, with irony that I toss around and fling back at them like a hot coal.

In the daylight, people stroll about as if nothing was happening, presuming that their five—or twelve—senses are in good working order. But most people walk in darkness, never seeing the important things, and on top of that, never dreaming. It's not just an accident, of course; because if you can't see in the daylight, how can you expect to see in the dark world of night? It is true that in the ambit of dreams, the senses, for good or bad, can't do anything, but sometimes they benefit from the body's complete attention to the wholeness of the universe. If the senses had eyebrows, they would surely raise them, but since they don't, they must simply *be* amazement without a face or a tuft of hair.

To continue dreaming, I'd stay on earth as long as possible, but not for any other reason. I've grown fond of dreaming animals and people, fanciful ones, of course. At the start and ever since, their influence on other people's lives has amazed me. For example, in matters of suffering or knowledge, not even Job or Doctor Faustus can aspire to more than they. This is particularly good for disbelievers, people who feel the knocks but learn nothing from them. In spite of the magic that surrounds them, the beings born of dreams have a rustic, polite manner; and if you look them in the eye, they shy away because they are humble, like country people. They know they're not human; yet, like people, they are ephemeral. They are happy in their own way, and we remember them as emblems of a region more solid than ours, probably, since theirs is invisible. As everyone knows, there isn't any form of matter that doesn't wear out. But invisible things don't wear out in the usual sense. In their roles as characters on a fanciful stage, they keep us company and ask nothing in return. Then in the end, when we're worn to a nub, we too become dreams and take our places in the fabulous dream catalogue.

Jursafú

*The only important news, the news of our own death, we'll never read
in the newspaper.*

I work at a newspaper, which is a pretty good indication that my desire
for information isn't what it used to be. I don't care much about details,
especially the ones that interfere with the broader view of things. I suspect we're headed for destruction, drawn as if by a magnet toward a disaster which will wipe out our youthful aspirations. The world smells like
a dead body; and I run toward my destiny with no illusions and only words
for tools, words pawed and rumpled every day, transformed by Satan into
conjurations of a desert. Twenty years remain until the second millennium. My life will never last that long, to that most ominous of figures
marking twenty centuries. I respond without the slightest grimace. I was
condemned from the beginning, at my feverish origin. But what I never
suspected was that the signposts which guide travelers on their way would
disappear from the horizon. The play has ended and the most treacherous animal has reappeared, yawning with the tiredness of many centuries
but still ready to do evil. I don't feel tired, but I'm not in the mood for
jokes, either. When the hour is at hand, I won't move a muscle, terrified
of an approaching storm that can't hurt me in any way. I'm not worried,
but sometimes at night I think the most frightening thoughts. I've just
crossed the boundary into the world of things never spoken, where I discovered who I am and where I'm going. Goaded on by the wisdom of the
ages, I move swiftly toward my destiny. My job is my job, and I do it as I
should; nothing more, nothing less. Why? Maybe it's because I'm haunted
by something a dead friend once said to me: "The only important news,

the news of our own death, we'll never read in the newspaper." It made me sick but didn't kill me. It made me immune to everything I read. I don't even give it a thought. I am a souvenir of communication. Between stupid jokes and long faces, I attend the desanctification of language, a rare occurrence in other ages. I have no idea who will survive this mortal challenge. I hear tell that papers and documents are being burned, some of them insignificant, others important. I won't escape the bonfire; I'm sure of that. This is nothing new. But I will save the ancient symbol, the allegory of having been alive.

In this besieged city, paradoxically called "La Paz," terrible things have happened: murders, tortures, terror. Every day the stench of an animal rotting in the darkness becomes more intolerable. We accept the rot and hope that it will become the seed of a luminous day. "That's not rain you hear," says a voice from the memory. I quickly answer, "I see the wet trees and hear the bolts of thunder." My stubbornness comes from having been trained in the lost province of certainties to confront the hallucination of life in a different way; in other words, from birth I was schooled in the highest form of useless work—living. I myself am a modest example of the impossible; I cleave through the "present" as a witness who cannot be bribed. Someday my limbs will grow tired and my body will be sucked into the whirlpool of light or glass. I still haven't thrown up my hands or tossed myself onto the junk pile, though many of my friends have deserted this uncertain adventure, one that, paradoxically, is basic to life. They've departed on their own or been forced to leave. So, those are the facts; and anyone who gets involved shouldn't be alarmed to find me waking up lost, half dazed in this broad land of nostalgia.

The Other

Life said to me: I love you. Then I asked it for a mule and its foal.

Why not ask the rock what it has dreamed for thousands of years? Why not question the dream about the secret gauze that separates it from reality and makes it unreal? I have no need to ask these questions, since after dedicating so much time to interrogation, I became a question myself and thus spared myself the anxiety of the questioner; in other words, I have managed to draw a line between myself—illustrious stranger—and the famous depression which is the source of metaphysics. For precaution's sake, I've become well-informed, with craftiness to spare—not when I confront the humble rock, but when I find myself immersed at noonday, at the precise moment when shadows disappear, the ones that serve to guide us, the dark copy which, with the sun's aid, we project upon the ground. It's common knowledge that at noonday the tricks we learn disappear, outshone by the talents we've always carried in our hearts.

The rock is a final, hardened dream. And therefore, it is a full miracle. It has no notion of what it is or what it means to others; but its clarity is more dreadful than any other form of human knowledge: it should suffice to note how rocks are easily lost and then found; they have such patience that by comparison, time would seem immoderate and space, unruly. The rock is the only idea which has become incarnate—it would be erroneous to call it "concrete"—and therefore seems to be a divine message if not a material form of the divine: a distant, ultimate objective, yet strangely enough, it is found both under our very noses and at distances so great that it emits rays of light. On the earth it causes us to stumble, and in its celestial state it produces the kinds of spiritual somersaults that humans fervently strive for. In the first instance, it causes us to become harder and more cunning; in the second—when it leads us toward the kingdom of poetry—it polishes our illusions and shows us who we are—vile creatures, easily replaced. A fellow countryman, seduced by legend, has aptly described the relationship that exists between the rock which causes one to stumble and the celestial memory, "What we learn from books, we remember; what hard knocks teach us, we never forget." And I might as well add my two cents' worth, "We each get the memory we deserve."

As for my part, I must confess that I've always wanted to be a rock's apprentice: it's the only bit of humility I feel beating in my chest. But since nature accepts me the way I am, I wouldn't dare mention it, even when I'm alone with the wind, the mountains, and the trees—even less when I find myself surrounded by silence. It never enters my brain, or any other part, for that matter. But when I'm alone, I religiously and unceremoniously prepare myself for the uncertainty of waking up either alive or dead. I have no idea what saves me, but in the morning I wake up smiling, my eyes beaming with gratitude.

I'm not a rock yet, but I still carry the magic of my first dream in my heart, a map with a vague, glowing outline of the ultimate. An ending that only a sketch of a stomach devouring itself can illustrate.

My life is the image of nostalgia. What existed before me was ungovernable nostalgia; and nameless besides. It became incarnate in me; I didn't ask why or how. I don't know how old I was when I first realized that I was wrapped in luminous shadows and surrounded by a holy wood that still accompanies me with its prickly gentleness. That afternoon the old folks began to arrive, and I was ill. So they spread out in the forest as usual, leaving me behind in an adobe house, possessed by a gentle, unknown fever and drenched with sweat. If some evil genie had flattened me, I wouldn't have shown any sign of pain; but that wasn't what I felt when I fell asleep and suddenly saw thousands of little yellow dots on the ceiling and a ghost wearing a big hat and making faces at me; and, terrified as I was, he forced me to share the space where he presided as the all-powerful, though momentary, judge.

The world was full of smiles and innocent jokes, but that time no one talked sonorously on the patio. I haven't forgotten; I remember. The first dream that I pulled from the shadows illuminated the day's uncertain steps, and that is how I obtained the images that would put my memory in motion, and now—with a body marked by copious activities—I traverse the past and, in a certain way, cross into the future.

I stopped being a completely disorderly creature, but the apparition of the supernatural among waking people arrived many years later. The natural magic of dreams was the precursor to the luminous irruption into the daytime universe; and in the final analysis, if there is a difference at all between one and the other, each person must discover it in his or her own way.

I'm surprised to find myself addressing for the umpteenth time a subject that doesn't affect me in the least—not profoundly or even superficially—for the simple reason that this kind of scar cannot be removed. I was playing with some of my friends on the moonlit patio at school, when suddenly they all disappeared except Salomón and the one speaking or remembering. Salomón thought that he could run away from me by darting into one of the classrooms; I ran behind him, but the person I encountered in no way resembled the boy I was chasing, because in the first desk next to the blackboard, I found a little girl sound asleep, a tired, gentle ghost whose glowing image seemed perturbed by my intrusion. That night a devil visited me in a dream and gave me a long, narrow magazine to read, and that's when I began to tug at the thread that would eventually tie me in knots.

I'm not a sad person or an interpreter of dreams. That is not my condition or occupation. To the contrary, if I listen to the melancholy music inside this skeleton, which I manage to transport rather noiselessly, it is because I'm a specialist at understanding the succinct language of reality. I am aware of this, whether standing in a private garden or watching a bee buzzing around a flower in a solitary wood. These two dreams are the pivot points on my map of the heavens. And now that I have deciphered their mysterious signs, the only remaining task is to read the message. Understanding it is another matter. "There are no roads; we make them as we travel," some mediocre person once said. In my opinion, if you want to read dreams you have to live; or to put it another way, you must learn to read at night what the night composes during the day. That's why it's the same as asking life for a mule and its foal.

Jursafú

I'm a dull, colorless translation of the beginning. But I presume, at any rate, to read that translation as if I were predicting my own outcome. The fruit is prefigured in the seed.

For years I was naive and wildly ambitious. That's how I ceased to be sympathetic to human discourse. The world is full of sounds emitted randomly and unceasingly by the featherless biped. And the fresh sounds of nature, vanished from the earth, linger only in the memory. This is a warning, and I, not my fellow creatures, should be the first to heed it. I no longer feel at home with words. I'm like a caged parrot. But the promise of the word's counterpoint keeps me going. I guess it's superfluous to add that I am silence incarnate.

I used to talk to my friend Adrián—he was a geologist—about many things, trying to figure out what could motivate people to live in harmony with one another. That was in 1966. One afternoon we were listening to a very moving speech: "The demands for social change must come from the working class, and the tool of the oppressed is revolution." Tonight, in 1980, my friend is dead—he fought with the guerrillas at Teoponte. The masses are still oppressed. And here I am, alive, without my friend, and with all these meaningless, powerless words swarming around my head. So it's not just because I'm bored that I say, "I've ceased to be sympathetic to human discourse." And to make matters worse, I wouldn't lift a finger to change any of it. Why should I? So this stupid world could knock my block off? Now you see why I say I'm like a caged parrot.

I don't take anything for granted; I stick to the facts—what I see, smell, and touch; and if I sometimes play dumb, it's because I'd rather not get mixed up in it; I'm as tempted as the next person, though I'm just a guy from dreamland. It's obvious. Some people never change in the least, as if the world weren't going to change either. I'm not amused. Some people are the way they are because that's the way their families taught them to be. I know that, and maybe that's what saves me.

My ignorance means more to me now than gold. I should have learned that years ago, before it was too late. But it is too late, thanks to a few things that have happened. It's not that I know more than anybody else. If it's me we're talking about, I'm just a poor sucker trying to straddle two worlds and fend off what I can. That's why my eyes are swollen in the morning and I laugh when people say, "Someone's coming back," as if to say that some folks know everything just because they've run the whole route, when it's as clear as the nose on your face that they only went halfway. Anyone who goes to the end of the line doesn't turn around and come back. They're so far away that you can't reach them, but you can sense them, in the noiseless things in nature, in climates and landscapes that allow the earth to speak. Because the best lesson is the footprint left by accident; and the ones who travel this seductive land—and leave behind their bones but not their souls—learn that lesson well.

Why should I bother with words when I might as well keep silent? You can't be a question unless you look befuddled. But silence has enough blood running through its veins to find answers to all its questions. That's why it sticks to a very simple truth: some are silent by nature, because they're scared or because they're born that way. The only thing we know about them is that they have a great need to talk. Could anyone who never shuts up understand such a paradox? Besides, temporary silence isn't a condition but a kind of delayed action, which some learn so they can identify with the infinite rhythm of organisms, the ones that watch us with their mysterious eyes, that look at us with irony and fear at the same time.

We tend to associate animals with unintelligent human beings. A talkative dimwit is quickly given the nickname of "parrot," a bird that from the point of view of human beings doesn't even know the meaning of ordinary words, much less words that have a double meaning. Actually, you only lose the word's meaning and its music when you don't value its silent truth. And when you stop to compare, you get "shorn," standing by yourself between the walls of the dream, crushed by the nightmare of helplessness; and angry because the fly doesn't listen, the tree doesn't talk, and somewhere on earth someone dreamed that "sociology is the science of hypocrites."

You don't pay attention, and that's the way it goes.

In 1951, a professor from the provinces was teaching his students— besides language, Incan history, and the rudiments of geography and arithmetic—the world's oldest occupation, imitating nature. So the children managed to learn how a potato becomes several potatoes and how to get rid of the darnels that can stop the blossoms from forming. Another professor—who had only watched the parcel of land being cleared—thought that pulling weeds was hard work and useless to boot since the weeds would grow back anyway. "It's logical," he called from his window. That was the first time I'd heard the word "logical"; afterwards, there was a whole "logical" string of them: "logic teaches us," "logically," "it's logical, *hermano*."

But to me, other types of evidence were more appealing. I liked, for example, the idea that we learn about life with our hearts, that the law doesn't make tradition, that the laws of human history are discovered through a full understanding of work that some would consider useless— a fine example of generosity. Because, if the people who pay taxes did what was "logical," the man at the window wouldn't have time for boyish enthusiasm—or anything to eat, for that matter.

By the time the potatoes were ready, I'd learned a new way to use words, by forgetting what they usually meant and allowing them to mean something a little less clear. Years later the new meanings would become more definite. Everywhere I went I would think of these arbitrary, luminous meanings. Children learn to repeat, like parrots, what their families—their most patient conversationalists—remember and pass on. They mimic the words because they want to be able to talk to others without stirring up the world of theory. Later—a lot later, if ever at all—the mystery of the erupting word arrives, and they realize the power it has over others and themselves. How does anything so deranged come about? I can't speak for others, but what happened to me was, first, I learned how to identify qualities which never change, and then to identify the ones that could change suddenly. This discovery provided a constant source of learning.

I'd like to mention the place where I spent my first years on earth, where I saw trees that changed form with a subtle, harmonious slowness. I looked at a straight path and sadly recalled a man who suddenly found himself six feet under; that's where I started listening to the wisdom of my elders who taught me the art of distinguishing between delayed actions and ones that suggest irrevocable absence.

A word is a gift from life, a gift and also a convention that allows us to identify things without getting ourselves mixed up in a lawsuit. But it's also a tradition imposed by the blood of our dead ancestors, whom children revere automatically. The likes and dislikes of the forefathers are inevitably passed on as preferences and prejudices in their descendants. This rudimentary code ends up complicating our lives and confounding our spirits; jokes don't seem funny anymore, and pranks fail to make us laugh.

The stage I've described concerns speech, which is the anteroom to written language. Back then, I was satisfied with empty notebooks. But the happiness I felt when I received my first printed volume, I owe to my uncle Antonio. I still remember that book with its blue cover, the sections separated by rose-colored pages printed with strange Latin words. The first part contained words of common usage, refined by history in a way that only philologists understand. Beyond the thicket of rose-colored pages, the symbols of orientation were found, and then the stumbling blocks of the homo sapiens: names of heroes, rivers, countries, cities, and books paraded through that section with rare splendor. Though, in truth, those pages contained nothing more than the respect we owe the incorrigible past; those terms could change their order but not their meaning. The words from the first part weren't like that: they were an invitation to the future, to a game of lawless invention that only required the apprentice to follow the rules of good taste imposed by the invisible magus.

By obligation and inclination, I began to cleave through an ocean of books, at first frightened but enthusiastic, later fearless and reckless but without the eagerness of youth. At a certain age I began to suspect that there were traps hidden there. Now, after reading nothing for many years, I can ask myself unashamedly, "What is a book?"

Whenever I held a book in my hands, I thought that I heard a voice from some remote place inaccessible to my present. It seemed real, but since it couldn't travel the dunes of time, it found other ways to place itself in the perpetual present of mankind; paradoxically, that voice achieved its goal through the silence of signs. Thomas Rourke, for example, the author of *Bolívar, the Man of Glory,* reached me through the medium of the book.

There are books, nonetheless, that strike like bolts of lightning and are ancient when we first read them. These are the ones that reveal the true nature of human writing, which after all, is nothing more than a presumptuous reply to the earth's unshakable word, or, to take it a step further, to the silence of the cosmos. Whenever I came in contact with these books, I became nostalgic for a dead world and for its failures. At the same time, I understood its occult language, which authors on rare occasions perceive; the idiom that exceeds their best intentions, their worst vanities, and, paradoxically, depicts them accurately, without defaming them pointlessly or attributing more to them than is rightly theirs. These books, the ones that strike like a bolt of lightning, provide a counterweight to some others, those rare ones that illustrate accurately the basic miracle of human language. These scarce tomes—that qualify as Works with a capital *W*—perpetuate the splendor of life (people, with their golden wake of failures, heroic deeds, voyages, and unexpected returns among trees and cities lost in the fog of history); and, simply by their presence, they tell us that the oral tradition, though important, is not enough.

The oral tradition relates to a specific human group, united by a common language. It is a walking marvel, because it polishes and passes on, through many years, crystalline truths or axioms of diverse interpretation. It is the perfect, convincing mixture of events and unattained desires, which can be said of other disciplines, except that the members of the latter proudly deny that this truth applies to them. The oral tradition doesn't have any prima donnas, probably since it's a collective enterprise.

Books are also a tradition, but are universal rather than oral; and, essentially, they are translations. They translate *being* into words and then are translated themselves, as long as they can be poured from one language to another, passing from sieve to sieve until they come to rest upon the pure solidity of the metaphor, provided their temperaments can tolerate such a sifting unharmed.

But all that aside, what can I do with a book that hasn't been translated into my language? I'm left out in the cold, to put it mildly—lost, befuddled, in a wilderness of signs, page after page of pure madness, to the finish. Then, at the critical moment, the translator shows up, who can at least do battle with two languages, though he or she may destroy the music of the mother tongue. These comical characters should never be told, to their faces anyway, how inept they are, how incapable of doing the things most mortals do. But deaf to such insults, they climb toward the top of the hill, falling and getting up as they go. But at the top they look at the world and smile, accepting the sneers and amazed that their detractors don't ask what's happening on the other side. Since they've never seemed like madcaps to me, I ask them about the landscapes that remain undisturbed. Because what is translating, after all, if it isn't revealing another's secret without disclosing the magic that sustains it? Let us consider an example, the banana tree, the beautiful monocotyledonous plant. How can we not humble ourselves before its mystery? The horse, by roads forbidden to man, discovered that the antidote for snakebite—a cure recommended by the gods—is found at the top of the banana tree. The pig, also aware of the danger of the viper's poison, knows that animals like himself, hardly able to lift their heads above the ground, would never survive if they had to rely on the banana blossom. When this essence of filthiness—swine, hog, sow, or whatever—suffers the attack of the enraged snake, it stanches its wound and restores itself to health by eating the root of the banana tree—the root.

The Other

It would be beautiful if one didn't forget. But remembering is like cooking, and if you risk it, you may get blacker than an old pot.

If I should bring up a memory from the distant past, it's not for the emotion it might cause (a matter which the client's pleasure doesn't dictate). To the contrary, I am guided by a modest hope, veiled by all the years that have passed.

I have no idea where we were going; I only know that in the night the plain seemed unending, that dogs were barking in the distance, and that we finally came to rest among dark trees, the mules in one spot and my parents and I in another beneath the iron cart. Although the dictionary says something else, this is what I call "province": the establishment of a vast world on an insignificant parcel of land, by people who, innocent and invulnerable in the warm morning air, believe that they have nothing; the experience of such simplicity and poverty never disappears from the minds of those who live it with their entire being.

Later I learned to call it Bolivia. It was an honor to live in that country until, during a trip, the heaviest one of all the men, women, and children riding in the truck proclaimed that our country was going to disappear, that the neighboring countries were simply going to divide the nine provinces among themselves. He added that this wasn't just something he'd thought up; his grandmother had learned it in a dream, and she'd never made a mistake in her life—God rest her soul, wherever she might be. Without a doubt, worry and ignorance were responsible for fat Pascual Medina's premonition, worry surely born of a lean economy, and ignorance, well, it can't be explained: it's another world where, in spite of the efforts of my youth, I continue to dwell, having convinced myself that it would be pointless to move beyond its borders.

Of course, I'm perfectly capable of distinguishing between ignorance and stupidity; I'm not an idiot. For example, everybody knows the world is round, but where walking is concerned, the man on the street is better off thinking of the world as flat. The first fact is all right for conversation. And though no one would try to convince us of the second, it's something we all agree upon. Another example, we all know we're going to die, but we act as if we were immortal. By the time we begin to see the other side of the coin, it's too late to go crazy and too soon to give up; so we just accept it and walk straight ahead with our eyes tightly shut.

It was wonderful being ignorant, until the smart people decided to do something about it. They decided it was up to them to pull ignorance up by the roots, and they did such a good job of it that now we're all a bunch of malcontents. There's no two ways about it; we'll never know what was taken from our memory, leaving us trembling with nostalgia.

They sent me away from the village fairly soon, because only two things could happen: you either allowed yourself to be exploited or you got an education. I avoided the first, but as I rode away sadly on the train, I didn't know that my departure would be bad for the others.

In the good old days, some rode horses while others could only watch. I remember the day my father went riding off into the woods with a gun, leaving my mother and the relatives crying. The memory seems clearer now than before. My great-aunt, a small, wrinkled woman, stopped crying first and went to light a candle to her favorite saint. My father wasn't the only one to ride off with a gun over his shoulder, but he was the only one in town who didn't believe in saints. One night the men who had left came back and quickly left again for Argentina because someone was chasing them.

Luckily for us, we were on the winning side; and the plainsmen, who were peace-loving people, decided to parcel out the fallow land, though it must have belonged to somebody. I was already fairly grown up when I realized that some people speak the same language, and they're alike in other ways too. Some sit down all the time, and others don't ever have time to sit down. I'll never forget what I saw, though some have tried to hide it from me or make it seem better than it was, putting words into my head that I could memorize but couldn't understand. Some of the words actually said something; others just hid something; and these were the simple ones. The words that really caused trouble were the ones that seemed to say something but actually hid something, or vice versa. Later on, I decided it was easier and more fun to talk to the people who didn't sit down because even the hardest work isn't so bad if you talk while you do it.

I can vaguely remember the Indians who lived on the plains, but not enough to be able to say they were "marginal ethnic groups." The Chacos, for example, I remember fairly well: they passed through the village from time to time, stayed for a day or two, and then took off like a streak of lightning.

We were ignorant compared to the educated people, but compared to those wanderers, we were really ignorant; or at least that's what I thought until a light came on inside my head and I became convinced that all of those valiant, nomadic groups—Chacos, Chiriguanos, Tapietes, Tobas, Chorotis—were ignorant. They were like the wholeness of the night, perfect, fearless, with a single star on the their foreheads—a determination to disappear without a word.

It all started one night when my parents asked me what I wanted to be, which was the local way of asking someone what he wanted to do when he grew up. I was no more than nine then and only knew my parents and the family members who were still living; I knew nothing about my grandparents or great-grandparents, or any distant relative. That seemed normal to me, and only later did I discover that my roots, unlike those of many people, were rather shallow—practically nonexistent—except at the point where they converged with nature, to disappear and reappear at the most unexpected moment—in my joy at beholding a landscape, my illumination at sharing that enormous, fervent melancholy that becomes strength for daily living. So, when they asked me the question on the enormous terrace of the night, what I noticed first was the barking of dogs, the gallop of my own blood in the quiet sounds of night, the moon shining on unknown regions of the earth, memories and hopes sifting through the branches of trees emblazoned on an immemorial summer.

I feel a tightness in my chest when I remember that I was once a child. My answer was directed not toward their illusions but to the shadows of destiny, to the corpulent hand of absence. "You want to be a doctor?" They were worried. "What kind of a doctor?" they wanted to know. I said I wanted to study medicine, not law. It frightened them to think I wanted to be a lawyer and line my pockets at poor people's expense, earn a living by pitting people against each other. "Nothing like that," I assured them, looking up at the star-filled sky, the clarity of space, whose greatness reached down with rare neutrality to the land of men. That was the first time I'd dodged an important question, and since, as it turned out, I didn't study anything, it was good practice for the more difficult sleights of hand that lay ahead.

But at some point you slip up, because no one escapes this world unscarred. In that special place long ago, there wasn't room for conjecture or artifice. There was no time for history or mathematics, nor time for time, nor a cubbyhole for the cycle of civilizations. There, people were tied to faithful reality: you work so you can live; and if that constant should give rise to an idea, then welcome it with a round of applause. But you can't get blood from a turnip. The desert grows larger and larger, but our thirst remains the same. It was a given that I was supposed to be ignorant. I was born ignorant. It fit me like a glove. And going away to school did nothing but confuse me and expose me to other people's madness.

Years later, I was talking to two Chacos; we were standing quietly, painstakingly choosing our words as if they were vipers. The cleverer of the two had spotted an artificial satellite in the sky, and without beating around the bush, he began to question me about it. Years earlier, he had thought of that celestial aberration as a bad omen; that was during the time when his body was nothing more than an anchor to his soul, a steady light in an unexplored territory. I, a more worldly rustic, was able to explain how such new human inventions worked. Remaining calm, he told me that the first time he'd seen such an object traveling at an uncommon speed, he was so frightened that he took off running as fast as he could toward the nearest village, preparing himself for the worst possible outcome, yet hoping he might find someone who could explain what he'd seen.

He viewed the sky, the beautiful firmament, from his wanderer's soul, convinced that nothing bad could happen there. When he lifted his eyes toward the heavens, he did so discreetly and reverently. The other Chaco remained silent, his eyes fixed on the ground, as if meditating on the words of his companion; and, protected by the noise of our conversation, he seemed to be clarifying puzzlements of his own. At least that is how it seemed to me, and so I asked what he thought about satellites and if he'd been frightened by them. "I don't look up," he replied, without blinking an eye, thus taking his place among the ranks of those who never lift their heads. Like hogs, domestic or wild. Like those who ask to be buried face down so as not to see the face of God. Like those who have fallen and broken their backs and can see things which people with good backs cannot. People who possess wisdom know that it always comes late. It never arrives on time. The curious task of making honey from bile can be attributed to such wisdom, which was also late in coming. No moral is intended here, just fidelity to the work ethic of our ancestors, which was taught to them by blows from a rod.

Jursafú

Our fellow creature is like a mirror of our invulnerable country.

Everything seems simple until a person reaches a certain age, when true interests surface, putting an end to appearances. Attaining basic maturity is different from learning how to sew or sing; sometimes it takes a lifetime, or only half a lifetime if the person is really keen; in some cases even several lifetimes may be insufficient for such a task. Perhaps that's why we say that someone was born too late or born before his time. At any rate, it is our duty to get along with our neighbors, whether they're brave or cowardly. Experience has convinced me that life would be more liveable if people were born some twenty years before their time—or thirty, or forty, or any number of years before the predestined date. When primordial man executed his first dive, he gave rise to the first mystery: was he pushed or did he commit suicide? The countenance that survives him is always a mystery, a seamless, unfathomable mystery.

We are the only examples of the impossible, the unpleasant aftertaste of a belief, madness barely tempered by the promise of abundance, in any order one supposes. And for those who are unaware of this, it would be useful to stare deeply into any human face. The writing on a face is a ciphered language, but writing all the same. It is terrible to read what is written there, finished in spite of its bearer, undisguised by proclaimed ideals. What is admirable in human beings is precisely what is inhuman, that element which relegates them to the animal or vegetable kingdom. Nonetheless, they perform their parts blindly, with a loyalty that is almost ludicrous, and they're happy in their roles. Encouraged by the splendor of the production and at ease in their parts, they muster the courage to reveal their sadness and the ideals they proudly carry between their chests and backbones. Though, in truth, they carry nothing except the print of apocryphal things, learned yesterday and therefore not entirely digested— a fact their confusion belies, as they assume a modern air and strut across the stage like indolent gods, far removed from the modest human condition. True enough, their sense of humor is somewhat disconcerting—an unusual quality in those still governed by invariable instincts. If paradise exists, their jovial nature will take them there (faith is another matter); in other words, they will reach it because they have laughed at themselves, either out of fear or good taste. And they have done it convincingly, with the same passion they demonstrate in destroying things not of their own creation. Perhaps this explains their preference for paradox. No other animal declares the opposite of his own belief so eagerly and unashamedly. It suffices to consider the expression "I die of love for Eulalia."

To fully understand human destiny, one must pay attention to the effects of these illustrious actors' capacity for sublimation. They sublimate everything in order, no doubt, to live out their lives with a smile. They couldn't stand themselves if they didn't expect the unexpected, precisely because they are inept at dealing with life's sudden changes and, thus, are tortured by the thought of being taken by surprise. They're able, nonetheless, to find solace in the notion that the ability to adapt instantly to unforeseen situations is proof of intelligence.

And then for a stroll through the cemetery, man's greatest invention after humor. It doesn't matter which of the two we put in first place, since both of them can be explained and justified as the source of a terrible joke. Together or separate, humor and cemeteries negate the dramatic roles that human beings assume with such enthusiasm. They have never suggested anything more adverse; and from that small triumph, sympathy surges for featherless bipeds, fraudulent and spoiled, intolerant of the slightest sign of fear. The cemetery and humor are their only authentic inventions; the rest is mere imitation, the art of observation carried to the limit, triviality and talent of all kinds—interpretive, inductive, quantitative, and qualitative, all the "-tives" you want but nothing more.

It's true they can fly through thin air, but with the airplane they've only imitated the pleasant motion of birds and insects; true, they've made use of the pulley, and yet they look in amazement at waterfalls which seem to go away but don't go away and are always returning. Guided by their industrious patience, they've made a jumble of all that pertains to the heart and body in general. On the other hand, their imaginations cloud over when they must look at what they have never seen, perhaps because they sense that an authentic creative act often demands life, or perhaps because when they first took a risk, they got their fingers smashed. "Knowing what lies beyond me is the same as knowing myself," they've said, observing themselves at a distance. As far as death is concerned, they know that some day they'll disintegrate, and that is as much as they know. As far as seeing themselves is concerned, they know what they see in the mirror, but it immobilizes them, and when they pass in front of objects that mechanically reflect their images, they cannot conceal the fact that they are acting; in other words, the images seem false, and they hide from their own eyes. Because acting, what really qualifies as "acting," is only possible for one's neighbor; frankness expressed so coldbloodedly to the ingenuous neighbor violates the code that people adhere to when they are by themselves.

But even their best contrivances derive from subtle variations on the comportment of the animal kingdom's only member dressed in mourning yet exhibiting a malicious sense of humor; I'm not referring to any outlandish character, but to the crow.

At any rate, it is our duty to get along with our neighbors, whether they are present or invisible, haven't yet arrived or have gone away. Of course, "neighbor" also refers to ones other than these; it includes those who no longer bear the human form or any state resembling organic matter, and yet live. And even if extraordinary steps beyond the normal scope of human relations must be taken, we must try to understand our neighbors. We cannot hope to learn anything from observation—whether looking at an insect or gazing at a star—if we don't have understanding. I'm at a loss to understand why the first lie was told, and this disturbs me. Certainly, there must have been some reason. Lies per se don't really interest me; they're like repentance or backsliding, mere roads of redemption. The first lie, on the other hand, leaves me befuddled, incapable of mental exercise or metaphysical calculations. Saying yes when the answer is no, or no when the answer is yes, or, in other words, saying the opposite of what one believes, is more intriguing than the dilemma of the chicken and the egg. The first liar deemed it necessary to keep his interlocutor in the dark; take Cain and Abel, for example. On the human stage, lies can only prosper among people who are abjectly ignorant though possessing perhaps an unusual knack for popular sayings, because people are an incarnation of the law of compensation. "What you don't know can't hurt you," says the man who made something cruel out of a mere trifle and stuck it like a small but painful thorn into his neighbor's side. The lie enriched the universe by adding to it the reality of fiction. And it carried humor to the limit, or rather to the cemetery, if we accept the pantheon as a symbol of something that doesn't exist.

Nevertheless, people don't have the backbone to lie to themselves. Not even the lowest of the low could do this, not because they don't want to, but because it's impossible. The first really stupid thing they did was to create a "mirror" of themselves: "If the other thinks so, I must do it." But as soon as this phrase was uttered, the terrible fear of the self was born. Next to such fear, the mirror of the "other" is the consolation of fools and, in the best of cases, the evanescent reality of nostalgia. Narcissus embodies—more than the excesses of self-love—a tribute to absence, the absence of the other, the being who without knowing it demands the truth from us. But who can tolerate the truth? People, its inventors and spokesmen? They're the only ones who don't accept reality with their bodies or their minds. They prefer to hold onto their illusions, no matter how absurd, rather than grapple with the truth. They feel a dark sympathy for the devil because they've forced themselves to believe that he is the only stranger who would allow them their lies or promote their illusions.

I am totally convinced of all of these considerations, and yet, when I apply them to my own life, I always come up short. They can be used as a catalogue to measure oneself from head to toe. And I do that from time to time without ever cheating in any respect. And this isn't just talk.

In the final analysis, jokes always end up at the cemetery. There, in a town apparently without a population, our loved ones dwell—ones who lied and ones who fought against the lie—capering among themselves and with the darkness. They never stray from there no matter what. But in spite of that, human beings always end up lugging the dead around; they can't leave them alone, because they are the heroes of their unexchange-able country, the purified territory of nostalgia, the graveyard that at one time offered us the invulnerability of being pure. The dead person was once the cordial other who listened to our falsehoods without batting an eye. They are all there. But our fear and ignorance of the great beyond prevent us from contemplating the luminous dissolution of life. We not only have an other; we are someone else's other. Paradoxically, we are the other of a dead person who can no longer put up with our lies. It's good to know this. Reduced as they are to silence—and to fiction in human terms—they only answer our ravings when we tell the truth (valid for any world) by way of the damp trap of dreams.

Notebook Number 2

The Other as the Dead Man Sees Him

All of these things lose importance and eventually become insignificant to those who obey a tradition, hold a patrimony, and, out of homage to the law, do not change it or ever question if such homage is due.

Once a bearded man crossed the jungle by charming the big cats with the noises he made with tin cans. The leopards allowed him to pass, not because they liked the clanging sound but because the old man's confidence in his seductive powers seemed hilarious to them.

Safe from the felines and thinking he'd reached paradise, the bearded man said, "Around here I pick the tune, and they dance to it." But several months later, he found a dead sparrow that seemed to bear a message from the earth: "We all depend on one another, the living on the living, the living on the dead, and the dead on the living." The sparrow, who kept him company in his loneliness, eventually made him sad; so he gathered up his tin cans and headed out of the jungle, but this time he wasn't able to make it through before the tigers devoured him.

The bearded man's life, as we could say of any life, inspires reverence and devotion. Feelings that were once confused are soon resolved because the man is dead, which places him beyond hope or rebuff.

If we are to avoid such misfortune, our view of life must be broad, unlike that of the man in question—who is now six feet under and can't rectify his mistakes or even decline a compliment. When we look at history, for example, as the tiger, insect, or rock might see it, our attitude should be one of amazement; however, if we look at history from death's perspective, from its deceptively inert pedestal, dismay seems more appropriate. But as some have said, if we were to live our lives that way, how much passion or motivation could we muster? Though we could avoid catastrophes, no doubt, like the one that befell the bearded man.

Allegories teach us that from the beginning of time, conquerors have determined how events would be interpreted. The opinions of many people have vanished from the earth because of the victorious sun's privilege of burying what it doesn't understand. And many more landscapes will be plowed under before those designed by people who have asked nothing of no one come into view.

I'm going to direct my attention toward a single individual. But my goal is not to vindicate. I don't believe in absurd redemptions, and the word "posterity" disappeared long ago from my reduced vocabulary. My obligation is of another kind: I want to uncover the secret tendon of human and inhuman events, with the single, paradoxical goal of destroying wild illusions. I am here now to praise the linchpin of existence, and only if I should come again, would I deal in shades and variations—without altering, of course, what is most essential.

My most important tool is my blind eye, which no one except the ingenuous dares to scorn or ignore. The speculations of the rational, civilized world slip through people's fingers, but my immemorial eye catches them in its net.

I spoke before of the victor's interpretation.

Bolivia, a backward country of the Southern Cone, is an example of the silly contradictions that the victor's interpretation allows. This land existed for many years, far from the beaten path of human history, but suddenly it was conquered by the Spanish, who had just escaped the grasp of their Arab conquerors. They arrived sick—sick with desire for gold—and forlorn: how else might you describe a band of men getting off a ship without the company of women? Illustrations depicting their arrival contain no examples of your typical couple; and the faces of the men reflect no desire to settle down. And as a Bolivian psychiatrist has pointed out, their state of mind was quite the opposite. In fact, the first case of insanity in Latin America involved a Sevillian who went berserk when, at the most unexpected moment, a long-haired Indian girl squatted down to relieve herself right in front of him, just as dark shadows began to settle upon the earth. This may seem only an amusing anecdote, but it is not if we regard its premonitory character.

After the conquest, prints of a past splendor remained unsoiled in the memories of the native people and have persisted to the present as negated history, as a kind of subterranean influence. But it would be absurd to try, as some have done, to return to the past, though the desire to do so is understandable. Perhaps such attempts are suggestive of a last farewell.

Many years have passed since the conquest, and what survives is a new language threatened daily by conflicts that seem to be unsolvable. The people who have become Bolivian, willingly or reluctantly, are melancholy at times, but usually they are content, especially if they are ignorant of the languages of the "sub-people"—those who were defeated by the newcomers and have yet to score a single victory against them. The native people continue to think of "civilization" as the enemy, which it is, because it oppresses them; and they rely on mother nature as their ally—an indecipherable one in the minds of the foreigners. When the latter cross the shrubless hills, they are frightened; the natives, on the other hand, tread with confidence, listening to the silence of their gods who are their authentic forefathers rather than their adopted parents.

"Here's a rock, and this is the way around it," said someone who seemed to comprehend the problem. And that's really all there is to it. The fruit is prefigured in the seed, and those who eat the seed will soon perceive the form.

"How can I make my life meaningful?" asked the man who lost his way in the barren land of his memory. "What good is it to be born, if sooner or later you must confront the inevitable and breathe the peace of the forefathers?" "Of course, you must work," answered a ghost. "But how can I do this without guilt destroying me?"

All of these things lose importance and eventually become insignificant to those who obey a tradition, hold a patrimony, and, out of homage to the law, do not change it or ever question if such homage is due. In a well-organized community, even death is proclaimed as natural and proportionate. But when two cultures crash together, creating a "third party" that is uncultured and confused, the new being will question and pry—what else can he do? And those who are born along such byroads carry whatever they can in their saddlebags, and often it is gold, which necessity or ambition requires. The "third party" isn't shortsighted in the least, but he is frightened when he wakes up from a dream, looks at the country around him, and, still panting heavily from his night's work, realizes that he's been saved by the skin of his teeth: "It isn't easy to breathe ancient air, but it's a problem of the lungs, not the mind. We only learn its value when we need it to save our lives; then we breathe it and it is pumped away by the blood, carrying a vague sketch of death in its flow. The ancient air of Latin America can be lethal unless it is needed to save a life; and people who do not understand death have not learned that death makes it possible for the blood to breathe. This is why I stare in amazement at the faces of the magic medallion."

I prefer to look at life, which is beautiful and worthy of greatest praise. It doesn't fear complexity, but simply brings to earth—without disturbing the earth's silence—prototypes of a different form, uncompromisingly beautiful and completely untransferable. Responsible, too.

The Other—whose questions were never idle—appeared one morning in a province, in the rustic dominion of birds and wild animals, and looking at all the beautiful trees, said to himself, "These forests, which cradled me as child, have a soul."

The Other was born the same way that ordinary people are born and saw many wonderful things that seemed eternal: vegetation moistened by lights older than time, mornings rumpled by the breeze of summer, skies bending under the weight of stars, and a profusion of lovely names for all beings, both simple and complex. And after he had seen it and then dreamed it for the first time, he was certain that he was living some divine adventure. But later on, when he learned about death, he was sorrowful and confused, and the bright images of his birth shone even brighter than before. He also knew, as do all human beings, that someday he would be held accountable, and that his actions would be judged, regardless of their importance, according to an established hierarchy.

The Other's past experiences had been of a firmer kind; they had been based on traditions that were sensible and perhaps more healthful. But he also possessed the gift of the universal. His parents were muleteers, honest, open, country people. His father was full-blooded Indian and his mother, Spanish; both were tied to the earth and sought sustenance with their hands, which is as it should be for all people who walk the earth. But it is pointless to analyze their bond with the natural world. Let it suffice to say that their love for nature was boundless, and this was their greatest virtue.

Earth is old, as are its people—this is obvious. But those who have just been born have no memory of things past. Everything seems new. For them, the memory is a "crevice of mystery." And many years later they are even more intrigued when they learn about the vastness of "history"—or that portion for which we are responsible: twenty centuries under the sign of Christianity, and, before that, an unending path toward the origin or night of time. No one has returned from that place except the Founder, who became frightened and decided to name all the things around him, to help him find his way. Then he died, and yet he is immortal—as are all legends—the happy, invisible magician of our memory. On any given voyage, one might easily be astonished, and confused as well, at having to find one's way among numberless footprints disguised as art, geography, science, philosophy, et cetera—all forms of knowledge which have slumbered in the terrestrial memory since time began. The important thing is not to lose one's way in the great totality of objects placed there by our ancestors.

A special kind of objectivity is required to recount the Other's first years of residence on earth. While he was growing up among the paths of the forest, the Second World War was being fought, and his uncle Jesús León was baptizing his dogs with names like "Hitler" and "Stalin." Some time later, when the bristly rustic was enrolled in grammar school, the National Revolution occurred, which was transcendent in the country's history because of the reforms it brought to an anachronistic society and also because it failed.

The Other wasn't able to see these events in their full dimension since he was young and couldn't place them in any rational order. So he waited for them to settle while he continued with his life, innocent—though he was the object of great curiosity—protected by nature, and, for the time being, removed from the shadows of the solar night which eventually reveal a man's destiny and thereby test his fortitude.

In other words, he lived in the forest and went to school.

With the support of his family, he finished his secondary education and then knocked at the door of the university. He left behind the land of his birth, the music of simple deeds, and went to a place where the horizons seemed clouded, because The Other didn't produce the desired result in the Superior House of Studies and quickly gave up, expecting never to become a professional.

This is the external version of what occurred. Its resonances, however, are more delicate, but not because our subject is made of an especially delicate fiber. Actually, he is rather tough and responds more easily to the structures of an archaic, rudimentary universe. And though it is nothing to be ashamed of, it was around that time that my dreamer friend began to have nightmares.

If you watch an ant in danger—standing before a big leaf, a rock, or a human being—you can tell if this celebrated creature realizes that he is about to take a risk. In other words, you can tell if he has been pro-grammed by some former error or if he is a virgin to pitfalls. Such matters that pertain to memory can be tested in all living organisms, and, in the majority of cases, the following adage—invented by some crazy earthling—applies: "Where danger lies, there also lies the cure."

As for human beings, anyone who wants to survive in a hostile environ-ment, without renouncing what he or she considers most fundamental, should be prepared to take on a whole host of demons, and death to boot.

The Other, who didn't know how to read or write, had no idea what he was getting himself into. So he gave up the idea of preparing himself for a profession. Instead, he started paying attention to stories that caught his interest, such as the one about a German with a cravat who thought that the serpent was the sturdiest animal on the earth because its entire body seemed anchored to the ground; or the one about the son of a British miner who had written a tale in which the main character was a yellow viper who was all alone in the garden of nature yet quenched his thirst in a trough. In short, the Other possessed a rudimentary understanding of the metaphor since he had inherited the analogic capacity of the muleteers of his native grasslands, where the humoristic metaphor was an accepted, even noble gesture.

From the beginning, my friend the Other had been seduced by the rural people's talent for expressing themselves. He had heard someone say that no one escapes "unbranded" from this world; and availing himself of the silence and gratitude of his heart, he was able to comprehend such wisdom, which came from the forest of his ancestors; and with that gift in tow, he was able to survive difficult situations and to muster courage to deal with life, without losing his faith. In the language of the common people, "unbranded" is the term used for wild animals, the ones that don't have a mark or an owner and are free because they haven't been broken or haven't felt the sting of the red hot branding iron. And then there's the story about the farmer who once asked his neighbor, "Do you know why the crow wasn't saved?" The man said he didn't know. "Pay attention, then, my friend. One time, a soldier had to carry a large block of calamine, and he was carrying it on his back very carefully to avoid losing his balance. But suddenly a violent gust of wind came up and nearly blew him away, calamine and all; but being a stubborn country fellow, he wouldn't let go of what was his. The sight was so strange that a marauder who was riding by said the man looked like a gorged crow."

About that time, a mysterious dream took control of the Other; he dreamed it the same night that he'd seen the little girl sleeping in one of the classrooms—the ghost who in real life was called Laureana Medina, Salomón's sister and Pascual's daughter. That dream was the first in a long series of dreams that eventually tied my friend to a language whose scope he barely suspected and whose powerful message he never failed to trust. If anything can define the Other, it is his faith in the music that exceeds him; in other words, he has used dreams as a defense against his involvement in a world of outcasts, a world that was finished and that spun him out to go on living as a survivor.

He came from a buried universe and now passed over the earth like a sleepwalker in someone else's world. But along the streets where he walked in solitude, he came to realize that he could never live with things that weren't his own. He must have his own life, of his own blood, illuminated by the memory of previous ages. His rustic spirit, a devotee of that light, coined a phrase to protect him from the impervious theatrics of foreign beings: "You do not love me, but you need me. I love you, and therefore do not need you." And in his estimation that phrase said it all.

But all was not said, at least if one agrees that a person's adventures can best be understood by another person and that hard thinking, even of the deepest kind, may never disclose what is readily obtained through direct observation.

The Other is totally ignorant about many things, but he is not stupid. He always pays attention to the messages of his dreams, and perhaps that is why he dreamed one time that he was in a grove of enormous trees of a kind often seen in his province; the trees seemed familiar, not because of their size, but because of their luminescence, which was a strange mixture of dryness and melancholy. He was trying to remove the bark from one of the trunks, just as he had done when he was a child, so as to reveal the deep holes in the cortex left by certain tree-eating animals. He continued pulling the bark away until he was able to go inside the trunk, and there he beheld a magnificent set of doors, like the doors of a cathedral, covered in hieroglyphics. They were, in fact, the doors of the great temple, and a voice announced that the symbols were the "language of the birds." He kept the dream to himself, as was his custom, and it seemed to him that he had benefited from some immemorial light and that an unsuspected thirst had been quenched. His only vanity was in feeling himself related to the things around him, without any desire or capacity to do harm; he felt close to the lament of "the internal," if it is possible to apply such a jaded term to a highly spiritual state of being. The Other wasn't able to interpret the dream; he had no notion of its premonitory meaning and, of course, never suspected—as experts have implied—that the language of poetry is a remnant of the language of birds, of the original word which established a dialogue between nature and beings long before the Fall—a biblical term used to threaten people when they misbehave. True, people have learned a lot from the sacred text, accustomed as they are to a life of narrow horizons, but their own experiences have also been a source of enlightenment.

Such was the "setting" bestowed upon the Other, and such was his personality: An archaic country, traversed by prophecies and relentless winds. A being tied to ancestral customs that took the form of memories in his soul, memories too silent to be heard by anyone attuned exclusively to the incitements of contemporary sounds.

Beings such as this should never leave their native habitats, that is, if they wish to lead normal lives; but isolation can also prove fatal, especially if they are aware of the speed at which the world is moving. So, for an innocent brute from these lethargic provinces, while leaving the native village can be damaging, not leaving it is fatal. Under such circumstances, it is better to test one's wings than to remain like a parrot, tied to a stake and teetering back and forth between a yes and a crack of the skull.

Such struggles take place in intimate quarters out of the sight of those who dance the rumba on the solar stage, since these festive types, if informed of an approaching catastrophe, would never want to miss it; strangely enough, they take no notice of other people's lives unless someone is about to blow a gasket. This is terrible, but it is true, as the Other found out when he was living in a city he no longer remembers. There, a forlorn human being who had been diagnosed as a "neurotic" climbed to the top story of an enormous building from where he hoped to get a view of the great city; but, as it turned out, he could hardly stand to look at the place which had caused his madness. He stood watching the hustle and bustle (he himself had been unable to adapt to such a routine) until, finally, the passersby noticed him and suspected his suicidal intentions. Small, silent groups began to form, waiting for the individual, who apparently had said he would jump, to carry out his threat. And soon the solitary man, as if seduced by the abyss of their eyes, dived headlong off the building. The curiosity seekers, having pocketed his loneliness, began to disperse, murmuring among themselves and seeming more or less indifferent to the tragedy which put an end to one man's dreams.

"My birth wasn't a communal effort," says the wayfarer, "so I'll follow my own destiny and ignore what my neighbor has to say. If a rock's a rock, isn't a man a man, or is he some traveler always moving toward his original form? No matter how much a rock is hammered or knocked about, it never pauses to meditate on its condition as a rock. And people, no matter what befalls them, have a forceful weapon at their disposal, though at times it may seem ineffectual. I'm speaking of nostalgia."

And if this is the music of the cautious approach, how did The Other choose the path which would lead him toward his destiny? He must have chosen the path of nostalgia for a reason; and it was probably to save his greatest gift, which was the luminous echo at his core.

So, how did this rural man earn his keep, for a time at least?

But before continuing, perhaps we should say something about the "rural man." Generally, he is thought to be a crafty animal with great capacity for pain since he never screams. He probably doesn't think it would do him any good. He is said, euphemistically, to have a "marginal" existence, unsuited to the subtleties of a spiritual life; for this reason it is considered natural for him to serve as a beast of burden. If, in addition, you keep in mind that he has a harsh life, you will have a fairly good idea of what his reality is like. As recompense, life has given him wisdom to confront pain, misery, and displacement. To deal with such adversity, he has created a solid faith for himself, which makes him privy to the secrets of nature, his faithful ally. And thus he lives, awed by a horizon which no one else notices, his feet planted firmly on the ground, and his mind free of all illusions.

So many injustices have been committed against this rural man that the only law he trusts—and by which he feels defended —is the law that takes some time but at least fulfills its purpose. People who haven't had their sensitivities dulled or their hearts hardened may be able to recognize their own arrogance and stinginess toward the rural man who for reasons of his own has chosen to remain near the campfire and make the elements his constant friends. The rural man suffers magnanimously the worst kinds of rigors, and, by doing so, he develops a grave virtuosity. Many topics are beyond his grasp, not because he is stupid, but because he has learned to remain silent in fifteen different languages. He can tell, nonetheless, the direction of the wind; and, when there are clouds in the sky, he knows whether to expect rain or only thunder. He is pure, animal prudence, and only madness could induce him to do anything contrary to his own welfare.

His attitude toward death is mysterious, which is understandable in one who expects the worst to happen at any moment and yet is aware at every second of the beauty of being alive. It is most unusual for a rural man to commit suicide. Numerous explanations might be offered, but regardless of the reason, it demonstrates his tendency to regard every gift of life, important or negligible, as a blessing and therefore a duty.

He possesses only the minimum needed to live, and by living so precariously, he often meets with hardships. Poetry is not a part of his life, and apparently he knows nothing of this celestial phenomenon. And yet he seems to engender poetry through the mere act of living and displaying his uncomplaining profile as if he were prepared to receive a bullet at any moment. Nonetheless, he doesn't consider himself a victim or a rebel, and he wouldn't draw attention to himself or to his cause. That wouldn't be the way of rural people, for their life is hard and leaves no time for rabble-rousing.

Anyone who has spent even a single night among rural people has suspected perhaps the existence of a different vital order. For them, life is always naked, whether they are sitting around the fire after a rain, shucking corn in the shadows of a slow sunset, or killing a pig at daybreak. Nothing seems to get in their way, and maybe that's why their voices sound strange in the morning, which is when they talk about the harvest or the weather or other important things.

Rural people are ruled by an ancient science which teaches them to respect things that are ordinary and to expose themselves to bad circumstances when necessary, which is a rather practical way of doing things. Their legendary offspring meet life head-on, and perhaps that is why many of them die at birth.

Anyone who has sampled the "bounty of civilization" would never consider adjusting to such an environment in which life is a struggle to survive and offers little more than small passions in their more brutal forms. In these rank-smelling villages, the biblical passage, "The wind blows where it wills, and you hear the sound of it, but you do not know whence it comes," is likely to be taken as a joke in poor taste.

Since having a decent life in such surroundings seems unlikely, rural people are becoming more and more uncommon and will probably die out completely. But the earth is not going to swallow them up; instead, they will become modern farmers, well-prepared technocrats, efficient engineers, or even experts in the professional lie. And without realizing it, they will cease to be what they once were.

At any rate, no one can presume to have a destiny all his own. Each person depends on the community; and if the individual leaves the community, he must do so with the knowledge that his own organism—itself a painful memory of a disintegrating collective—may regard such an act as fatal to its historic identity. If the person who wishes to break away is thoughtful, he must carry out his plan as transparently as possible. And in breaking away he must prepare himself for the challenges he will face, above all, loneliness. If he does these things and is mindful at all times of the promise of a better life, he will maximize his chances for success.

If a sociologist were to study this kind of situation, his or her conclusions would be simple. In the worst of cases, the Other will end up on the rolls of the unemployed; but if the winds are in his favor, he may join the ranks of highly motivated professionals who deny their background and know nothing about their culture. One of the two, with slight variation, is likely to occur to a rural man like the Other. If he experiences the first, he will be despised by society, which finds such people loathsome, yet supports them through taxes. If he experiences the second, those in power will accept him, but he will lose his authenticity, a well-known fact to all who resign themselves to an alienating existence.

There are other possibilities, though little known, since their benefits are small, and they wouldn't astonish anyone except perhaps a very honest person, a person who would never waver from the truth, a person whose linchpin might go out on him in the middle of the desert. People with contemporary tastes, especially those who prefer a good tragedy, will find these adventures colorless. But, as the saying goes, a road not traveled is still a road.

For such things to happen, a person must know how to say yes; not yes to anything that is suggested but to things which exalt life when exaltation seems totally out of the question.

One day the Other was standing next to a horse and watching a woman when a poor man went into a pharmacy to ask for something he could never expect to find there. Later on, in another town, the man worked really hard to become a lathe worker. While he was there, he was given some advice that has been given to many dreamers, advice that no one except a fool would disregard. Someone told him to stop using the word and start serving it. At first, writing didn't seem to suit his rural makeup, not that he didn't try. But then suddenly, it became his calling, one that had been with him all along since his life began. At that point, he became the voice of his dead ancestors, the voice of a memory that wished to affirm itself in a world sorely lacking in happy memories. He stood holding a book and offered his opinion: "This is complicated. And even though I don't understand it, I'm beginning to see what it's saying."

Jursafú as the Other Sees Him

Because he went away, he began to remember like a person who is awake but talked as if he were walking in his sleep. Because we must go away to become conscious of the language we speak, the language that redeems us.

I lost track of Jursafú in Salta, the city where he went to study lathe working. And it was unfortunate that, being away from home, he should try his hand at something for which he had no preparation and that was contrary to his nature. I started to notice a distance between us when one day he heard a poem of rare beauty; and that same night he started twisting and turning in bed; and the next day I was shocked when I saw him because he didn't look like himself. Then I saw him writing down a dream in a notebook of blue-lined paper with wide margins, and I knew that the change was permanent.

That was one of his many disappearances.

A lot of people, both ignorant and educated, believe that we choose our own destinies when in fact the opposite is true: events attach themselves to certain people and not to others. And in such instances, certificates of good conduct aren't worth anything—with no intention of offending people who really apply themselves. But there's a great deal of difference between one idea and the other. My personal belief rests soundly on experience, which I wouldn't lie about, of course, and I'm not one of those people who expects to be paid for doing nothing.

The poem I mentioned set the tone for all of Jursafú's decisions. Some things were decided unconsciously, though they were important and would change his life forever. In other words, he gave up lathe working as a way of putting food on the table. It wouldn't be entirely true to say that things have gone well for him until now. The way I see it, he could have taken his time and done things more patiently, but he chose instead to get the job done quickly, either because he was good at it, or maybe he just liked doing everything at once.

Now that he's living on the other side of the river—in a world where everything that glitters isn't gold—he's happy, because he says he's read a lot of books. When I was boy, I also read a lot of books, novels by Alexandre Dumas, Vargas Vila, and others whose names I don't recall at the moment. That was the extent of my encounter with literature, but it soon lost its charm, because life is hard and quickly puts an end to childish illusions, even before a person is grown. Though some people manage to hang on to their illusions longer than others, this can be dangerous, especially if you get too old before you discover that taking risks can get you into trouble. And if you're Bolivian, it's even worse, because we seem to be born with a losing hand, and if you take a trick, it's better to keep quiet about it. So you go through life feeling as if you'd been punished before you began—or at least that's the impression one gives.

Mentioning these things and watching the sun sink into the prairie, I attempt to recall my friend Jursafú, a Bolivian who doesn't even know his own country, though, strangely enough, he believes that he can feel its geography throbbing in his chest. Being born on the frontier caused him— without his knowing it—to feel a special attachment to unimportant things and to worry about being tied to a place that he might never understand, no matter how hard he tried. And it is a well-known fact that a frontiersman can express more with his eager heart than a city person can with his vague terminology. I've also learned that it's no joke living in a place that borders on another place, and that belonging to one side places you in a different position, even if you're a lot like the people on the other side.

At any rate, after Jursafú had finished his first years of schooling, he suddenly left for Argentina. He tried hard to find a job that would allow him to support his eight brothers and sisters, but he couldn't find anything. He had failed and was ashamed. And to make matters worse, it all happened in a foreign country. Contrary to what he had imagined, he had more than enough skill to do mechanical things, but poetry, which struck him like a bolt of lightning, clouded his vision. After the dream, he managed to fill a whole notebook with poems written by trial and error, without getting any help from teachers. Frightened by insights and nostalgias he didn't understand, he stuffed the verses into a green bottle, and when he returned to the village, he buried the bottle in a dark place in the forest.

In some respects, Jursafú seemed to be reliving the adventures of his uncle Antonio, who as an adolescent had done well at some prestigious school in the same Argentine city I mentioned earlier; his uncle's success was in vain, however, since for many years alcohol controlled his life, until decades later, in old age and after a tremendous struggle, he managed to stop drinking. But his triumph came too late, when his friends and family expected nothing but the worst and didn't really care if he drank or not. Such a victory was out of sync with his failing health. It wasn't surprising, then, when Jursafú's father—who prided himself in knowing when to throw in the towel—told his brother Antonio, "You've already got one foot in the grave, so you might as well go on drinking."

I wish I'd remembered to mention earlier that when Jursafú was fifteen he fell in love, which brought him great joy and more than a little sorrow. He centered his attention on Laura Medinaceli, a girl with long braids and a country smile, who came to the village about the time Jursafú went chasing after Salomón Medina and stumbled upon a young girl asleep in a classroom. His state of mind was such that on one occasion he refused to go hunting with the rustic men from the woods.

As it turned out, Jursafú left for Salta and came back, burning with love for Laura. After he finished high school and was still in love with the girl, he was determined to become a geologist, which seemed a good way to make his way in the world of credits and debits. But that didn't work out, and he got involved in some secret business, which he never denied. He ran around as if someone were after him or the devil were guiding him from the depths of some terrible horizon, like in a nightmare.

At this point in the story, I begin to feel a little uncomfortable in the role of narrator, because I'm at a loss to explain some of the things that happened to my friend, though at times I get a sudden flash of understanding and am able to capture about two-thirds of the main events.

Unlike a dog, I can lie down without running around in circles. So I stayed in the province. "If I'm not going to be happy," I said to myself, "why should I leave? I wouldn't be any better off than I am now, and obviously, things aren't going to improve." And my friend stayed on in the city and had a hard time making ends meet, and every time he came back to our village to see the trees and wild animals that we grew up with, I would follow him around like a dog and must admit that much of what I know I learned from him. And his effort to teach me things so that I wouldn't get mixed up with the law wasn't in vain. Later on it was very useful to know—as I heard from his mouth—that they couldn't keep you in jail for more than twenty-four hours, because I was always getting myself into trouble by blurting out, "Take me to jail if you think you can."

But people do get old. And their enthusiasm for new things begins to fade. Before you know it, you're on your way back to the ranch with a lot of loose ends to tie up, some of them easy to handle and others more complicated, but most of them will involve simple everyday matters. As I matured, my relationship with my friend became more objective. At its core, it became more intense and around the edges, more elaborate. This was the natural course for it to take, which I can quickly explain, words permitting.

The world has changed, actually quite a bit, and I'm aware of this. Nobody is said to be dumb anymore, and even people who are tongue-tied are considered smart. But I'm not one of those people who changes just because everyone else does. I can't, or rather I don't want to. What good would it do for me to become a different person when I live in a province where only memories are important? As far as I can tell, it wouldn't make any sense at all. But it's different in Jursafú's case; he takes what he can get, since he is committed to substances whose values increase as they become permanent, under the pressure of rapid change. But no matter how knowledgeable I became, I could never get along in that kind of world.

That's the way Jursafú is now, at least on the outside, because inside he hasn't changed, and even a fortuneteller would never suspect that after so much time of wandering over the earth, he'd be the same. Especially if you consider that just getting away from village life is supposed to refine a person. Of course, I don't agree with that for a second, and I would never try to hide it. But a lot of people do believe it, and that's not going to change from one day to the next. All you have to do is look at the big parties they give for the ones who go away and come back—few as they are. And the parties are even bigger if the visitors have made a name for themselves, which is hard to do in a small village. It's just a lot of silliness as far as I'm concerned. It's like your better class of rooster. When you open the door to the chicken yard, he doesn't do what the more ordinary kind does, which is to head for the nearest shit pile, never to be seen again. The high-class roosters just strut around a bit, crow a couple of times, and head back into the chicken yard. What suits the city dweller doesn't suit the farmer. And though I imagine such behavior is likely to continue, at least it isn't generalized, because even the dumbest country people know that, rich or poor, the same fate awaits us all. And who would try to put on airs anyway, after what Pila Ramos said: "Friends, I don't believe in beating around the bush, so I'll just say what's on my mind. If you know your way around, the world is like a big pasture, and if you happen to lose track of a donkey, it's bound to show up sooner or later."

The only things I can talk about are the things I understand; and in this world, that is the only knowledge that counts for anything, as Jursafú well knows. What anyone might have predicted has occurred; in other words, the years have caught up with us, and now each of us has enough vision to judge his own life and to understand the lives of others. This kind of project demands a whole panorama of memories, visions of a world that could have been different but was not different and, therefore, turned out to be the world as we know it. But we hold it at arm's length as we would a dangerous animal.

Our village, which was full of lovely trees and had a strong vegetable odor every spring, was at one time far removed from the rest of the world; its inhabitants could make contact with other parts of the universe only through the stars. And to some extent, the warm climate, the rains, and the necessities of daily living made the people a little crazy. We were rural people then, and we continue to be rural people now, and those of us who tried to be something else ended up as phonies, apes from head to toe, but without the charm of a real ape. And instinct, which at one time saved us, eventually pulled the rug out from under us, leaving us where we are today, a bunch of lame-brained monkeys up to no good.

The most luminous memory I have of Jursafú is from our school days. One typical Chaco summer, a boy of eight appeared, and everyone swarmed around him because it was said that he already knew how to read and write, and we had to see it to believe it. The usual sociable types said that he hadn't come before because he lived in the forest some five kilometers from there and had had to wait until he got big enough to walk four leagues a day.

They sent him straight to the second grade, and in two days' time he had fallen in love with one of the girls in his class who was called Ignacia and was his same age; and, given his fine character, she had no right to treat him the way she did. It was his first love, deep and pure, though without success. And what really drove him to distraction was that, under such circumstances, one of his own cousins began to fancy him. But gradually, his unrequited love for Ignacia faded as he traveled back and forth from home to school and, on his way, saw many kinds of shrubs and enormous trees, wild flowers and animals of all sizes, thorn bushes and soaring birds, the freshness of things in the morning air and the secrecy of things at night.

One fine midday he was returning calmly to his home, but in the middle of the road—in a well-known patch of sandy ground that was hard to cross barefooted—he suddenly asked himself a question that, with age, we learn not to ask: "Who am I?" Though he well knew that his name was Jursafú, he didn't really know who he was or why he was there under the sky and upon the earth. He broke a barrier we shouldn't even touch, because if we demand an answer to such questions, the results can be devastating; he went on not knowing who he was, but worse than that, he couldn't remember his own name. When he realized what he'd done, he fell flat on his face in the hot sand. His fear of questions that have nothing to do with reality dates from that time; in other words, he has an aversion to questions that human beings can't possibly expect to answer. Though I ought to mention that for a long time after that he was secretly proud of his strange experience, which he thought contained many symbols. And he suspected that during the fainting spell he'd received a special gift or idiosyncrasy that would always be a part of him.

The National Revolution took place shortly after that, in 1952. The people who lived in the forest—listening to the only radio in town—

heard the voice of an announcer from the nation's capital; that voice, affected by the weight of the tragedy, said the streets of La Paz had turned into a river of blood. What was happening then on a grand scale in the heart of the country had already occurred on a smaller scale in the frontier zone, when the people returning from Yacuiba, pleased at having fulfilled their civic duty at the voting booth, were received by a round of gunfire from the soldiers stationed in our beloved village—which, by the way, is still called El Palmar. After the disturbances, a lot of the villagers fled and some were taken to jail; Jursafú's father had to hide for a few days in a field of tall grass near the railroad station. And Jursafú went there several times at midday and during the afternoon with a bucket of food for his father and some other men, some strangers who had revolvers and were committed to a cause that the boy, who innocently took them their meals, could hardly understand.

But eventually the world changed for us. It turned around. After April of 1952, life seemed to be telling us that now it was our turn. Strange people began to appear in the province; and in El Palmar the rural people especially began to attend meetings and participate in demonstrations led by angry men who carried guns. Every now and then, you could hear shouts of "Long live the martyrs of Catavi!" and "Long live the Revolution!" And finally the rural people managed to carry out what seemed impossible for a minority. They divided up the land and tore down all the fences and barbed wire; some of them carried pistols at their waists and others carried shovels, hoes, and tools of every size and shape, and all of them shouted the slogan: "The land belongs to the people who work it." The lazy ones slacked off fairly soon, but everyone was willing—some of them more than others—to work to achieve the goals set by the union. The greatest benefit would go to the people who had very little, which was almost everybody.

They started a soccer club that for many years was called "The Second of August," in honor of the Indians and the Agrarian Reform, and it was the best team in the whole province. The Revolutionary Command saw to it that the rural people were respected, and, for the time being, they did away with military rule. The people were still poor, but they were happier than they had been; though they didn't know why they were happy, especially since they were poor. Then from time to time a new kind of musical group would come through town, and as time passed, the appearances became more frequent. The musicians played on their *zamponas* traditional songs from the Altiplano, a region we knew very little about; and when the music was finished, they would shout "Long live the Movement" and "Glory to Villarroel."

The names of the candidates for deputy—supernatural beings who presumed to represent us without ever having looked us in the eye—were scrubbed off the sides of buildings, and in no time the Revolution did away with all such garbage, and we were happy until the next blow came, this time not from the enemy but from the new government representatives. Shovels, hoes, wheelbarrows, machetes, and a large load of medicine had been sent from the region's capital. Some of the shovels arrived and were handed out among the people, but nothing was seen of the medicine until it mysteriously appeared in a pharmacy owned by a deputy. Shortly afterward, the tractors ordered by the cooperatives arrived, but since they couldn't be used on sandy ground, they were used to transport gasoline to Paraguay. At first this illegal business was carried out with some illusion, but very quickly it turned to shit—not animal shit, to our misfortune, for, after all, animal shit is a good fertilizer and has a country smell. At least that's the way I looked at it, since I usually sniff the air and everything around me when I want to draw my own conclusions.

Jursafú and the devil himself know I'm not lying.

About that time, Jursafú finished grade school, and his parents sent him to Villamontes to continue his schooling because it was obvious that he should try his hand at some profession. When he received his grade report at the end of the first semester, my friend had nothing to be proud of since he had failed eight of his eleven courses. Embarrassed about the unforeseen results, he remembered that on one of his last walks through the woods with his father, the older man had told him, "My son, if you apply yourself and do well, I'll sell the shirt off my back so that you can finish your studies." And he proudly showed him the shirt that he was wearing, and since both of them were immersed in the conversation, they didn't notice that the devil was scampering about and laughing at them because the shirt was full of holes and its owner couldn't have found a buyer if he'd tried. But Jursafú never thought of that, since he wasn't about to let his father make that kind of sacrifice; on the other hand, he didn't want to have to leave school.

He was caught between the past and the present, and what was destined to happen did happen. Jursafú and his father were finishing their talk on the outskirts of Villamontes near the shore of a wide river that flowed past in infinite sadness; Jursafú's ears perceived the words which recounted his parents struggle on his behalf and the small recompense they had received from the budding student; but his soul and his body were in another place. Maybe he was remembering the warm day when he first arrived at the village and was full of hope in spite of having forgotten his lunch, the first one his mother had prepared for him. He had also forgotten a useless pigeon that he had cared for and trained, stuffing grains of corn in its beak and then tossing it into the air; it had never learned to fly, but several weeks later it arrived in Villamontes riding on a bag of corn, because while Jursafú was away, it refused to eat and just sat on the bag and waited for a miracle. After their warm encounter at the railroad station, the two went over to the boarding house, and as night fell, the pigeon perched on the bedstead, as it usually did, but at midnight, remembering their sad separation, it hopped down and got under the covers, which was the end of the pigeon, because Jursafú cuddled it too tight and smothered it to death. The pigeon is buried on the bank of the Pilcomayo in the overgrown garden of a house which at that time belonged to Doña Fortunata but now belongs to no one because it was washed away by the wide, infinitely sad river.

In Villamontes, Jursafú had carried around a splinter from the *urundel*—the sacred tree of the ignorant people—as if it had been a relic or something secret. He picked it up in the middle of the woods, and by carrying it next to his chest, he silently promised to protect his parents. Losing the splinter would mean bringing fate down on his head; thus he had borrowed needless suffering by indebting himself to nature, that wild part of the universe which appears to have no emotion but which my friend had suddenly involved in an entirely human matter. Jursafú had sealed a pact—his first definitive compromise with life—with the wind and the strong, quarrelsome solitude of our land. In such cases, it is impossible to know who has seduced whom, who has led whom astray. I don't have the answer either. And even if I did, I would say that I didn't.

Caught between the past and the present, Jursafú looked at the sad, wide waters of the Pilcomayo, and his father went back to his chores, which began at five o'clock in the morning and ended at nine at night. And Jursafú, in spite of the fine shoes worn by his classmates and the presence of Hilda Mendoza—his latest flame—began to fight the current as if he were trying to reach its source and finished the first two years of high school. He didn't get good marks but he didn't fail anything either, and without even realizing it, he had managed to open the doors of Tarija, the capital of the southern region, the City of the Guadalquivir, and other places. This was his first airplane trip because the old man and his fourteen-year-old son, Jursafú, decided to fly. From the air, the small scrubby bushes of the valley which he was seeing for the first time looked to him like black sheep about to be shorn in the middle of a lonely landscape—one that wasn't at all to his liking, which he was able to confirm once on the ground. And there he saw the treeless hills, narrow streets, and tall buildings of a city filled with the aroma of ripening peaches and the tired voices of citizens in their tidy square on the bank of a sparkling river bordered by willows and *molles*, the sacred tree of the Incas. Everything looked very different from his homeland, whose rough inhabitants now seemed pitiful, even as mental images.

Amazed by the abundance of delicious fruits, Jursafú thought of similar ones that grew in Gran Chaco Province and were just the same as these except that they were sourer than lemons. So he decided to send some of the delicious fruit to his relatives. He would send a basket filled with different varieties from the fertile valley, but while he was paying to have the parcel sent at the airline office, a condor that usually ran loose in the square noticed the basket about to be mailed to the frontier region. In human terms, it is a mystery how the condor managed to discover that Jursafú wasn't a native and was wandering around like a lost soul. But from a different perspective, communication among the three kingdoms of nature is a fact, not a mystery.

Going along such a road of trials and tribulation and always remaining close to the most elemental things, my friend became a traveler of many worlds, worlds that I have only heard about and that I have never cared to enter because I'd rather not become a monkey in silk clothing. After spending two relatively happy years in Tarija, Jursafú moved to Salta, where the revelations of poetry awaited him; he returned from that place with a disheveled look about him and a green bottle in his possession. He got his high school diploma in the City of the Guadalquivir and then applied at the University in La Paz, but after turning over an inkwell, he decided that, from then on, he would keep the following motto in mind: "It's better to do something badly than to do nothing at all." He asked Laura to become his wife, and during the first two years of married bliss, he wrote a book that summed up his first twenty years of happiness on the earth. He made friends, some that were like us and some that weren't, and he got himself balled up in more than a few contradictions, since he was used to doing things on his own without having to think of anyone else.

Trying to help people like Jursafú is like pulling a donkey by the tail. Moreover, the story becomes more complicated at this point because I'm not familiar with some of the essentials, though I certainly could be if I had followed the tracks of an invisible animal that stalks Jursafú as he merrily goes about his life and on occasion thinks of sending the choice fruits of other worlds to his familiar, unforgettable village; but his good intentions haven't amounted to much, and here we sit, waiting. And since we're good at waiting, we've remained here all these years, in the same spot where we were born. But now, the closer I try to get to him—in my memory—the more distant he seems. And what is my memory?

Sometimes, bending under the weight of many years, my memory pulls from the shadows the image of a miraculous village, a village where many people once lived but who now live in different places, have changed, and have adopted new manners and machinations. The place isn't different, but the warmth of our illusions has given it a flavor that can't be found in any other part of the world. In the olden days, no one knew that the world was round, and no one seemed to want to know. On moonlit nights, we ran around on the patio at school like a bunch of nitwits, illuminated by a light that wasn't natural, but it protected us just the same, as if by magic. It rained hard for days on end; it rained as it should, with lightning and great claps of thunder resounding in the distance; and the water rushed about our feet and touched our hearts which were simple and kind. In winter, the cold and dampness forced us to stay inside around the fire and to put on our overshoes, but if we looked up, we could see the heavens, beautifully cloaked in dark clouds.

All day and night we could hear the galloping of horses. Some of them, my friend, were real, others were mere inventions of the devil that the dogs warned us about with their howling, that boded presences from another world. Far, far from the thickest part of the forest, the loud, jangling song of some lost rider was heard. Maybe real, maybe a lie. Our fear was magical, so much so that it didn't paralyze us but stirred up our imaginations; we believed in apparitions and they believed in us; and because of this trust, we were able to form true friendships with different kinds of trees, trees of the dark waters and trees of morning clearness.

There were birds of many colors in the dense forest and in the open air. The birds of the forest—the militia of Silbaco—had a captivating song, a melody and nothing more. No one has seen them or will ever see them, because they don't exist; they only sing, but their song is more perilous than any existing thing, and their chirping can deprive unsuspecting people of their lives—but not the people who know them and never answer back no matter how difficult it may be to remain silent. The birds that live in the open air are victims of the hunters except for the ovenbird and the crow, which symbolize pleasant communion with nature that can occur far away from the forest and sometimes from life. It can be—as it often is—a lament for a loved one or the consolation that follows, the peace that comes from enumerating the loved one's virtues or from the wind, the blessed wind, blowing through the streets and many roads that lead to the pathless woods.

Each dawn was like the first in the eternal month of May. We knew nothing of the rest of the world and its long history, and obviously, since it wasn't ours, we didn't care about it, because in the land of God people carried the elements of the universe in their souls; and when they disappeared, they were gone forever to open the way for new roads of life. Our lives were full, intense, and without vacillation, and the word "solidarity" had no meaning, for it was the invisible axis of our lives. Must the air be named for us to take advantage of its vital presence? It simply is breathed and put back into circulation. Gratitude is what enhanced us, and therefore, death was a living consolation. The horizon ended in a distant green or blue, and above it rose a light blue transparency which is not beyond our reach as one might think; but that transparency changed us into inaccessible beings.

Wearing a broad-brimmed hat or with the wind blowing in our hair, we relied upon a language of proverbs, word play, and double meanings. And no one tried to get to the root of the matter because at the root there was nothing for us, only the earth, new and fertile, changing and propitious for the ardor of youth and for the nostalgia of those about to leave us. And like a promise from the other side, there was the morning star with its sudden burst of light, or the stars that fell and brought good luck to those who were watching.

Many people died in that scenario while we opened the door to life with its illusions. And eventually, we were able to carry on an active commerce with the dead, though they had no recollection of us in their pure state of death, tugging at us as we slept or appearing as white forms in the night or making noises in places where there was nothing that could make a noise. We were far from here and close to there. We loved and lived peacefully without sudden starts, half animal, half human, just as life demands if we want to breathe deeply and be who we are; and if we ever got a knot in our throats when we looked up above, it wasn't because of any neurosis or old-fashioned fear, but because of the evidence we saw of the infinite. The more removed we were from the origin, the more magical our tie with it became; and our memories grew stronger, memories of the first journey, of conception, and of the joy of being on the earth full of pastures, elaborate sounds, and silences conceived with rigorous precision.

Rural people say that "respect comes from distance," but to grasp the total meaning of such sayings, you have to be rural, for we express ourselves roughly yet proudly and in keeping with our particular needs and experiences, and we develop a kind of maturity, learned in part from hardships. We are not deaf, and from time to time nature speaks to us through examples, telling us what we ought to do. And we are all ears, even if our ponchos are tattered. No one but a stranger would tell us to make machetes out of wood or to roll *palobobo* into cigarettes. Only foreigners have died of thirst on the bank of an *aguada*. It's obvious; "respect comes from distance," because only distance allows us to remember everything with absolute precision. But then came the chaos that produced the chasm, and we peer into it with dread, knowing that we may drop down into the uncertainty of being neither of the past nor the future—which before we never feared—as though condemned to exist in a nebulous present, confused by some sort of spell, and yet finding ourselves in the same setting where in another age, by the grace of a primitive existence, we saw ourselves as a natural prayer rising up from the soul.

I'm not sure if Jursafú went away before or after the village lost its magical ambiance and the province was struck by misfortune. But he left knowing that he was condemned to remember our loved ones who as of yet haven't disappeared from life. Inhabitants of an endangered world, they remain without a word, as if beings such as they—indelible among the paths and trees—should ever need to speak. Or is it not so, Victorino Guzmán, Pila Ramos, José María Ruiz, Pancho Francisco, and Fortunato Gallardo?

And because he went away, he began to remember like a man who is awake but talked as if he were walking in his sleep. Because we must go away to become conscious of the language we speak, the language that redeems us. In these whereabouts, we still know how to remember, with language, that things are not immobile, and to communicate—through diabolic art—without altering the healthful silence of the word. It is even possible to "sound" an alarm in silence. Animals know this, just as did the ancient dwellers of the province, who could fall down stammering and cursing but were never afraid. What better proof that we should never disregard what our elders have told us?

Why did Jursafú go away? Why did he choose to live like a frightened animal? Did he prefer distance? Did he go away breathing words or, like a good mute, was he so in need of language that he had to distance himself in order to truly appreciate the hidden structure of our lives? In these parts, we all know, especially the Chacos, that there's an ordinary language and also an invisible one, and ancient souls possess the art of walking with one foot on the sunlit path and the other in the deep well of night, without one foot disturbing the other.

The Dead Man as Jursafú Sees Him

In the Andean city, ocean of rock and transparency, the place where the
dead and sages inhabit a world finished off in full splendor.

Last year, as I walked down a steep incline accompanied by my son
Alberto, I gazed at the enormous quantity of buildings constructed in the
city of La Paz. In the center of that monumental mass, a cubical form with
an infinite number of windows stood out. For a brief time it had been the
tallest building in the Andean city. My son, still a child, captured that image
with a statement containing a question: "That's the great city, isn't it?"

Involuntarily, I remembered the passage from Nietzsche's *Thus Spake
Zarathustra,* when the madman is trying to convince the philosopher to
abandon the city because it has become a nest of vipers and a den of the
most abominable iniquities. Zarathustra, who was no idiot, then asks the
madman—if I'm telling this right—why, instead of telling other people
what to do, he doesn't just go away himself.

I was distracted for only a second, for I remember quickly saying, "Yes,
that's the great city." Right after that, I recounted our odyssey, the origin
of our hardships and of the music of the province, and the forbidden
dream of the muleteer—all of which he was hearing for the umpteenth
time. But I repeated it, nonetheless, and as insistently as possible so that
he would never forget.

I arrived in La Paz exactly twenty years ago; in other words, I have now
left half of my life in this Andean city, the largest in Bolivia and the highest
in the world. I'm a person from a remote frontier province, not a province
of the central region. I decided to draw near the "fire" in hopes that I might
improve my lot; in other words, I decided to get an education so that I

could provide for my eight younger brothers and sisters. It's what anyone might have done. But life decided differently and spun me around like a top, over here, over there, until I had lost sight of my original goal; then it offered me a rough road, which, without knowing it, I had been avoiding for a long time.

The poverty of Bolivia is a lot like that of its poorest families; in other words, it's the most destitute country in Latin America. Its history is a microcosm of the history of the entire continent, and the trickery and the lies that our neighbors are able to hide are readily visible here. We're not proud of it, but we don't cry and scream about it, either. As you might suspect, its nine states are very different, so different that when Bolivians travel a few kilometers, they may well be heading into an unfamiliar zone. And the surprises or difficulties that await them are often accentuated by linguistic differences—a problem that no one has been able to solve and that no one pays much attention to, except for research scientists. Sometimes I try to imagine what it would be like if we only spoke Aymara or Quechua, especially since the official language is Spanish, which is the chosen language of the ruling class or whichever group happens to hold the reins of government.

I speak Spanish, or Castilian, as it's called; and I'm not bragging when I say this. It's just a confession. Besides Castilian, I speak a few words of Guarani, French, Aymara, and Quechua, and I know one word of German and one of Italian. And from my travels, I have come to feel what I once only understood; and I can truthfully say that I have come to understand the Bolivian majority, which is not Spanish-speaking, and I can testify to the fact that they are good eggs, though they have suffered limitations, and some would call them "marginal," which is basically a pejorative term. Everyone knows this. In a few words, being marginal means not participating, not from choice, but from adverse circumstances. But thanks to fate, everything in life is relative, which was already drummed into the human memory; but before some people would believe it, an Albert Einstein had to show up and prove it mathematically. To give an example, the first time I was in Paris, I had to put up with the most terrible inconveniences because I didn't know French. But as soon as I realized that "été" meant "summer," everything was fine. It seemed too small a word—a rather pathetic little word—for a phenomenon which in my estimation goes beyond the powers of language; and this is understandable if you remember that I'm from a torrid zone filled with trees, a vast plain with its own music rising up from buried dreams. I was at one with this world and knew that summer was its supreme event.

I remember taking my son by the hand and telling him many things at once, all of which meant, more or less, the same thing: don't ever forget your roots or pretend you're from somewhere else because life has a knack for putting things where they belong. He's still too young to understand what I was talking about. Sometimes he picks up my notebooks and reads them, just as I read my father's diary, written in a large, sloping hand that revealed his strong spirit and self-control. At any rate, regardless of what I want, my son will do and think as he pleases. If he's good, he'll remember things he never saw and only learned from others—or from books, which is worse. And if he's bad, the best I can do is pray for him to the kind spirits, because fate is not as easily corrected as the anomalies we pick up from the external world. Your fate will be your fate no matter what you do to avoid it. Your path will always be the one that was plotted for you at the beginning of life.

Until about twenty years ago, this city still had a provincial air about it, which, paradoxically, was a source of amazement for those of us who lived here. When I say "us," I'm talking about the ones of us who arrived from Tarija to seek a profession. It was a beautiful time because we were young or because the city wasn't so desolate or hopeless as it is now. Few of us remain, and when we see each other, the old fervor is gone. We're different. We have new obligations which have caused us to see things differently—things we thought would never change. As it turned out, we each went our own way, which is always how it is with animals and human beings. I've completely lost track of some of them, people I admired and was proud to call my friends. One of them lost a kidney; some of them are dead; some have returned home to work as bankers. But the ones who are really far away are the ones you meet on the street and they act like perfect strangers. Yet we continue to greet one another as fate dictates, though such greetings have no meaning or dignity. It would be better if we treated one another as strangers—real strangers—and passed without speaking, just as strangers do in a city when they look at one another without seeing, since it's been decided that loneliness isn't loneliness, which protects them from intimacy yet permits a certain familiarity, one that fills a common need. In such situations, pure instinct reigns, though I'm not sure what kind of instinct. Maybe it comes from anxiety—or death. Who knows?

This is the great city that Alberto pointed to when he was a child, the city which is Bolivia's seat of government and where the drama of national identity is acted out. What is our drama? The question is absurd, and because it is absurd, it reminds me of a young writer—not so young anymore—who, in 1961, called together a group of young people with literary affiliations. We met on the patio of a large house on Juan de la Riva Street, and there in the burning sunlight, typical of the Altiplano, he asked us a question which we normally wouldn't have answered, or maybe we would have answered it if he'd asked us at night, "Friends, what is life? And what is death?" I remained silent, not because I was wise—I was too young to be wise—but because I was cautious, as rural people are. I laugh about it now, but it wasn't funny then. I was ashamed, embarrassed; I felt as if I'd done something awful. I wish I'd written down what some of my friends said. It could be useful to know what innocents would say in a situation like that, which only an impertinent fool would create.

Twenty years have passed, and the guy who asked the question is as much of a jackass now as he was then, and the other members of the group, who thought they had a special gift for writing, have ended up doing various types of work—work they don't especially like—which often happens to people who believe in life and believe in their own calling. Some have turned out to be hopeless alcoholics; some were killed in political uprisings in our country; and others seem to have vanished from the earth, though probably they're out there drifting in the sea of anonymity, neither sinking nor swimming, which doesn't mean, of course, that they're treading water while the rest of the world rushes by.

I had just begun my adventure in La Paz and foolishly believed that a career in engineering might solve my problems. But in reality, what I wanted was to be pardoned for an old sin, not my sin, but one that had given me a lot of trouble just the same. I'm talking about the questions

64

that tormented me when I was a child, questions too tough for a kid. "Why am I here?" "Who am I?" "What was I before I was born?" "What's going to happen to me when I die?" Questions that educated people discuss, especially artists and writers. I got my first hard rap on the head, and it took me totally by surprise, because I thought the devil was somewhere else, not in my own front yard. The whole business depressed me, but I was ignorant and quickly put it out of my mind. Though I never really got over it.

Most of us were about twenty then—I wasn't quite twenty yet—and we were all searching for a deeper truth: we wanted to find the linchpin of existence. When we weren't involved in some harebrained scheme, we were going to meetings where the older people, most of them dead now, either repeated their worn-out phrases or, on occasion, sang some tragic ballad we'd never heard before. In other words, it was a real minstrel show and I grew tired of it rather fast. Today no one would attend such meetings, much less participate. But during one of those nighttime gatherings, something strange happened which I'll relate to exercise my memory if nothing else.

One night in January in Miraflores—the section of La Paz which has changed the least—I met a great poet who was old and wasn't going to live much longer. We were at a party, and while his daughter was dancing, he sat drinking, which was his major pastime, and every now and then he would mumble something unintelligible. I was happy sitting next to him, listening to what he had to say, which was nostalgic and nocturnal like his poetry; but suddenly he said to me, his eyes still on his daughter Jenny, "Do you know what I like most about my daughter?" I thought for a moment and could have continued thinking for a long time, for I hardly knew his daughter, since I'd entered that luminous world only recently. But before I could respond, he answered the question himself, "The best thing about my daughter is that she's my daughter." He then lifted his glass to his lips and quietly slipped away into a silky, Parisian ambiance filled with memories of a glorious past.

The poet's young wife was graciously attending the guests. She was like a figure that had slipped from the night, with her almond-shaped eyes, her long tresses brushed back and fastened at the nape of her neck, the spot from which feminine mystery flows. Her green eyes, like the eyes of some extinct animal, spied me lying lethargically on the couch, either looking like a party crasher or maybe staring innocently at the other guests—I don't recall. I only remember that she took me by the hand, led me out into the hall, and told me to wait as she went dashing up the stairs. Everyone was half drunk—a strange alcoholic beverage was being served—and half deaf, thanks to the music. But shut off from those infernal tones that sounded strange and distant, like in a dream, I stood waiting for her return. She came back carrying something in her hand, but I didn't see what it was, even as she slipped it under my jacket. Then politely yet insistently she asked me to leave the house. At the front door she said some things that didn't make any sense, but from what I could understand, she'd just handed me something that I'd wanted for a long time. I went away thinking about how strangely she'd behaved. She was probably neurotic, I thought, or perhaps an involuntary messenger from another world.

By the time I reached my room on the other side of town, my head was roaring. I had made my way through the dense, dark web of endless streets without looking at the envelope under my jacket. But the first thing I did after closing the door was to take it out and examine its contents. It was a notebook full of poems. They had been written by someone named Cranach—or something like that—and addressed to the woman who had given them to me. They were strange poems, and their author seemed to have been suffering from a broken heart.

Several years passed before I learned the author's true identity. They were years of continuous searching, fear, and restlessness, years when I had one foot in the geology department and the other in some slippery place which seemed purposeless but inescapable all the same. Something was pushing me in that direction—a direction that seemed contrary to my nature. For example, one day after my physics class, a young, blond math teacher who looked like a gringo showed me around the lab and then invited me to his home. He introduced me to his beautiful mother who was mending clothes for the family, and then he played some records, including a Bach concerto, and finally, recommended some readings: Franz Kafka, Antoine de Saint-Exupéry, Hermann Hesse, and Albert Camus, whom he considered the most important of the lot. I read *The Trial* by the first, *The Little Prince* by the second, *Damian* by the third, and *The Stranger* by the fourth. As I read, I suspected it was all going in one ear and out the other since I was preoccupied with other things, like my separation from Orana, the girl of my dreams, who was either in school at Tarija or Camiri, or she might have been doing something else, but regardless, she was a long way away from my eyes and my arms. Eventually I got fed up with my studies, and one fine day, after seeing a movie called *The Carpetbaggers,* I decided to quit school. I was suddenly left with nothing, and I wrote to my parents but didn't give them any real explanation for how I was feeling or what I had done. I stayed on in the city, alone.

I suppose that if such a situation were to present itself, I would do exactly as I did then, but only if I could be as young as I was then, which was twenty. But I wouldn't do it at this age, not because I don't have the strength, but because I've been in enough dangerous situations to know that you have to rush into them without worrying about what might happen to you. And after you've been through a lot, then you can talk about pain, exhaustion, fear, and all the other terrible things that can happen to you, things the featherless biped is always claiming to have suffered every time he turns around. And I'm still living by myself with nothing to do in the daytime, or as they say in my village, "chewing on a raw potato," remaining silent in fifteen different languages, and keeping the faith of the ancient dwellers of my province. And, apparently, I reached the end without uttering a word, but unless I'm wrong, it doesn't have to be that way. If a person keeps on living, maybe it's because he stays hopeful and trusts that things have an explanation no matter how baffling they may seem. And even though I stumbled around most of my life, I always believed that life holds a special meaning for everyone, and that everything happens for a reason, though sometimes life is hard. And I'm not just saying this. Anyone who's put himself to the test knows what he believes and what he doesn't. And I, for one, was saved by my particular brand of faith, which didn't always keep me from getting a beating; sometimes it even seemed that believing as I did was a sin, and that I was going to be punished for it whether I did anything wrong or not.

I gave up geology—without losing touch with the pure earth— and took up literature. No one persuaded me to do it. It was a crime I committed on my own, which makes me responsible for my downfall. My practical side rebelled against such an "unhealthy" pursuit. And for a long time I really didn't know what serious literature was all about. Even now I couldn't give an official definition, though based on my own knowledge and experience, I might be able to expound on it a bit with no other source than what I've learned roaming the earth and seeking truths that I am able to understand. My only goal has been to speak from my mute soul, and I measure my success according to my own opinion and not the praise of others who have watched the fire but have been afraid to touch the coals. I innocently knocked at the door of a world I didn't know and entered in good faith; but words locked me in, though I was never innocent enough to believe that they were good for anything—or so insensitive not to wish that they were. Literature is worthless if you ask the opinions of the so-called "practical people," and that's no laughing matter, since they're the ones who run things. And also the fact that so many vain, insincere people choose this profession makes a person wonder about the honesty and seriousness of people who claim to believe in the written word. It is true, nonetheless, that a lot of intelligent people find this material singularly attractive. Even members of the Bolivian military have found some well-written verses thoroughly illuminating, which might be funny except that it implies a dangerous truth. As a friend of mine once said, "It's like standing in front of a monkey that has a straight razor in its hand."

I used to never think about such things, but even if I had, it wouldn't have convinced me not to be a writer. When you're young, you act young; it's a good way to be, whether you're running the race or just standing on the sidelines. When you're young, you want to try everything. And though you may think you're listening to your elders, in reality, you're only listening to yourself. That's how it was with me. And it's probably that way every place on the globe. I happen to live in one of the more remote areas of the world, and people who live at the modern core aren't always aware of their power. Here, among the mountains and plains, I learned that culture can be a way of communicating, and it can also teach a person how to be alone and happy. Our culture, meaning the culture that floats on the surface of our lives, mimics something that is contrary to our nature. At best, it is a clumsy rehashing of what has been done in Europe or the United States, or, at worst, a hypocritical effort to recover native values which for the most part have been devalued, ridiculed by the social elite who controls them.

And yet there's a different kind of culture, a secret one whose distant rhythms were set long before we existed. Communication, with whomever and for whatever reason, lies at its very heart. After communication comes information—defined in modern terms, of course—and as far as I can tell, this culture's well-informed members can survive the worst of times. Based on this evidence, we believe that the dead man is in possession of all information, since life reveals its secrets only after death. These are important words, but not because they're mine. I, too, got involved in things that were mundane and lost sight of who I was before I could intuit the plan of the universe that overwhelms us with its splendor. I remember having written once, "in the blue garland of profundity," and was pleased that I could express in six words an emotion that needed to be expressed, which is a respectable thing to do. But right after I did it, I walked out on the street and caught a whiff of something frying and other food odors that were totally alien to the experience I'd had in my room, and my state of mind quickly changed. This was the first time I'd ever sensed a disparity between what I was doing—with good intention, you understand—and what was going on under my nose. While I thought about that, a light came on inside my head, and I was able to see things clearly. Maybe this isn't the time to go into the problem or what I was able to do about it, but what I figured out was that each thing has its own place, time, voice, and music. And this was terribly important for the course I chose to follow; in other words, it allowed me to see how confused our society really is, and that it is provincial and hypocritical in the worst sense. But in the final analysis, you can't close yourself off from it; you have to pay attention to what goes on around you, whether you get anything out of it or not. If people, in fact, could shut themselves off, unless they were stupid, they would knock a hole in the roof so they could at least see the sky, the pale blue firmament that faithfully summarizes all human events. And if they didn't, they might expect one fine day to wake up, planning to go to their favorite park, and discover that the world had disappeared.

I'm not just saying these things to be funny; they synthesize a number of things I've been thinking about for a long time, maybe my entire life, which doesn't mean, of course, that they are especially important. They are questions which have shaken me up, the way a sack of potatoes gets shaken up on a journey so that the potatoes fit better; in other words, I hope that thinking about these things has made me a better person. At any rate, when I started the trip, to make myself feel better, I said to myself from my muleteer's soul, "No matter what happens on the road, you can take care of it." And I'm halfway there, though I haven't left the country; and I know that people don't have any choice about where they're born; some people say that it's a matter of chance, but I say that it depends on a secret pact between our bodies and the land that is assigned to us at birth. Our land is wide, mountainous, diverse, and contradictory; but I like it, from the lowest valleys to the icy peaks. It's the guardian of a way of writing that, until it's deciphered, will hold us all as slaves, which is the way it's been since the republic was founded.

Around here the Indians who work day and night are the ones who suffer the consequences. At least some would say that—the ones who think they own the world. But anyone who roams the wide land knows that it's endless and full of surprises; it's inaccessible, however, to the lazy people who would mishandle its treasures, either as tenants of the Burned Palace or simply as owners of the wealth that circulates throughout the shrubless hills. This is hard to say and even harder to understand. I was always aware of it, but there are many thorns and sharp stones along the path, and it may take a while to get where you're going, especially if you're walking, and barefooted to boot.

When I reached La Paz, after many attempts to accommodate myself in a country that was and wasn't mine, I had an opportunity to examine these difficult materials and their no less difficult plots; I looked at them from my provincial point of view and with the uncertainty that is common to those who feel estranged in their own country. These were excellent years, though I could barely keep the shirt on my back and got pneumonia more than once, without knowing it, of course. During this time, I lived in a small room and worked there making packages for coffee. And I met quite a few Argentines—most of them young—who were wandering around the continent then, but now have made a name for themselves in places like Peking and Bolpebra. They were all determined to learn as much as they could about Latin America; some were truly dedicated; others were mere adventurers. They seemed to fit in perfectly in these parts, and they taught me, without intending to, that it's one thing to travel and another to stay in the same place; and some people have to stay at home so that others can sail the great oceans, just as some people are observers and others have to let themselves be observed. If it weren't that way, life would lose its savor. So thanks to the gauchos, I suddenly found myself learning about my own country from a wooden chair I built for myself so I could watch the world spinning around in circles. I think that I'm right—but please be patient with me if I'm not—when I say that Bolivia isn't like the rest of Latin America. It's as though our nostalgia for the past were turned to stone, and none of us can do anything about it, because all of us have been affected.

Our land has often been the victim of foreign greed, and its people have felt suffocated, boxed in. And if you doubt this, look at our history with its many barbarous deeds—and some noble gestures as well. After a hundred and fifty years of seclusion, we are Mediterraneans to the gills, but we are still alive and kicking and have miraculously been able to hold on to our dreams. But if we look out upon the hills, eternal and grandiose—to mention only two of their fine qualities—they seem to move away at nightfall toward their Andean dwelling, the cave where human life began. And in that sphere, frivolity cannot soothe us inside or out, for the only thing we feel is a burning transparency that emanates from fear. I sometimes ask myself if our irresponsible neighbors, who make fun of us, could have survived half of the disasters we have been faced with. Two politicians, Juan Manuel Rosas and Facundo Quiroga, nearly wrecked Argentina, for example. We, on the other hand, have had at least a dozen presidents—some elected, others put into office by force—who were worse than those long-haired cowboys ever dared to be. Not to mention all the other scoundrels we've had to put up with—so many of them, they hardly fit in such a small country.

If we've managed to survive, it's because we're governed by a different rhythm, one that keeps our memories fresh, and has left us with the legacy of a race whose descendants have kept alive the signs of its existence. There are no enigmas here, except for the tourists, who visit Tiwanaku but ignore the survivors of that mysterious culture. And while such visitors profess a deep reverence for the past, they live in a present which they cannot share with the guardians of that past. It's an ironic situation created, paradoxically, by people who have no sense of irony. And something similar occurs inside the country. I'm speaking not of individuals but of an attitude held by many Bolivians whose heritage is half European, an attitude that might prove ominous for the country. But if I were speaking of individuals, I would have to add that some are very sensitive to the situation; in other words, they are especially adept at sensing danger and are constantly on guard—for the sake of their own well-being, of course. Because, when all is said and done, it is a question of self-preservation and not of humanitarian ideals.

One night in January of 1980, while looking at a map of the election precincts, I fully understood the difference between people who act like proprietors and people who are proprietors but don't act like it. I was very surprised to see that the map of the Andean city was full of Aymara and Quechua names. Except for the few that alluded to the Spanish presence—San Jorge, San Pedro, and the whole saintly crew—most of them derived from the language of the conquering tribes: Pampajasi, Kaikoni, Següencoma, Sopocachi, Achumani, and so on—which made me believe that the real owners had had the foresight to name the places that they had inhabited since time immemorial. Or you might say that when a place is founded, it is also named, and a true founding occurs only when the word is present, which allows us to endure without disturbing the silence of the native landscape.

I don't know if this experience was the beginning or the end of a long slide; I mean the one suffered by my wayfaring hide, forest born and forsaken, forced to roam cities and fields, and marked by an indelible sign, as though I were bearing some delicate and dangerous load tucked into my bosom. For whom, I didn't know. But time, which resolves all things, would decide. And I carried that sign with me at all times, as I traveled near and far. After leaving the geology department, I had to earn a living, for it would have been shameful to do otherwise, considering the disappointment I'd caused my parents. Besides, I wouldn't have asked them to support my idleness; I've always said that if you want to be idle, you ought to pay for it with the sweat of your brow. That's the only way to really enjoy it. It's like eating a good stew after a hard day's work. I wandered from one place to another until I found a temporary job as doorman at a tall building on Ingavi Street, a building with balconies from which you could see the entire city; and when I looked at the enormous buildings, all I could do was stare in amazement. And my thoughts wandered toward my native province and curled up inside the word "summer." Many years would pass before that word was erased from my reduced vocabulary, years of external cold and internal heat. My job ended, and for a time— exactly during the time when the Nationalist Revolutionary Movement was being put down—I worked as a journalist, though actually all I did was correct galley proofs; and later on, I got my first job working for a production company run by Arciles and Patinuk. So as it turned out, I benefited from the money invested in the Bolivian film industry. I traveled through several parts of the Altiplano, first Achacachi, then Collana, Charazani, and Curva, and finally Isla del Sol, where an ambitious project was being carried out. They were filming the story of Sabina Urpi, a woman who had been raped by a mestizo and whose husband then sought revenge for the crime. The story unfolds in the middle of a landscape which became not only an ally but an accomplice of the relentless avenger.

During the time of the filming, we stayed at the island's most com- fortable ranch house, a relic of an ill-omened past. I lived for sixty days surrounded by a lake, Lake Sagrado, and in a setting that was very different for me, because of the relationships I made there and also because of the oppressive atmosphere which didn't allow for levity of any kind. After nightfall no one dared to venture out alone, and we would have pissed in our pants before we would have gone outside. One day, when some of us were poking around in the dark basement of the Mirador, we discovered the remains of the last descendants of the Incan nobility who had been cruelly sacrificed as though they were being punished. And we were relieved to know this, not because of the sacrifice, but because it explained the sounds we'd been hearing, sighs that didn't sound human but were capable of punishing those who were. I hadn't done anything to hurt anybody, and I never would have done anything to hurt my neighbor, especially if he was worse off than I was, and besides that, I think you have to be a scoundrel or have a stone for a heart to live off someone else's hard work.

Though I knew I hadn't had anything to do with such a terrible thing, it was so awful that I was affected by it just the same. The clincher came one night near the end of our stay on the Isla del Sol, when we were sitting around, relaxing and talking—everyone except a boy about fifteen who sat quietly smiling at us. He was from the island and had done odd jobs in the kitchen or anywhere else that he was needed. We had grown fond of him and hated to leave him in such a desolate place, especially since he was bright and we thought he might do well for himself in La Paz. At least that was what Fonical said, who had taken it upon himself to speak for all of us. He suggested that we take Justino back to the capital, find him a home, and enroll him in school. The boy responded enthusiastically—he wouldn't have dared to say "no"—but then he decided he should talk it over with his parents and went immediately to his shack.

An hour later, he came running back; he was calm, alert, and pleased about his decision. He said "no" right off. He wasn't going to the city because he had decided to take the advice of a witch doctor who was visiting his family, someone the community had hired to make it rain since it hadn't rained a drop for a long time and the earth was very dry. Yatiri, as he was called, had summed up the boy's future in a few words: "You will go to La Paz and at first everything will be fine until something turns up missing at your guardian's house and everyone thinks that you stole it. After they've seriously reprimanded you, they will tell you never to do it again, but by then you won't have time to do anything because they will be shouting orders at you every time you turn around. You'll have to give up your school work. Then they'll say you're lazy and irresponsible for not taking advantage of the sacrifices they've made for you, and when you least expect it, they'll throw you out on the street. Your situation will seem hopeless, and you'll have to go back to where you came from, which is where you are today but so eagerly wish to leave."

The man who had offered to be the boy's guardian, after listening to such accusations, told him not to be a fool, but Justino stood his ground, convinced that the community had advised him wisely. The boy's obstinacy made us want to meet the man responsible for his decision, and the next day the seer appeared among us—a clear presence in that world of machinations. I remember his eyes, his poncho, and his silence created from the sum of so many summaries of human history. Hard but sensitive, without the tricks of those who lack real talent, and without the gaiety of those who have never seen danger, he told each one of us our fortunes, not to prove his power—which actually was what we wanted—but because he had received sudden insight into our lives, which he was able to see at a distance and close up. He told one man that he was going to lose a son, and the man apologetically left the circle and went straight to Copacabana on the edge of the lake, where he received a letter brought by the scriptwriter, Patinuk, saying that one of his offspring had passed away. The seer looked at each of us in turn and told us what had happened and what would happen. And then he went away as he had come, with his poncho and his silence and his lack of concern for life's enigmas. That night it rained cats and dogs, and a wind blew up that threatened to carry off the house and the trees. It roughed up the lake, which grew very dark, as shadows fell on the earth and in our souls.

Several days later, we were going to leave and return to the land of fiction—our peaceful scenario with its little dreams and disappointments—where we liked to think of ourselves as momentary discoverers of worlds presumed to be full of darkness. But before we could go back to our mischief, our work forced us to stay on another week in Copacabana. We needed to shoot some more scenes that couldn't be filmed in La Paz. And while the work was being done, I was able to hear an anecdote that I've never forgotten, because it beamed forth like some mysterious object emerging from the sand at Isla del Sol, that universe of dead people and sages, of sincere victims, and memories of a life snuffed out in full splendor. One afternoon when I was looking at the lake and standing next to some modern canoes and traditional balsa rafts, a young girl came up to me and said: "My uncle died here. Every night he would wake up, leave the bed where his wife was sleeping, saddle his horse, and ride toward the lake. As soon as he reached the shore, he'd take off his clothes and swim as fast as he could through the icy waters, as though he were being drawn toward some remote past. After he'd finished his nightly exercise, he would get back on his horse, go back to his house and his double bed, and the next day, he would wake up as if nothing had happened. But his wife couldn't stand the thought that there might be another woman, and one night she followed him. When she saw him dive in, she became frightened and started screaming because she knew that by day, at least, her husband couldn't swim. Obedient to his wife's voice, he woke up. But he drowned."

That was my brief experience with the seventh art. Soon after, I became a secretary for a program organized by Sanguinetti to promote the plastic arts. It was the first time I'd earned a salary, and I could afford to rent a room that I didn't have to share unless I wanted to. I could be alone or with someone else, whichever I preferred. And seeing what eyes rarely see, I realized that a poet is a balance between the characters he creates and their creator. This may sound unimportant, but it was basic to my mental health. For years I had been stumbling around from pillar to post with a suitcase in my hand, living in places that would never be home, though I was always treated well. In my room in Miraflores, I could feel something stirring inside of me that I wanted to express. But every time I tried to put it into words, it disappeared, and I kept waking up from a nightmare and feeling I had nothing I could count on, nothing concrete to underwrite my existence. This has been the most difficult thing for me to overcome, and I still think of myself as marginal, living off my own dreams—in other words, by a miracle. But this conviction, which was absurd yet insightful, has given me a kind of blind faith and has allowed me to bare my soul at every instant, because I'm convinced that only spirits who are open to catastrophe develop the humility that redeems us from evil.

I was living in total solitude, but about that time Latin American literature became fashionable, and I, like many other youths of my country, become enthralled by books that told of a more lucid world and tried to depict us, heart and soul. I was overwhelmed by these scholars who had discovered the secret tendons of our geography; and, in truth, I felt like a slave, not only to all the books in the world but to the emotions of an entire universe. In this uncertain struggle, my youthful impatience turned out to be a blind alley. True, some of my friends were serious, not many, but I did have a few who had a certain mental prowess. The horizon seemed full of promise; but then Laura showed up, my provincial love was rekindled, and we got married.

My happiness was short-lived because I suspected that a secret would soon be revealed that would put Bolivia on the front page of all the newspapers. It had to do with Che Guevara, who had come here sick and had written, among other things, a brief farewell letter to his parents, telling them that he was back on the road "with his shield at his side." About that time, when the fate of the Latin American guerrilla was still unknown, another Argentine, a writer named Héctor Alvarez, was giving a talk in La Paz on the native cultures of our continent, primarily Mayan culture. A member of the audience became so enraged that he couldn't contain himself, sprang to his feet, and accused the speaker of being irresponsible. "How can you talk about the spirit," he yelled, "when the life blood is being drained out of the country?" The angry man was a gringo, a journalist by profession, and a friend of some left-wing Bolivian intellectuals. The Argentine writer reminded him that "many have been deceived by America."

Two years after the assassination of Ernesto "Che" Guevara, I had an opportunity to learn more about that unique individual who had been so concerned about the destiny of Latin America. It happened in 1969, in Paris, where I'd gone with a grant. I didn't know French but wanted to learn it so as to make my way among so many French strangers; I came across a magazine, a serious publication which—like so many others—had given full coverage to the events that rocked the world in 1967. It contained photographs taken from an American airplane flying at ten thousand meters above the Bolivian jungle. The ground was clearly visible and I was able to make out an oven for baking bread, but it didn't look like the ovens used by our rural families. The one in the picture was unusual because there wasn't any smoke coming from it; in other words, it gave no indication of human presence. It was a Vietnamese oven in Bolivian territory. Who had built it? I thought that the C.I.A. would know, as well as one of its agents stationed in Bolivia, the hot-tempered journalist who had become infuriated with the speaker lecturing on Mayan culture.

It was one of the many dirty tricks I saw in this world, and since I wasn't equipped to view the abyss as anything other than what it was, such deception affected me profoundly. But I didn't let it destroy me. Instead, I managed to discover, with the help of some people who were already dead, exactly what it was that bound me to life. As a child, I had learned that the universe changes drastically the first time someone close to you dies. From then on, you see life in terms of a "before" and an "after." In other words, vital time emerges. And curious as it may seem, everything changes because a person has disappeared, a person who the day before held out a hand to us and smiled, or laughed his head off at some fellow with a nickname. Slowly, as one marches along that blind alley called "life and death," groups of people begin to form, people who are no longer with us yet participate in our lives. We move along from one group to the next, from the groups formed by our dead relatives to the ones formed by people who are important to us all and who have left us "history" to guide us through a world of shadows. This is basic to my way of thinking, and it's too late to convince me otherwise. Events that concern all people shouldn't be called "history." It would make more sense to call them "The Book of the Dead for the Living."

This insight took me by surprise one October day, when I was looking at my country and gnawing on a raw potato. I said to myself, "If you want to get ahead in this world, you've got to be willing to get your hands dirty." And I got up from where I was sitting and gave thanks for that insight, which had come to me without any effort on my part and was a good summation of everything that had happened in the past and would happen in the future. For a few days, it seemed absurd to me how human beings live their lives: ambition seemed petty; vanity, foolish; the world of reason, narrow; and silence, entirely wise. Life seemed to wake up in the morning and go to bed at night, like some giant eyelid. It woke up another morning in La Paz and struggled to wake up in my hoarse chest. As the last shadows faded, I was still unable to chase the worries out of my mind because, in a fleeting night, I had traveled the entire universe with my enormous doubts and thin hopes; I was lost in the intricate brambles of human knowledge. But I saw a ray of hope when sounds of another time began to sift in through the closed window. And in came the aroma of a pure forest, the place where the muleteer dwelled with his shadow and his primitive woes. At dawn, with my eyes closed and my heart calmed, sleep brought me a dream that I have guarded beneath my poncho until now: "The people of a village who were seduced by a magical town called Tirinea, decided to leave their belongings—shacks and dreams—in order to search for the promised land; they started off with the children leading the way—because the devil might frighten the adults—and wandered tirelessly through the desert; dressed in rags, these illusive Canaanites finally reached paradise, exhausted but still lucid enough to react with amazement upon finding themselves in their own village, which they had eagerly abandoned and which turned out to be called Tirinea." A complete circle that clearly illustrates the magic that some call imagination. A metaphor that already existed in nature, since a meandering is only that: an enormous circle that reduces the distance. And when the circle is complete—a process carried forward by circular forces—the distance disappears for the sake of direct communication. The dream was a warning. Though I can be dense about a lot of things, I'm not at all dense about premonitions. So I prepared myself for what had already begun to happen. I gave Laura a hug and went to live with Orana, a girl with a quiet soul and hair that hung down to her waist. With her at my side, I stopped frequenting the so-called fashionable places and, with a maté in my hand, started listening to a different kind of music, the music of the muleteers, who lived poorly but without restrictions, with many problems but invulnerable to them, men who were always moving toward a point where fate turns to illusion, through mounds of kindly shadows and nights refreshed by the dreaminess of warm days.

Happy, impervious to our country's sadness, immune to the knavery of its officials, I was shocked to find myself suddenly writing a book, and sometimes, late at night, I felt as though I were gently falling rain. This was the last time that life allowed me to hear the brave, natural sounds of the frontier. Words darted back and forth in my mind like cross-fire, and sensations flashed like bolts of lightning. I was so far away that I hardly sensed them, for they belonged to beings that had drowned in the solitude of another land, of another hallucination, but where my soul, nonetheless, had found unexpected shelter. Orana was still asleep, with geraniums all around her. Alone, she and I, childless, with a bright future before us, we watched the world from a window trimmed with eucalyptus. In three months I was able to get rid of something I had been carrying around for twenty-five years. It choked me up to think I didn't know what I had done with my life; and though I had always been far from desecration, I would change it into words or destroy it. Suddenly I was tongue-tied in fifteen different languages, but held nothing back, and in sixty pages recounted everything I'd ever done or felt, in depth. But on the morning of June 13, 1967, feeling overwhelmed by certain events that were taking place, I threw up, then went back to sleep, and had a terrible dream. First I dreamed that stones were raining down on our house, and one of my hands was flying around throwing out advertisements of the film *Hamlet*, and finally, someone who looked like a building engineer, wearing khaki pants, boots, and a brimmed hat, was glaring at me and threatening to take hold of my hand, but I managed to grab it and squeeze it against my chest—thinking it was a frog—until it was dead; and then I woke up crying.

I was happy for a time, until I felt a void in my life. But gradually it was filled by my own being, which for the first time came into view. I was living in a different space, and my body could sense the power of the Andean world. True, I had been in La Paz some seven years, but you don't always see things just because you want to see them. The time has to be right, and you have to wait patiently. Though I was Indian, I was a stranger to the Andean setting. I knew nothing about the Aymaras or the Quechuas, and besides that, my body rhythms were different. That desert of stone and transparency felt contrary to my nature. But with my stranger's soul, I began to see a broader panorama crossed by brilliant ideas and heroic deeds. I perceived an earth filled with wonders, a world that proceeded from the night of time and where the mythic couple—a pair of rogues—had committed the inevitable sin, disobedience. I became a prisoner to my books, which I read endlessly, though they were of doubtful benefit; I knew a lot but my judgment was poor. In the middle of such an apprenticeship, a voice spoke to me, "If you aren't careful, you could end up on the street again." That scared me because I knew that I could be gullible; in other words, I doubted my own maturity.

I came back to reality when I heard about the death of Guevara, which, according to one source, "came as a terrible shock to many Bolivians, including some whose consciences aren't entirely clear and others who are ignorant of what has been happening in their own country." Spontaneously, my soul began to reexamine human history, our history, where, to my surprise, I discovered many lessons. Also, because of Che's death, I made new friendships forged by the heat of dormant ideals that had suddenly burst into flames. I'd never experienced real misery before, the kind of misery that people feel when their stomachs are empty and they are plagued by constant problems. I saw it for the first time when I visited the Bolivian mines, where the blood of our blood is spilled every day without a single complaint. The silence of those people gagged me; I had no desire to say anything about their problems, which, in my opinion, ought to be addressed by the sensitive soul of the combatant.

And living in a rapidly moving present, I believed that certain presences had always been with me. At times they were made of shadow, and at times they were as brief and dangerous as a bolt of lightning. Someone whispered to me from death, "Now that you've experienced every human event, all you need to do is stir your memory." I looked at my body, and when I was able to see deep inside of it, I was sorry for my anxieties, which at one time I thought would propel me toward the truth. But the "eyes" I was searching for were in the landscape, hills, plants, animals, and rocks, alien to the illusions of human consciousness. Then suddenly, in a gust of wind, my own face appeared, and it wasn't the face of an older man but of a beardless youth with neither the experience nor the courage needed to hear the earth speak.

One day I made a list of the dead people I'd known. Anyone alive has known many beings who are now bones, nothing more, indifferent to the changing seasons or the discoveries of poets. I remembered my cousin Ramón, who died at the age of twenty. I remembered Angel Vargas smiling ironically beneath a lemon tree in bloom and his words of wisdom just before the noose tightened around his neck, "Let us all return meekly to the earth." The dead filed by, smiling; and my heart shrivelled as I watched a bee buzzing among the geraniums on a Sunday afternoon in La Paz, with my companion, with hopes and thoughts that had acquired neither the form nor intricacy of real thought that emerges from death. Pensive, at a crucial moment in my life, I remembered a distant afternoon when my uncle Jesús León, who had served as a second lieutenant in the Chaco War and was now a humble man approaching death, offered me a carob drink under the shade of a *garbancillo*. And after I'd spent time with the dead of my own past and of my country's past, I returned to the world of the living, to the Andean world of pure twilights and morning hubbub, where everything seemed haphazard but was so perfectly put together that the soldering was invisible to all except the solderer. It was at that time that I began to conceal certain convictions, not from others so much as from myself. I entered a no-man's-land, and there I was able to prove that knowledge found in books is worthless unless it is rigorously tested; and in this barren land, the only thing to be done is to wait for the trusted voice, cordial and enthusiastic, of our own limitations, a world of our own founding, with stars that are within our grasp.

Of the many friends I made during that time, one of them left a vivid impression. It was a young engineer, who was normally a serious person, but with a couple of drinks under his belt, he became hilariously funny. And there were other contradictions in his personality. On the one hand, he had the intuitive powers of a medium, and on the other, he was a hard-core revolutionary, who fought and surrendered in the jungles of Teoponte. His name was Adrián. One day I looked into his eyes and knew that he was going to die very soon; and from then on I could only think of him as a dead man among the living, which to a certain extent is true of all people, but in his case it was different because what I knew I had learned through direct perception. I lived with that strange knowledge— knowing I was communicating with a dead person—until he died from a bullet wound in the back as he had dreamed would happen.

From the time he was a child, he had dreamed again and again that he was in the heat of a battle and shouting orders to the other troops. In his first dreams, he was only a soldier, but in successive dreams he gradually moved up in the ranks. By the time I met him, he had become a captain, but was still getting shot in the back. He was a good man, far from a weakling, and was incensed by any form of injustice or hypocrisy. While others were desperate for contact with the supernatural world, Adrián was constantly besieged by a host of inhuman forces. He often woke up with his eyes swollen—like a cat that had been bitten by a snake—which was a sure sign that he'd been roaming the rooftops of the city all night or had been reading books that he remembered nothing about in real life. He was no fool and was fully aware that he had an "other" inside of him. My hair stood on end when I found out about the amazing numerical relationship that figured in his destiny; but I said nothing about it then, or later, when I discovered in a dream that he had died and in the same dream received some good advice that I always carried with me in a secret compartment in my billfold. Why deal in facts that don't earn you anything—anything material, that is? Only a fool would do that. I've always suspected that human beings aren't especially suited to the delicate petals of wisdom; sportsmen that they are, to them wisdom is just intelligence or a gift for words. And wouldn't we all sell our grandmothers for a nice turn of phrase?

Bolivia is like a bucket of cold water when it comes to such tendencies—which is a blessing. Anyone who wants to triumph is likely to go astray, but those who do go astray but don't lose faith find protection. Just look into the eyes of our authentic heroes or shake hands with the people who work from daybreak to dusk without saying a word, because complaining is foreign to their lips. Along the rugged road of human suffering, they only learned to speak quietly, and next to them, the rest of us sound like fools. Some of us, more than others, know that they are made of a tougher metal than we. The engineers know it, the ones who get drunk and travel the Altiplano. They couldn't do it sober. They speed along the landscape, their elbows pressed against the windows of the train. They are alien to the stony Andean presence, to the clean, cutting edge of dawn. They close their eyes so as not to see the llamas waiting for someone to come and melt the frozen waters. They close their minds. But at the base of that existence lies the active loneliness of the Quechua or Aymara women, for the men have gone. At dawn they have departed for the other side of the hills—where the devil lost his poncho—toward the meadows where the beans are waiting to be looked after and loved, so they will grow. This is life that has been put to the test, life so powerful that its passions, kindled by precarious triumphs, endure on the mental surface of the Bolivian collective. In the face of so much certitude, it's laughable to think of all the commotion made by the upper class as they award their illustrious citizens for twenty-five years of rectitude—though without the bait of the prize, they would have behaved as complete scoundrels.

Apparently, the book in question was destined to remain unpublished, without a future. But the sixty pages I had written had opened their own road—and opened another one for me, one that was different but well trodden nonetheless. My new direction was greatly influenced by the arrival of the writer who had lectured on Mayan culture—a man whose preoccupations were not at all like ours, which is not to say that he was worthless like some of his fellow countrymen. Something told me that here was a person who could uncover the very pillars of Latin American life, hidden as they were amid the most forbidding undergrowth. He was a first-generation European, and later on, he proved to be an anguished soul, unable to take part in the frivolous deceptions of his country. Above all, he was intelligent and knew how to make use of Western culture to orient himself in unfamiliar terrain. He was marginal, as all authentic creators are, and he produced a work that has allowed me to understand what is essential to all precursors. He wasn't a good poet or a good novelist or even a brilliant essayist; he wasn't a mediocre eclectic, either. It's one thing to fail because you're useless and another to triumph through apparent defeat. My friend Héctor had the disarrangement and the character of the perfect outlaw; and instead of floating in the supposedly harmonious stream, he was happier on the bank, longing for harmony. Like so many of my earthly friends, he has already drowned, but he fought to the death in an effort to make his way upstream toward the source. Now the river has carried him away, downstream, to the vast ocean.

I have lived with these dead in active trade; and because they went away but returned, they have acquired the silky transparency of the Great Beyond. This is how my life has been until the present. But a gap exists between one state and the other, which will be filled when the memories arrive and illuminate the perpetual present of my soul. That gap is my trip to Europe, which took place in January of 1969, after I had visited my native plain. I never thought that I would be able to make such a trip, not because I considered it anything out of this world, but because of my material limitations, which were my condemnation from the beginning. But it took place, for someone on the other side was manipulating the invisible strings. Unfortunately, that voyage caused more suffering than one could imagine, and I returned home totally debilitated. Before I left for Europe, I said good-bye to my parents and other rural relatives, and one of them threw a wet blanket on the whole business when I saw him standing with his usual plow in the sunny afternoon of the magic plain of my youth. He wished me good luck without asking my destination or what was carrying me so far away and in such a hurry. When I returned, debilitated and with a bad kidney infection, I was surprised to find him as cordial as ever, stuck to the same plow and identically sincere, as once more he wished me good luck. That's how close and personable Pila Ramos was. That night, the night of my return, I looked at the sky and understood the meaning of the phrase "the stars of old"; I began to tremble like a child before the ancient purity that I had been politely denied, as if my presence, my illusions, my wild plans had offended the most defenseless humility. I raised my eyes—I remember it quite well—and in the serene sky saw the morning star.

A new life began for me. I don't know how. I only know that in Buenos Aires, the night before I caught a flight to La Paz, in February of 1970—after a year of protest in Europe—I had a dream that stirred things up quite a bit, and I decided to look again to the faith of old. I dreamed I was on a mountaintop, looking at a circular lake which was very small and clear, almost sky blue; and, suddenly, without warning, the waters began to toss and swirl, turned dark and threatening, and then moved in my direction. I was able to catch a final glimpse of the plain that stretched before me, but it was too late to do anything; the waters knocked me down into an abyss as deep as an ocean. Struggling in that infinite dimension, I couldn't save myself, so I rolled up into the fetal position, pulling in my arms and legs, ready to spend eternity in a place with no echo, to pass inopportunely into oblivion. In the final bastions of silence, I heard a voice, "Now you will know true death." I woke up frightened and went over to the window, opened it to get some air, and felt the warm breeze of Latin America, represented at that moment by the paradises of the River Plate, by the brightness of the Argentine poem, and by the friendly accent of lazy madcaps who call us *coyas*. I rested for a long time in the warmth of the evening and could see my own face in the deceptive tameness of another sphere, made of stone, transparency, and the light of the high plains.

The next day I reached El Alto de La Paz. That enormous surface looked like a giant chunk of calamine basking in the sun. Its inhabitants looked as if they had never moved from that spot, and for an instant, I understood the value of expressing oneself through silence. I didn't find work in the seat of government. I went to Cochabamba and lived there jobless for nine months; in the City of the Valley, I heard about the death of the guerrillas in Teoponte. I had a thousand dreams, sleeping or gazing at the hard, tiresome earth, but I didn't find work and went back to Tarija. There weren't any jobs in the City of the Guadalquivir, either, and finally I came to the end of my journey, Gran Chaco Province, and greeted my relatives and friends, who hadn't moved from the spot since I'd left. The military coups and assassinations began, and I returned to La Paz. Just as I had decided to become a cab driver, since there weren't any other jobs available, someone took me by the hand and led me to the office of a newspaper, a daily newspaper, where the news of human events is printed.

Notebook Number 3

Jursafú as the Dead Man Sees Him

One travels with what one is, unburdened of pointless weight. God grant that the trip enrich but not pervert you.

Jursafú is thinking about the previous night while flying over an ocean that doesn't seem real in the darkness yet is like the map he saw as a child in his village, a map of the world that filled him with wonder. It is dawn, and suddenly lights appear in the distance, probably the lights of Spanish towns illuminated by his imagination.

Less than a month before, he was in his native village with his wife, son, parents, and friends. Then came the long, difficult journey to Buenos Aires by train, the loneliness of the station, his arrival at the airport, the aimless search for a reservation, and a fixed itinerary accepted with some reluctance. He had learned as a child that he was incapable of such undertakings and that two things should always guide him, two things that together were sheer madness: a faith that moves mountains and a duty to live with as little as possible.

I can see him sitting there stiff as a board, which would be alarming except that in that fascinating world he's happy as a fly in a bowl of milk. From time to time, an ancient sadness comes over him; then suddenly he is calmed by an unyielding solitude. Fortunately, he's oblivious to everything. He always was oblivious to everything. He has no idea what's ahead of him, and like all people of his race, he moves along with his eyes closed, cast inward toward impalpable certainties. He suddenly feels that he is speaking, but actually he is thinking, "I wouldn't want to die among all these gringos eating salad and not looking at one another, pretending not to know that we're flying at a high altitude and that the slightest movement could be fatal for a machine like this, no matter how safe it's supposed to be." He is silent again, like a rock, and feels only the blood pulsing in his veins. He is afraid of the unknown. February of 1969 finds him amid the lights of Spain, an immemorial land, a part of Europe where he will travel for an entire year. Sporadic songs in Spanish might help him remember. But he doesn't hear them. He doesn't want to remember. He's got something more important on his mind. He's thinking about himself and all the others like him, cut from the same cloth, identical and alone in the green fields or on the chalky plains. They ought to have been trees, migrating birds, lizards in the bright sun, the most humble piece of creation, but not this terrible sadness which the innocent never know.

Suddenly he turns around and speaks to me, "*Hermano*, how are you?"

I remain silent in fifteen languages, looking at his anemic body wrapped in a blue suit, his pale skin, so many dreams squeezed into such a flimsy satchel. Since he is fright incarnate, he doesn't feel afraid. He's filled with joy, a joy purified by the sacrifices of his ancestors.

"Jursafú," I ask, "do you remember how you used to make a plan that stretched from the day of your birth to the day of your death? You'd guess all the things that would happen and draw lines on a map to indicate your comings and goings. You were just a seed, but you wanted to look ahead to the seed's destiny. You thought that was where the secret lay, the unmoving axis that controls the frenzied movements."

"I'm sad, and the animal who is carrying me has forgotten how to whimper."

He closes his eyes and silently thinks to himself. He is sinking into a dream. I stop talking and give him up to the reality of night. Jursafú is traveling toward a continent his ancestors never knew, and the novelty has shaken him, though he knows that life—enigmatic from start to finish—is the most difficult journey of all, because its hermetic laws have decreed that no one can know what lies past the river and beyond the trees. It's the only way the whimsical creature called man could be brought under control. Pretending he's going to behave himself, he mutters humbly, "the only thing I know is that I don't know," which he promptly forgets as soon as the clay is dry.

"You can lead a horse to water but you can't make him drink," says the passenger with the blue suit, who has come equipped with ample sayings and proverbs which he hopes to use to his benefit in the world of credits and debits. He looks at the other travelers gobbling down their succulent meals and supposes that their complacency prevents them from noticing the magic of the trip.

Because of a curse that I'd rather not go into right now, Jursafú and I fight all the time, and our feud is not going to end until he is transformed into the supreme joy of the countryside, and only the wind knows when or where that will happen. In the meantime, he's traveling. He's always traveling toward the unknown, in hopes that someday he will be able to communicate. This is something we learn at birth, but we don't know how to say it. If people communicate, they travel, though some never move a muscle. One of my clearest memories of Jursafú's travels goes back to his childhood when he was struck dumb gazing at a beautiful, blue sky, while a warm breeze blew, carrying the smell of dead trees and whispers of fertile life. Happiness penetrated him to the core, and never again was he able to distinguish between "subject" and "object"—terms authoritative texts would insist upon. Trapped in a language that functioned above and beyond reason, he began to communicate in very human terms with his surroundings. One day this innocent task led him toward poetry, which, as everyone knows, tends to ignore the rules of communication in order to commune with the universe. So Jursafú was tempted to forget about trivial human pursuits and to gamble his life away on every phrase. He suspected that he was getting himself into something dangerous. "It's like throwing the *taba*," he thought, remembering a game he'd played as a boy. "If you sling it too hard, you might fall on your ass."

After heeding this calling or blind passion, Jursafú became a poet overnight, though nothing in his background prepared him for such a venture. But I must say on his behalf, that human concerns and calculations have nothing to do with the undercurrents of creation or its laws; and my young friend had known this from the time he was born. Not as a twenty-six- or forty-year-old might know it, for he knew it purely and completely. Those who spoke the country's official language were unable to turn him away from the challenge to seek the untranslatable music of human dreams, dreamed in the many different languages and dialects that still thrive in Bolivia, a vast region of villages which have warranted the attention of no one except the stars, a conquered land, a nation brought to its knees, defamed to the roots, shaken by the throws of destiny, but in spite of all that, stubbornly defended by distant gods.

"I hesitate to take such a risk, to live in this beautiful land," says Jursafú, remembering something a friend had said—and that he would never forget: "People are the same size as their country." But he'd said that many years before, when he was a boy and didn't know that words couldn't be taken back and that a fish's mouth is what gets it into trouble.

But now he's scratching his head because he can't seem to find his way into this strange world in spite of the fact that a pretty stewardess is coming toward him with a flower tucked behind her ear. This young Spanish woman reminds him of the girls back in Tarija, though she is telling him in a friendly, professional accent that she couldn't possibly look like the girls in his remote land. With aseptic tenderness, she hands him a red rose. He courteously receives it, realizing that this gesture has nothing to do with human love.

All the same, this is a feather pillow compared to New York, where he rolled around like a bowling ball for seven days, hearing a foreign language and wondering why he was alive. One week was enough to send him packing from that terrible place. Jews displayed their ethnicity like an open wound; blacks had hate in their eyes; whites were proud "conquerors," but knew that a thousand blades and curses were after them. He managed to fight the forces of winter—which calmed the forces of violence typical of summer—and to arrive at his hotel on Forty-second Street in the middle of the red-light district. There he began to think about his country, and after imagining some half-dozen Bolivian landscapes, it dawned on him that he was missing the point of his journey. He wondered where that madman Walt Whitman was, and his heir, Henry Miller. And the nephew of them both, Norman Mailer. They must be lurking somewhere in the shadows. So he dived into his adventure, headfirst, though his own soul told him that he was a dumb foreigner and could easily get himself into trouble. He enthusiastically visited two museums, and for a while it didn't occur to him that his headache wasn't caused by the different food he was eating but by the quantity of paintings he had looked at without stopping to catch his breath. It was too much for him, and he caught the next plane to Europe.

He had read that the United States, whose population consisted mainly of people who had come from the Old World to conquer the New, was suffering from the same disease as Latin America, and after being there, he was sure that it was true. In spite of its technology, it was different from any of the areas occupied by ancient traditions—France, Italy, Germany, and the other European countries. "I can get to the bottom of this without working my head off," he said, a little full of himself. ∎

On the airplane, he began to feel something that he'd had a vague sense of in Buenos Aires—a fear of taking part in a luxurious life that was alien to the forest and the silent huts in the deserts of rock and transparency. When he saw the first lights of Spain, he thought about the meaning of the Nativity, which for him was a strange image contrary to his experience because he'd never been exposed to that kind of religious celebration, not even as a preamble to the great carnival of the world. He'd grown up like an animal, without a birthday, without shrines; and his only baptism had been his promise to live on the earth without disturbing anyone. Now he was looking at Christmas on earth, like Arthur Rimbaud's illusion that was later destroyed by his words of farewell: "My journey has ended. I am leaving Europe behind. Yes; I have closed my eyes to your light. I am a beast; I am black. And I would be wise to leave this continent where madness has made its home." For Jursafú, the premonitions of the young Frenchman were a puzzlement, and by the time he reached the ground, he was as imperturbable as a stone and protected by the voice of silence. At Barajas, there were many Spaniards and gringos beneath the hot sun with their feet upon a bare earth which reminded him of the Altiplano. But the people were very different and spoke with an accent that transformed them into sheer emphasis, pure thunder, with no gentle rain.

He began to sniff the smells of Madrid on his way to his lodging. They were unlike anything he'd smelled till that time. He couldn't tell if they were pleasant or not, because the sounds of Spanish words kept getting in his way. They came at him so furiously that in five minutes' time he was ready to pounce on the first Iberian to hit him with another *vale, chaval,* or *joder*. While riding toward his boardinghouse on Guzmán el Bueno, he thought about the Spanish people he'd known in his native land. He smiled at the thought of José Mendesoto, an older man who had been his benefactor in Tartagal and who ate all sorts of herbs for his health and never tasted a bite of meat. He could see him pouring oil and vinegar over a bowl of purslane and beets. He was murdered one night by four thugs who thought he had a lot of money, but all they found was a pantry full of empty oil containers. When he'd finished the memory, he set his suitcase down on the pavement and started to stare at a woman, the only one to his liking he'd seen in Spain. She came and went away, with her long dark hair softly waved, her black eyes, her adolescent lips, and a body bathed in the light of a jungle never trodden by any man—a jungle that Jursafú came away from like a listless survivor. And several hours later, his condition hadn't changed, as he sat eating breakfast, having learned that Spaniards eat lunch at three.

In the company of four strangers, he gobbled up his Spanish lunch, feeling as though he were nineteen again and immersed in the cordiality of a college dining hall. Somewhat relaxed, he forgot he was a foreigner and entered into the conversation, while at his back, they locked the exits to a world that would hold him captive for twelve months. His four friends included the three Hurtado brothers—descendants of Alonso de Mendoza, founder of Nuestra Señora de La Paz—and a young man called Gaztambide, a fanatical believer in extraterrestrial beings. He didn't care about life after death; life on Mars, Saturn, or any other sphere bobbing up and down in space was what caught his interest. That was his illusion, as Jursafú soon discovered, and though he himself was not entirely hostile to the notion, it bothered him that a person would waste energy on such a thing, which to his way of thinking, was just an escape from what was in front of him. Jursafú saw through Gaztambide right away, but the heated exchange of words kept him from detecting the later's physical limitations. "How could anyone with eyes," he said to him, "behold the earth and feel anything but amazement? You could see in a day how magical it is. Just being alive is so overwhelming that I don't have time to sit around wondering if life exists on Pluto or Venus." He was putting all his energy into expressing himself rationally, but finally he noticed that the

Hurtado brothers were no longer responding to what he said. Their attentiveness had turned to stupefaction. He broke off his speech in the middle of a sentence because at last he could see that he was speaking to a blind man. Gaztambide had been blind since he was ten. Jursafú felt miserable for the rest of the afternoon, but that evening he went out and bought some cold cuts, bread, and a knife. Then he went to sleep, leaving his body at rest on Spanish soil.

The next few days were days of discovery, when he forgot about himself. During the sunny February mornings, he walked through the parks, avenues, and narrow streets of Madrid. He went into bookshops and walked out of movie theaters, scratching his head and looking for a museum. But instead, he would direct his steps toward a small square where an old man would be sitting near a very large oak tree. The old man always smoked a pipe and watched the horizon without blinking, with the skill and serenity of an experienced actor. He told Jursafú that he'd been to America and fought in the Mexican Revolution, but not on the Mexican side. When my friend asked him if he'd known Pancho Villa, he abandoned his pose and answered angrily, "Of course, I knew him, and don't mention that son of a bitch to me again!" Then he sank back into the horizon. "You're as much of a son of a bitch as he was," thought Jursafú, looking over at the modern horizon, the skyline of tall buildings, and the sign accrediting one of them as being the tallest building in Europe. He remembered another sign, "the most luxurious movie theater in Europe," and then recalled his confusion at the use of the preposition "of" denoting possession in street names: the Street of the Duke of Cádiz, the Street of Santander, etc. After walking for many blocks, he found the Prado Museum, where Francisco de Goya's dark period and *Saturn Eating His Children* awaited him.

It was late when he arrived at the boardinghouse. The door was locked, and no one was around. A man with a large ring of keys, who was hanging around on the other side of the street, crossed over to where Jursafú was standing, opened the door, and asked for *cinco duros* in return. He looked like a simple doorman, but his duties as a spy gave him control over other people's lives. Jursafú suddenly remembered that he was in the land of Francisco Franco, the dictator who several decades earlier, at a meeting in Hendaye, had driven Adolf Hitler a little mad—the latter making all sorts of demands and the former sitting there quiet and stubborn as a mule. But later in bed, he forgot all about the incident. He drifted off to sleep—the memoirs of Eugene Ionesco hadn't been able to hold his attention either. And wrapped in dreams, he began to hear a soft tinkling of bells which he confused with the chirping of birds in his native province. But then he saw that the bed was shaking. He laid his book of Ionesco aside and wondered if the ghosts of his dead relatives had come to see about him. But it wasn't that. It was an earthquake, and the boarders—all but one, who was combing his hair in front of a mirror— were already standing down on the street. Jursafú quickly joined them, and for hours they walked the streets of the city like old friends, telling each other their secrets, drinking wine, and waiting for the fear of another tremor to pass. The whole town seemed to be doing the same thing, sharing childhood memories and strengthening bonds of friendship that would easily last in a world free from danger.

"But they didn't last so easily. They never did," thought Jursafú a week later, as he sat by himself, regretting the night of wine and songs with a Bolivian and a Guatemalan, both students of literature. The latter, supposedly an heir to an ancient American culture, had ridden for two days on the back of a mule from his native village to the country's capital, where he'd caught an airplane and arrived in Madrid, with one saddlebag filled with dreams and the other with misgivings. The night of the earthquake, he'd gotten into an argument with a Spaniard over a joke that either the Spaniard shouldn't have told or that the Guatemalan had misunderstood. And having drunk two bottles of wine and dredged up several centuries of misunderstanding, the latter whipped out a gun and fired at the Spaniard. The police came and restored the peace. But the Guatemalan was too incensed to stay on among the offenders; so he abandoned his scholarship, literature, and Europe, caught a flight for his homeland, rode for two days through mountains, valleys, and cowbells, and arrived back home as a new day was breaking, roosters were crowing, and his parents, brothers, and uncles were plowing the fields, which they did every day from sunup to sunset.

Jursafú could still feel the wine in his system, and he wanted to go to sleep, in spite of the curious image of the Guatemalan. On the table beside his bed there was a copy of *Doctor Faustus* by Thomas Mann, a book that hadn't interested him in La Paz but that he now read enthusiastically. He picked it up and began to read but immediately fell asleep. As soon as he closed his eyes, he began to dream that he was walking along a path, like one in Tarija, that ran along the bank of the Guadalquivir and was lined with willows and *molles*. A fresh morning breeze was blowing through the trees, and groups of noisy students were walking along the path. Jursafú was carrying a book in his hands and appeared to be reading, but suddenly he looked up as if someone had called to him, and his eyes collided with a group of European girls who were laughing and talking, and one of them motioned provocatively to Jursafú. He didn't hesitate to follow her, ready to take her up on her amorous offer; but suddenly, by the side of the path, several of his dead relatives rose up out of their graves and stopped him in his tracks. They were dead but had faces like living people, beautiful faces with coca leaves arranged on their cheeks and foreheads, suggesting some ancient emblem. They moved as if guided by a medium and, without saying a word, made threatening gestures in Jursafú's direction. When their cryptic message was finished, the dream ended. Jursafú sat up, scratching his head. He was too agitated to think about his stay in Spain, a country that was very much like his own except for a few advantages and disadvantages.

The day before, he had decided to leave Madrid and bought a railway ticket to Paris, realizing that while he was preparing to go to a place that was really foreign, his Guatemalan friend was on his way back to his native land. "I'm going to France," he thought, looking at the pile of books and papers on the small table, which contained some of his own writing, some books on biology and physics, the autobiography of Carl Gustav Jung, Karl Jaspers' study on Nietzsche, plus several volumes by Ortega y Gasset in which the philosopher of "me and my circumstances" and other topics recalls the months it took him to refute Arnold Toynbee's theories on world history. Jursafú was pensive. From a distance, his handwriting looked like it had gotten smaller, which puzzled him. He also noticed that it wasn't as neat as it once had been when he was starting school. And there weren't any frills, just clean strokes representing as honestly as possible a new, unsteady reality. He had learned some interesting things in the last month, but he couldn't stand the thought of staying on in Madrid, wasting time with pretty Spanish women and hardheaded Spanish men. The Hurtado brothers had turned out to be the soul of hospitality and with them he renewed his acquaintance with Béla Bartók, whose concerts he'd first heard in La Paz and had listened to repeatedly in his room in Miraflores. Also, the Escorial was a wonder and Toledo, magical. And what could he say about the Alcazar, where, with the help of a guide who took him through the rooms on the Civil War, he had discovered the real temper of the Spanish people? He dutifully paused to think about the Francoist general who sacrificed his own son, captured by the Republicans, in order not to hurt his cause. "Pray to God, my son," he told him. "Your captors have placed too high a price on your freedom, and I cannot yield. Pray to God." My friend didn't like that image getting mixed in with the others: the eternal presence of La Pasionaria, the deep emotion of the rural poet Miguel Hernández, and the profile of Pablo Neruda, consul, gazing at the distant towers of Castile. Jursafú had bought his ticket, and he was determined to move on to another place. He got out of bed.

In spite of his dead relatives' warnings, Jursafú went to France. He crossed the border by train, in the company of several Morocans, who spent a good part of the journey curled up on the cramped floor as if they were sleeping in the middle of a beautiful desert. He gave them some bread and, making gestures with his hands, was able to break the barrier of their mysterious language. At the end of the trip, he got to know two Latin Americans in whose company he arrived at the French capital. By a stroke of luck, he found a place to stay, and as soon as he was inside his room, he opened the window. In front of him was a dingy, colorless wall corroded by time. But in a matter of minutes, the wall began to take on a whole myriad of colors; and hundreds of years of history, like a rare flower, started to open up before this rural man's eyes. In 1961, in La Paz, he had learned about Modigliani, Chagall, and Picasso from his friend Galarza—the one who lost a kidney during a hard Andean winter—and on his own, Jursafú had learned about some others—Camus, Rimbaud, Edith Piaf. He put film in his camera and took a picture of the part of the city that was visible from his window. Just one. And then he left the hotel.

It was the beginning of summer but without the raging heat of his primitive world. Here there was a different vision, a more elaborate one, arranged by men who were born old, who were bored with life before it had begun. Jursafú stood staring in amazement at one of Boulevard Saint Germain's innumerable corners. Wrapped in the warm air of a season he didn't understand, he was being carried along by the human tide toward a world that he had idealized but which was sensual all the same, as up-to-date as fashion yet fearful of its own demise. The weight of ancient Europe was crushing in on one side of him, and on the other, a transitory modern life that demanded high comedy, verbal music, anonymity, and dissipation from its participants. Just as he was about to go under, he caught a glimpse of a feminine figure. It was she. Floating in the tide but managing to appear lucid, a beauty was coming toward him, dressed in a metallic sheath of bronze brocade or maybe just a bathing suit that stretched from her neck to her thighs, enough to drive the passersby crazy. Jursafú could guess the exact form of her body, rhythmic movement turned to flesh beneath the sparkling sheath. The crowd closed around her, but didn't pull her in, as though to hold her up before his eyes as a rebellious image of life in motion. The revelation of an autonomous world, a world that made its own rules, shook him for a second. A mixture of weariness and animal excitement ran through his body, his life now posited in a language frequented by spirits from other ages. He closed his eyes and, with his imagination, traced the path of a star.

The night was being played out in a land settled by the Gauls; but somehow a thick undergrowth had taken hold of him. Luckily, he'd seen the danger and was preparing for it. "This is just the beginning," I warned, in my dead man's tongue. But he didn't hear me. He was absorbed in memories of the distant town of Villamontes, in Gran Chaco, where at the age of thirteen he had first known a woman, not as a temptress, but as a young girl, generous with the caresses nature had taught her. Fifteen years after that miraculous experience, he could hear the barking of the dogs, the voices, and a farewell that abandoned him to the mysteries of a seductive city, both friendly and terrifying. Someone was approaching to accompany him toward Notre Dame and Porte Saint Denis, but he remained in a beloved wood, alone for the first time with a girl who was opening herself to him, softly, tenderly, captives of an overwhelming passion, a passion that made them barely conscious of their existence on a tiny planet in an enormous solar system. While he remained there in that mythical dwelling, a real presence from his soul directed his steps. "I'm in hell," he thought and fell asleep, not suspecting that the night was confining him to an insane asylum.

He woke up wanting to see the City of Light beneath a radiant sun. On the night that he arrived, after leaving his baggage in the hotel, he strolled haphazardly from one place to the next, seeking a spontaneous view of the city. He wandered from corner to corner, walking by chance into the old Roman section—shining beneath the light of other centuries—stumbling into the Latin Quarter, and ending up at Notre Dame. He walked a few more blocks and decided to stop at a cafe, but suddenly found himself in the middle of a riot, French style: bombs, tear gas, sirens. He could see the violence, but he couldn't understand it and, under the protection of his own ignorance, walked calmly back to his hotel.

"You were lucky," said Danilo Romero. "Things got pretty rough last night for de Gaulle. He had to resign."

Danilo, who was from the Argentine Chaco, had been in Paris for twenty years. He was a painter and a writer, who reluctantly had acquired the necessary customs to get along in that cold world illuminated by the occasional limpid phrase. His face was tired, but his noble spirit was intact. Jursafú met him the first morning of his stay, when he went to buy something at a nearby market and got into an argument, as one might expect. It was as though someone had given him a kick in the rear, but he didn't let it get him down, nor did he bother to ponder why he was in Europe, especially in France. To the contrary, he decided to learn ten French words every morning before he got out of bed, a few more before lunch, and some more before he went to bed. The pact was sealed, and he started to leave, but a friendly hand stopped him in his tracks.

"Can I help, *compañero?*" said Danilo, and then, addressing the French clerk, asked for a "kilo de gros pain, si'l vous plait" as well as a "douzaine d'oeufs, un litre de lait et une libre du beurre."

"Ce sera tout pour aujourd'hui?" the smiling woman inquired.

"Oui, madame, merci."

The woman was looking at Jursafú, but Danilo departed with these words, which would occur only to an Argentine: "La parole est d'argent, le silence est d'or."

Jursafú became such good friends with Danilo that he left his hotel and went to stay in the room offered him by the gaucho, who during his first years in the city had lived off the money he earned selling parrots and other exotic pets that Parisian merchants were willing to pay a good price for. In the room, Jursafú saw a very large photograph. From the subject's clothing and combative stance, he appeared to be a Japanese karate expert. The apartment belonged to him, and he had rented it to Danilo, who now was renting it to Jursafú for a small sum. Jursafú asked Danilo if he himself knew anything about the martial arts, to which his friend replied, "I don't feel that I'm being attacked by anyone." That was the first significant sentence he'd heard in Europe, and as he might have predicted, an Argentine had said it.

Several days later, while looking through an open window at a long row of closed windows, Jursafú confessed to his new friend that he hadn't the slightest desire to attach himself to a culture that seemed irrelevant to his own existence. Danilo sat smoking a cigarette, and Jursafú could smell the aroma of cheese, vegetables, and fruit coming from the marketplace. "I know you think you're a rebel," his companion replied. "You think you're the only one going against the current. But you're wrong. Everyone else is going against it, too. Here and over there. So don't think you're so different, and don't go making yourself out to be a victim. If you want to get along with Frenchmen or Chacos, don't worry so much. And remember that people are like eggs; they're a mystery, but once they're broken, nothing can put them back together again."

The afternoon drifted slowly into the room, bringing with it a perfume of old conflicts. The French were in a frenzy waiting for summer, as they always were at the beginning of a new season. Jursafú breathed in those aromas—polluted by men, embellished by history—with a kind of naturalness typical of those who accept whatever life gives them. He continued to think about the absurd situation in which he found himself and was convinced that he would never fit in, especially if it meant giving up what he held most precious. He suspected that Danilo had been too quick to criticize, maybe because Jursafú was like a mirror of his former self—the young man who, twenty years earlier, had arrived in Paris with no money in his pocket and a bunch of paintings under his arm, but determined to make a name for himself in the art capital of the world. That didn't happen, but Danilo did manage to get his name listed among the best sixty painters of the sixty thousand who lived in the more romantic sections of Paris. "Too high a price for my middle-aged friend," Jursafú decided. "So what if he was a good man and had a nice girlfriend like Francine? Like a good frontiersman, Danilo would have to intuit the inviolate center."

"Danilo, can you guess the first word I learned this morning? *Radeau*. The rafts the Chacos use in Gran Chaco Province."

"That's good," the Argentine said, laughing. "Now, forget about the dictionary and find yourself a girl. It's the best way to learn French, and you won't have to be alone."

Jursafú went for a walk along the Seine; the sun was sparkling in the water, and it reminded him of the walks he took as a child, except that the natural habitat which protected him then was missing. About twenty meters in front of him, a crowd was gathering, and he hurried along to see what was happening. What he saw left him limp. The people stood silently watching an old woman who was seriously hurt. Someone said, "Elle es mort," and the crowd obediently began to disperse. The girl in the brocade dress, the one he'd seen the night before on Boulevard Saint Germain, was standing in the crowd.

"My name is Francine. I'm also called Barbara Kochan." She had light brown hair, blue eyes, and a magnificent body.

"What a terrible way to die," said Jursafú, referring to the scene they had just witnessed.

"It's our style, and certainly there are more trivial ways of looking at life," she answered, with a touch of fantasy in her eyes. "We've eliminated nature from our environment, and we see life as it is, difficult and absurd. We don't have to use euphemisms. You people are more optimistic, but it's not just a coincidence that the most perverse, the most poisonous animals in the world come from Latin America. Hope is an illusion held by people who live in hell, and it's always been that way, hasn't it?"

"Maybe it's better that way," said Jursafú.

"Better than what?"

"Well, for example, better than letting the poison into our brains. But here, hell is other people."

"Ah bon? What was your first dream on French soil?"

"I'm sitting in a cafe on Boulevard Saint Michel, thinking I'll scream if I hear one more *ah bon* or *c'est drole*. Then I'm lying on the ground, looking up at an enormous tree. Suddenly there's a circle of fire, and it's burning the trunk of the tree. Flames are darting around the bark, and animals start jumping from the branches, and just as the flames are reaching the top, I hear a voice that says, 'Beware of betrayal.'"

"It's a dream about the elements. That's strange. What do you make of it?"

"And in France, of all places," he added. "The language of the dream seems too obvious. I think it would be a mistake to interpret it literally. The only way I can figure out my life is to live it. Maybe someday I'll understand the symbols."

He was about to sneeze, but he caught himself and asked her if she'd dreamed anything recently.

"I dreamed I was a mute," she said smiling.

His attention was on Francine, and he had no idea where they were walking. When it got dark, she said she had other things to do; so they said good-bye, and she walked away, carrying with her a vague promise of the unforeseen.

Jursafú also returned to another world, where Danilo confessed to him that after two decades of exile the only thing that he had managed to prove was his own marginality, which was typical of artists, but in his case, belonging to a foreign culture also had something to do with it. He confessed this to Jursafú when they were at the home of Jean-Claude, Danilo's girlfriend's brother, who had invited them to look at his most recent designs.

"Primitive objects make lovely decorative pieces," said Jean-Claude, pointing to several bright objects displayed on a shelf.

"But don't forget that Picasso used primitive art in one of his most important periods," Danilo added, placing a container of pickled beef on the table.

"But Picasso uses Western art to transform primitive African art," their host noted.

"And what about so-called primitive powers?" asked Jursafú, imitating the young Frenchman's pejorative tone.

"I think modern civilization is superior. And I don't see anything extraordinary about that. What powers do you mean?"

"Magical powers, or maybe they don't impress you."

"Have you ever known anyone who could perform magic?" asked Jean-Claude, suddenly intrigued.

"I can, and I'm pretty good at it, according to people who know about such things. I could do bad things if I wanted to," answered Jursafú, somewhat uncomfortable in the role he was being forced to play.

"I admit that strange things do happen," confessed the Frenchman, somewhat shaken, "things that science can't explain."

"Don't worry," said Jursafú. "One day science will be able to explain them, but it will never be able to eliminate them."

"Of course," Jean-Claude confirmed, "and besides that, you look like a reasonable person to me."

"I'm more than 'reasonable.' I accept responsibility for my powers."

Danilo and Jursafú exchanged a knowing smile at the door of the apartment, and the latter left for the room on Faubourg Saint Denis Street. As usual, he crossed the bridge over the Seine on foot, walked up Boulevard Sebastopol looking at the Tour de Saint Jacques, and then disappeared into the darkness of his neighborhood. Every night he managed to elude the dragnet set up by the police to catch prostitutes, but that night he fell into another kind of trap set for him by a woman with large breasts and a ruddy complexion. His loneliness had become intolerable in that quarter—which some forbid but are eager to visit—in that apartment owned by a Japanese man who was a European champion of martial arts. Jursafú's violent encounter with commercial sex together with the terrible linguistic barrier was more than his rural Bolivian soul could bear. That night he decided to leave Paris.

He went to Geneva to see his young blond friend who in 1961—at the University of La Paz—had recommended some books whose authors (Camus, Kafka, Hesse, and Saint-Exupéry) he now knew well. A group of Bolivian students, mostly engineering students, took him in, and the week passed rather pleasantly until news arrived from the Bolivian capital that his brother Cope had been arrested for alleged contacts with urban guerrillas. The same source reported that the painter Julián Tuercas had been involved in an action that resulted in the death of Inti Peredo, the only survivor of Che's activities in Ñancahuazú. Under such a cloud, Jursafú returned to Paris. And the night he arrived, frustrated at his inability to adapt to a foreign environment and nostalgic for his homeland, he drank an entire bottle of wine by himself and then exploded like a Roman candle. He went back to his room and kicked the door in. But the next day nothing was said except that he would have to pay for the damaged door. Not that the manager was his friend. It was simply that no one gave a damn what anyone else did, especially since all the insults—twenty-seven-years' worth of insults—had been shouted in a marginal language, in other words, a language that no one understood.

Jursafú felt confused. He remembered his friend Adrián. He knew that Adrián was living in some dream world, where they were planning the destiny of Latin America. He had last seen him on September 13, 1968, just before Adrián had left La Paz to work for the Revolution. Jursafú and Adrián were such good friends that they had never bothered to ask each other about their more mundane pursuits, literature for the former, theater for the latter. But for sure they both wanted a world that was solidaric and just, though Jursafú suspected that Adrián was one of the few good, honest people he had known during that time. And now, in a foreign city, a concern that was more than personal had taken hold of him. He knew that his friend's principles were no different from those humanity had always strived for, but how far would Adrián have to go to accept reality and stop involving himself in a lot of useless wheeling and dealing? For reasons that Jursafú respected, Adrián had gotten rid of all his books before going to the Islas Afortunadas and had given his friend a number of volumes, including *Thus Spake Zarathustra,* which now formed part of the small library of a provincial man who knew nothing about the grave melancholy of the Superman.

From his own collection, Jursafú had given his friend the teachings of Lanza del Vasto, an author who was popular in his day because, according to legend, he had crossed the African jungle by charming the tigers with the noises he made with tin cans. He also gave him a rock from the Gran

Chaco, a rock with mystical powers because when he'd picked it up one wintry afternoon he'd heard the song of a bird that had lost its way. When Jursafú was saying good-bye to Adrián he suddenly received a flash of insight and gave his friend the following advice: "The troubles suffered by people who dedicate themselves to causes have nothing to do with their importance or their lasting value. When we remember all the martyrs who hid their triumphs in their apparent failures, we ought to celebrate the former yet never detract from the latter."

Jursafú gazed at the repaired door, wondering why he was still in the City of Light, and thinking about his friend who was in the Islas Afortunadas on the continent of hope. But little time remained for him to wonder. A dark call that he couldn't ignore would decide. He would go to Germany, to Berlin—not Munich, Heidelberg, or Düsseldorf. Sitting comfortably in a train compartment, he realized that a fascination from his childhood was leading him in that direction. He remembered the stories his parents and aunts and uncles told about Hitler and Stalin, like second-class magicians waving their wands over their troops, commanding them from the Third Reich to the Soviet Union, the Soviet Union to the Third Reich. Now he was traveling toward the divided city, a city that had fallen under the spell of contemporary history. But Jursafú couldn't fool himself; he was also running from the French language.

He boarded a train on the international line that ran from Lisbon to Moscow. In Paris, sitting in a compartment with eight total strangers, he began a journey that would take him to the former German capital. But if French was difficult for him in Paris, no language seemed to work in that crowd, since not one of them would utter a word. "Eight dead flies in an imaginary universe," he thought, taking a good look at each of them. Most of them were blonde, a couple were brunette, and there was only one dark-skinned girl, who was either Arabic, Indian, Filipino, or Armenian. He was amazed when he spotted in her purse a copy of Julio Cortázar's *Final de juego* in the original Spanish. As soon as he had confirmed that she really did speak Spanish, he continued speaking with a natural fluency that he had longed for since his arrival in the Old World, the part north of the Pyrenees, that is. The young woman said she'd been born in Chile, was twenty-two years old, was on her way to Moscow, knew twelve languages, and that the others in the compartment had remained silent for the entire trip. But at that moment they all began to talk, as though they'd just regained consciousness, and with the help of the capable interpreter, chattered constantly, each one telling his or her life story. As it turned out, some of them knew Spanish. Ilsen, for example, dressed in a little cap and looking like a character out of Thomas Mann, was able to give in full detail—using the language of Cervantes—an account of her recent trip to Spain; and speaking more privately to Jursafú, she told him about her stay in a sanitarium. Why was she there? She smiled. She'd gotten addicted to drugs. And now she was out and had fallen in love. Would she get married again? She was traveling and hoping to regain her faith in life. The old woman sitting to Jursafú's left tried to engage him in conversation, but without much luck because she was also given to amorous dialogue and began to recount an unfortunate affair that had taken place in her youth, and though she was seventy years old, it seemed to her that it had happened only yesterday instead of many decades before. "I'll never get over it," she said wistfully. Her story was a sad, brief story that many people might have told. She had been seduced by a promising young violinist when she was one of the most beautiful dancers in the Baden-Baden ballet. She was only eighteen and hoping to find a primrose path where she might linger with the violinist for an entire life-time. But he turned out to be a drunk and a spendthrift and eventually went to prison. "I still love him," she muttered, her face turned toward the window. With her light brown hair pulled back behind one ear, her entire figure looked like a melancholy rendition of life's drama. Could anyone see her eyes looking toward the past? The tears running down her cheeks? She was talking to herself as the train rumbled slowly past the guards at the German border and moved toward the famous city of Berlin, with its legends known to every German citizen. Legends that were now on the lips of a thirteen-year-old schoolgirl who had spoken only German during the trip; her language was so precise that her listeners felt them-selves transported to the spiritual depths of a race that oscillated between terrifying moans and hymns of celestial splendor.

He accompanied his Chilean friend to a hotel and said good-bye. He then walked along the street to get his first taste of German life, and on

Kurfürstendamm Avenue, he saw a Bolivian face that he recognized from some years before, a man he'd casually met in La Paz at a party where everyone was intoxicated except him, and now, on September 6, 1969, Oscar, his sober acquaintance, was offering to take him to a student hostel where he would spend two weeks among students of many nationalities—German, Chinese, Iranian, and so on—who temporarily found themselves in the country of Schopenhauer and Nietzsche. Unfortunately, he was forced to continue speaking French, since German didn't allow for improvisations.

One sunny day, he found himself alone in the city and decided to enter a large establishment to look at a collection of constructivist art. To his surprise, the woman he'd seen in the brocade dress, now wearing different clothes, was entering the same museum.

"Francine," he called out to her.

"In Berlin they call me Barbara."

"A barbarian amid beauty," said Jursafú, trying to make a joke by slightly altering the title of Héctor Alvarez's enigmatic book.

They left to look for a cafe. About noon she asked Jursafú about his first dream on German soil.

"I'm in a country I've never seen before, but I know that it's been occupied by the Germans, and I'm with a girl who's Jewish. The war has started, and we're surrounded by Nazi soldiers. There are lots of cars in the street. Some have been stopped by armed guards; others are racing by. I'm not afraid, which surprises me. My friend, on the other hand, looks terrified. Then I remember that I'm a foreigner. Suddenly guns are firing all around us, but I'm looking toward another part of the city where there's a beautiful mountain. For some reason it looks to me like a Japanese volcano; then suddenly it begins to erupt. But instead of lava coming out, the head of a Greek philosopher emerges, exactly like the one we just saw in the museum. The mountain makes all kinds of movements trying to push out the head."

"I must be the Jewish girl," said Barbara. "I could be African or Indian as well as what I am."

"How can you say 'what I am' when you're one thing in one place and another in another place?"

"I'd like to see you tonight. Meet me at Cecilienstrasse 1471." ■

Many German professors participated in the meeting, not young professors but old ones with venerable beards. They were friends of Barbara's, and like them, she was a prestigious university professor. The owner of the house thought that he was talking to a member of a guerrilla organization or at least an active revolutionary. Settled comfortably in his paternalistic posture, he asked Jursafú a question which Barbara translated into French. And Jursafú in broken French replied that death was too prevalent in his country to be taken lightly, and that he wouldn't tempt death without a very good reason.

The professor was alarmed and said, "This isn't reality; this is mental masturbation!" Without thinking, Jursafú switched from French to Spanish, not giving a damn if he was understood or not. "Yes, of course," he continued angrily, "you can think about death, discuss metaphysics, listen to Beethoven's Quartet No. 16, and plan all sorts of mad schemes that you will never put into action—protected all the while by a healthy bank account, no doubt. But to make you happy, I'm supposed to run around with a machine gun over my shoulder."

"There's been a misunderstanding," said the professor, alarmed again.

"Or maybe I'm just not good enough to explain my own actions. Goodbye, my dear professor."

Jursafú and Barbara left immediately and walked downtown. They went into a place where a light was constantly flashing and sat down at a table full of young people who said very little but behaved hysterically. They danced madly to the infernal music, a music that made dialogue impossible, so they all smiled at one another and melted into the night.

To get away from the crowd, Barbara and Jursafú went back to the hostel, and the latter took off her shoes and followed her friend up the stairs. From a dark window, they watched the illuminated city.

"Schopenhauer and Nietzsche were born here," he said.

"Don't talk to me about those two. They hated women. Why should I like them?"

Jursafú was still leaning on the windowsill when Barbara began to undress. He could sense what she was doing but continued by the window, thinking about what he might be doing years from then in Latin America, where he'd never felt like a stranger. Then he turned around, embraced

Barbara, and lost himself in her beautiful body. Before, the lights of an adverse present had disoriented him; its order besieged him; he wanted nothing to do with it. But the two of them together were now breaking the order, breaking past the language barrier, and drifting into a sea of remote origins, silence, and nostalgia. The entire night Jursafú listened to French spoken by a woman whose body surpassed the power of all languages. They lay unprotected in a distant place, talking to each other, feeling connected to other beings who performed necessary tasks and lived on the earth, but differently from them.

"For a long time I thought that Africa was the most beautiful continent," she said.

"I like your name," said Jursafú, drifting in a sea of dreams.

"Francine or Barbara?" she asked. "But what do names matter tonight? We're trying to find out where we belong. That's what really matters. Some people seem oblivious to everything. Isn't it awful?"

"Barbara, ask another question, anything that comes into your mind."

"What's going to become of you? You seem oblivious to everything." Then she covered her face with the sheet.

"I know what's going to become of me. But two people can't love each other if at the end of the day one of them doesn't know where the other has been."

"So then what happens?" she asked with an ambiguous smile.

"The only way to be faithful is to remember, and I should know, I live from one memory to the next."

"Have you noticed how American Paris has become?"

"Since I'm a foreigner, I can't tell. But I can tell when a bird is pregnant."

"It's where I was born, at least I think I was born there. I grew up in Saint Germain and the Latin Quarter, but then I renounced Paris and forgot all about it."

"Why are you always renouncing things and forgetting about them?"

"I like the black, African sun better. What's your country like?"

"Say it, and you'll know it."

"I can't know it. I can just tell it's there, like an old piece of buried metal, a vast space where day and night triumph, things that are dark and unequal in a vulnerable night. Is it a mirror of hell?"

"It's wet and luminous. And sometimes too sad to be comforted. And there's no turning back. You either die or fight your way through."

"Then it is dark. Do I surprise you? We only act ourselves when it is dark—neither good nor bad, just as we are. The light sets a trap—darkness—before the careless. What would happen to light without darkness? You must know this because *you* come from darkness."

"Maybe I knew it before, but I know it better now. Barbara, how did you discover darkness?"

"I can only remember how the story ends. I was in love, and I wanted to be loved, but the one who was supposed to love me was naked and wore a mask. Masks and nakedness. When they appear separately, they mean the same thing. Both are luminous symbols. But together, they stand for sterility and castration. When I learned this, I discovered my own darkness and the darkness of other people. I was sixteen, and it was taking me a long time to find out who I was. I joined a commune where everything was shared, from the forks and knives to the children. Ridiculous, isn't it, like all things man-made. None of the men knew which children were his, so there couldn't be any fathers, though everyone was a parent. But a woman always knows who her children are, no matter how much of a whore she is; and that's the subtle but decisive distinction between the masculine and the feminine in the celestial realm. And the same distinction is made manifest on earth by the penis and the vagina. I didn't think this way then. Actually, I didn't think at all. I loved all of the men faithfully, until a special man came along. I didn't want to share him with the others, and he didn't want to share me. They threw us out for being selfish, and maybe we were glad to leave. But we didn't realize that our love would die as soon as we were free and on our own.

"Do you like the story? I want it to sound like a great paradox. They threw us out, and that was the end of everything. That's how I learned to hate people who don't care about the community, because I already detested people who had to be pressured to do what they were supposed to do. I ran away from that ridiculous world. I don't know why. You seem so old to me, maybe because you remind me of someone who went away chasing after the unfathomable. Are you an ear listening to the silence of the universe? You can ask the magic circle if you're doing what you're supposed to do. You've never heard of it? I'll show it to you some time—now, if you like. The circumference of the circle is the mundane sphere and everything inside of it is sacred and untouchable. The universe is so vast that we have to limit it, in our imaginations. There must be some reason for people wanting to make a universe out of the darkness. Come here. If I have wisdom and you don't and you offend me, I can kill you and it won't weigh on my conscience. The hierarchical principle of the universe, ruled by God and the devil, is like that. Most people don't know about the friendly relationship between God and the devil, but sometimes they find out about it when their lives are at an end. And what is living? Making love. You will find me again in Rome, the lovely, open city. I will be dressed in white and make you smile. We'll make love in Florence and also in Paris. This I will have told you in Berlin, while watching a city with no secrets from a dark window. But that's not true, at least not entirely true. Do you remember Wolf Vostell's nude woman showing off her beautiful body except she has a piece of cement in her vagina? That's his vision of Berlin, the divided city. That's where we embraced for the first time, and now we're making love in a Roman bed, which means that we're safe.

"It's hilarious what you said about German parks with their perfectly straight paths, without even a shadow of a curve, which is a typical false interpretation of the Aryan spirit, like the cloudy horizons in the distance. Those are false too. In Paris, the parks are round. I detest Bruckner because I can't stand distance. Have you noticed? I'm full of beautiful curves and my anxiety is round. I'm an open city: I show you the danger so that you may leave with peace of mind. Paris isn't like it used to be when I was a child. The American touch did away with its rebellious spirit. Me, a rebellious image of life in motion? A shimmering brocade on Saint Germain? Don't fool yourself. I can make love to you in the City of Light with the passion of an African woman giving herself to a man on a lonely beach. I want you to make love to me, even if you are pure oblivion. Do it tonight." ■

They were in Spain.

"I'm glad you stopped me in the Latin Quarter, and one day you'll know that Handel's suites are ours. I was never here before. I learned about Spain from Ortega y Gasset's descriptions. Is that the way you pronounce it? I never thought I'd learn about it in bed with a man who had arrived on a plane and was leaving on a boat called the *Michelangelo*, in the feminine waters of life, immersed in the embryonic depths. You find yourself; then you lose yourself again. The sign of our time. We'll meet some other day, in different skin, and you will know me by the mark of this farewell.

"Do you think I'll like Barcelona?" she continued, asking questions. She was standing near a window and an early morning breeze was blowing in her hair.

"It's time to leave," Jursafú either said or thought. He gathered up his belongings and said good-bye to the European night. His brief stay was coming to an end. ■

Jursafú was sitting in his cabin aboard an Italian liner—the cheapest cabin available—and glad that he had chosen to spend two weeks getting to know the immensity of that vast monster, the ocean. He was from a country that was Mediterranean, in spite of its mountains and unending plains. In a few minutes he would be moving away from a history-laden continent, with its many enlightened people and also a great weariness. He wasn't sorry about his stay, but now he wanted to leave, to think things through and separate the important from the trivial.

"Life is trivial, especially if you aren't a serious person," Jursafú said suddenly, as though he'd just woken up from a long nap.

"When you get to that country of yours, that nostalgic country, you'll understand why things are the way they are. You'll know that the world is round without stopping to think about it. You'll believe in silence again," I said to him in my dead man's language.

"I don't care if it's round or square. I just want to hear the sound of my own voice, the way I used to speak." He dropped his dark head to one side and, as if he were sobbing, deeply breathed the air of his eternal convictions. "If they only knew who was among them."

"Nobody, Jursafú."

"So, who are you?" he questioned angrily.

Only in the night air, only leaning over the railing was he able to appreciate the rhythm of the voyage. Shadows crowded around him, but he couldn't tell if they were the clouds that appear at birth or fearsome primordial images; the strangest part of life was coming into the world and leaving again, possessed by night. He was still a prisoner of Western culture, of ancient Europe, but he couldn't remember anything he'd read, only what he'd seen. He had saved only a hundred pages of what he'd written, not that it was valuable, but he liked the paper it was written on and it took up little space. He suddenly looked at me, and his expression was as it had been months before. He couldn't hold anything back, regardless of the water or the other immensity beneath a starry sky.

"I know you're the incarnation of things that don't exist in this world, or any other. The Dead Man who travels by my side, with his soft melody. But you don't live inside my skin. You're the ethic of an incorruptible universe, for which I'm grateful whenever I'm at my wits' end, and I never forget it, in spite of my ignorance. I only wish I could understand the delicate workings of the universe, so I could put the things that confuse me in their place. Don't bother me anymore. You know I'm not out for myself, and if you ask me what I'm doing here at this hour, I wouldn't know what to say, because I don't know what I'm doing, I don't know why I'm alive."

I interrupted him. "So you can discover that the world is round."

"Not only is it round, the fire that lights it up is too hot for anyone's comfort. Besides burning, that fire veils the origin or makes it incomprehensible. At any rate, we persecuted people know the origin. But I won't say any more. I don't want to get myself into anything I can't get out of." He was looking down at his hands as though he were talking to himself.

"So, why do you want to write?"

"I don't want to. It's not my doing. I was happy to be a rock, though maybe that was too much to ask. I was being presumptuous. I would have been happy being the father of six children and working as a lathe worker. Though that wouldn't have worked either. When I gave up such common pursuits, I lost the chance to lead a normal life. But if I could see why things are the way they are, just for a second, I would be happy and satisfied, no matter what happened to me afterwards. And just when I'm about to find it out, I close my eyes and turn around. Why?"

He remained silent. A mysterious sky reached down to his shoulders with its eternal, celestial lights. The season made no difference. Beyond the earth, it was all a matter of temperature. On the other side of time, the seasons and the path of the stars become meaningless. From that dizzy pace, a hymn rose up from someone who was lost and far away, removed from the magic circle, permanently nostalgic. I smiled and said to my curious companion, "The stars will return, Jursafú. The seasons will return. If eternity is what you want, you must be willing to travel blindly with your enigmas, without yielding to the temptation to decipher them, even if the devil falls at your feet and begs you to."

My opinions seemed to startle him. But he sank back into silence, into unending preoccupation, as he stood watching the immense waters.

"Don't you know why I'd rather not talk?" Jursafú spoke quietly. "I'm pure silence, manifest silence. Do you know why? Precaution. I could open my mouth and start babbling like a sleepwalker or a fool. But no matter what beautiful things you say to me about life, you'll never get me to tell you what I'm thinking when I go poking around in things that would be best left alone. And that's why you're here, at my side, when you know it's a waste of your time. It's your misfortune to have a shell of a man for your interlocutor. No one lives inside of me, not a grouch, not a pleasant soul. Not death nor life. And for that matter, anything we say to each other tonight, on the high seas, has already been said a thousand times, at the beginning of the world and today, in ancient and modern languages, in all sorts of tones, in clear, reasoned sentences and melancholy ramblings. I'm not a poet. We explain ourselves by means of the Other, other people, our neighbors. The only essence which is explained by its own mystery is woman; you know that as well as I. And women can come to an end, because of sex or a love that slowly dies, but they never cease to exist. At any rate, that's something we can't talk about. Only a man and a woman can speak of that, and only when they're alone. But, of course, they never talk, they only function, like the bees and the flowers, moving softly toward despair, preparing the road with their perfect breath. A man and a woman will always end up in a jungle they've never seen before, but they never get lost. Perhaps this is why we see them in the end bathed in a light of primordial melancholy. You and I can't speak of men and women. So, what can we talk about, my dear shadow?"

I left him looking at the couples talking and laughing on the deck. He was suspended between the reality of his desire and his memories of women. It was a beautiful night, but he had been the butt of a bad joke, and he was taciturn.

Jursafú's soul was on fire, but the sea was calm, and the days and nights passed quickly. By mid-trip, he had finished reading Plato's *Republic,* which he was able to do in spite of the constant interruptions of a young Argentine who was concerned about the outcome of certain sporting events in his country. Jursafú wasn't especially impressed by the Greek's discoveries, since he was riding the crest of his own experiences and couldn't concentrate on anyone else's. But he did decide to retain a living reminder of the episode about the people who saw the light and didn't want to go back to the shadowy world of human beings, though we consider it the duty of enlightened people to return to the darkness and get along as best they can. But it occurred to him that such behavior was typical of human beings and that rarely did one encounter a case of "pearls before swine."

Jursafú thought that by the time he reached home his head would be clear, and this helped to keep his spirits high during the trip and to make daily annoyances like the shipwreck drills more tolerable. Someone always took pictures of the make-believe victims, photographs that surely would be lost along with their subjects in the event of a real catastrophe at sea. Even though Jursafú was feeling tired and nauseous, these exercises provoked a little ironic smile which broadened into a big grin when he saw the older passengers enthusiastically acting out their parts.

"Obviously, nobody wants to pass to the other side," Jursafú said to me. "No one is willing to give up his place, though sooner or later you have to. You have to leave, so that others may come and receive the same hugs and kisses that we received. I feel locked into a space of light and shadow. And here I stand, awaiting my fate with open arms, vulnerable to whatever comes my way. It's useless to be on guard, and besides, it's a waste of energy because we all get to stay, but no one remains unchanged. The ones who didn't amount to anything will be split down the middle, no matter what human defenses they may try to use. You can be sure of that. But even if I'm passing through the valleys of shadow and death, I won't forget the most important thing: once you've seen the world through the heart's eye, you can find it again with the vision of the soul."

The boat docked for a couple of hours in Rio de Janeiro, and Jursafú breathed in the fresh air of Latin America. He sat awhile on a bench in a large square, and everything seemed less serious to him, though he was suffering mentally and physically. He felt better there, amid pure instinct, in spite of the honeybees on the trip who made everything sugary sweet, even silence. He didn't even like Florence, for example, that city turned into a museum, where art had overtaken life and the past made the present seem unreal. The oppressive European ambience was fading away, had taken leave, without a gesture of farewell. A laborer walked by whistling. A bee was buzzing in the afternoon sun. The honey of little, tender things, comfortable things, was rising up in his memory. From the trip, only the image of Barcelona remained, the conversation with Francine or Barbara Kochan, a young woman who was either Jewish or Arabic, who helped him the best she could, with her ancient heart, her race, and her secret crying. A disillusioned heir of the cabala, she wanted only worldly knowledge, but what she had inherited from her ancient bloodline singled her out when her lovely face changed into an endless premonition. He remembered that day in the room on Maire Street in Paris, when they were playing question and answer with a group of Frenchmen. Jursafú asked a silly question which Barbara translated, "Who is the devil?" A voice that seemed to echo from the desert answered, "Whoever is present while God is sleeping."

But Jursafú knew where the answer came from. He was calm, or calmed down—which were different things to Jursafú—when he disembarked in Buenos Aires, feeling like someone had played a joke on him and he had taken it rather well, at an age when jokes didn't seem all that funny anymore.

The Other as Jursafú Sees Him

Working is resting on oneself rather than upon the backs of others.

"Aruskipasipxañanakasakipunirakispawa" is important if not fundamental to the Aymara language; and though it has thirty-six letters, it is only one word. To even roughly express the same concept in Castilian, you would need four words: "estamos obligados a comunicarnos." From Castilian it passes easily—and deceptively so—into other languages and reappears dressed in its original mystery. But it remains faithful to its context, even under the most adverse circumstances, and carries forth its beauty and wisdom to the end.

An approximate translation in French would be "nous sommes tenus a nous communiquer." In English it would be "we are forced to communicate"; in German, "wir müssen uns mitteilen"; and in a regional language like Catalan, "necessiten comunicarnos."

In the open air, "aruskipasipxañanakasakipunirakispawa" might look like some obscure message written in hieroglyphics, but it is too full of life to be relegated to such archaic music. True, it belongs to a ciphered language, but its daily use by the people of the Andean plains has carried it beyond such simplicity. And while it doesn't have the ill-deserved prestige of more obscure or difficult terms, it bears the luminous, seductive quality of things which endure over time. Numerous human beings who have communed with the universe, summed up their knowledge of the world, and then transmitted it through purified forms, have exercised their seductive powers through the word "aruskipasipxañanakasakipunirakispawa." To an illiterate observer, the word might resemble a serpent, consistent from one end to the other, totally articulated, and maneuvered by invulnerable means.

Ernst Jünger has said that the serpent is the most solid animal on the earth because its entire body rests upon the ground. But this metaphor, with all its suggestibility, doesn't exhaust the complex connotation of the snake's presence among human beings; and instead of solving a riddle, it simply concocts a new one. The serpent creates a magic field much greater than it needs to live and to defend itself. With only one-forth of the displeasure that it unleashes upon its surroundings, it would have more than enough room to move securely through life. But no, it isn't satisfied with this limited domain. Some would have it symbolize the Fall, understanding, of course, that not even this ophidian could escape such damnation.

"Aruskipasipxañanakasakipunirakispawa" is an invisible serpent which a race of reprobates used to create a defensive system much larger than they needed to survive. The Aymaras, far from losing their way in a broad terrain, create vast dominions where those who do not fall are at least likely to trip; for "we are forced to communicate" isn't a conventional phrase or momentary courtesy, but a net that traps the products of the most exalted imagination as well as shadows that the image cannot contain: animals with specific forms and some that have no form; creatures that frolic in the mire of life and those that death has calmed; all that has gone before and all that is yet to come, and today's respite as well; things that a hand cannot touch, but two or three jubilant shudders of a lifetime can foresee, if the life has been meritorious and deserves to shudder in such a way.

Like other animals of its kind, the serpent often bites its tail and creates a mortal circle for all creatures on the earth. Some remain within and others without, and consequently, our vision of the world is divided into two parts, two kinds of life that are quite different if not opposite. In daily life, if one should discover that these factions are irreconcilable, it would be wrong to attribute such opposition to bad intentions, since the people who embody these archetypal extremes do so unwittingly.

Whether one stands inside or outside the circle, it can be fatal to anyone who is unaware. The viper knows this when it is overwhelmed by life and falls asleep, giving itself up to the dominion of death; and the toad is aware of this and doesn't hesitate to condemn the viper to death, coating it with its foam.

That beautiful, distant girl, Barbara Kochan—either a Jewess or an Arab—knew this secret. And in spite of her flirtations with the modern world, her blood still bore the mark of the cabala, a gift for tracing the magic circle upon the earth.

"Aruskipasipxañanakasakipunirakispawa" in the high, lunar night of the largest Andean city, a metropolis where for some life is an invulnerable presence, perpetuated in the accent of those who seek tranquility in the sound of their own voices.

In a room in Villa Fátima, a section of La Paz, a man walks back and forth before the world but lags behind the shadows of his own destiny. The future seems clear, and he wants to read the exact message of his last days. Burdened by unending chores, his body wants to hear once and for all the rattle of gunfire that will put an end to the life of Melquíades Suxo. Who is Suxo, an astonishing creature? An Aymara Indian, accused of having raped a girl who was underage. Since he doesn't speak Spanish, he is considered mentally retarded. And since he doesn't defend himself—because he is ignorant of the charges brought against him—he is presumed guilty. The dictator's flunkies have interpreted the Aymara's silence as a tacit confession and have condemned him to death, as though his disappearance might atone for some ancient crime. Melquíades Suxo illuminates his presence on earth with powers of other evidences, and the regions he inhabits are untouchable, so much so that a newly arrived justice means nothing to him. Toward the end, he never asks for clemency; he would never lower himself in that way. He only requests permission to visit his relatives on Friday nights. He could bear any affront except a violation of his communion with his own world.

The man walking back and forth in the lighted room in Villa Fátima— a man who is called the Other because of his relationship with dreams— has recovered from a serious illness to then fall into the bottomless pit of unemployment. His fear of not having the minimum needed to live still afflicts him; and in fact misery is knocking at his door. But a more immediate concern, his concern for the life of Melquíades Suxo, has silenced these cares. Memory, which is neither selfish nor generous except when it so desires, passes indelible images of other scenes along to the Other: a small village at twilight, a plot of overgrown weeds, a Guarani Indian lying face down on the ground with his hands cuffed behind his back, a man armed with a revolver and aiming it at the Indian's head.

The world is divided into hangmen and victims. The man in Villa Fátima stands before destiny, his hands cuffed behind his back. He has reached the limit of his resistance, but this is nothing new to him. He has always been a victim, which he views as a prelude to a future good. He has been waiting all his life for a luminous image which others would consider pure conjecture.

Looking from the window of his humble room, the Other remembers a story that his friend Adrián repeated often. It had to do with an uncle of his who couldn't sleep for worrying about a convicted murderer named Caryl Chessman, whose execution had been postponed several times. A kind of knowledge that rises up out of the abyss had turned the murderer into a new man, a man who regarded his own past as a terrible nightmare.

The Other was also familiar with Caryl Chessman and had followed the story from Tarija, where he was trying to get a diploma. During that time, it often occurred to him that men preferred to recall a person's past rather than allow the present to shed light on past events. That had happened in the case of Caryl Chessman. Each time the execution date drew near, Adrián's uncle would play a scary game of solitaire in order to know beforehand the fate of his North American friend; and every time the execution was postponed, the cards predicted a favorable outcome. But one afternoon the cards were against him from the start, and he left his room feeling very sad and walked down Landaeta Street with the weight of the world on his shoulders. Someone in the crowd reached out to him, grabbed him by the arm, thanked him for the nights he had lain awake, and then moved away with the human tide. When the startled man reached the middle of town, he discovered that his friend had just been put to death in the electric chair.

The Other recalls this story in order to prove that constant attention can exert an unexpected pressure on the world and force it to reveal its sacred face. He walks back and forth in a room in Villa Fátima with all kinds of sensations spinning through his brain. He has nearly lost hope of becoming a decent carpenter. He doesn't have enough money to realize his dream, and besides that, an ironic Hebrew phrase keeps running through his mind: "The poor always say they do not wish to be rich."

Thanks to the skill of Marcos Salazar, his kidneys are no longer diseased, though they bother him from time to time. He asks himself what this short, stocky person with a soul split between goodness and an ironic smile might mean to him. He met the healer in his native village just as he was about to go to Salta for an operation. Marcos arrived that morning when the perfume of spurges and guaranas, damp with warm rain, filled the air. The Other could hardly shuffle along in his *alpargatas* (his shoes) but, nonetheless, he was heading out toward the land of morning transparencies with no clear destination but guided by ancient instincts about life and death. The leaves of a beautiful guarana, submerged in a continuously renewed world, fluttered in the distance. Marcos opened his mouth and muttered something about the leaves of that plant being a sacred cure for a particular malady—I don't remember which. The Other, hardly able to drag his body along, was so ill that he would have welcomed any suggestion, but he was in no mood for jokes and found it hard to believe that his Callawaya friend knew anything about the guarana, since he was an Andean through and through, and such plants were unknown in Curva, Marcos' native village. But Marcos, unaffected by the sick man's doubts, spoke at length about the properties of the guarana in a language that seemed strange to the Other and might have made him mad had his companion not spoken with an honesty that seemed incapable of deception. Then they gathered flowers of various kinds, many of which were unknown to his friend, but Marcos was able to appreciate them for their peculiar forms and colors. He made a paste out of all the flowers, and to the paste he added honey and a gutted lizard. Then he covered his sick friend's waist in the animal and vegetable mixture and confined him to his room for three days.

Lying in the dark room, the Other could sometimes hear Salazar's loud laughter out on the patio. Sometimes the house was silent; sometimes he could hear the hubbub of daily living. When he left the room, he was like new and could live in the present, or foresee it, as he sat on a rustic bench beneath the star-filled sky. Marcos Salazar also gazed at the sky rather playfully, like a cat watching a snake. The Other broke the silence and asked him what he thought about the many wonders of the heavens. "If we could just *be*, like that, nothing more, whether things are okay or they aren't. Just be, like that, nothing more." It seemed he was going off on a tangent, but actually he was only expressing his people's view of the sky. Soothed by a nocturnal breeze, the Callawaya continued looking at the sky. What an immemorial sky it must be.

Thus, in March of 1971, Marcos Salazar looked at the warm sky of the Other's native province while the convalescing man thought about the Callawaya's land, Bautista Saavedra Province, or more exactly, Curva, a town he had visited in 1965 when he was working on a film. As he had traveled through the dark mountains, it had never occurred to him that six years later his life would rest in the hands of a Callawaya, and not in the Andean zone, but in the interminable plains of sun and fire, among spurges and other trees so familiar to his plainsman's soul.

After he'd been on the earth for twenty-four years, he'd gone to Bautista Saavedra Province in pursuit of his dreams, but with no experience at all in the Andean world. In spite of his lack of sensibility, he had been impressed by the transparency of the sky and the infinite variety of medicinal plants. He'd remained for two days in Charazani and then gone up to the high village of Curva. Full of legends and inhabited almost entirely by women, the region had seemed to project a strange past into our time. Like good nomads, the men had all gone away except for a few who were waiting their turn. The Other had spent the entire night conversing with one of them. With only the light of a candle and without the inducement of alcohol, they'd touched on every possible topic, abetted by a joyful serenity acquired through endless hardship. The following day, the descendant of the Andean wise men had given him a poncho and a bag, identical to those of Marcos Salazar.

Disturbed by other matters, the Other scratches his head in his room in Villa Fátima and remembers the gift of Marcos Salazar: "Just be, like that, nothing more."

It is possible that Melquíades Suxo has already gone to the other dominion. Terror has emptied the streets. So how could he receive any word? Laura has remained in Gran Chaco with the children while he looks for work. He hasn't found anything, and things aren't going well. He hadn't been able to find work in Cochabamba either, where he stayed from February to December of 1970. He recalls that Adrián suddenly appeared in June, fleeing and carrying in his pocket the stone that the Other had given him in September of 1968. When he saw a small air conditioner in his friend's room, Adrián couldn't help but say something about acquiring unnecessary possessions. "Whether it's cold or hot, our bodies can adjust to the temperature," he said with a smile. Walking through the apartment, he added, "If things don't go well here, I'm going to Brazil or Nicaragua. It doesn't matter as long as it's in Latin America. I believe our time has come." Several times they ate lunch together. Laura and Alberto usually joined them, and on one occasion they heard Wolfgang Amadeus Mozart's *The Hunt*, which was Ernesto "Che" Guevara's favorite quartet.

Adrián died in Teoponte on September 13. The Other read the news of his friend's death two months later in a La Paz newspaper, though he received his first notice of the tragic event in a dream the same night his friend was killed. Just as in the dream, his friend died of a stab wound. He dreamed that he was out in the fields, and suddenly he looked up to see his friend on the other side of a stream. He seemed to be in good health, except that his head was shaved, not entirely, but just down the middle, and his long hair fell to his shoulders on both sides, giving him a somewhat strange appearance. They began to move toward one another to embrace, but suddenly a black, authoritarian figure, similar to a British policeman, appeared between them and held them apart with a sword. The Other woke up with a start.

Later on, when he read the names of those who'd died at Teoponte, he dreamed the same dream again, but the second time the setting was a tavern, and many friends were there; or at least they were friends in the dream, because he didn't know any of them except Adrián, whom he was toasting with a glass of red wine. He and his friend left the tavern and went to the field where they'd been in the first dream, and while they were walking around, the Other tried to explain how sad he was about losing his friend. But Adrián politely interrupted, saying, "I'll be back, and besides, something important is going to happen in forty days." The Other went on with what he was saying and recounted the first dream in great detail, including the part about the field, the stream, his joy at seeing his friend—even with his head partially shaved—and so on. Adrián, in a very sad voice, told him he shouldn't have spoken to him. As soon as he said that, the policeman from the other dream appeared between them and very angrily put an end to their dialogue and to the dream, and the Other woke up with a pain in his kidneys. He turned over in bed and looked at Orana, a girl from his distant youth. He fell soundly asleep, but the next day he was upset to hear about Northon Castillo's death. A student, Northon had been the only person killed during a demonstration in La Paz. The photograph in the newspaper remained fixed in his mind: the silent protest of politicians, college students, and workers, and Castillo's body being carried to its final resting place.

As December was approaching, the Other spent a lot of time in the Cochabamba libraries and hills. He would stay up at night reading anything he could find, from the decalogue of young Nazis—as well as Che Guevara's edition of a young communist's decalogue—to Bertrand Russell's popularized version of Albert Einstein's theory of relativity. Between both extremes, he managed to squeeze in geometry, Egyptian pyramids, a study on bees, a book on biology by the Spanish physician Gregorio Marañón, Arnold Toynbee's study of nomadic tribes, and Carl Gustav Jung's work on synchronicity. In the hills where he walked with his son Alberto, he observed the flights of birds and the activities of insects; he looked at everything caringly, as though a kind gesture toward the life that prospered in those hills might help him to recall the corn fields of his native province. When December arrived, he left for Tarija. At first he felt spiritually ill and eventually, after reaching Gran Chaco Province, became physically ill. In August 1971, the bloody coup that many Bolivians had been expecting finally occurred; and since the Other was able to do very little, he spent his time building some rough benches in an equally rough garden. One day when he was working and listening to the radio, he heard that the University of La Paz had been bombed. Two weeks after the coup, he traveled to the Andean capital, and during those difficult days he again crossed paths with the harmonious Marcos Salazar. ■

The Other looks out of a lighted window upon the town of Villa Fátima; at that hour, his is the only light burning in the village. Well, almost the only one. The other windows are dark but not deaf to the hoarse groans of the army trucks passing in the street. Marcos Salazar, his wife, Peta, and his daughter, Teresa, are sleeping on the ground floor of the house. All had grown tired from their individual chores. That morning the Other finished a set of four chairs; that afternoon, with a saw, hammer, and nails, he and Marcos tried to make a frame from a thin piece of laurel, the hardest and least serviceable of all woods. Talking as though he were a real carpenter, the Other said to his friend, "Cheap wood is expensive." But it was important to the Callaway to finish the frame; like all Aymaras, he considered himself handy at any craft. "Zapopeta," as he was affectionately called, thought himself a tinsmith and a cabinetmaker, and to hear him tell it, he could do anything at all in the area of construction and mechanics; and, of course, he was a cloth maker, able to weave intricate patterns, which he did enthusiastically, in his own way, and without the slightest hesitation.

"Poverty is awful," the Other says to himself, trying to graze the truth without damaging it. Of late, he feels lonely in the city. Walking back and forth in the lighted room, he feels deceived, and understands the man who had gone into the forest with a gun over his shoulder and knows that he, too, could do the same, but not necessarily in the same place. For days he'd walked the streets of La Paz looking for work, and though he remained optimistic, he knew that things might not turn out as he'd hoped. And after seeing poverty in every alley, hopelessness in every zone of the Bolivian capital, he felt especially discouraged. Finally, he realized that he had lived in that city for many years without actually being there, and that he had miraculously remembered everything he had seen. His country had seeped in through his pores and now it was coming out of his mouth. "My country is like a perfect dream," the Other murmurs, "where every desire seems possible." He scratches his ear and suddenly remembers that he is waiting for the arrival of Orana and the children, who thought they were crazy to let themselves be taken in by his enthusiasm. Surely no good would come of it.

He is very tired but doesn't want to sleep. He's always admired people who can rest for five minutes and feel completely revived. Like the other members of his race, he has to be really exhausted before he can fall asleep. He is quite sure of this and doesn't have to think about it twice. He'd become aware of it as soon as he was able to string together a few phrases in reaction to life's enchantment. So he picks up *The Possessed* by Dostoevski—a ferocious novel—and turns to the first page; but suddenly he is distracted by a song on the radio, "When you fall in love . . .," and the secret waters of his soul began to stir, because every sound of daily life seems to him like a love song. In a car, train, truck, or airplane, in any kind of vehicle from a mule to a bicycle, in a movie theater or the dark of night, all the melodies of the earth inevitably referred to romantic encounters, happiness that becomes fear should the lack of love appear on the horizon. Silence accompanies love only if it is fulfilled.

The song on the radio brings back distant, tender memories; and though the words allude to a Spanish town, they remind him of a very healthy, animal-like experience from his rural existence. In the dark recesses of his being, a strange creature had remained, marked by a feminine presence. He had directed himself toward that feminine world, armed with the unfaltering weapons of poetry, and without hesitating, had titled his poem "Orana." By the time he realized what he was doing, the poem was finished, but its creator remained melancholy. Filled with desire, he had written a love poem to the women he had loved since he was a boy. He coughs sadly. Laura and Orana are the same person; they are exactly alike, except that "Laura" means gift and "Orana," the grave tenderness of suggestion. A stranger to the world of concrete meaning, The Other coughs sadly and thinks of seducing Orana.

But given the extent of his loneliness, love offers little respite. The time for pondering has ended. He will have to make up his mind to either stay in the city or return to the land as a farmer or truck driver. He hasn't depended on anyone before and doesn't want to now. He won't allow his job to depend on people who think they've made a world for human beings but have only made one for fools, and the devil take anyone who disagrees. The Other pushes such ideas out of his mind and thinks about his family instead. He tries not to think about El Alto, a place where he spent several days trying to get a job doing work he knew nothing about; the entire time an icy wind had been blowing, chilling him to the marrow. He went away feeling as if he'd been living among the dead. Though he'd been determined to get along in that mountainous environment, something broke in his soul; but instead of sitting around moaning about it, he built a fire, a fire that would either lead him to the precipice or guide him toward salvation.

He turns off the light and slides under the covers. He becomes silent and entrusts his life to the shadows of memory.

But he doesn't close his eyes, and begins to see the images that his memory brings to mind, some laughable, others unpleasant, all of them stirred by the voice of silence which directs him through passages he thought he'd forgotten, like his stay in Cochabamba, another town where he'd looked for work. His stay there had affected him deeply, had even caused a physical weakness in his lungs, though it hadn't taught him anything about carpentry. But in spite of the congestion in his chest, he was sure that he had done what he was supposed to do. And he'd felt happy, seized by a joy that ran through every muscle in his body. His memory then transports him to Santa Cruz, to a street where he could smell the pleasant wetness of the trees on a rainy night. It carries him back to the City of the Valley, Cochabamba, and leaves him standing in his room with a Yugoslavian named Sulkievich, one of Marshal Tito's ex-guerrillas whom he'd run into by chance in La Paz when the Other was working in an art gallery. Laura prepared a meal to celebrate the happy encounter with this old friend whom he'd gotten to know because of a mutual interest in chess. Over a few glasses of wine, they discovered that their friendship had not grown cold. Sulkievich asked about Adrián, but the Other thought it best not to say where he was or what he was doing. The Yugoslavian understood his friend's reluctance, accepted it as a sign of discretion, and changed the subject, inviting him and Laura to a picnic in the country the following weekend. They accepted, and one morning after breakfast, headed toward the countryside with some Italians, engineers, and children. They sang songs that some of the participants remembered from their youth, but the Other was feeling old that day and didn't want to sing, especially since the songs had nothing to do with his life. While the truck rambled along over the rough terrain and his companions sang at the top of their lungs, the Other looked out at the mountains and recalled entire sequences from Italian motion pictures on the Second World War.

That day Sulkievich offered him a construction job at a cement factory in Irpa Irpa, forty kilometers from Cochabamba. He said it would be an opportunity for the Other to learn to use a theodolite, but actually Sulkievich wanted to help him get out of some political scrapes he'd gotten himself into. So one luminous day, Sulkievich and the Other went to Irpa Irpa, a very lovely and tranquil area with a promising future. The ex-guerrilla, who was the general supervisor of the project, went back to La Paz after introducing him to the man he'd be working for, a Polish man who had some knowledge of engineering; and under no circumstances would he allow the Other to use the theodolite, but instead put him to work driving a truck, which he thought would put an end to the new-comer's enthusiasm. But that wasn't what happened at all. The Other turned out to be an excellent truck driver, better than he thought he would be when he was a child and played with trucks. What had been mere child's play then was now a wonderful combination of play and work. Also, at work he became friends with Manuel, a young man from Cochabamba who was very bright and capable of getting accepted at any night school. "You don't have to stay ignorant, and if you do, they're going to exploit you," the Other told him between one load and another. Manuel wiped the sweat off his face with his shirt tail, and instead of answering him, asked, "You think it's possible?" The Other dumped the load of sand and encouraged him, "Of course, it's possible! All you need is a little polishing." The dialogue continued between the two for a week or so, until one day the Other was reported, not only for being a rebel but for insti-gating others to be the same.

On his last night in Irpa Irpa—or what was going to be his last night—the Other was very tired and quickly turned out the light in his room, which was actually Sulkievich's room. Since it wasn't a week night, it didn't surprise him to hear people coming in drunk. He could hear several men—whose voices he couldn't identify at once—carrying on a rather silly conversation, which they did quite freely, probably thinking that the Other was sound asleep. He was able to recognize only two of the voices; one belonged to the Polish man who fancied himself an engineer, and the other, to a man from Santa Cruz, who acted as if he'd stayed out in the sun too long.

As one might expect, the conversation eventually turned to women, and each participant claimed to know more than the others and to pos-sess an iron will when it came to the weaker sex. One of them who sounded as if he might be a high ranking police officer said that he couldn't believe the hypocrisy of some people. "The other night I saw something that left me dumbfounded," he affirmed. "I was making the rounds and saw this automobile. It was dark inside but strange noises were coming out of it. I peeped in through the window and who do you suppose I saw? Miss Bolivia and some long-haired gringo who'd come to Cochabamba trying to pass himself off as a basketball player. They were naked and going at it. 'What the fuck's going on here?' I shouted, just to scare them, because I wasn't going to arrest them. Not that I didn't want to, but it would have looked bad for the girl, not to mention the country. Can you believe that every year we pick the most beautiful woman in Bolivia and then she fucks some foreigner right under our noses? What are we? Chickens? That we keep throwing the meat to the dogs?"

Through a crack in the blinds, the Other could see the sky and a few stars and imagined a cool, rural breeze blowing in the dimly lit night. The drunks got tired of talking about women, and for lack of another topic began to discuss work, leaving the policeman sitting there like a knot on a log. It was the others' turn to talk, and the Polish man, who fancied himself an engineer, began by bragging on the excellent job he was doing and said it was outrageous that the real boss was away in Italy, making money without lifting a finger, and showing up twice a year for appearance's sake, and every time with a different lover. And then all of a sudden he threw out a threat. "I'm coming back here in twenty years, and I'm going to bring my son with me, and I'm going to tell him about the Italian, and I'm going to say: 'See that factory? Your father built it. But if you don't toot your own horn, no one's going to toot it for you. See—the assholes forgot to put my name on it.'"

At first the big man from Santa Cruz didn't say a word in response to what the Pole had said, but eventually he loosened up and said what it was really like to be a Bolivian, the kind that won't let himself be led around by the nose. First he coughed to prepare himself to speak: "I don't know if I'll ever have a son, and if the truth be known, I'm not sure that I need one. I don't know if I'll be alive twenty years from now, and I don't know what difference it would make if I were. And I don't know if I'll ever come back to Irpa Irpa. But if I ever do, with or without children, the first thing I'm going to do is see if the linchpins I put in this afternoon are still in place. And if they are, I'll be happy, and I'll say, 'Look, I put those linch-pins just as I was supposed to, and after all these years not a one of them has come loose.'"

The Other nearly split his sides laughing. What a beautiful story, he thought, though some would have called it "old fashioned" or "banal." Then, remembering a very lively girl from Tarija, he said to himself, "Some of these gauchos would make a person afraid to be an Argentine." She had aptly described those people who in her opinion had become pure fluff, all thunder and no rain, so to speak. He fell asleep, oblivious to the drunk men's voices.

That would be the Other's last night in Irpa Irpa. He made up his mind the following afternoon while strolling in the hills with a piece of willow in his hand and sniffing the air, which smelled of goat droppings. He was looking for rocks and twigs that were of an unusual color or shape, like the ones he'd looked for years before in Isla del Sol. Suddenly he stumbled across a shotgun shell left behind by some hunter. He was surprised to find a second one but not at all surprised to find a third. He continued gathering them up until he had sixty in all. He placed them in a row and made some mathematical calculations that only he could understand. And then, without any effort on his part, the sixty pages he'd written in 1967 began to come back to him, pages that he had bound together as a book and titled *Tirinea*. And after thinking about the chapter headings and studying the facts of his own life, he came to the conclusion that he would die on August 14, 1977. He knew that on that night, still far away, he would not be able to sleep but would lie awake contemplating his own death. He thought about the time that remained to him on the earth and immediately was soothed by a firm conviction: people go on living because they believe that they are in control of their own deaths. He quit his job, which held little promise, and went away from the City of the Valley. ∎

But now he can't sleep. He tosses and tumbles under the blanket, an old poncho from the Gran Chaco, woven by Doña Clemencia Ruiz in 1956; it has a patch in the middle which somehow makes it more dignified, since the owner alone is aware of the grave circumstances that caused such a scar. The Other, who is well familiar with them, opens his mouth and begins to curse, "*Me cago en la reputa madre . . .*" But nothing happens. The world hasn't come to an end. He has only recovered the peace he was searching for. The city is alive, and he is also alive, though within the confines of a small space created by his own anxiety. He is aware that pain is often a prelude to discovery, that most people don't have the vaguest idea what they're doing, and that only lazy people go around questioning the purpose of their own labor. But he doesn't even have a job to become lazy about. And he doesn't have any place he can call his own, except the space he occupies by virtue of being alive. It is a territory he occupies very well. Just as many people could travel the whole country without getting lost, the Other knows the deserts and the swamps, the jaguars and the doves, and the hidden, woodsy cave of his private dream world. And though he is worse off than he's ever been, he wouldn't trade his life for a mundane existence. He has an aversion to people who think that to make a place for yourself on the earth—a crummy little spot where there is no time to enjoy beauty or vent your emotions—you have to have property, houses, land, bank accounts, and stocks and bonds.

In the same Andean city, while the Other is fighting to stay alive, Melquíades Suxo is no longer a reminder of a dull community's doubt and bad faith. The Indian from Villa Fátima is only a handful of memories, languishing solitude, the present come to a halt. There wasn't any city he could have called home because he had given up his dreams very early in life and walked from one place to the next, half naked, knocking at a door from time to time, since "words traded with one's neighbor are a kind of rest for those who have crossed the desert," especially if that neighbor, by definition and habit, was open to the mysteries of human madness and could repeat the inaugural words of the great sacrifice. But the neighbor might be insensitive and take the pilgrim for a delinquent. In that case, it would be better to continue on along the lighted street, cursing as he went: "And what does he know about pregnant birds? And what the hell am I doing looking for an intermediary to talk to the man who cursed the fig tree for not bearing fruit at a time when figs were out of season? I can make up my own prayer and pray to whoever put me on this earth without giving me the good sense to stay out of trouble."

In the silence of the night, he hears a mournful cry, a cry that is choked, torn out by the roots, like a tooth. A tooth, that small link between a body and pain—and the body, like the tooth, entails all possible links with the universe. And the louder the moan, or the laughter, the closer we are to revelation. The body never leads us astray, though many have gotten lost in its multiple languages. And the Other knows this very well. Not long ago, soon after he left the Gran Chaco, he had an unpleasant surprise. On top of being broke, he woke up one morning with a swollen face, but he didn't have any pain. He looked at himself in the mirror and knew without a doubt that the swelling was coming from a molar that had a big cavity. He remembered that the following day his landlord was coming home, and he still didn't know how he was going to pay the rent. And now this. "When it rains it pours," he said to himself. And then suddenly he remembered his friend Jáuregui, the dentist, whom he'd known for quite a while but hadn't seen for some time, maybe because he hadn't had any toothaches. He washed his face and went to look for him, expecting to find him pulling teeth at his office on Comercio Street. And though it was too good to be true, there he was, just as the Other remembered him, and they greeted each other as old friends. But the dentist, ignoring his friend's swollen face, said he had more important matters to discuss. *"Hermano,"* he said, "you've come just in time. I have a house in Villa Fátima that I need someone to look after, and I've been thinking that someone could be you. Here, take the key." The Other forgot about his molar and left with the dentist. He dropped the key in his pocket and heaved a great sigh of relief. He was glad to be a housesitter again. He looked at the infected molar in the mirror and comforted himself with a saying that was popular among the poor: "If it doesn't rain, sometimes it sprinkles." And later on, he curled up on the bed and felt happy, repeating to himself: "I'm not anybody's man. Of course, they keep me running. And I run, thanks to the devil and the Unnameable One. But as they say, there are two ways to destroy a person. And the spirits know it—the ones symbolized by the faces on the magic medallion. Everyone knows that they ruined Job by taking away everything he had, and even what he didn't have, as though some pleasure was to be gained from taking everything away from the haughtiest man on earth. And they destroyed Faust by giving him everything, including the title of doctor. So it's better just to stay in the same place, like a rock, come what may; and if the place itself changes, that doesn't affect me. And no matter how frightened I become, I'm not going to leap into thin air."

He tries to stop thinking but can't. He'll have to keep on thinking till he falls asleep or lie there all night waiting for the dawn, like a snakebitten cat. Cats have a great time playing with snakes. They paw at them and rile them up. But if the cat slips up, he may end up with a swollen head. His only vulnerable spot is the tip of his nose. It's not so easy for a snake to bite him on the nose; but it is possible, as anything is possible. Just ask a dead cat.

"When I think, I want to die. When I work, I want to live. Now I don't have a job to make myself want to live. So I think and I think. Because tonight, it's all I have to do." And he tosses around in bed until he finally gives up and accepts things the way they are. He is always ready to do that, not because he is lazy, but it seems crazy to him to fight reality. Laura is waiting for things to improve before leaving Tarija. The Other thinks he is in love with her, and maybe he is. He doesn't know that people either get better or worse as they get older, which can be trying for a marriage.

In her last letter, Laura told him about a dream she'd had: "I was looking at myself in the mirror to see how long my hair had grown; but instead of seeing myself, I saw a dark woman with long, black hair and greenish eyes. And I felt like something bad was going to happen." The Other had become angry. He was in no mood for superstitions. Her interpretation seemed ridiculous, and besides, she could have kept her mouth shut, knowing he was too poor to buy himself a *locoto*. Holding the letter in his hand, he'd looked at the geraniums caressed by the wind and written a long message to no one, to Nadia, to Orana, to Woman. "Goter and Nadia, I know I'm playing with fire," he'd said. As far as he was concerned, he didn't mind taking risks, but it was his duty to stay healthy so he could complete a mission which, in spite of all his efforts, he hadn't been able to accomplish.

He is tired of listening to talk, and his youth has left him permanently scarred. Now all he can do is wait patiently and continue to work on things, things that have nothing to do with business. Tears roll down his dark cheeks, but he can't feel them; he is trying desperately to hold on to his sanity. He knows that the gap between what a man has and what he wants can drive him insane. "Because a man isn't Man if he doesn't have desires," the Other thinks. "And that's the way the world is because it's real. And life wouldn't exist if men, the most willful of all creatures, were not present. But this biped, dull as a dead fly, doesn't arrive on the earth empty-handed. He comes with both saddlebags stuffed full of desires and illusions. And he uses his dreams to write about his life on earth. Such documents are often interesting, though they offer little to anyone seeking objective, scientific data. 'You talk the way you live' is a saying I truly understand, as if whoever invented it had been thinking of me. I don't care if no one else finds it meaningful. Some people wouldn't know the truth if it bit them."

What are the Other's desires, and what is his reality? The man in Villa Fátima can feel the barbs of injustice piercing his chest. He tries to sleep but can't. The long night is like a party when most of the guests have gone and only the closest friends remain. He understands his reality, which he's learned about from the beat of his own heart, his own insights and intuitions that eventually changed into words. He needs only the bare necessities to live, since certain revelations—the ones about life's meaning—can be understood only by a naked soul. "For any specific knowledge to rise above the common place," he'd once said to Sanguinetti, "it must be judged by fully independent criteria. And it's the same with people. They can never realize their own distinct qualities if they are chained to human interests that take away their authority. The distance that separates me from myself is the greatest distance of all. It's a simple truth, but it's taken people an eternity to figure it out. No matter how hard you try, you'll never get very far loaded down with possessions."

What he never says is that his greatest desire is to translate his experience on earth into words, knowing he will die very soon. And though he never says it, he hasn't been able to realize his dream because he can't get the kind of job that will allow him time to write. And now he has plenty of free time, which he's come by in an awful way, and besides that, he has nothing to eat. He yawns and curses his luck.

Just as he closes his mouth, he hears gunfire in a distant part of the city. "As long as I can remember, all I've heard is gunfire in this country of revolutions. But no matter who wins, we lose out just the same. No one gives a damn about us. It's all the same to them."

He tries to sleep, but when he closes his eyes, he opens the more dangerous eyes of his soul. He gets up instead and sets the kettle on the fire. While waiting for the water to boil, he fills a *poro* with leaves and sugar. He is finally able to clear his mind of the memories that have haunted him during the night. He yawns again and says, "Oh, shit." He is still tired, since he hasn't slept, and strange notions drift in and out of his brain. He isn't surprised. In the few books he's read by Latin Americans, there are always characters who can't or don't want to sleep. Some have wonderful memories, some are happy, and others behave like fools but can't change, as though controlled by some awful fate.

"It seems only natural for me to die when this ordeal has ended," he says, unconvincingly, maybe because he is still thinking of the future, August 14, 1977. Through experience, the Other has learned that just when a person gets used to being happy or starts to understand how the game is played, it is over. "I'll never get a chance to enjoy myself. I'm going to die, just as I've taken hold of the reins." He drinks the first maté, reminiscing about his friends. As he watches the sunrise, he feels surrounded by human warmth, as though he is in the company of a muleteer or some other rural person. Then he is gripped by an uncontrollable need to cry, but the tears won't come. His eyes are fixed on a sky full of bright, neutral stars that have nothing to do with human affairs. He is trembling all over but doesn't try to control himself. He brings the straw to his mouth and tastes the warm liquid which has been his companion on other occasions.

"Hey, don't let them slap you around," says a voice from the past. The Other smiles to himself. "There are some things I refuse to remember, even in my dreams," he'd heard a man from his province say, a man who was very poor and had caught a train one day to be immediately thrown off by a policeman for no reason at all. He'd thrown him down like a sack of potatoes without even saying why he'd done it. But as the poor man walked away, he unleashed a long string of curses upon his offender. "You dirty son of a whore. Don't you ever lay your dirty hands on me again. And if you think you've seen the last of me, you're wrong. I'll find you, when you least expect it, in some dark alley when you're all alone and out of uniform. Then we'll see . . ."

"Don't let them slap you around," says a voice which comes from far away, from a damp, tropical place with *tártagos* and, like a dove, tries to make a nest for itself in the Other's chest. Life? A fight that must be fought.

But against whom? His only foes are shadows, and what can he do but curse them? That's why the days seem harmless to him. During the daylight hours you can see your enemy. "But in silence and total darkness, it's harder," he thinks to himself, preparing another maté. At this particular moment, there are no shadows or ghosts. He remembers something that happened the week before when he stopped at a store to buy bread. It was a store he'd never gone into before since he always did his grocery shopping in the market below his apartment. But that day the market was closed. In a part of the street that he'd never frequented, he bought a few things and stood looking at the city. It was about nine o'clock in the morning, and La Paz seemed very pretty. The sky was clear, and people were going quickly about their business, pleased to be lost in the crowd.

The Other understood such solitude but wasn't used to it. He had his own solitude of a different nature. "How could such a small difference shape a person's point of view?" he wondered. But before he finished the thought, he turned around and looked up to see the back of his own apartment. Beyond the walls of his room, there was nothing but empty space. It was a frightening sight. Ever since he'd lived there, he'd heard all sorts of noises coming from the other side of the wall and could understand why people complained about the lack of privacy in modern buildings. Sometimes he grew tired of all the noise, of the voices of women and children, of furniture being knocked about, of clanging pots, of the heavy breathing of people caressing and mounting one another during the long nights, or of the voices of those who fell asleep and dreamed of God. And without moving from the hill of Villa Fátima, he stood looking in amazement at the back of the building. There was nothing there, absolutely nothing. With great curiosity, he waited for night to fall, and now, aware of his mistake, heard not a sound. But the power of silent energy was even worse and disturbed him more than all the familiar sounds he'd imagined on previous nights. The silence of those nonexistent creatures was intolerable, frightening, foreboding.

"The back side of a thing that seems perfectly natural can be awful," he says to himself, pacing back and forth in his room, after walking like a somnambulist through some other spaces that he also inhabits. "Those who live in a real world have no idea of the price that others pay so that such a world can function harmoniously," he adds But he doesn't want to think about ingratitude. He wants to think about his life and how he can get back on his feet. He imagines himself as a truck driver on his way to Paraguay in someone else's truck, carrying gasoline to Puerto Sajonia. He can see one side of the city, and the other side he knows to be as it always has been. That is the rural part with its green fields. He remembers something his father said to him back in 1961—"You're cut out to be a rural man"—which has been his curse for life. This is experience talking, not resentment. He's been thrown off a train once, and now, after many years have slipped away, he is trying to get what he wants, without going against his nature, without letting other people slap him around, and without getting himself in over his head.

The faint light of dawn is illuminating another world. The Other comes to, standing up, with the *poro* in his hand. He feels as if he's been doused by the waters of the past, and now he is ready to take the first step. His eyes aren't yet accustomed to the reality he will have to share with other people; however, he is disposed to love that reality. He doesn't make any final decisions, not because he is hesitant, but the decisions aren't entirely his to make. Other people and other factors will also have a hand in it, people he doesn't know and factors that are abstract, anonymous, phantasmagoric.

What is propping him up? What is keeping him awake? The inaudible blow of destiny, the call that must be heeded. His faith has been pressed to the limit. He can't go another step on his own, and all he can do is pray. For several months he's tried to become a carpenter. He's only been able to earn a fifth of what an unskilled laborer is paid. With such a wage, he isn't going to make it through the year, much less if his wife and children come to live with him. So he decides to go to the Chaco, which means giving up his dream of living in the city. He buys a ticket on the only bus that goes to Tarija during this season of the year. He buys some pants that will do for working in the country and a pair of boots. Then he goes to say good-bye to his friend who hired him as a carpenter, a movie director who has begun to make his own films. They talk for a long time, and he makes a sketch of his parents' house in case the director ever decides to make a documentary on the Chaco War. Judging from the people who come and go, he decides the director's office must be an important place. It is very different from anything he's known. There are photographers, scriptwriters, and other people who are competent at jobs he knows nothing about.

The Other says good-bye to the filmmaker; and on his way out, just as he is about to run into a brightly lit doorframe, he bumps into an old friend whom he hasn't seen in months. She is walking fast, as if she is being chased, and catching her breath, she says to him, "I've got a job for you. They need a copy editor at the newspaper on Pompilio Daza Avenue." "For how long?" he asks, for lack of anything else to say. "Just for two weeks, while someone's on vacation." It seems like a waste of time to accept a temporary job, especially now that he's made up his mind to leave the city. His decision to abandon his dream and leave La Paz is costing him dearly, though no one knows it, nor do they need to know. To some extent, he's already distanced himself from the city, and now it is as though he is looking back at the cruel joke they are playing on him. Suddenly, a city that has denied him everything for a full eight months is offering him a chance to stay on for two additional weeks! He tells his friend that he can't change his plans. Oblivious to the Other's state of mind, the tall girl in the black boots says it's all right and then asks if he'd mind stopping by the newspaper to tell them to look for someone else. The request seems reasonable, so he hugs her good-bye and starts off for Pompilio Daza Avenue. He arrives at the office and heads up to the second floor, but halfway up the stairs he runs into a group of people he doesn't know, one of whom is the news editor. As soon as he's introduced himself, the Other receives an order that catches him off guard. "Run over to Ballivián Street and ask for Señor Vilela. They're expecting you." He walks through the offices of the newspaper like a robot. "Tomorrow I'll be passing through Patacamaya," he thinks, touching the bus ticket in his pocket.

But that doesn't happen. For two weeks he sits at a desk they assign to him. But it isn't his desk. It belongs to a member of the permanent staff named Carlos Vallejo, a man who is well prepared to carry out his job. But he is on leave because of illness, nothing very serious. After a couple of weeks he will be back at work, earning a living for his family. The Other knows nothing about the job. His fellow employees, who are all strangers, seem to enjoy teasing the newcomer. "You'll be ready to throw in the towel before a week is up," one says to him in a joking manner, attempting a sort of backhanded friendliness. The Other is thankful for the gesture and begins to open up like a tropical flower. At one o'clock in the morning, he thinks he hears music mixed in with the other noises of the newspaper. It is an old Bolivian melody which seems to make the work of the proofreaders and typesetters go faster. He suddenly becomes sad. Actually, it isn't sadness he feels but a kind of resplendent gratitude. He is working to earn his keep, even if it is just for a night. And he is going to work hard so he can eat his bread with joy. He works as carefully as he can, trying to catch everyone else's mistakes without making any of his own, which is impossible. His nerves are on edge, so he gets up and walks around for a while, but his legs can hardly support his body.

About two in the morning, or a little later, he walks out into the dark street where there is no one except some drunks. He heads back to his apartment, walking along streets that seem as lonely as he is. Human dreams have mysteriously come to rest in the Andean night. He can see shadows moving in the distance, thugs who roam the streets at night carrying chains in response to a call for violence. In recent months, these groups are seen in every part of the city. He walks out into the middle of the street, prepared to receive a beating. What do these people know about his dreams, the crossroads of his life, or the fields he plowed as a young boy? They know nothing, and why should they? Likewise, what does he know about the motives of a pack of merciless wolves? No one seems to know anything about anyone. He crosses in front of the drunks and walks on along the street, preferring not to think about all the strange things that have happened this day. But once he is safe in his room, he can't fall asleep. He doesn't know the meaning of the Aymara word that mystifies the lives of the plainsmen; he doesn't know the magic power of "aruskipasipx-añanakasakipunirakispawa." On the other hand, he knows well that a snake that falls asleep is lost forever.

With his eyes fixed on the lead-colored hills, he stares into the future, holding tight to his last hope. Abused by goings and comings, he decides to stay on in La Paz for two more weeks. He walks over to the kettle and serves himself another maté.

The Dead Man as the Other Sees Him

"We are the only examples of the impossible, and that is why love delights in torturing us," said a careworn man. Then Love said to the Devil, "Don't go easy on me because I'm not going to go easy on you."

There's an animal called the *guanaco* that lives on the plains of the Gran Chaco. Obviously it's not the same four-legged creature that scampers about the wide Altiplano, because the one that inhabits the dense forest region of the Chaco is very small and feisty. His bite is nothing to laugh about, and it's better just to leave him alone. But if you're ever bitten by one, expect to spend at least three days under a blanket, nursing a very painful wound. I've never been bitten myself, though as a child I often played with them and thought about what the world must look like through their eyes. The expression "swallowed up by the earth" suits the *guanaco* to a *T* since most of the time he's underground. And though it's hard to catch sight of one, you can usually find them by looking for their "caves," which actually look more like upside down pyramids or inoffensive little holes. But inside hides the *guanaco*, ignoring anyone who calls, friend or foe. You can't even root him out with a stick; to the contrary, the more you poke at him, the farther down he goes. A muleteer would never even try to get one out that way.

But what could never be gained with threats and supplications can be won with the help of traps and trickery. And if you don't believe it, ask the *guanaco*, who is quite familiar with such methods. Normally he's content to stay in his hole, but let an absent-minded ant slip into his pyramid and he's up in a flash.

That's when you can catch him. So if you want to see a *guanaco* alive and kicking, the best thing to do is look for ants, which are his perdition. Then, as soon as he sticks his head out, you can rescue the ant, which would be the humane thing to do, and at last come face to face with this nocturnal creature.

Not that the *guanaco* isn't an able foe, but I've never had any trouble getting a look at them since I usually have a couple of ants in my pocket, or at least one. I've been studying them for a long time, and it seems to me that they've got things just backwards, which I say with all due respect, for actually I'm quite fond of these night creatures, maybe because they look sleepy, or worried, as though they had the weight of the whole world on their shoulders. Of course, a lot of them are nearsighted or blind. But even so, they go about their business and the business of others with great care. It's not out of any particular goodness on their part; it's just that they're born with some sort of aptitude or sensitivity. At least that's what those who presume to know say. So *guanacos,* without dragging free will into it, just do what comes naturally. Though they might learn something from the old saying, "The stars may guide us but never oblige us."

I, on the other hand, see things in a different light. To me it's a classic case of bad luck. Sooner or later something bad is going to happen to all of us; it just happens to them first. Everybody knows it, but nobody thinks about it. And I'm not going to waste my time thinking about it either. I'm good for a lot of things, but philosophizing isn't one of them. But some-times I lie down in the sun with a maté in my hand and try to understand the way things are. Actually, I probably put more heart into it than head. But I wonder, for example, if it's possible to know from one minute to the next what's going to happen. I think not. And if anyone does know, they'd rather keep their mouths shut about it and let it catch us by sur-prise. I know that for sure. They're all keeping quiet in fifteen languages, whoever they are. And it's probably for the best, even if it hurts us. Because anybody who knows us, knows that if the stakes were high enough, we'd sell our own grandmothers.

Speaking of people who are knowledgeable about *guanacos* and simi-lar creatures, I'm dying to say what happened one night when my dear friend Adrián, Argel, and some other companions were having a beer at a place in the City of Illimani, La Paz. Everyone was pleasantly drunk and not at all rowdy, when all of a sudden, with no warning at all, a big fight broke out, and it got so bad that even the police refused to intervene. One of the waiters whipped out a revolver, fired a few shots, and hit a man in the head. The victim, totally removed from the battle zone, was sitting at a table, facing a man with whom he was talking. Neither was paying any attention to what was going on in their midst. In spite of the waiter's excellent aim, the man didn't die, though he was rather shaken by the bullet which lodged in his brain. No one tried to remove it, thinking the man was going to die anyway. We heard later that a couple of quacks split his head open like a ripe melon, and there sat the bullet. Without touching it, they began to poke the nerves around it; and each time they touched a nerve, the man would respond by raising his hand, scratching his ear, or whatever. Since no one in Bolivia dared to perform so delicate a surgery, they took the man to the United States, where he's remained the same, neither dying nor regaining consciousness; and every time they press the right nerve, he waves back at them.

This strange incident has made me think. And when I've been with friends who were philosophers or sociologists, I've let them know my opinion, which a few said sounded like an old wives' tale and others have respected as ancient wisdom: "It makes perfect sense. You poke the right nerve, and like a robot, the man does what he has to do. But what about the rest of us whose heads are in one piece? Who is it who's touching the right nerve to make us happy, sad, or excited, when all the while we think that we are in control of our senses?"

So even if I laugh at "free will," I don't sit around like a bump on a log, either, and I'm not so stupid as to think that everything's going to be handed to me. I couldn't do it. Adrián and I have talked about this a lot, with him taking one side of the argument and me, the other. And now my friend is dead, but he still talks to me about the man who got shot in the head and other mysteries which to him aren't mysteries anymore. And I'm not afraid of him and listen to what he has to say, just as though I were listening to an older brother; and that's how it ought to be, because dead people by nature are older than the living. There's no two ways about it. I think about these things often, especially when I'm watching the sun set and suddenly become nostalgic, for no reason. And I look at the sad, lovely sky and say, "For every sorrow there's someone to express it." Sometimes I think for so long that I start out thinking one thing and end up thinking another. Then I wonder if I'm being controlled, if some idle so-and-so has put an ant next to the hole of my quiet existence. Need I say that my memories have kept me afloat? Having just turned forty, maybe I ought to take inventory and admit that, thanks to my memories, I've been able to do a thing or two. But I have no intention of taking inventory. I will continue, however, to stick to what I can do and not what I want to do, and I'm not ever going to stray from that enormous truth that an old fellow said to me in the shade of a carob tree: "The really big rocks, the ones too big for me to carry, I set to one side, and the others, the ones I can manage, I push along in front of me." And then he added, as if what he'd said to me weren't enough: "What's a rich man going to sing about if he has no sorrows to tell?" And I said to myself, "Holy cow!"

My memories have started coming back to me just as my life is drawing to a close. I'm not long for the grave, and it's not just a lot of foolishness. But there's no point in worrying about it. Besides, I have a whole stack of memories just as fresh as if they'd happened yesterday.

I live by myself now, though I haven't left Laura. I decided to live alone after I met Constanza, a beautiful woman who's everything a woman ought to be. I live alone—alone and worn out from so much running around—but I have Constanza's shadow as my constant companion. I've never wished anyone any harm, but I have wished I were dead. A thousand times I've thought I'd be better off that way than having to put up with the things people have done to me. And I'm not just saying it. I'm past being a romantic, not that I ever really was one. The only romantic things about me are my dreams, which are dangerous in themselves. Every one contains a message, though it takes patience to figure them out, to take them apart and then put them back together. There's no two ways about it. I didn't dream them just because I went to bed on a full stomach.

The best way to interpret them is to go step by step, which is a cliché, of course, but true, nonetheless. Because, in the first place, dreams pass through the mouth of an interlocutor who doesn't exist in the same dimension that we do; and second, because things that happen in a dream occur at their own pace, unlike that of the sun, and if our special needs demand it, several events can occur simultaneously; and third, because the memory is like a net where our interests are trapped, twisted, and turned, to then reappear even brighter than before.

So let us proceed, step by step. The first thing that comes to mind is a cemetery. I am thinking of the little graveyard, in El Palmar, which is where I lived till I was twelve. I remember going there one afternoon, though, as far as I knew, no one had passed away. It was on a hilltop, and a cool breeze was blowing, a breeze so soft and cool that in poetic terms it might have been called "a crepuscular breeze from the trade winds that were passing through the province." It was cold, and when I looked up and saw a small bird sitting quietly in a treetop, looking as if he had no place to go, I felt chilled to the bone. I doubt the bird was really sad or that anything terrible was about to happen. It probably was just the time of day, the hour when things on the earth come to a halt. All those who have lived and traveled through forests, towns, and fields know perfectly well what I'm talking about when I refer to that special time when all the hustle and bustle loses its meaning.

I'd seen cemeteries before, so that wasn't the cause of my sadness. I'd seen a lot of them. The first was in Aguayrenda, the Guarani graveyard at the foot of the hill in Peima. The second was in Campo Pajoso. I was just a child then, and I couldn't imagine why they'd taken me to a cemetery. But later I came to understand, for while I was playing among the *tala* trees and the wild Syrian rues, my mother was praying before my father's tomb. He was the first close relative I'd lost, and I can remember seeing his body in spite of the layers of dirt that covered it. I don't remember anything about the deaths of my father's parents or where they were buried. For all I know, life itself may have carried them away and sprinkled their ashes through the forests of my native province. I can still feel them in my blood; and through my silence they breathe the warm forest air. And sometimes I am quite certain that they prefer to be with me rather than anywhere else.

So you see, I get along well with the dead. I've tried to avoid run-ins, which can happen if you aren't careful, just as it happened to Santarra, a loudmouthed bully who one night, when it was so dark you couldn't see your finger tips, lost his way in the woods with some burros he was tending. I don't remember if they were his or someone else's, but at any rate, all burros look the same in the dark, and that night you might have even mistaken the devil for a friend. A light rain was falling, and it was icy cold. Suddenly Santarra ran into something, most likely a barbed wire fence; and he turned around and went the other way, but nearly fell into a deep gully. So he looked for another path, and again ran into a piece of barbed wire, which this time scraped him across his back side. Cursing his fate, he decided the only thing to do was to lie down and go to sleep, which he did as soon as he'd found a rock to prop his head on and had covered himself up with his wide-brimmed hat. But all night long— according to what he told us many years later when we were standing on the patio of an abandoned house, waiting for the rain to let up—he was never able to get to sleep because every time he closed his eyes a voice would say, "Move over a little, you're taking up all the room." And one time a very sweet voice that seemed to come straight up out of the ground said to him, "Hey, big guy. Stop cramping my space. Can't you see there's room enough for both of us?" So he decided just to lie there with his eyes open, not that he could see anything, but it seemed like a good idea, since he was sure the voices he'd heard belonged to dead people.

And as soon as the sun rose, he saw that he'd been right, and took off running, losing his *alpargatas* in the process, because he was standing right in the middle of a cemetery and had been lying on top of a grave. That was the first and only story I ever heard Santarra tell. The next week he came riding through town on a train, a freight train with open cars that passed through the village every seven days. He was alive and conscious and was lying there with his elbows propped on the railing, as sure as anything that he was going to die. His insides were hanging out from the stab wounds he'd received from the husband of a woman he was humping.

So you see, I try get along with dead people, with Santarra and all the rest. And I don't go around bragging about it, like my deceased friend. Now and for all time I'd like to say that I've nothing but the most profound respect for the dead and their lovely existence. And anything else I might say in their regard is said humbly and sincerely. But sometimes I start to brag about my dialogue with the dead, and as soon as I do, good-bye dialogue. How could a loudmouthed braggart carry on a conversation with someone whose entire existence is based on silence? Impossible. Of course, talking about it is one thing and doing it, another. Talk is cheap, very cheap. Anyone who's been in the desert knows that there's even a right way to be thirsty. But the first thing you have to learn is how to be alone. So it's better to forget about water till you've learned that.

Whatever I've accomplished, I hope that in the process I haven't thought too well of myself. But I can't be the judge of that. I'll leave that up to the wise and honest judge, the one who stands above our petty lives. I hope I've done right by the dead and all those who were about to die and those about to be born. I owe them a lot, in every sense, the material as well as the ineffable. My debt to Vallejo, for example, is very great, though I never knew him. Sadly, he didn't know me either, but without a moment's hesitation, gave me his place. From October of 1971 to June of 1972, I didn't have a job, so I decided to go to work as a truck driver. About that time Vallejo got sick— nothing really serious—and gave me his place for two weeks, only two weeks, till he could get better and support his family again. But he didn't come back; he got worse and worse and finally died. So I never even got to see him, but you don't have to see a person to know him and be his loyal friend forever. My children needed to eat too, and I wanted to earn a living by the sweat of my brow so I could deserve some time off. From that time on I continued in Vallejo's place, as a copy editor at a La Paz daily. And that's how Vallejo got into my life. One time in a dream, Vallejo said to me, "The dead are grateful beings, and they can see everything clearly. They don't have to tax their brains trying to understand things because nothing's hidden. Everything is clear."

And I suppose that's the way it is. But it's not that way with dreams or the devil. If they're involved, you'd better open your eyes wide and watch what you're doing. There's no time for lying down on the job. It's strange that my first dream, or at least the first one I can still remember, had a ghost in it. I didn't know it was a ghost then, but now when I think about it, with its long, yellow polka-dotted tail, I'm sure it was a ghost. And I'm even more sure when I remember that I was alone in the room, and my parents and other relatives had gone for a walk under the trees. Because it's a well-known fact that ghosts only appear to children, and not just any time, but when they're alone.

With the devil, it may seem different, but it isn't really. Lots of books have been written about the devil, but once you've seem him, you forget everything you ever read about him and think of him in the context of your own life, and you'll see him in terms of your own symbols. It's all a matter of keeping your eyes open. The first time I ever saw him, he appeared as a woman, actually a little girl who was only eight years old. Her name was Laureana Medina, and she was sleeping in a classroom at Rufino Salazar Elementary School, when I was barely ten and was playing chase out on the patio, which was lighted by the moon. But thinking back on it, I don't believe it was something that just happened; it happened for specific reasons that I have discovered after many years of painful searching.

I remember that several days before I saw her, I'd gone to Campo Pajoso, some five kilometers from El Palmar, with a man who drove a red truck. We dropped off the passengers and started home about ten o'clock that night, which is like midnight in the country where they go to bed early so they can get up at dawn, unless they have to take care of something urgent. I don't think the driver was afraid, or maybe he was and that's why he carried me with him. Because it's a well known fact that a ghost won't hurt a child. But for my part, I wanted to go along because I really liked riding in the cab. On the way back, I started talking to him about some pretty serious matters that just popped out of my mouth as if somebody else had put them there. One thing I talked about was God and goodness on the earth. We discussed one thing and another until my friend, who was driving, couldn't contain himself anymore and pulled off the road near a wooden cross where a log truck had turned over many years before. I can still remember the illuminated darkness of the trees, the innocent sounds of the crickets and other creatures of the night, the treetops reaching up toward the sky in an aura of pure, natural innocence that I was seeing for the first time. I never forgot any of it. The man was kneeling on the ground, sobbing with his head between his hands. He was trying to say the right words, words that would make a difference in my life, because what he was doing was offering me up to God. "Receive your servant," he said, concentrating on his prayer, "and don't abandon him, because he was born to serve you. He's one of your own." Thirty years later, I was able to read for myself a verse that says, "Child of life, you have struggled hard to see the summit." But at that beautiful moment so long ago, my friend's prayer did me a world of good; and when I returned home to find my mother ironing my father's clothes, my brothers and sisters running around the house, and my father drinking maté, I was surprised that they couldn't see the sudden, luminous change that had taken place in me. I was transfigured, my life didn't belong to me anymore, and by force I had become the dwelling place of a high, incomprehensible divinity. And on top of that, three days later I had to put up with a ghost and a dream in which Lucifer—or Mandinga as he was called in those parts—gave me a long, hard inspection. I was scared to death and ready to wash my hands of the whole business. And I put it out of my mind until many years later when I came to understand what had happened.

In time I went astray; but the years had a way of bringing me back to the fold. If a man never makes a mistake, how's he to learn the meaning of forgiveness? Though some people just go on acting like fools no matter how many times it gets them into trouble. There have been plenty of times when I was really down in the dumps, and I cursed myself as others have often cursed me. But every time, after I'd gotten started back down the right road, I realized that if you don't give yourself to God, nothing bad is going to happen to you, absolutely nothing. The problem is that sometimes it takes a long time to get around to giving yourself to God, and in the meantime, the devil takes hold of you and doesn't let go of you, from sunup to sunset. And though getting along with God is no laughing matter, getting along with the devil is even more serious. I confess that before I started back down the right road the second time, I really was a good-for-nothing. I'd listened to a lot of foolishness, mostly from my friend Cranach, about the world of darkness and about wicked things, and I decided to try my hand at it, which a person should never do out of sheer idleness but only in the case of absolute necessity. But as everybody knows, changing a person's mind is like trying to pull a donkey by the tail. And the more advice I heard, the further in I went until I was in it up to my eyeballs with the devil. And a lot of terrible things happened to me till one day my own soul was able to show me the way. But all of this happened over a period of years and will have to be told bit by bit.

The following, for example, is something I wrote back in 1972; and only God knows why I wrote it, for I certainly don't: "The mountain. I stand alone before the world. I am surrounded by ordinary things, things that I have always known. But my eyes are playing tricks on me, and these same ordinary things have taken on a mysterious character. I'm lucky to have my words, which might have fled, robbing me of my most important tool. I'm a blind man wandering alone in a desert, and now Life has come to vent her anger on me. Sometimes I catch hold of her and make her scream, and then all the ghosts of an entire lifetime flood around me and in a moment set her free. For I come from the mountain, and the mountain is where I learned to sing. Actually, I learned everything I know there. It's where I made a pact with the devil, as had been prescribed, a pact that suited my being. To each his own, as the saying goes."

Later on, a fire that I'd set as a joke threatened to burn me alive. And even then, frightened but still contentious, I wrote an "Ode to the Devil" which I tried to publish but was politely turned down, thanks be to God, for there is no reason for such torpid private documents to ever reach the public eye. The text, which has remained in my hands, I now offer to the reader: "The land where I lived had many trees. Summer arrived quietly without the interruption of a single voice. The boughs of the trees gently sloped toward the sky. The sweet aroma of water lingered on in streams. In summertime, travel meant a happy trip, and if anyone in the countryside felt uneasy, it derived from a need to praise in silence the sacred lands of long ago. I was born in that enchanted land; and by an evil sign, which had left its mark on my chest, night would shroud the path of my love. But I was blessed, and my first years ended happily there. For you appeared. I know you, as one must know the person whose chest he pierces with a sword. My night is stained with blood, but my eternal wandering redeems me in your presence, and my memory praises you, as it praises all that was left behind."

My relationship with Orana apparently dissolved any illusions of love, and now I am involved in a very unpleasant affair with Laura. One human being houses an infinite number of beings, and it's erroneous to suppose that such multiple—or a least double—personalities should be assigned only one name. I know that. I knew it intuitively from the time I was born, and therefore wasn't the least bit anxious about giving a second name to love. Since I'm telling this story bit by bit, I suppose I ought to include here a poem, "The Fire of Night," which I wrote over a period of several nights at a time when I knew that Laura was about to blow up at me, though I was still insane about her long hair. We were having little daily spats that, like a trampoline, were the impetus for more important battles. I have paraphrased the poem's thirteen verses as follows: "You will be carried to the desert by a woman, where the trees that witnessed your birth cannot accompany you with their gentle shade of water and wind, nor the sacred star hold you back with its music. You must suffer as the founders of a religion suffer, as those sleeping souls who profess a strong, secret bond with life. You are what has been called youth and gold-filled ignorance. Your heart beats rapidly, a captive of exotic flora. You must suffer deeply if you are to know the highest peaks. Your wisdom is a treasure that only children can discover. Nature, gentle nature, is perfumed by a dream that surrounds it. What is near and what is far silently await your song."

How should I know if this was a literary voice, if it contained the pleasant, dreamy tones of the imagination, if the creative spirit reigned over it. I could not have cared less about any of that because what I knew for sure was that between one thing and another I'd gotten into something that I'd have a hard time getting out of. For more than ten years, I'd forgotten just about everything I'd done, convinced that in certain situations no amount of experience would do any good. I often recalled a lesson on hope, summarized in the following parable: "A big storm hit the middle of a valley. It was thundering and lightening and large pieces of hail were coming down. A man in the valley thought that the big flood had come, the one that would destroy the whole world. He saw no way to escape and bid farewell to life, not realizing that on top of a nearby hill another man could see the storm and knew that it was only local." I never liked that story, in spite of its valuable lesson, because it's one thing to watch it rain and another to have hail beating down on your head. The first man actually felt something. The second man was only thinking. And in order to pick the best solution, you'd have to be in both places at the same time. I put the lesson on hope out of my mind and happened to recall a famous line from Franz Kafka, "I am persecuted; I am chosen." The Austrian author's words only confirmed my lack of confidence in books. In other words, I realized that there were tons and tons of books, and any hypothetical reader who wished to become an "authentic" reader would first have to travel the rough roads of life in order to appreciate how much you can learn from things you haven't experienced, and words allow a person to do that. But experience permits the reader to judge the importance of a book, a work that through a dead medium speaks to us of life.

The easiest way to do anything is to do it bit by bit. When I went to work as a copy editor, I knew right away that I wasn't earning enough to meet my expenses. So I decided to cut back any way I could. For example, instead of catching the bus, I started walking to work. It was a fairly long walk, but I had no choice, so I just went out and bought myself a good pair of boots, because otherwise I was going to wear out the only good shoes I owned. The first three nights—actually it was about three o'clock in the morning—I walked home alone; but the fourth night I realized that someone else was doing the same thing I was, trying to save money any way he could—and that person, whose name was Jorge Arce, lived in the same section I did, Villa Fátima. God bless his soul, because not long ago he died. He was about sixty-five years old, and he and I quickly became friends, mainly because of his fine sense of humor; I like people who laugh at their own troubles but take an interest in the troubles of others. He knew a short cut through a darker and more desolate part of town, and one night we suddenly heard whistling noises coming at us in all directions. He began to quicken his step, and though I'm a pretty fast walker, that night I couldn't keep up with Jorge. As soon as we were out of danger, he told me that we had narrowly escaped being assaulted.

It must have been experience talking because, as I found out later, Don Jorge Arce had been attacked just two months before by some young thugs who'd stolen his watch, the only thing of value he had on him. After that, we took a different route through wider and better lighted streets, which eventually led past a large square called "Gualberto Villarroel" in honor of the late president who was hanged from a lamppost in Plaza Murillo on July 21, 1946. Every time we passed the square, we remembered that kindhearted colonel who'd often said that he wasn't an enemy to the rich but a friend to the poor. And after many talks with Jorge Arce, I came to agree with him that we shouldn't expect too much out of life when the purest Man on Earth was forced to climb up Golgotha carrying a big cross on his back, and a beautiful child who cursed the fig tree for not giving fruit out of season was crucified by men who were terrified of his innocence. Don Jorge always stuck out his tongue before or after he laughed; but that time I didn't see even the tip of his tongue or so much as a faint smile on his lips.

Walking to and from work, either alone or with my friend, I often thought that sooner or later my situation had to change and that I ought to be prepared so I wouldn't be taken by surprise. Clearly, I was walking because I couldn't afford a car, but if I could get a raise, I could catch the bus. And if I could get another raise, I could take a taxi. But if things didn't go my way, I'd be walking again, and I might not have even the most necessary things to live. And that's exactly what happened, and here I am walking again, lost in an enormous tide of pedestrians.

The windows of my small room are boarded up. There's only enough space for a cot, a few books, and the utensils I need to make maté. There's a river that flows near the house, and during my first days here, I felt like I was in the country again, not just any country area but that beautiful part near Narváez in Tarija. When I think back to that lovely place where I spent my lost youth, I am overcome with nostalgia. Trapped in a city that will always seem strange to me, I often think of the afternoons when I would go down to the river to fetch water for the truck driver. The sky would look sad and overcast; dogs would be barking in the distance; and I would watch the darkness settling into the valley, erasing it from the landscape. Suddenly, in the middle of that scene, I saw a corral with many deer. It glistened in the dark and seemed to be moving. The fence wasn't made of ordinary wood but snakes that the owner of that solitary place had tied end to end. I broke out in a cold sweat, and then a plump, green man came up to me and said, "I don't know why you'd want to go where you're not wanted. If you stay with me, I'll give you all these deer, parrots of many colors, and any tricks you want to learn." I didn't get to answer because he was gone before I knew it. But remembering that lonely place, I pretend it's the river that flows near my room, leaving behind the music of human dreams. In order to reach such an inhospitable place, I had to open my heart to many human beings. And to reach the shore of this blindly flowing river, of this endless loneliness, I had to spend five years separated from Laura. Now she and my children are living in La Paz. A tremendous amount of energy has been consumed during these five years, and though my *alpargatas* haven't been scared off of me yet, I've had my troubles. I've been burned, but I haven't had the desire to put out the fire that burns me. So why brag about it? I'm the same man I always was, but I'm not who I used to be.

It's the last night of December 1980, which for me is the present. The country is passing through a grave economic crisis, and as I walk down from Villa Fátima, the city looks as though it were wearing a somber mask. I, too, am wearing a dark disguise, not that I especially like it. The great, worldly feast day is approaching, and as the hour draws near, I decide to spend the evening with Laura and the children; we will enter the new year together. What will the approaching cycle have to offer us? I'm not sure, but I've got my suspicions. I am sure, though, that before the night is over the need for a casual embrace will carry me to Orana and a scenario that human couples desire more than any other. Some time ago I began to have tender feelings for her. I also burn with desire for her. One day I suggested we engage in an intimacy she knew well, and in a moment, we'd returned to a forest of warm air and humid darkness, and without a warning an animal was attacking her from behind. It wasn't the first time it had happened, but that time I lay there with my eyes closed, picturing her dark, beautiful skin, her radiant face, her long, black hair, her sensuous body that responded without hesitation to mine. Her whole being—aromatic, transfigured—had quickly surrendered to frolic, and she fought back, as would an enemy, in a dark, crystalline spiral of intimacy. Orana, with her lovely breasts and firm buttocks, is as sweetly affectionate as Constanza, a long-legged, flat-chested brunette; and both can work their feminine magic on me. Starting out like a feverish youth and then progressing toward skillful maturity, my body goes crazy inside of them, and afterwards it's more powerful than before, emerging from the vegetation of a seductive, unknown world. A captive of a sensuality split between Orana and Constanza, my body has turned me into a happy navigator, a renovator of landscapes trodden under by neglect. Then I come back to reality and take up my daily course, only to pursue them again in memories of nocturnal magic. They are both there, nude, transparent in the silent darkness, reaching out across the distance, sweet and simple like wildflowers in the morning air, swaying back and forth in the province of my dreams. Constanza is now twenty-seven; Orana, thirty-seven; and this rural wild man has been forty years upon the earth of inconstant light. I met Constanza on August 14, 1977. The first time I saw her, my head was filled with memories of my native land and with the sweet smells of the forest. And when she first surrendered to me, triumphant yet defenseless, her skin emitted that same aroma. She was like a mount whose owner, an intrepid romantic, had permitted me to ride, a mare who to his way of thinking, couldn't be tamed. So I freed her from the reins of a daily reality that no longer pleased her, and in the shadows of a bed that wasn't hers, inflamed her with irreverent, intrusive caresses. During that long-awaited afternoon when I was mounting Constanza, the beautiful animal's owner strayed from the path of his dreams and, pacing back and forth in the cage of his insomnia, became enraged.

Meditating on the mysteries of life is not an aspiration of mine; but here I go, sticking my snout into murky waters. Why? Because they're murky, and I've got a snout. I know that I'm never going to sprout wings, and it would be stupid for me to hope for such a thing. But I do hope to catch the attention of someone who knows the meaning of forgiveness. What person can hope to be goodness incarnate? Not I. How could I? And I'm not stupid enough to pretend to be what I'm not. Certainly, there are some people who are good, especially those who haven't been tempted. But to become good, first you must be an apprentice to evil. Goodness is never a talent, and sometimes when it's achieved it leads to pride, as Job knew well and so did Faust. Grace is another matter, and you can't buy it or earn it with suffering. Like all great gifts, it's always undeserved. No two ways about it. Sometimes I look back on the low points in my life, and the beatings I've taken seem to lift me up, and I think that maybe I'm ready to drift noiselessly into the harmony of the universe. I wonder why my memories haven't helped me out; maybe they went on ahead of me in that treeless field of solitude; I don't know. I only know that they must have put on boots for a long journey, because they've abandoned me, left me without even a grain of insolence in my saddlebags. Could it be that everything that's happened, one thing so close on another, ended up perverting my spirit? Or did the shadows grow tired of my obstinate soul and go away, cursing me as they went? It's true, I mount two women; but before I knew it, the sluts were mounting me, practically forcing me to do it, until suddenly I managed to find my way to a clearing in the woods and knew one thing for sure: I'd managed to catch the attention of someone who offers protection, asking nothing in return.

I've loved a lot in my day, and I go on loving. Satan knows it well, as I found out when I met up with him on the high seas, and at the time, as far as I knew, I didn't owe him anything. But the worse time wasn't then, but on St. John's Eve, when Laura and I were living in a three-room apartment in San Pedro—a section of La Paz—that must have been occupied by some witches from the Altiplano before we moved in. Now that I'm in constant contact with my soul, I've got the time to figure out why things turned out the way they did. And with so much time to think about it, I'm convinced of one thing which I suspected from the start: when you get the pants scared off of you, you just sit there like a knot on a log; and the opposite, people who think they've seen the devil but really haven't are likely to squawk like a parrot. It's the same with a novice dog on the field of battle; he'll bark and bark but never cross the river. But a dog with experience will jump right in, and as he paddles across the stream, he'll beat the water with his tail if he considers it a valid commentary.

As a prisoner of the indelible present, I've got memories up to my eyeballs. Everybody would like to occupy a place in the bright, invisible center. Only God knows if I live and breathe in that luminous circle. And I might as well confess that I've done what a man has to do, and I've been an ass for long periods of time, sometimes longer than my body could take, and if I could stand it, it wasn't because I was tough or intelligent; far from it. It was pure luck, maybe because I've never lost touch with the stars. Though, once, to get my compass working properly, I had to lie on my back without moving for a long time, which got longer as the days came and went. Nothing's free in this world, which everybody knows. When somebody hits you, it's a lot easier to fall on your butt than to just stand there half dazed, not moving a muscle. It all started in the middle of a dream on October 9, 1974, when the title of a book and its length in pages suddenly came to me. Things started to come together on that St. John's Eve I mentioned before. My brother Demosthenes was there when I got the news of what was going to happen to me. We were sitting on the patio in the dark, watching the fireworks and the smoke that was enveloping the city. It must have been about nine o'clock, and after a couple of drinks we started reminiscing about the Gran Chaco and our family and the good people we had known there. And after we had talked, we just sat there quietly, feeling pretty good about things in general. I was still enjoying the silent, brotherly reverie when our next door neighbor appeared, wearing a hat with a brim and some short boots and looking like a rural man dressed up for the weekend. I couldn't see him clearly, but I thought I saw a long nose and white, wavy hair. The strangest sensation came over me. When he knew that I'd seen him and had been taken aback, he forced a smile. That sinister creature had been living right next door to us and we'd never suspected. I was ready to go a few rounds then and there, but holding back, shouted a warning: "Don't go easy on me, my friend, because I'm certainly not going to go easy on you." For a split second, I could feel my fist sink into his face, but I wasn't punching anything except air.

A few months later, in August of 1976, I met Constanza. Our meeting took place at the Black Light Theater where I'd gone to hear Franz Schubert's *The Trout*, presented by a quintet from Heidelberg. I've got a bad habit of talking to whoever's standing next to me, and that night, before I realized it, I was deep in conversation with a dark-haired beauty, not knowing who she was or where she was from. She, on the other hand, knew perfectly well who I was. After half an hour, she told me her name, but I later forgot it. I didn't see her again for a long time, and by the time I did see her, I'd almost forgotten her face. I happened to run into her at a lecture on "The Badly Assimilated Feminine Principle as Motivation for Nocturnal Art." We made a date to have coffee the following day, and she showed up wearing a pretty flannel skirt; I remember quite well. After we'd ordered our coffee, we suddenly realized that we didn't know why we were sitting there. We didn't have anything in particular to say to each other, except for the obvious, which couldn't be said on the first date. So we smiled and tried to carry on an intelligent conversation, until we gave up and faced things as they were.

After several dates, we became friends, never stopping to think about where we were headed; and on the night of May 3, 1977, standing under the tall, dark trees in Plaza Gualberto Villarroel, I kissed her for the first time. And I kept on kissing her, as we lay in the grass under a faint moon drenched by a sad, gray horizon. Laura, who was already expecting some sort of calamity, left for Tarija the following week. Though she didn't say it, she was going away intentionally, to let me learn a hard lesson on my own. But I was happy again; someone loved me and I loved them, with the simplicity and warmth of youth. But between our first embrace and Laura's departure, I had a dream that left me in suspense. I dreamed that Orana and I were together, and she was sitting on a bench. Constanza was standing in front of me with her face all aglow. Looking at me, she said, "I promise to be faithful to you." And that was the end of the dream. The days came and went, and on August 14, in an alley so dark I could hardly see her long, wavy hair, Constanza's body directed itself toward its destiny; a door opened that I should have kept shut; the last article of clothing that deprived me of her body fell away; and without anyone suspecting, the devil's lusty penis penetrated a lovely, young maiden.

The days came and went and my dreams became increasingly frequent and bizarre. I don't know exactly why, but one of them stuck in my memory. I was walking into a church in the Altiplano, and Constanza was by my side. We entered through the main door, and many people were going in and coming out. On the inside, it didn't look like a Christian church; it was more like an enormous Aymara dwelling, with large patios for the wagons of the muleteers. But for minutes at a time, the entire place would take on a sacred character. We went up to the second floor, and from there we could see what was going on below. Suddenly we were talking to an old Aymara who could tell that we wanted to get married and began to list the requirements of matrimony: "to survive the night of fear, you must sacrifice the White Llama and a big tray full of geese."

In April of 1978, I dreamed that I was passing through the university and to my astonishment saw the sacrificial White Llama in the atrium. In an instant I knew that the pact was sealed. We were of one flesh, and from that time on, the bee and the flower would be the symbols of our souls. I still remain in this invulnerable present and do not regret it. Seven days ago, Constanza came back from Cuzco and brought me a kneeling llama, the most precious animal in Andean culture. Maybe this suggests that a cycle has ended. But whether we are inside the circle or outside of it remains a mystery. Maybe we are together or maybe we have been separated by a golden band. I'm slowly learning about such things through my dreams, but I'm not especially anxious to receive messages from my dead protectors, among them Adrián. He, however, seems to be reaching out to me with a certain urgency. In a dream I saw him sitting on a bench in a small square. I was with Constanza, and I noticed him and went over to talk to him. But he covered his face with his left hand, signaling that he didn't want anyone to see him. His face was gleaming with a kind of wisdom unknown to human beings; his eyes were transparent and he looked very kind, but suddenly he became harsh and judgmental. I wanted to introduce him to Constanza, but he refused to look at her. And calling me to one side, he said, "They've decided to put me in charge of the defense of balkanization."

In the meantime, during the last five years, some terrible things have happened, including a whole series of coups and assassinations of both government officials and workers. With the help of the Argentine army, the country has turned into a living hell, with violence breaking out at every turn. Many Bolivians have been killed, and many others have left the country. Those who remain have done so either because they can't leave or they prefer to die here. The country is divided by constant conflict and to such an extent that it may explode at any second. I think the members of the resistance are right when they predict even greater violence because there's a limit to how much people can take. Maybe I'm not the only one who's ready to take up the gun; surely there are many. But not everyone said from the start, as I did, that the military were not to be trusted. I've learned a lot about Bolivian society. I learned one thing about it from a relationship with a woman; and I learned some other things from watching people suffer. I'd rather not even think about it; it's so awful. And not only that, I thought I was going to be killed. I was so sure of it, the thought of a normal death never crossed my mind. But now when people talk about revolution, I don't feel anything, because ours ended in disaster, thanks to the scoundrels who were running things. They always did manage to come out ahead, but now I think it's their turn to lose.

I don't understand why I don't want to talk to people anymore. Maybe it has to do with something a mute once said to me: "Just as I'm about to speak, sorrow overtakes me." In order to complete my apprenticeship, I allowed all kinds of obstacles to get in my way; and every time something happened, I'd offer a prayer to the heavens. It never would have occurred to me to ask for something I hadn't lost in the first place, and all I asked for was a chance to wash my vision in the broad expanses of the world so I might see my neighbor's face. Once in the insecure realms of the imagination, I met two quiet visitors who'd come from the Middle Ages, by way of what magic I wasn't sure. They were wearing purple habits with hoods so that only their faces showed. Since they were inclined to remain silent, I did the same, and the three us stood without saying a word, which in itself said a great deal. I would have done whatever they'd asked if they'd spoken to me. But they simply returned to their abode where nothing of any size can be put, no matter how small. There's no getting around it. The desire to talk went out of me. And now as I come to the end of my life, I'm starting to remember everything. Things about my parents and brothers and sisters, about Orana and the children. Someone had to be alone in the world, and it was our fate to be alone in a city. We were alone from the beginning, watching our sad reflections in a world we'd left behind. As far as my relationship with Constanza is concerned, I suppose some remote God tried really hard to return us to our original selves— identities we cast aside without a thought to their worth.

I don't want to give any false impressions about myself. I'm a rural man of about forty and consider myself normal, more or less, though I don't believe that "normality" really exists except as an ideal. And I'm far removed from ideals. I never did want anything to do with them, because for people who do what they're supposed to do on the earth, ideals are nothing but a burden. I'm not joking. And anyone who thinks I am ought to remember that crazy Arthur Rimbaud, that luminous adolescent who, after leaving a small book that revolutionized poetry, wanted to come back to earth to do something he was supposed to do—make a dent in reality. I don't have any need to go back anywhere because I never left my world in the first place, not in my dreams or in reality. Because for people like me, our country is a solitary stage. I knew it from the start and took it like a man. That's the way it is, and I said to myself jokingly to hide my sadness, "Patience and good humor." And I went about my business, alone, surrounded by the multitude, and in the company of my hidden gods. I never could understand people, maybe because I could size them up in an instant and was never far from right. I'd explain this better if I could: I can get along with anyone, but I can't accept the way that most people think, modern people, that is. I don't mean to be critical or flippant. It's just that right in the middle of a structuralist interpretation, I'm likely to get a vision of a desolate plain with stars overhead, horses in the early hours of the morning, and perhaps a melancholy tune like soft rain.

Nobody understands why I have to live in the city, and that's fine with me. For a long time I've had a part-time job translating a city language to a rural language, and vice versa, pouring the rhythms of country people into the innocuous mold of a metropolitan tradition. I translate forms into symbols, which are neither compliant nor submissive, and in doing so I destroy the precarious order of the forms. Life has taught me to steer clear of impartiality, and I'm too old now to go looking for it where it oughtn't to be. It's a matter of pure, simple truth, and to illustrate it, the following double example may be valid.

There's a poet named Cranach whom I heard about by chance, or maybe I should say "spontaneously" since I don't believe in chance. It happened in 1965. He was kind of a misfit, a *poèt maudit*. Back then I knew what "misfit" meant—but not *maudit*. He was said to be an out-and-out scoundrel, but the man I discovered was nothing more than a child who had distanced himself from the world to love it even more. I said to myself from the beginning, "Here's a great poet, a disillusioned master." It's not surprising that he fooled me, but it backfired on him. Not that I'm smarter than anyone else. I'm just used to being around people who take the direct approach and come out better for it. They learn from the bad things that happen to them, and they turn out to be good and caring people. But Cranach was reenacting the drama of the fallen angel. I watched for about a year and went away without causing a ruckus, though I must confess that I can give as good as I get. Cranach ruined a lot of people, people he didn't even know. And having said that, I might ask, "What is a world, anyway?" Doesn't it start out as one person's way of doing things but eventually end up as a way of life? Of course, such codes of conduct wouldn't get off the ground if others didn't accept them and go along with them. But whatever is accepted, be it material or spiritual, is what I'd call a "world," and all who want to be a part of it have to do their share. No drones wanted. A lot of people got involved in Cranach's world, maybe because they didn't have a world of their own. But that doesn't make him any less to blame for leading a whole group of people into the abyss. I must confess that I learned a lot from Cranach. I was barely twenty-four the night I went with him to his room, and on the walls saw photographs of holocaust victims, shortly after hearing him carry on about the benefits of Nazism. I wanted to tell him a thing or two, but didn't. At any rate, I hate what he did, trying to pass himself off as some kind of hero to a lot of defenseless people.

Since I said I'd illustrate my point with two examples instead of one, let us look now at the other side of the coin. Of all the people I remember from childhood, my favorite is Don Victorino Guzmán, a prosperous carpenter and farmer who went to work every day with a smile on his face. He is very old now, but when I was a child, he paid us visits with some regularity. That was when we lived on the outskirts of Aguaragüe in a locale that was known by two names, Water's Eye and the Coast. One sad day, Victorino, who was an ordinary, jovial man, became ill. He didn't have just any illness; he had asthma. That was the start of a real Calvary because he couldn't die and he couldn't get well. He lived that way for twenty years, wondering what he'd done to deserve all that suffering. Every time I went home for vacation, they'd tell me about Don Victorino and how the doctors couldn't cure him or even ease his pain without killing him. Things were looking pretty bad, and he'd stood it as long as he could. Then one fine day he woke up determined to take matters into his own hands; so he said good-bye to his wife and children, picked up his axe, and headed for the woods. He didn't stop at the edge of the forest but went deep inside where not a sound was heard above the silence of the trees.

I could guess the outcome; Don Victorino had made a pact with the devil. He'd become a witch doctor. Not another word was said about his asthma, and according to all accounts, he was completely cured. One day when I was drinking maté with my parents, I decided to ask them about our friend's miracle cure. My father turned to me and said something I won't ever forget. "Son," he said, "when a person's been sick for twenty years and he doesn't die and he doesn't get better, if he ever does manage to crawl out of his hole, all he can do is praise the Lord and practice witchcraft."

I had to speak to Don Victorino Guzmán. Compelled by a force bigger than myself, I went to look for him one day about seven o'clock as the sun's light was growing dim. I wasn't going in search of any cure. I was just going. I directed my steps toward the middle of the forest, thinking all the while about the good-natured carpenter I'd known as a child. A fine mist was falling, and it was slowly growing dark. A puff of cold air came out of nowhere, and suddenly I was reminded of hidden sources and sad trees, landscapes that in spite of their desolation offered a gentle comfort to passersby. I reached the corral gate and a troop of dogs rushed out to see who was there. I stopped to pet them and then went on toward the house. Don Victorino stood watching; he had a long, white beard and was wearing a wide-brimmed hat which protected him from the wind and rain. I didn't expect him to know me, but he did, and we hugged each other tightly. I felt the warmth of an old man who had reared many children, and I hoped he could feel the affection of someone who had gone astray but hadn't abandoned his faith.

Once we'd gotten over the shock of seeing each other after so many years, we began to talk of many things. What happened after that, I would hope to tell as accurately as possible, but I may be missing some of the details. I'd barely sat down inside the cabin when a man came riding up on horseback. The dogs didn't make a sound, and the rider didn't get off his horse, even after a short time had lapsed. All of a sudden I became drowsy and lay down on one of the rustic cots that Don Victorino had built. Sometime later I woke up, feeling as if I'd been put through some sort of preparation so that I could carry on a dialogue with my friend. And we immediately began to talk, first about simple things, and then went on to more complicated subjects.

I don't know exactly when I realized that I was talking to a wise man, a man who'd come face to face with evil without recoiling. But what really struck me was that here was a man, in the middle of the forest, who had reenacted a great human adventure stripped of all the ornaments of a more worldly setting. The hardness of his features was illuminated by a flame from a rustic lantern flickering in the wind. The fire in his eyes spurned deception of any kind, here or on the other side. And yet in a second, his face could change and his eyes fill with compassion.

"Don Victorino, when did you first see the devil?" I asked.

"I saw that scoundrel more than forty years ago," he told me, in words that bore the untranslatable mark of the forest. "You weren't even born yet. I had a small piece of land near Aguaragüe; it was new land, recently cleared, and I decided to plant sweet potatoes. The weather was good and my family was willing to help, so I went ahead and put in the potatoes. The week after that I started digging a trench for watering the plants. One morning, about four o'clock, my lantern blew out three times. I went on with my digging till I hit something with my shovel. I looked to see what I'd hit, and it was a clay pot. I put down my shovel and brushed the soil away with my hands to see if there was anything inside. And I found another clay pot, a white one, inside of the first pot. The next day I gave it to a family who were friends of ours, and according to what they told me, when the wife washed it, it broke. About that time my ears began to itch, and I got a big boil on one ear. I couldn't sleep it hurt so bad, but I didn't have time to sit around, so I went on working. About a week later I was back in the same field at the same hour. It was cool and raining. I was watering the plants, and just as I was finishing up the alfalfa, I saw a man in my neighbor's field, walking in my direction. He asked me if I was through with my work. I said I was. But I was in a hurry and didn't want to get into a conversation. He wouldn't leave and kept following me from one row to the next. As I'd reach the end of a row, he'd be standing there looking at me. My back was tired, so I stopped to take a drink and roll myself a cigarette. Since he was right there next to me, I offered him the bottle. He took it in his hands, like he was going to take a drink, but instead, he emptied it on the ground. Then he said he had some tobacco for me, but the pack was empty. He was starting to get on my nerves, and he was beginning to look familiar. But I was wrong, and I knew it when my lantern blew out again, and he loosened his tongue, 'When I give somebody something, they don't go giving it away. Why did you give that pot away? You ruined everything.' I was young and didn't know as much as I do now, so I just dropped everything, coca leaves, bottle, shovel, and all, and took off running through the potato patch."

After a brief attack of laughter, Don Victorino resumed his former seriousness. He told me that for years his asthma had made him sicker than a dog, and in desperation he'd left his home and come to the middle of the forest. Still depressed, he'd started looking for wood, and that's when his friend—who from the beginning of time has struck fear in the hearts of human beings—showed up. In spite of his experience in the sweet potato patch, Don Victorino had never flirted with the idea of witchcraft, or with any other idea for that matter. And though his asthma had kept him up all night, the sudden apparition jarred him out of his stupor and carried him away to a different time and place.

Don Victorino went on with his story: "'Good afternoon, sir,' I said to him. 'Good afternoon,' he answered in a hoarse voice that sounded like a hoe raking across the ground. 'Who are you?' I questioned, feeling bolder, because there wasn't any going back and the time for being afraid was passed. I wasn't a kid anymore and had learned that fate carries us where it will before it hurls us off a cliff. 'If I'm the one he's come for,' I thought to myself, staring down at his polished shoes, 'he's not going to leave till he's seen me. And besides, I've got a thing or two I'd like to ask him.' 'Why do you want to know?' he asked me, without moving a muscle."

According to Don Victorino, the visitor was a big man, strong, and well dressed, and he promised him good health and the knowledge to heal himself and others, especially of illnesses that had no cure. Don Victorino didn't tell me anything else about that night that had slammed the door on all curiosity seekers. But even if that hadn't been the case, this writer would be hesitant to tell the whole story but would repeat, at any rate, what the old carpenter said to him in a very serious voice, "Never fear. There's a certain order to the universe, and every intelligent, honest being must respect that order just as it is." I said good-bye to my friend and walked away into the dark night, tracking through the mud and bumping into trees; and every step took me farther away from the quiet solitude of a Doctor Faustus, though I would be listening for his voice for the rest of my days. When I reached my parents' house, I curled up on a sack of corn and felt comforted, as if I'd seen a comet moving slowly through the sky of my province.

And now I'm in La Paz, trying to figure out what these two episodes— about Cranach and Don Victorino—might have in common, and also wondering about my own life, recognizing, of course, that all people have their own ways of learning things. I don't know if anyone ever really sold his soul to the devil, as I've heard said. But, at any rate, I wouldn't do it because you can't give away what isn't yours to begin with. What happened to me was different. I just bumped into the devil on several occasions. And as far as I could tell, it's not a pleasant experience, especially if you like being alive and hope to stick around awhile. But, paradoxically, you have to make him your friend if you ever expect to see the dark side of the soul, which is the only path to divine splendor. I take my hat off to anyone who takes a different route. I had two women and still do, and their bodies have led me to some of the weightiest conclusions. I travel the night alone knowing that dawn can't be far away. Because no matter how often I've rubbed elbows with the devil, I'm still human, try to do what's right, and lead a reasonable life.

The universe, as I see it, is neither good nor bad. And at my age it would be absurd to espouse a facile moral position. There's something out there that can hurt people and that knows about the changes in people's lives. I know it's hard to distinguish between good and evil, especially if you believe that both can serve as purifiers. I don't think I'm better than any-one else, but I'm not any worse, either. I can usually muddle my way through without making too much of a fuss. I keep a cool head and take things as they come—keeping in mind that my greatest ambition is to become a rock. I haven't made it yet, and sometimes I get depressed about it, though for the most part I'm a pretty jovial guy. I'm always playing jokes on people and they on me; life would be a bore without humor. I didn't come up with that idea; it came to us from the earth's most ancient dwellers. On the other hand, I imagine that enforced loneliness—the kind you don't ask for—is awful, though I came into the world alone and I've stayed that way so that I could better understand other people and learn to appreciate both the living and the dead.

Fortunately, I've had a job for some time now, and with that obligation taken care of, I've been able to work on my own projects. I'm grateful to have the chance to earn my own keep and in my spare time to put my talent to the test, that is, to write things that nobody tells me to write, because it's one thing to suspect that you can write and another to actually do it. Working with other people has taught me respect for my fellow man. Some call it "solidarity." I've been working for some time now, first as a copy editor and then a reporter, which meant that someone else would be putting in the tildes. I said good-bye to my wild ambitions, but not all at once; it was a change that occurred spontaneously over time, since I was used to staring into the future from a window that lets in a light capable of transfiguring us. I live in the perpetual present of my soul and know all about my country from one end to the other. I feel a sincere affection for everyone who lives here, whether they wear hats or not, whether their pantries are full or they travel God's roads with their bags empty, whether they live in the past or the future.

It chills my heart to think that life has to be taken seriously. I'm reminded of this when I think about a letter I wrote back in 1965 that bore the title "Letter to a Friend Who Died before My Birth" but could have been called "Letter to a Child Who Died before My Birth," because in spite of the subtle difference, the topic was the same. My topics may seem confusing, but I assure you I know what I'm talking about. And when I revise and polish my work for external consumption, I can calmly say, "I can't imagine what to expect from a story introduced by someone called the Dead Man and carried forward by an illustrious stranger known as Jursafú." But there they are. By nature, I'm a man of firm convictions; in other words, I'm not the least bit afraid to use the word "I" in this country thoroughly afflicted by insecurity and sorrow. For example, in a few minutes, my feet, which have been programmed by a mysterious call, are going to carry me out onto the street, and I will stop as usual at the Mirador to lift my unknowing eyes in silent prayer. The stars have stayed the same. I know that. And they're as far away as ever, deaf to our requests for a harmoniously constructed universe. I'll move on then through the breath of the city, skillfully making my way among a crowd of lost strangers and guided by the lights of a modest world where everyone is forgiven and accepted. Making my way through an underbrush of dreams and expectations, my body will find a definite route through the streets, recall old friendships, and shake the hands of loved ones. All of this is possible and fits neatly into the dreams I've chosen for myself in this city, without taking anything from anyone. Because what's a city anyway? A valid question, but maybe a little strange, like asking what life is. Such matters are better left to the idle. I only know that I was born practicing not to sell my dreams. Pushing pride to one side, I repeat softly that I'd rather die than renounce my convictions born of terror and homelessness. Because it's one thing to elaborate theories in the peacefulness of everyday life and another to come up with material—provided by your own hide—for those happy disquisitions. I recognize the right of people to do as they will with their own life. But when the judgment day rolls around, forget about playing hooky. It'll be too late then. If my soul was tempered with a delicate instrument, it was only so I could learn to shake hands sincerely with my fellow man. That's the sum of my experience. By the warmth of the hand, I know immediately what kind of beast I have before me. And then, the eyes, where all future actions founder. It's a well-known fact that powerful eyes can change the complexion of a life and make it sparkle in unpredictable ways. Isn't that the way it is with the eyes of children, especially the children of the dispossessed? They contain a vision of a better life. I know because my eyes were my greatest gift during the painful period of my illness. They could talk to me of healthier, purer days—of life distanced from misery—because the images contained in those pupils were above suffering and would never drown. No two ways about it, eyes are the greatest gift.

My preference for naked life comes from my rural origins; it's not a question of any special sensibility, and my ambitions could be as dangerous as anybody else's if I didn't have someone to draw the reins in whenever I get out of hand. That someone is the Dead Man, to whom I wrote a letter before I was born. And now he uses an unheard of method of controlling me: he tests me with the devil and with love. It's been a hard course, full of twists and turns, because as a man I haven't always known how to make my way through the thickets of figurative language, and sometimes I get lost before I make it to the first turnaround. For this reason, many people prefer the direct approach and, like the elk—that thick-skinned animal similar to the donkey—move straight and fast until they run headlong into the cashew tree, the innocent, continuously blooming tree of life.

Notebook Number 4

The Other and Jursafú
as the Dead Man Sees Them

You can see, I can hear; I speak, you listen; you dream, I remember; I write, you read; you sing, I'm the suffering for which you sing; I act, you are pure, trembling nostalgia. And that's the way it is and will be indefinitely, until we reach the place where destiny is taking us before hurling us off a cliff.

One day of a long-forgotten year, some wisecracker, who was trying to make a joke, called Epifanio Cliff by another name. Not only was the name wrong, the occasion was inappropriate because a funeral isn't the proper time or place for making jokes.

"Good evening, Señor Epifanio Cavern," said the man, looking very solemn.

Don Epifanio greeted the man and discreetly corrected his mistake, telling him that his name wasn't Cavern but Cliff.

"That depends on how you look at it," replied the wisecracker, smiling. "If I were down below, looking up, I'd have to say Cliff. But since I'm up above, looking down, I ought to say Cavern." ■

One summer afternoon he was in a rural barbershop where people told jokes or read whatever they could find to pass the time away. A customer usually encountered old issues of magazines, rumpled and torn from the careless treatment of other customers. The one he picked up contained a little bit of everything: book reviews of doubtful merit, articles of a pseudoscientific nature, notes on world events, and toward the end, the sports news, of course.

"There's nothing here worth reading," he thought, flipping through the pages—wrinkling them as he went—hoping to find some piece of news worthy of interest.

His mind a blank, he sat holding the magazine in his hands while a Figaro meticulously shaved the back of his neck. Then his eyes fell on the centerfold, which contained a large photograph of a two-headed dog, the product of an experiment conducted by Soviet biologists. There was something disconcerting about the picture, aside from the fact that a head had been grafted onto a normal dog. The animal, which was of a dark bluish color, was pictured with his own head and that of another dog of the same breed. The dog's own head drooped and its expression was very sad, while the new head panted enthusiastically with its tongue hanging out. The contrast between the submissiveness of the dog and the excitement of his new head was unsettling, but, as the accompanying article explained, the "scientists" had been unable to maintain the new head's disposition for longer than two weeks.

The new head didn't die, but the dog with the bluish-colored hair did. Still holding the journal in his hands, he thought about Janus. He recalled a recent dream in which he'd been trying to pull a big tick, filled with his own blood, out of his body; and just as he'd tossed the tick into the fire, he'd woken up. He continued to think about the way his face looked when he was asleep and how he smiled when he was dreaming. He thought about how a person—who had enough to do just being a person—might not have any reason to laugh and how nice it would be if he had someone else to do it for him. He supposed that at some point in the distant past this "other" had grown tired of smiling and had become melancholy for a time in order to get some rest. ■

In Miraflores, the mansion of the architect Arturo Posnansky is still standing. The monumental edifice, later made into a convent, housed people of diverse sizes, shapes, and colors. And Adrián figured among them, still a student of engineering and occupant of a small room where he was able to keep a few personal items and a large drafting table. It—the room, that is—looked like the hull of a ship tossed about by a dark, threatening sea; the whole house, as far as Adrián was concerned, was equally dark and dank and might easily have been called the House of Terror. But, as narrator, I ought to mention that such a name was based entirely on supposition and also that Adrián had read the complete works of Edgar Allan Poe, that sleepwalking writer who denied himself the benefits of the sun's rays and locked himself into the music of the world's most significant night.

A particular geology student spent only two nights in Adrián's room, not special nights but ordinary work nights like any other night in a student's week. His reason for spending the first night was of no particular interest, and—come to think of it—the same could be said of the second night. The first night, he noticed that a comb fell off the dresser onto the floor, propelled by a force beyond human understanding. Adrián explained to him that such things happened all the time. Some gesture on the part of the listener must have encouraged him to continue his story, which seemed to have ended, because the host went on to explain that the whole house was strange and full of potentially evil spirits; and this was the only explanation he could offer for the fact that a few nights before, when he'd been pouring over his geometry homework, he'd heard a blood-curdling scream followed by a woman's uncontrollable sobbing. Believing her the victim of a violent attack perpetrated by the accomplices of some fiend, Adrián had jumped up and run out as quickly as he could, prepared to rescue the victim. But he found nothing except the usual things, things that were in a state of flux but were always there, like the clear moon, a fresh, gentle breeze, dead trees, and an open, stellar serenity which could only be altered within the minds of thinking individuals, people who suffered and, through their suffering, believed that they had reached the anteroom of real thought. He'd retraced his steps, this time slowly and silently as though he'd drunk down in one gulp the entire secret liqueur of the evening. Some gesture on the part of his visitor must have encouraged him to leave off telling his story, which seemed to have ended, because, for a few seconds, the host remained silent in fifteen languages and then went on to discuss more mundane topics, things that were typical of a student's daily routine.

On the night of the second visit, the comb flew off the dresser again. The visitor couldn't remember exactly what had happened next: a lapse of time, the repetition of the same signs and gestures as before, the discarding of the possibility of a trick or momentary insanity, and finally, the acceptance of man's lack of free will and the limits of his understanding. And then what really happened: Adrián suddenly took up the story he'd been telling on the first night. He'd gone back to his room, intrigued by the strange goings-on that bore a trace of the unreal; but forcing himself to rise above that reality, or unreality, he headed back to work, hoping to finish his designs before midnight. He opened the door to his room and stared long and hard at the occupant who was sitting in his chair; he stared at his own hand holding the drawing pen, at his other hand guiding the ruler, at his forehead slightly detached from the world of firm objects, at the familiar shadow of his body, and at his entire body absorbed in the problems of descriptive geometry, with its precise, invisible laws, a whole universe where there was no room for nostalgia because only in living, moving realms could melancholy—the sign of things past—prosper. ∎

José María Ruiz lived his entire life in Zanja Honda, in the southern part of the plains of the Gran Chaco, where the word "south" had no special meaning, since the landscape was no different from any other part of the region—north, east, or west. Wherever your eyes fell, you could see the same rickety trees that looked dead but were alive, trees whose branches came into view only in moonlight, stretching with the help of their own shadows toward the lofty realms of foliage and exuberant vegetation.

José María, who was the eldest of four children, lived with his family, which consisted of his wife and mother—women with miraculous hands for weaving ponchos—and three children, Estéban, Eleuterio, and Hernán. The firstborn was no more than fifteen when something happened that would change the course of all their lives.

Land in Gran Chaco Province, especially the plot where José María Ruiz lived, wasn't good for raising crops. The sun, the marly terrain, and constant droughts made it unsuitable for growing corn, tapioca, or other crops that prospered on the slopes of the Aguaragüe, a chain of mountains bordering the vast, arid plain.

But what amounts to nothing in Chinese may seem magnificent in another language. And that's how it was with this particular land. Its lean surface was incredibly suited for raising animals. Maybe it was a miracle, maybe it was the nutritive value of the rickety trees and shrubs, but it was evident that the herders didn't have to go far to provide their cattle with a substitute for sophisticated fodder and with the necessary water, which, though not abundant, could be found with regularity in the lagoons inhabited by wading birds and other kinds of animals.

Ruiz was a cattleman and a happy man besides. But it was his sense of humor, not his animals, that was responsible for his happiness. He liked to say jokingly that he was "young, noble, merry, and poor." He offered his friendship to everyone, but didn't mind telling you that in his opinion people who didn't laugh weren't to be trusted. He was of slight build but strong, wore balloon trousers year round and, in his better days, boots that laced up and that he adorned with a pair of handsome spurs left to him by his paternal grandfather.

He'd already lost his money when one night a troop of Bolivians were spending the night at his home, a place where travelers were always welcome, friend or stranger. They found him cheerful as ever but humbly shod in a pair of old *alpargatas;* his body was a great deal thinner than before, and his face was reduced to little more than a mustache. That night the youngest of the travelers made off with a poncho that had taken Doña Clemencia, Ruiz's wife, six months to make. This occurred in 1957.

Two years later, hard times hit the province. None of the truckers who usually carried merchandise to the frontier between Paraguay and Bolivia dared to cross the marly terrain. It rained for days on end, and the only way to reach the outlying posts was on horseback, which was how the natives of the region had always traveled. But bad weather wasn't the only problem. By 1959, the rumor was already out that a bad man—who controlled a whole gang of other bad men—was stealing cattle in the Gran Chaco. And according to the rumor, he wasn't a stranger in those parts. Pascual Delfín, who was José María Ruiz's *compadre,* the godfather of his son Estéban, had recently given his godson a beautiful, tame calf, and the young boy looked after it as though it were a jewel, which is what was expected of a young man who received a gift from his godfather. And everyone who knew anything about animals said the calf would grow up to be a fine cow.

In the forest, evenings are different because the people who live there are different. The people who live on the plains follow a different light and have their own codes. And it is natural that such peculiarities would manifest themselves in situations of crisis. During one of those different evenings, Ruiz and Delfín were drinking wine together. A rustic table in front of them supported their elbows, and a slender shadow cast by a *garbancillo* shaded both men's backs. The thin man with a mustache was trying to keep his spirits up despite the fact that he'd lost fifteen head of cattle. He knew who the responsible party was and, quickly changing the subject, said to his friend, "Listen here, Pascual, I want you to stop stealing my cattle." Delfín was a thick-skinned type and said he didn't do it. Ruiz calmed down, drank to his companion's health and to their friendship, and told him he'd kill him if it ever happened again. "One more cow and that's it," he said, laughing at Pascual, who smiled back at him.

It was true that Pascual had stolen his friend's cattle, but he had done it by mistake. It was one thing to steal and another to steal from your best friend and father of your godchild. The whole business weighed on his mind. And what really made his life miserable was a repeat of the same scenario. A few weeks after the toast under the *garbancillo,* a couple of Pascual's men rounded up some cows, and among the herd was the beautiful, tame calf that he'd given Estéban. By the time Pascual realized what had happened, they had gone too far to risk taking the calf back to the corral, and after a sleepless night, Pascual took the animal and tied it under the shade of a *sombra de toro.*

As soon as Estéban realized that his calf was missing, he took off like a bolt of lightning. With a rifle over his shoulder, he set out on horseback to look through the woods and other likely places. The hours passed without a sign of the animal, and he felt worse and worse about having allowed his godfather's gift to be stolen right out from under his nose. But by midday he found the calf. He jumped off his horse without letting go of his rifle, joyful for having fulfilled his duty by finding the lost calf. He was untying the animal from the *sombra de toro* when he heard a strange voice, "Leave it alone unless you want me to put a bullet through you."

He didn't understand the trick that was being played on him by a masked man on horseback who'd emerged from the trees at the edge of the forest. He didn't understand that he and the man had ridden at different speeds and along different trails but had come to the same place at the same fatal moment. For the first time in his life, he couldn't think of a thing to say, but before throwing himself on the ground and shooting at the stranger, he managed to say, "All right, let's have it." Because of bad luck or bad marksmanship, the unhappy godfather ended up stretched out on the grass with his forehead bathed in blood.

Estéban ran away and spent several weeks at the house of the boy who'd stolen his mother's poncho. The police booked him and were about to catch up with him when, trapped in a web of suspicions, he decided to take off for Argentina. ∎

On January 15, 1962, three young men were talking at one of the main intersections on Busch Avenue in Miraflores, a section of La Paz. It was a typical afternoon, no different from any other in the city. But it was special for these three youths who were at an age when the world seems full of premonitions and far removed from banal matters.

The three agreed that not a single day on earth ought to be trivial or ordinary.

The first, whose name was Julián Tuercas, was a talented artist—hysterical but very talented. His father had died when he was only a child, and now he lived with his elderly mother. He was fierce as a trapped animal, but his eyes, which were intolerably sweet and innocent, showed not a trace of meanness. He was Bolivian, had studied at a religious school along with other privileged children, and for a long time had wanted to become an architect. But he'd chucked it all without a second thought in order to dedicate himself to painting, and had taken decisive steps in that direction. He had no idea what lay ahead of him and didn't seem concerned. But he was only twenty, so why worry? And besides, he was the center of attention of Bolivia's reduced circle of artists.

The second youth, whose name was Germán, was the same age as the first; in other words, they had met in school and been friends for a long time. They were seeing each other for the first time in sixty months because Tuercas had been in La Paz and Germán in Buenos Aires.

When friends are reunited, they remember old times, and a common intimacy surfaces between them. But this isn't what happened. Germán appeared to be calm but wasn't, and the effort he was exerting to maintain a tranquil exterior gave him away. His life was filled with trials and tribulations that no ordinary person could have imagined. Not even an expert could have detected what was troubling him or what was needed to restore the harmony he desperately wanted.

The dialogue that took place between Julián and Germán was reduced to a brief exchange of words connected by long, tedious silences.

The third youth didn't open his mouth except to say hello and good-bye. A geology student, he was more timid than the other two, shyer than a rabbit, as Galarza, one of his classmates, liked to say. He only spoke when it was necessary, which was rare.

After a long lull in the conversation, Germán said good-bye, leaving the other two to discuss his life at length and without interruption.

"Your friend's weird," said the third youth.

"He has reasons to be weird," Julián Tuercas replied. "His life is like a bad joke."

"I don't even know his name, much less his life history," the geology student replied.

"Oliva, Germán Oliva. You've heard the name I suppose."

"I've heard the name, but I can't place him," said the third youth, scratching his head. They walked on along Honduras Street.

"I feel sorry for him," said Julián. "What he went through wasn't just a personal tragedy; it was a tragedy for the country, too."

The painter summarized a recent and well-known chapter of Bolivian history. The events had occurred in 1946. Shortly after the execution of Colonel Gualberto Villarroel, president of the republic, the panopticon where prisoners were being held, including three officials of the defeated military regime, came under attack. The ex-officials were Pedro Oliva, José Rodríguez, and Juan Peña. Angry crowds sacked the offices of the panopticon and freed all the prisoners, but they were unable to find the three men for whom they were looking. No one had bothered to look into a back room that the men, terrified by the mob, had made their hiding place. But someone with the devil egging him on retraced his steps and found the missing officers. The angry mob acted out its revenge and later hung the bodies from lampposts in Pedro Domingo Murillo Square.

"Any Bolivian knows that story," said the third youth to his friend.

"Yes, and it would be terrible if they didn't," said the painter, pretending to be irritated. "But I bet you didn't know that Pedro Oliva's son was there. He was only four years old, and no one seemed to know why he was with his father. When the mob first appeared, he was quiet. But later on, as they were going away, he let out a yell, not like the scream of a child but more like an alarm set off by someone carrying out a role assigned to him by destiny. Hearing the scream, the people stopped in their tracks and then turned around. Everyone remembers what happened after that, but no one seems to remember about the child being there, which is strange."

The geology student suddenly held his breath. He could vaguely remember an Oliva who condemned an innocent man to death around the turn of the century, a man who'd been accused of killing General José Manuel Pando. But before he could ask if that Oliva was Pedro Oliva's father, he was interrupted by his friend Julián Tuercas.

"Germán is strange all right, and now you know why."

"I can see why he's strange, but what I don't understand is the tragedy itself. It can be explained but it can't be justified. There's no reason for it. Why did Germán have to get mixed up in it? He was a innocent little child, so why did he have to be the executioner? And he wasn't just the executioner; he was also the informant. And he couldn't even control what he was doing."

"My dear friend," Tuercas replied, "innocence has nothing to do with it. All tragedies are incomprehensible to human beings," he added. "And if they weren't, they wouldn't be tragedies. The Greeks figured it out thousands of years ago. They learned it from watching the gods, who did some pretty scary things. But let me ask you a question. Why bother with human ethics—usually grounded on fear or a desire for compensation—if you take into consideration the capricious unfathomability of the universe? I know that modern thought says that people are the masters of their actions—and of their destinies as well—but the ancients, without forgetting about duty, knew that such vanity was mostly useless. ∎

They aren't called "violinists" but "fiddlers." They've come from a distant province to perform their music, thrilled at the prospect of making known the music of the muleteer. They will soon perform at a coffeehouse in the largest Andean city; but now it's Sunday, and they're staying at the house of a friend. Maté has been passed from hand to hand; they've eaten the roasted meat and drunk the wine. There are other guests present, people who aren't familiar with the world of the muleteer and who are interested in things that are different or primitive.

The musicians include Fortunato Gallardo, Alberto Choque, Amancio Zeballos, and one other. One of them has attracted the attention of the house's owner. He looks familiar. He is the youngest of the quartet and plays the bass drum. The two men are drawn to each other as though each had reminded the other of a landscape hidden under the brambles of a solitary existence.

Hernán's hands are large. The other man notices this when Hernán pulls out his wallet and, thumbing through the memorabilia, locates a small photograph, which he hands him as proof of his friendship.

"That's my father," he declares, proudly.

At that moment they are interrupted to listen to the soloist of the group, who is about to play a well-known tune from his native plain: "*Vámonos, compañerito, vámonos; que vengan otros, que les hagan los mismos cariños que nos han hecho a nosotros.*"

The man in the picture is on horseback; he's wearing a hat with a wide brim, and the horse has a leather saddle. The owner of the house is surprised, but remembers quite well having taken that picture—many years before in Zanja Honda—of José María Ruiz, sitting proudly astride his horse; he remembered promising to send him some copies. That was the last time he'd seen him.

"I took this picture myself."

"*Ejuayjuna,* things do change! Unless you're lying to me," he said with a chuckle.

"You were just crawling when I passed through Zanja Honda and came away with this poncho, made by Doña Clemencia. Whatever happened to Eleuterio and Estéban?"

"Eleuterio is still there, sometimes looking after other people's cattle, sometimes his own. Estéban left for Argentina; I don't remember how or when. I heard he was doing all right, working on a farm that belonged to somebody from Salta. But he got caught in a storm in the country and was struck by lightning."

"That's awful. Poor Don José María."

"He never knew about it. He left us before Estéban did. I was still a kid when some men took a knife to him. They said they'd come to collect. Collect what I never knew. I didn't know we owed anything. I remember one afternoon they called to him from the other side of the fence, and he stopped what he was doing and went to see what they wanted. He never came back. The last thing I heard him say was, "Bring me the knife." When we went to take it to him, he was all covered in blood and couldn't talk. He just died right there without saying a word." ■

He found out from another painter, also Bolivian, that his friend Julián Tuercas was in Paris. He jotted down the address and went to look for him. The landlord of the apartment, which was on the sixth floor of a spacious, modern building, looked him up and down and told him he had no idea who Julián Tuercas was. He walked down the stairs, disappointed that the people of the French capital hadn't heard of his illustrious friend. He walked along the edge of the road on the outskirts of the city, defending himself from the rain and thinking about all the years that had passed and the unpleasant-ness of being in a foreign city "because there was no reason to be anywhere else"—as the author of *The Stranger* would say. He smiled mechanically and, like a robot, turned on his heels to look again at the skyscraper he was leaving behind. In one of the rooms on the ground floor, he saw a familiar silhouette sketching lines on a large, white canvas. He took a closer look and was sure that the artist was his old blue-eyed friend. After greeting each other, they walked the streets of the city remembering old times.

Like school chums in a crowd, they felt far removed from the brothels on Boulevard Sebastopol. They felt close, nonetheless, to another sensitive matter. Tuercas at all cost would try to prove his innocence and would explain, without being asked, that he wasn't an informant and that things had happened differently. Emerging from the dark European night, an Algerian policeman looked at them suspiciously and asked to see their iden-tification. Julián, visibly shaken, handed him a small book that proved him to be a person without citizenship. Their walk came to an end. But the next day they met for lunch and again that night to say good-bye. Tuercas had just returned to Paris, and the other man was leaving soon for Latin America. After an awkward silence, the artist confessed that during his militancy he had never vacillated for an instant. Even after he'd been arrested, he'd never had any second thoughts. But when they showed him the bloodstained clothes of his wife and child, he lost his nerve and told them what they wanted to know, facts of little importance, facts that his interrogators had known about for some time. All they wanted was an informant. His friend remained silent in fifteen languages, and Tuercas went on with his story, adding details to what the other already knew about recent events in La Paz. He wasn't willing to judge anyone; he'd never been tempted to do so. It had never even crossed his mind. He thought that Tuercas's decision to return to Latin America and resume his role in the Colombian guerrilla movement was crazy. He was going back for revenge. He knew that, but still thought it was crazy. He decided not to tell him that he—Tuercas—had almost been killed in Ecuador and had been saved by a miracle. A man who traveled from La Paz to Guayaquil for the sole purpose of killing him, for some unknown reason hadn't carried out his mission. The man had eaten lunch with him, his wife, and child, and when the fatal moment arrived, he'd looked into the painter's blue, curiously innocent eyes and with his finger on the trigger decided not to go through with it. That image came back to him in a tenth of a second as he stretched out his hand to his friend on Maire Street in Paris, shortly before he walked on along the street, thinking about another encounter, an encounter that had taken place years before on Busch Avenue in La Paz. Germán Oliva had been present—that tense Germán who years later would put an end to his own life with a revolver in a room in the enormous city of Buenos Aires. ■

A detestable animal in the opinions of those who know, good taste sets it apart from the apparently lucid, charitable world, and the joyful universe would prefer not to count it among its members even for a fleeting moment. This malevolent tradition has been secretly transmitted, and even children—normally tolerant toward the things of the earth—view it as an ominous sign, an emblem of evil.

The crow flutters alone in his merriment. Pure solitude is its glee. Because whenever it is beheld by human eyes, it is transformed into sheer sadness; its appearance lending itself entirely to the act of mourning.

In an evening's landscape, when things either acquire meaning or relinquish it, the crow appears; and all ambiguous feelings are pushed to one side, the side of sadness. Sometimes the crow holds its beak above its blackened wing and watches the ground, supposedly in search of food, the putrid flesh that frightens all who regard life from an erect position. It would be wrong, nonetheless, to suppose that crows are interested only in things that have begun to rot; their fear of all that has passed is what inclines them—incarnations of unwavering grief—toward the brown earth.

Faithful to their mission, they distance themselves from all who regard them as an impertinence in the solar world, and with a caw, scare away all sorts of dangerous creatures. They never prey on living things but take what can no longer defend itself, what has given in to time, rain, and oblivion. Pure oblivion, they swallow it down, though a more degenerate type prefers the peanut, but man's threats keep it at bay.

It lives out its life on the sidelines of human tenderness but with the same worth of more favored kinds of birds. It could not care less about what people think, connected as it is to the sky and the ground by a frightening link: the knowledge that it is the source, the symbol of a higher wisdom which reveals its secrets only to those who aren't afraid to climb the craggy slopes and to let go of life willingly.

The beauty of the crow. ■

It was usually afternoon when Don Gabino Castillo strolled through the streets of El Palmar, accompanied by his faithful dog Speckles—though in truth the dog hadn't a mark of any kind on him. His entire body was pitch black, so black that if you stared at him awhile, his beautiful coat would take on a bluish tint. Don Gabino lived by himself and no longer had any living relatives in El Palmar. But that didn't prevent him from behaving with spontaneous familiarity toward everyone in the village, about whom he seemed to know everything, including their family histories.

In the tropical zones, there's a time of day when the land is cooled by breezes blowing in from the forest. At that hour Don Gabino could always be seen on some street corner in the village. He might look as if he were wasting time, but he always left his home with a particular route in mind, and neither rain nor wind prevented him from reaching his destination. He visited all of the homes in El Palmar, and a year was plenty of time to make the rounds. He would sit for an hour or two, talking about old times, but if his host guided the conversation toward more recent events, Don Gabino could follow the thread just as well. He was a great conversationalist and a hardened addict to maté drunk from a gourd.

In spite of his familiarity, no one knew where Don Gabino Castillo lived. It was known that his shack was behind the hill and in the vicinity of the graveyard, which was an area covered in thick vegetation, but with the exception of certain curiosity seekers and liars, the villagers couldn't say that they'd ever entered his house. The main problem was the dog, which was gentle as a dove when he was on the street or in someone else's house but would change into a ferocious beast when anyone approached his master's yard.

His life wasn't typical of that of a dog, and for many years he hadn't associated with other canines. He was serious, servile, and unpretentious, as if it were his duty to behave in a reserved and honest manner, like people; and, like people, he was subject to bouts of sadness, which showed in his eyes. From Monday to Sunday he occupied himself with things that were basic and necessary. For example, he would go to market carrying a basket in his mouth and return with it full of bread, meat, and whatever else Don Gabino needed to prepare lunch and dinner. All the vendors said he was their best customer. Also, the people of El Palmar would set aside a ration from their own pots for Don Gabino, and it was Speckles' job to carry these tributes to human solidarity back to his master.

One unfortunate morning—for whom?—Speckles neglected his normal rounds and took a different route. Early in the day a young boy saw him near the railroad station, at first running around on his own and later playing with other dogs, as if he'd totally forgotten his daily chores. No one saw him after that, and Speckles, with his lovely black coat, seemed to vanish off the face of the earth.

Later that afternoon, Don Gabino ran into one of his neighbors who hadn't learned of his recent loss.

"You aren't eating very much, Don Gabino," said the man, trying to make conversation, for, in fact, Gabino had always been a very skinny man.

"Yes, my friend, I eat very little. And for that matter, there isn't so much to eat." He stared at the horizon with his blind eyes and walked away.

Don Gabino Castillo had lost his sight in an accident, and several years later, because of his blindness, he'd stepped on a poisonous snake and gotten a nasty bite. Not only did he lose his right arm, which had to be amputated, he could no longer hear the sounds of the earth, or if he could, they sounded like the echoes of a waterfall or the buzzing inside his own head. So he decided to be exactly what he was: deaf, one armed, and blind. It was then that Speckles showed up, unnamed and still a pup, untrained but able to learn certain skills, skills that would require discipline and sacrifice on his part. But the pup accepted it all, maybe for lack of a temper or maybe because he'd developed a taste for regular meals. The next years were happy ones, as happy as possible for a being that has given in. Don Gabino taxed his memory, forced himself to remember everything in order to fend for himself in a world of darkness. Speckles, his faithful companion, held his animal instincts in check.

And now Speckles had suddenly decided to rebel and return to the innocent efficiency of primitive life. He went away, old and worn out, toward the land of animal reality. Don Gabino, who was aware that nothing could be done to change the inevitable, seemed resigned and not the least bit upset. He strolled calmly through the village, not heeding the repeated suggestion that he go out and get himself another dog. In so many words, he was saying good-bye to all his friends but without wasting emotion on things that couldn't be fixed. He managed to get to his house, stumbling as he went, and quickly found a rope which he used to hang himself later that evening. ∎

He met Cranach in 1965, when the only aromas the world held for the former were those of rural innocence, of wild vegetation and morning dew. Cranach, on the other hand, was from a different world, made up of tiresome darkness, and his only source of light was music composed of mist and exquisite nocturnal emanations. He was La Paz incarnate, not the La Paz of today but of the turn of the century. In the beginning he told the young rural man that poetry, or writing in general, demanded total commitment. But the young man didn't seem to object, since he liked the demoniacal ambit that Cranach was proposing. But later on he realized that his attraction was without passion, a mere mental exercise, an effort to understand something that could only be learned from hard times, over a period of years or during a particularly difficult episode.

At forty, Cranach had lived life as he'd seen fit. He'd learned to follow his own instincts, and, in his writing, he'd broken with all traditions at a time when no one else dared to do such a thing. Cranach used the expression "burn your ships" only once, but since he'd followed that advice and managed to avoid the abyss, he expected others to make the same sacrifices and to follow similar routes. The rural man was willing to do what was necessary to prove his seriousness, but he wasn't keen on the idea of following a route that would take him far away from his native province.

Despite the fact that he was at an age when it is easier to imitate others than to explore one's own inclinations, the rural man was influenced by Cranach for a very short, though significant, time. His break with the writer didn't stem from his own merits, which were certainly meager, but from the impossibility of a city dweller recreating the life experiences of a villager.

For a long time he couldn't appreciate the practical lessons which Cranach, out of the goodness of his heart, had taught him:

"Translate a language spoken by everyone to a specific tongue."

"Isolate yourself from the world so that you can learn to love it."

"Have an ironclad faith."

"Know that what matters in life isn't life itself but works which make life meaningful."

"Never allow others, who for the most part are busybodies, to confuse being humble with being docile."

"No matter what befalls you, be grateful that you're alive."

"Translate a specific tongue to a language spoken by everyone."

One night, of the many nights they spent conversing and drinking tea, the rural man confessed to Cranach that he had one of his manuscripts in his possession and that he had received it from an oriental woman, who had given it to him for no apparent reason. He never returned the manuscript to Cranach because when he told him about it, the author became very grave and said, "If it came to you in that manner, it must have been for a reason."

The evening didn't end with this confession. Cranach, author of a voluminous, unpublished novel, told the rural man that he had thought about the novel for a long time, since he was a young man, in fact, until one night he suddenly felt obligated to begin writing. What led him to take the first step was the smell of something burning, a smell that had blown in through his window mingled with the aroma of evergreens from the garden. It was a smell that he associated with a married woman whom the rural man eventually came to know at a time when she still possessed a spark of youthful beauty, though today, in spite of her years, she seemed old and pitiful. He didn't meet the young man in the photograph which Cranach handed him, because he was dead. He had been Cranach's intimate friend; and something suggested to him that the relationship had been unnaturally close, abnormal, maybe perverse, because before he'd died he'd given Cranach a couple of his teeth for a keepsake.

For some vague cause, the rural man and Cranach—after an intense, intellectual friendship—parted ways forever. However, the real cause had been foreseen by the rural man at the conception of the friendship: "Our paths, my sorry friend, are not parallel or identical and never have been. At some moment in time they had to cross, and now that moment has ended."

And that was the end of it. ∎

The village, which is man's modest attempt to block the advances of nature, watched Pila Ramos grow and caught a glimpse of his intelligence and vigor, qualities which would prepare him to confront dangerous situations.

An energetic person, there was something splendid in his manner that suggested the presence of a victor in this distant, rural sky. Those who knew him only in passing and those who were his friends have testified to the plenitude but not the turbulence that reigned in Pila Ramos's life.

The steadiness of his youthful vision, captivated by the beauty of the countryside, would lead one to believe that his life was balanced and normal.

Perhaps it was pure instinct that led him to finish his primary education and to acquire that token of happiness referred to as culture. But one fine day, Pila Ramos defied the teachings of his elders, made a shambles of his family's dreams and expectations, and took off for the woods, the dense forest, which man with great difficulty had managed to abandon. There he remained, holding his breath, until the incomprehensible Pila Ramos, reduced to rags, was considered dead by human recollection, which, as everyone knows, is incapable of dealing with absences of great duration.

The thoughts and feelings of that solitary man, representative of a race that considers itself superior to animals, were a mystery not to be easily solved either by great understanding or simple curiosity. But, as if by magic, after many years of absence, Pila Ramos returned to the village. He returned several times at great intervals and stayed only briefly, as if to prevent himself from becoming attached again to human contact. But he was such a changed man from what he'd been before that his precautions were unnecessary. His heavy beard and disheveled hair were the least of it. He'd become a complete stranger, not so much for his coarse manners and ruffled appearance but because he had thwarted every code, broken every law which had taken generations to construct.

Paradoxically, and precisely because he was a stranger, he evoked a warm response from the villagers. Even those who didn't know him soon exchanged their indifference for clear sympathy.

Though the forest had become his permanent home, Pila Ramos increased his visits to the village. And though horticulture was what he liked, he didn't shrink from duties of a more burdensome nature or from things he knew little about. Enthusiastic yet inconstant, he was a combination of great virtue and great shortcoming, a contradiction that strangely seemed to escape him. In the dark of night, his tired figure could be seen forcing water up the steepest channels, but since he was shyer than a rabbit, he never accepted praise for such skill and would always take to the woods in the nick of time—in other words, just as he'd earned the affection of some stranger, or wiped away the last doubt of an admirer.

Pila Ramos's small contribution to the community consisted of jobs performed at night, and all in all, his activities didn't seem to amount to much. But in spite of that, there wasn't a person in the village who wasn't prepared to do him a favor. Such unsolicited protection became a homage, which a community usually renders to those who travel unknown paths and expose themselves to inexpressible risks. Artists and inventors are citizens of this type. What Horacio Quiroga attempted at Misiones, honorably but without success, Pila Ramos, ignorant in matters of meta-physical anguish, achieved in his provincial cloister: to live according to the dictates of the heart. Free by vocation, he was willing to take the blows that destiny meted out to him in exchange for his independence.

Before he died, Pila Ramos allowed a cousin to visit him in his wood-land refuge. It was a cold, windy night, and Pila held his hands in front of the fire. He chattered happily, stringing together a series of popular say-ings. There he sat, with his eyes half-closed and an incredulous smile on his lips, until finally, when it was nearly dawn, he got up, stretched like a cat, and said to his visitor: "Listen, cousin, I wasn't born yesterday, so don't start treating me like a snotty-nosed kid, coming around here sticking your nose into things that aren't your business. Maybe I don't have any money. I've got seven jobs and twice that many debts. And so what if I'm poorer than a church mouse. I can take care of myself. Just you wait and see. After all, the world's a pasture for people who know their way around, and if a donkey goes astray, he's bound to show up sooner or later. It's one thing to get lost in the city, but I bet you it's worst to get lost in the coun-try where there's nobody to tell you where you are.

"Why are you looking at me like that? Or isn't a bird in the hand worth two in the bush? There are two kinds of people in the world, the kind that learn and the kind that don't, and thank goodness we're not all stupid or there wouldn't be anybody to tell us what to do. I wouldn't be surprised if the devil and all his children were buried in this very spot. They could scare the pants off of anybody. They could scare the smartest man in the world into wishing he was on his mother's knee. They could make even a brave man's skin crawl. Better safe than sorry, and if you can't stand the heat, get out of the kitchen.

"I thought I was getting somewhere, but there are people in the world who don't know how to do anything but collect. They've taken it out of my hide more than once. We all want what's coming to us, and nobody likes to be last in line. Isn't that right, cousin? Life pushes us to the limit. But when we're by ourselves, you'd think our heads were a plot of hard ground, because the ones who were here and left didn't come back, and the ones who were supposed to come never showed up. But since there's not much in there, everything looks clearer. The world's got to be old.

That's why it's good-bye to the pig that stays in the sty. The pig that runs away keeps on running, and that's the best way to learn that if you run, there's no where to go and no place to stop. Don't pray to saints who don't perform miracles, and don't waste your gunpowder on mosquitos. And before you go acting like an elk. You remember about the elk? But why should you? The elk's a thick-skinned animal. And it marches straight ahead till it drowns in the river or butts its head on a cashew tree. Yes, you know about that. Or maybe you forgot. It would be good, cousin, if you could remember everything. But remembering is like cooking, and sometimes when you start remembering things, you get blacker than an old pot." ■

"What a fine filly!" exclaimed the twenty-seven-year-old man with the big mustache to his companion upon seeing a young Paraguayan woman passing along the corridor. Her husband was also Paraguayan and both were professors at a university near Paris.

The observation was addressed to Danilo Romero, an Argentine painter and writer who lived in Paris. Somewhat offended, he responded with dead silence. Maybe it was because he knew the woman—a tall, shapely redhead—or maybe it was because he wasn't used to hearing that sort of phrase applied to a woman, even when the rhythmic movement of her hips inspired such a description.

The man with the big mustache, who had recently arrived in the French capital, ignored Romero's silent response and went on with his work. His desk was piled high with all kinds of publications, folders, and files, all having something to do with Latin America.

After an uncomfortable pause, the painter suddenly turned to the man with the mustache and said, "Hey, *pibe,* I think I've got something for you, something you can use to practice your French, which certainly needs practicing. The best way to learn a language is to speak it, but it's not the only way. I know what I'm talking about. Another thing you can do is to translate—articles or anything. Of course, it wouldn't be easy and you'd have to use a dictionary. "There's an article in there," he continued, handing him a magazine, "by Martín Solano, a Latin American author. I translated it myself. It's pretty straightforward, no fancy stuff. It's an interesting article. You might try to translate it back into Spanish. Then we can compare your translation with the original. Take a couple of days to work on it and let me know when you've finished." Then Danilo Romero smiled good-bye to his companion and left the office.

By the end of the week, a rather tedious week except for an occasional stroll or visit to a museum, the twenty-seven-year-old man had managed to return the article to its original language. Proceeding one paragraph at a time, he ignored the overall meaning of the essay; but as he went along, he began to appreciate Martín Solano's views on language, which was what the article was about, language. It contained the following excerpt:

"From One Extreme to the Other"

Forceful language has no need for capital letters and by its nature distances itself from emphasis of any kind. It only requires the simplest elements to describe the things that occur from day to day.

Whenever writers write, no matter what the theme, there's always a bag of tricks at their disposal.

But forceful language doesn't avail itself of any devices other than the rhythmic flow of language—a topic often addressed by stylists or those who demand style. It's probably correct to assume that authentic rhythm corresponds to the physical rhythms of writers, to their individual methods of taking in a landscape, of effortlessly breathing it in, of making themselves comfortable amid the hills and valleys of the world.

From whichever angle we approach it, we do not exaggerate when we say that writing reflects a person's breathing; and carrying it a step further, perhaps it is accurate to assume that successful prose is a sign of the author's physical satisfaction, a sign of honest self-expression. Writing is like unrobing; but the nudity revealed is a mere consequence of the act of writing, not its high and glorious end.

It's a well-known fact that even the most arbitrary human movements are life sustaining, except, of course, ones that stem from insanity; and this is doubly true of breathing, which is basic to man's existence and never leads to harm. A curious mechanism, it combines the material elements of the external world with the blind harmony of the interior universe, and it accomplishes this with a certain immediacy. The circulation of the blood performs a similar function but requires more time and takes place "backstage," so to speak, veiled in darkness, jealous of its caprices and laws of concordance—a trivial difference that no one who is genuinely interested should overlook.

The writer must follow the rules of punctuation, which is nothing more than a set of symbols that regulate the flow of the sentence and allow the reader to breathe. And as one might expect, there's more than one way to punctuate a sentence. In this field—as in all fields—the rules are mainly for orienting the writer, and people who follow them to the letter usually have little to add to the richness of the universe. The rest tend to ignore them.

There's no one who can force us to choose between a comma and a semicolon. Nor is there anyone who can require us to put a period at the end of a sentence. What really decides the question is the need for a short pause or a long one; in other words, the important thing is the need for air.

People whose fate it is to become writers need all the signs and symbols they can get their hands on, no matter how insignificant they may seem: from the hermetic word to the trite expression, and everything in between—quotation marks, parentheses, ellipses, and anything else, so long as it doesn't mar the page.

A blank page can mean two things: either the writer hasn't begun his or her work or the work has been successfully completed. It's the most important sign. And in comparison, all others seem opaque, insipid, and deprived of splendor.

Despite trickery, the adequate or inadequate use of signs reveals the conceptual wealth or poverty of the writer, as well as his or her grip on reality. Writing is the only mirror which time doesn't darken. Whether writers choose to be stylish or dress up like monkeys, their particular ways of organizing words will paint a cold, accurate portrait of who they are, without adding anything or taking anything away, without supplying them with any kind of camouflage other than that provided by their great equanimity with *blind, mute wholeness.*

Though the research may say something different, there isn't a good writer alive who doesn't write the way he or she talks. In other words, writers will only put on a page what readers can read without stuttering, wearing themselves out, or running out of breath. Writing and reading are the same thing, identical entities responsive to their own instincts, watered from the same fount, where life in its totality is praised.

It's a well-known fact that breathing provides a rhythm for the body to follow. Or perhaps vice versa, the body chooses from the start a rhythm that it finds suitable. And here we find—decked in other foliage—the irreconcilable theories of Nominalism and Realism. In ideal terms, rhythm should be the meeting place where body and soul can frolic merrily. And, in fact, faulty breathing may suggest an environmental problem, while proper breathing has been the highest goal of communities and individuals since time immemorial.

By listening to people's breathing, it is possible to know something about their backgrounds, where they are from and whether their beginnings were felicitous or not. Talented examiners may discover if individuals have gotten along with their peers or if their lives have been an arduous struggle to survive a collective rhythm that has become disorienting.

Because of their sensibilities, certain individuals may become documents of their communities. But the great creator of language is the people, its renovator par excellence, and its unsubornable guard. This isn't an attempt to wax sentimental or to give lip service to a cause. The truth has a way of disentangling itself from transitory praise.

Everyone knows that sayings and proverbs are dangerous because they are petrified language. No one would dispute their wisdom, and yet when paraphrased, their messages are likely to be contradicted. People can't be sold an artificial dilemma; in other words, they abandon sayings and proverbs that no longer have any meaning, and they keep the ones that speak to the times. With great skill and accuracy, the people cut the dead branches away from the *form* without harming the *content,* and this is how wisdom is preserved, dressed in words that are modern, active, and sometimes vulgar to the dismay of the experts.

The people are successful in their efforts because they tend to jump from one extreme to the other; otherwise, they might not be heard. At first, the color you see is blue, and then all of a sudden you're looking at green without noticing the change, or vice versa.

And that's the way the people are. They're either working hard to earn a living or giving full rein to their joy, which is generally lawless. In either case, their breathing attains its full potential, working hard to fill the lungs with air so that the community may go on darting from one extreme to the other, from green to blue. Thus, by instinct, it prevents the breathing mechanism—which is also the mechanism of life—from becoming atrophied.

This phenomenon may elude those who place a high value on moderation, which has often been seen as a virtue, though in essence it is little more than a fear of taking risks and one of the worst forms of complacency. Not only do they fail to understand the phenomenon, they make moderation their standard and use it to mold the destiny of a nation.

Since this elite refuses to take any risks, it contributes nothing to the community and lives unashamedly off the people's labor; and through a curious perversion of values, it claims the right to establish norms and to create a paradigm for life, which—as one might guess—is nothing more than an imitation of life. Thus the elite jumps from a misunderstanding of moderation to the inanity of considering itself a depository of communal virtues.

The anonymous man is not uncouth or vulgar; he has his own standards and respects them completely, but he isn't so stupid as to consider them sacred. His traveler's status inclines him to keep his standards in motion, to throw them out ahead of him and then to pursue them as a hunter would do; perhaps this is why he is cruel and cutting in his expressions, which is not to say that he uses a direct language or that it enslaves him.

The use of parallel languages, along with the cleverness that such a task presupposes, is common among the people who live on the fringes of official history. Anyone acquainted with the Chaco Indians knows that they pick their language before entering into an honest dialogue. A lucid representative of these *primitive* people once asked someone from another region, "Shall I speak to you in Chaco or in the Chaco's invisible language?"

The anonymous man prefers to deal in metaphors and allusions and to involve his interlocutor in the discourse, which may come as a shock to the unsuspecting listener. He tends to share events of common interest, even trivial or domestic affairs. A clear, human conviction leads him to converse on matters of interest to every-one, which is the source of his strength and power. Though he may know nothing of linguistics, his fine instincts steer him away from weak terminology. He grasps the totality of things without entan-gling himself in the undergrowth, which is quickly choked by lusher vegetation.

Untouched, untouchable language, whose essences are con-tained in dictionaries, offers an enormous scale of meaning that popular tongues traverse, meanings that run from one extreme to the other without hurting themselves or others. And though mean-ings sometimes change, even irrevocably, they could never be so ungrateful as to deny their origins.

Pick up a dictionary of the Spanish language and look at the word *escatología,* for example. It's a word that, like a snake, can bite its tail; in other words, it easily joins two distinct and even contradictory meanings. On the one hand, it refers to things beyond the grave, and on the other, to excrement.

Between one extreme and the other, a whole range of meanings come into focus, and the talented writer is able to detect them and put them to use.

Words that can't be found in any dictionary are like unbranded cattle, powerful and free. But they are tamed by constant use and become worn-out, docile creatures whose brands give them away. Then they pass into that luxurious but limiting corral, the dictionary.

For some reason, the word *linjitsear,* also Spanish, isn't in the dictionary, which doesn't prevent it from being an appropriate means of expression. Not a single authority has managed to tie it down because it's part of a secret code that certain communities have elaborated to protect what can be heard but not said, perceived but not expressed. It's a word that at the same time is so proper and improper that it is used by the good and the wicked, scholars and fools, brutes and people of good breeding, the golden-tongued and the tongue-tied, people of high moral character and the lowest of the low. Which suggests that though people may use the same language, they rarely share the same point of view for very long.

If a Bolivian man were in love with a woman named Eulalia, he would never allow the word *linjitsear* to be used in her presence. He would consider it offensive, not because he's puritanical, but because he views their relationship, which may be neither here nor there to other people, as something special or miraculous. He chooses a word that allows him to pursue animal-like conduct without blushing. In other words, to penetrate the corporality of the feminine universe, the man must create an atmosphere that the occupied person recognizes as inexpugnable. The word is "wife." Isn't it obvious? Maybe not to those who confuse bondage with seduction and thus damn their own souls to hell. On the other hand, there are words like "whore," which perhaps wouldn't affect men who aren't in love, even though expressions of that type could easily offend the woman his neighbor adores.

There's a part of language—or of the human heart—that reaches up to the heavens and captures an exemplary vision, exemplary for its splendor. Yet needs of a sensual nature give weight to the celestial sphere and anchor it to the earth. More important than moral concerns, there's a practical consideration, a need to maintain a true *balance* between the two extremes; and man, the most confused of all living creatures, encapsulates the potential for such a balance.

Words themselves—and everyone knows this, even children— are neither good nor bad. It's their complicity with human beings that gives them a certain tonality; and this tonality has, in fact, an aesthetic value. The only ethics arises from aesthetics. It's the same with actions; they only interest us if they affect us spiritually.

We're indifferent to nothing in life, no thought or deed. And those who have been chosen to keep us abreast of this mind-boggling business invariably stay in close contact with language; and if they so choose, they may avail themselves of words that have been censored by the current morality. If they recognize the difference between imitation and talent, they will make use of the great linguistic repertory (human and nonhuman), the enormous memory which silence has woven, but they will never abuse it. And they will interweave their words with silence if they are practiced enough to wield such a powerful weapon. They will never remain at the warm center or limit themselves to words contained in the dictionary. Without blinking an eye, they will borrow words from the real dictionary. And for another matter, they will always be mindful of the fact that even the simplest expression, once it has been transmitted to another person's mind, may produce unexpected variants.

The problem is that not a single word means the same thing to everyone. Translation makes this apparent by teaching us not only that man longs for linguistic unity but also that he has failed to achieve it. Unity is possible only in theory, and those who have earned it are usually dead and therefore reconciled with the inert world; and if they're alive, they've received something which isn't intended for human beings: the gift of living silence. Words are what they seem only in theory. In practice, they oscillate between the trivial and the unspeakably grand, dependent, of course, on the sojourners' dispositions, since they may be novices or experienced travelers of life's perilous roads. Allow me to close the discussion for the time being with the following query: If I say the word "table," why should I expect two individuals, one who has never seen a tree and one who was raised in the forest, to react in the same manner?

He finished the translation and went to Danilo Romero's office. He told him he would like to write a commentary on Martín Solano's article and would prefer to go to a more appropriate place to write it, like a cafe. On his way out of the office, he crossed paths with the pretty Paraguayan.

"You may not like hearing it," he said to the Argentine, "but that's a fine filly of a woman."

"Don't be a jackass," Romero replied.

Under the pretext of showing them a new journal, Danilo motioned to Eulalia and her husband, Martín Solano.

After a warm and friendly introduction, Martín said to the man with the big mustache, "Tourist or expatriate?"

"When I'm not in Bolivia, I'm neither, and when I am, I'm both at once," said the twenty-seven-year-old, with melancholy in his voice.

They talked for two hours at a cafe in the Latin Quarter. The Paraguayans had jobs teaching Spanish at the University of Vincennes. They were exiles and had only recently arrived in France, but Martín had already made friends with Julio Cortázar, the author of *Rayuela*. ■

Because it's an invisible, fleeting sort of creature, it's considered the most dangerous bird in the forest. Called a *silbaco* by those who frequent wooded areas, it has also been called by other names that in some ways have modified its mysterious nature, not always friendly to lost travelers.

Different from the barn owl and other nocturnal birds that man has considered harbingers of bad tidings, the *silbaco* is even more frightening and can't be trapped no matter what. It emits a terrible, shrill whistle which riders can't ignore, especially if they're traveling by themselves, with only their shadows and memories for companions. When it whistles, everything in the forest becomes silent in order to hear the sound that isn't animal or human and that inspires nothing but abject terror. No one claims to have seen one, and yet many well-adjusted individuals have behaved like idiots in its presence. And though it has no substance, people who have heard it and those who haven't seem to agree that it has the properties of a nocturnal bird. A creature unaffected by good and evil, it doesn't know that its mere existence is harmful to human beings. Just from hearing its sound, many have died from terrible hemorrhages. Others have been so shaken by the sound that they took refuge under the foliage of a *guaranguay* and never again set foot in the forest. Only on rare occasions has the mysterious bird gone to roost in the city, which has more often been the domain of the barn owl, symbol of death, which prefers the environs of people and sometimes makes its nest in a tree near where children play late into the night. The *silbaco* is more at home in the forest, and when it travels beyond its own dominion, its powers are severely weakened; in cities, where people no longer run from invisible things, it's considered more of a legend than a danger. What's a *silbaco* going to do in a city where the language of concession prevails? A rudimentary and magical creature, it carries out its obligations in other places. It goes where it's needed, scaring people but not causing them to surrender. Relieved of its own flesh, it lives among trees and bushes, a pure embodiment of silence in dark and glorious places. ■

I have no idea how many people ever came face to face with Francisco González, but thereabout 1967, when he was one of the world's best playwrights, almost everyone knew him by name. As proof, I can point to numerous articles in newspapers and journals announcing performances of his plays at the most important theaters.

He managed to call even more attention to himself by doing all sorts of outlandish things. Spanish by birth, he had been living in exile for ten years, when at the age of thirty he announced that "though he loved his country, he did not love its autocratic government." These and other words criticizing Spain's dictator put an end to any hope of his returning home.

Even in La Paz, the isolated Andean capital, people who stayed abreast of cultural matters heard about what González had done. And many young people became his fans without knowing anything about his talent as a playwright; I'm thinking of one young black-haired rebel in particular.

The same year that the offensive statement came out in the newspaper, the magazine *Remolinos del Sur* published one of his plays that was being staged simultaneously in New York, Paris, and Munich, according to the editors' brief introduction. The young man with the black hair doesn't remember the name of the play—maybe *The Labyrinth*—but he does recall that a large number of white sheets were to be hung from wires and placed capriciously about the stage. They were supposed to look like roads, the idea being that the playwright was trying to confuse his characters, who were enough alike to be the same character, by placing an infinite web of possibilities in their paths. In order to save themselves from some vague danger, the characters were supposed to run away, choosing, of course, the correct path to follow.

The young black-haired man, who discussed the play with some of his friends, thought that Francisco González's play was little more than an intelligent series of variations on the main theme, which was the anguish of a well-known author from Prague—in other words, Franz Kafka. And besides that, he thought that most of these variations were already common in modern literature.

Soon afterward, *Remolinos del Sur* published another text by the same Spanish writer. The second piece, however, had nothing to do with theater or even literature, but a great deal to do with the blind rage of social protest. The text, less than a page long, proved that beauty is often found when least expected, and, in passing, it also revealed the author's true nature. What was Francisco González really about?

Someone is standing at the doorway of existence and hears a monstrous animal splashing on an unknown shore. It isn't clear if this is the ocean or the prelude to an actual birth, but noisy waves seem to threaten to carry away this innocent creature—carry him away or dash him against the rocks. The child senses that his life is in danger and that he may be near death. He can't have been born only to die. Suddenly a pair of powerful hands put him in a safe place. Those hands, a symbol of brotherly love, remained forever fixed in the mind of a man who became one of the most successful playwrights of our time.

Francisco González is famous, but he doesn't know his own father. Despite the adulation of critics, he won't accept this fundamental absence and continues to search for him in vain. Of course, the mother knew who the father was but carried the secret with her to the grave. Years of searching produced the following results: his father was an important leader of the Communist party in Spain. His political involvement kept him from leading a normal life; in other words, he only lived for a short time with the mother and spent very little time with the child. The hands that saved Francisco from the monstrous animal, as he later discovered, belonged to his father. And the beach was nothing more than a watering trough. Before he wrote *The Labyrinth,* González researched his father's life and discovered that he and some other members of the party had been arrested, but instead of being tried for political crimes, they were simply certified as mentally incompetent and put in an institution. With Christmas approaching, Francisco's father became terribly depressed and, breaking the window in his room, like a madman, escaped from a world of madness. He sneaked away like a wolf over the white snow, through the dark night, wearing only his pajamas. No one followed, not his friends or his incarcerators. It wasn't necessary. The whole country was like a concentration camp. From that time on, his destiny became a broad desert with oases and continuous undulations, the creations of a solitary wanderer's loneliness. Many years had passed since the Spanish people lost the last battle against the dictator who later ruled them with an iron fist; but that night a man slipped through the autocrat's fingers, a man who would later be unmasked by his own son.

The young man with the bristly, black hair read the story with his friends in La Paz and several months later repeated it to a man with ruddy skin and a broad smile. They were sitting with their elbows propped on a table, defending themselves against the burning heat of the plains. His friend was the same rural man who had once said to him: "I close my eyes and attack life head on. I push the big rocks to one side, and the little rocks

I kick along in front of me." The elderly man sat listening quietly to the story of the man who had broken the windows of his room and slipped into the night. A gesture of recognition crossed his lined face. He choked back tears that had been choked back many times before. Scratching his head, he tried to hide the sensitive part of his existence but finally appealed to a word that no one can reject: "My father's name was Domingo. I lost him when I was four and my mother when I was fourteen. But I'd have given them up when I was a baby for the sake of life and freedom." ∎

The route descended from the high valley between shrubless hills and eventually ended somewhere on the vast plain. The truck driver's helper wasn't with him, and a boy of fifteen, his only passenger, helped him to pass the time. It wasn't a long trip, only a day and night, unless the roads were bad. The truck was empty, but its owner had hopes of picking up passengers along the way, to pay for the gas. If all went well, he would return in two days with a load of gasoline cans from the Sanandita refinery.

It was starting to get dark when they stopped at the side of the road, beneath a sky filled with large, black clouds. The boy took a pail and went to the closest brook for water. Going or coming, he heard the sound of dogs barking in the distance and smelled the sad aromas of the earth, wet by a light rain that had fallen for several days. They poured water into the radiator and went on their way. They were supposed to stop for half an hour because of the so-called "neutral light." "When the day hasn't ended and the night hasn't arrived, no kind of artificial light does any good," said the driver, pointlessly turning on the lights of the truck. After successfully maneuvering his vehicle around several dangerous curves, he added, "Most accidents occur at this time of day. It would be better to stop and wait till after vespers. But who has the time?" He talked as if he were conversing with himself, asking and answering his own questions.

Around the next hairpin curve, with a cliff on one side and a ravine on the other, he put on the brakes, shifted into reverse, and raced backward. "There she is, that damnable creature. That's why we're in the shape we're in." A big, black snake with yellow spots had just crossed the road. The driver had tried to run over it, but the snake had escaped unharmed and was slithering into the damp, red soil at the edge of the ravine. Both the man and his younger companion sprang from the truck and tried to halt the snake's progress with a torrent of stones. The boy managed to hide his lack of enthusiasm for trapping animals and also to overlook his uncertainty with respect to the driver, a rural man who was known in the city for having killed someone with one blow from his powerful fist. He was really a peaceful soul, but because of that one unfortunate accident, the people had started calling him "Iron Fist." In spite of the stoning received at the hands of "Iron Fist" and the young boy, the snake slipped away into the ravine.

Without realizing it, they had stopped for the full half-hour of "neutral light." By the time they returned to the truck, it was night. The driver turned on the lights and they drove away into the dark forest of tall trees, very different from the shrubless hills they'd left behind. They couldn't see anything except the road, but they could smell the new aromas of a different land. As the driver had predicted, they were able to pick up passengers along the road, and since two of them were women, the young helper was obliged to ride in the back with numerous strangers who sat quietly, like shadows from another life, protected by their wide-brimmed hats.

The boy was also silent. But once more he saw it demonstrated that when you ride in the back of a truck with other people, the real problem is your feet. You can adjust the rest of your body with the help of sacks of potatoes and onions, but it's impossible to situate your feet. They seem to stick out all over the place and get in other people's way. Feet can't seem to grasp the fact that they aren't needed on a trip. Though the passengers stayed awake the entire night, it was as if they'd slept soundly, with their eyes open. A man draped in darkness said jokingly to one of his neighbors, a man he didn't know, "You either sleep or you don't, and that's all there is to it." The waking man's voice was different from the drowsy voices of the other men, who were wearing sombreros and by pure habit tried to talk the way he did.

At four o'clock in the morning, the truck went racing down a hill at full speed. The trees, now short and sparse, were illuminated by a clear, ashen moon. The first day of the trip was behind them, nothing more than a memory, because the air was warm and silky, purified by the new dawn. The truck suddenly came to a halt, and all the passengers looked up to see what had happened. The more curious ones peeped through the railings. From the short forest, intertwined with rickety trees, shadows, and light, a rider was emerging, a man who seemed to have come from far away. He got off of his horse and handed the reins to a child. "Now run on, son," he said while he struggled with an enormous white sack.

"Have you got something there to sell?" asked one of the men on the back of the truck.

"Some rounds of cheese," answered the rider.

"How much are they?" asked another passenger.

"Not as much as they're going to cost when I get them to the border," answered the rider, sardonically. "That's why I'm taking them there—so I can get more for them."

"He's smart," said one of the passengers.

"Neither smart nor dumb, but that's what you get for asking me before I've even had a chance to sit down. Already wanting my cheeses," mumbled the rider. "I don't even know who I'm talking to," he said, now laughing. "All donkeys are brown in the dark."

"Go to hell," said the man to whom he'd referred.

The rider without a horse was wearing a white, short-sleeved, embroidered jacket and short boots nearly covered by his wide-bottomed trousers. He hadn't loosened the cord of his wide-brimmed hat, but since he wasn't herding cattle, he'd let the hat slip down over the nape of his neck. He wanted to talk, so he probably wasn't tired from his journey. He fell in with the young helper and ended up telling him that many years before he'd gone to fight in the Civil War of 1949.

"And what made you want to fight in that war," asked the boy, "if you don't mind my asking?"

"The country was in a mess, and I was sick of being poor. And I figured that if we won, things were going to change because it was high time that things went our way," he said, as though his memories were crowding in around him.

"So what happened to the men who went to war?"

"We lost. That's what happened, my friend. We're used to losing, but I'd rather not think about it. Thieves took what little I had because I'd left and gone to war. And besides that, I had to keep running from the law, all the time, like I was the one who'd done something wrong. That's how it was."

"But there are laws. Why didn't you take the thieves to court?"

"What for? You can't get blood out of a turnip. They didn't have any money, either. So why take them to court? Just so I could say I'd won? You don't know what it's like, taking someone to court. And it wouldn't have mattered if they'd been rich. I'd have come out on the losing end no matter what. Everybody tries to encourage the poor people, but when they lose what they've got, they're damned to hell. That's why we fought the revolution. And for what?"

"Well, all that happened a long time ago, and things are better now . . ."

"Sure they are," replied the rider, sarcastically. "They're better for them and worse for me. No, my friend. I rode away full of hope and rode right back to where I started, to my cows and my farming, and you may not believe it, but a man can break his back working and still end up with nothing. I hate to say it, but that's the way it is, and nothing's going to change it. I tried to change things and nearly lost my hide in the process. What I did get was peace of mind. I sleep like a rock. But even when I'm sleeping, I dare them to touch me. The peace that comes from experience—nobody can take that away from you," he said, yawning, plainly tired of the conversation.

He closed his mouth and fell asleep. He was dog-tired but managed to hide it until he'd slumped down like a sack of corn on the floor of the truck, dreaming of the child he'd lost in the woods on his way back to the corral, of the diligence of a mother, the noisy play of little children, the singing of the birds. ∎

As a child, he'd often seen a blurred photograph whose frame, when new, was gold. It sat in a room that was nearly always dark; it was a picture of a young couple. The woman, with long braids and a face that showed a life of toil, had a maternal look about her; she'd probably given birth to several children. The man wore a wide-brimmed hat and had a big mustache; his calm eyes seemed to stare far into the distance. His forehead had been lined by the practical demands of living, not by thoughts of unfathomable depth. It was obvious that he was a realist, had been reared strictly, and could handle a horse as well as anyone.

They were his paternal grandparents, but he never got to see them, or his maternal grandparents, for that matter, though he remembered a woman with a smiling face who once said to him, "Come, child, run along behind your grandmother." Maybe he'd just dreamed it, and after he'd thought about it so many times, it seemed real to him. He knew nothing at all about his maternal grandfather except that he was a rural man with curly, blond hair.

But the man, his paternal grandfather, had an air of darkness and a look of exhaustion that comes from many years of self-control. How he died was a mystery; he'd never dared to ask his father. His father, however, did tell him that his grandfather had founded the town of two names—Water's Eye and The Coast—and that, near the frontier, he'd gotten into a fight with a gaucho—the reasons were never clear—and after swimming across the Pilcomayo with a rope tied around his head, ended up seriously hurting the man. Years later he became the magistrate of Campo Pajoso, at a time when the cattle thieves would stop at nothing. But they never got the best of him, and he managed to get through it alive.

At that time the child didn't know that, because of family sentiment, people tend to exaggerate the virtues of their ancestors and descendants and to overlook their defects as well. He didn't know that this is one of the few formulae which human beings willingly learn and apply. The years passed and that wide forehead beneath the hat continued to symbolize a laborious life, one that had come to earth not to sit back and be poor, but in one way or another to muster up the courage to live.

For long hours the child would sit absent-mindedly beneath the flowering lemon trees, saving himself—without intending to—for a time when he would contemplate more serious questions, peering at the landscape and discovering his own aptitude for deciphering its symbols. He was only half right when he thought of his grandfather as having led a normal life of raising children, earning money, and dying of old age. True, he'd worked like a mule, but he'd never had any money and had left the earth at a relatively young age so that his eldest son hadn't known him either, except from his photograph, which he examined tirelessly, wondering if what he felt for his father was devotion or idle curiosity.

"He was an honorable man and was famous for his marksmanship," his father had said to him one day when they were walking through the woods.

"Where did he come from? Where were his parents born?"

"I don't know much about the family history," his father told him. "My parents came down from Valle de Concepción and their parents came from Atacama after the War of the Pacific. The roads the blood takes are often hard to follow and unpredictable as well. We're from this place, but we could have been from any place. It doesn't matter. But you'll know your real country when you've girded up your loins and defended yourself against the people who try to hurt you. That's what your grandfather did, at least that's what they say he did, because I didn't know him either. I've heard he could take a revolver and, standing a long way from his target, break an egg without grazing the lip of the bottle. Try as I may, I can't remember him except for his hands, which seemed large to me then. As the years pass, things start to get fuzzy. His hands . . . that's all I remember. He died first and then my mother, so at fourteen I was an orphan. Of course, I remember my mother well because I was half-grown when she died. But when my father died, I was just starting to crawl." ■

The ovenbird, an insignificant looking fowl, partakes of terrestrial life in a rather grand but discreet manner. It loves flowers and chirps merrily with every change of season. It's a steady creature, but its prudence never stifles its spirit of adventure.

Lively and sociable, the ovenbird is a stranger to depression and melancholy, which can take hold of dreamier spirits, especially when twilight catches them in the top of a *lapacho*.

The ovenbird could have become a hero, but lacking the vanity needed to conquer others, it rejected that path, conquering itself instead and becoming a saint. Its affinity for goodness and responsibility won it respect among people, sparrow hawks, and all birds of high flight.

Even the *tarajchi*, a sly and menacing fowl ignorant of the rules of social conduct, gives the ovenbird its silent approval. Hunters don't seem to be interested in the ovenbird. A strange devotion to its diminutive figure, passed from one generation to the next, has managed to save it from acts of violence. It exudes an undeniable sense of authority that others have come to respect, though it earns them not a peso.

But its nest, built at the top of a carob tree or cashew, is a target for storms and lightning. It's like a small oven whose spiral-shaped entrance protects the baby birds from rain and curious eyes. Without being compulsive about it, the mother and father birds have a good idea of what lasts and what doesn't, and make their nest of clay and straw, which hardens to a cement-like material and provides the warmth of any house built with love. This nest isn't just protection against the storm; it's a symbol of arduous labor, and its builders, like typical biblical characters, only rest on Sunday, a day of singing, removing fleas, and relaxing.

Let it be known, the ovenbird has no enemies, and if it finds death frightening, it isn't for lack of internal fortitude or because of a guilty conscience, but because that's the way destiny intended it.

Hummingbirds, the venerated jewels of rural people, have more colorful plumage, but the ovenbird arouses a special sympathy in man. Nature seems to have worked magic with this innocent creature by embodying its wise laws in this modest bird.

In order to carry out its creative labor, the ovenbird works from Monday to Saturday with a joy uncommon in our time. Despite its incessant coming and going from one limb to the next with its beak full of clay, it never puts on a long face. Also, its home is considered a masterwork by expert masons and wandering birds alike. And there it dwells with its mate and offspring.

The *tarajchi,* which lays its eggs in dove nests, could never get away with such a thing in the cool nest of our little-known friend. Though a hospitable sort, it's not likely to adopt the progeny of other birds.

Among thirsty trees and unusual insects, lost on a January afternoon—which could have been the first day of the world—someone must have seen an ovenbird and thought of it as the only creature that lent beauty and meaning to his life.

But where Paradise thrives, there also hides the devil. The ovenbird, just like the human race, finds in the serpent an inevitable fount of suffering. Though used to living on flat land, the snake is able to intuit in which tree the ovenbird has built its nest. And as though by magic, it slithers up the tree, penetrates the nest, devours the baby birds, and drifts into a world of unending sleep, because the mother and father bird immediately prepare some clay and seal up the entrance to their usurped dwelling.

In the solitude of Gran Chaco and some other Bolivian provinces as well, sealed "ovens" are commonly found with their malign intruders inside, condemned to eternal darkness by the ovenbird's harsh decree. ■

"People who work shouldn't gamble, and people who gamble shouldn't work," said the old rural man to his older brother, sick of seeing him working himself to death and getting nowhere.

"Why so drastic?" asked the older brother. "One of these days I'm going to get back everything I lost along the way."

"You're wrong," replied the old rural man. "People who work are supposed to know what things cost. And they aren't supposed to bet their hard-earned money on just anything. And anybody who gambles," he added, "if he's a good gambler, doesn't have to work. He can make his living off fools like you."

"But the fact is, I gamble, and I know what I lose and what I win, and I'll do as I please," said the older brother angrily. "If you're scared of gambling, that's your problem. It's not for everybody."

"Fine, fine, do as you please," said the old rural man. "Talking to you is like pulling a donkey by the tail. People who gamble do it because they think they're going to win. Otherwise, they wouldn't do it. But the ones who know they're going to win are cheaters and aren't allowed to play. There's only one game that you can't lose, and the only way to figure it out is to work and sing at the same time." ■

Patinuk, at fifty years of age, has published several volumes of short stories and is considered one of the founders of Bolivian cinema. If that weren't enough, he's also an ardent Indian scholar. He has dedicated himself with such passion to the topic that once a mestizo student asked him, with all due respect, "Señor Patinuk, what are you going to do when there aren't any more Indians but just human beings?"

But criticism doesn't faze Patinuk because he's the soul of sincerity and goodness, which makes many of his colleagues wonder if sincerity and goodness are guarantees of profundity and intelligence. Such conjectures don't interest Patinuk because, for reasons no one seems to understand, criticism doesn't faze him.

His friend Fonical, who is the same age as he, has a different sort of temperament. In other words, he's a rogue and a swindler. He's talented enough to imitate other people's work, but in the end he loses out because he can never surpass them. Over the years, what he's amounted to is a decent chess player, swimmer, actor, cameraman, model-airplane builder, geologist, singer, politician, and anything else a person can do in an under-developed country.

When Fonical figured out that people thought highly of Patinuk because he had a good heart, he decided to be good, too. So on Isla del Sol, where they were filming a documentary, Fonical offered to take care of Justino—who, by the way, was as good as gold—and to send him to school. But he ended up shooting himself in the foot, because he couldn't actually take a sixteen-year-old *isleño* back to the city. But the Judgement Day itself didn't frighten Fonical, so why should he upset himself about a slip-up among human beings?

Fonical worries about Patinuk's literary success. He loses sleep thinking about the fact that his friend is not only a well-known short-story writer but also one of the best scriptwriters in the business. Worry and insomnia finally pushed him to ask Patinuk to read a novel he's had under lock and key for three months. He wonders if he has promise as a novelist, and "Patinuk," he thinks, "is the best reader around."

But Patinuk, who is never fazed by criticism of any kind, keeps forgetting to look at his friend's book and always gives Fonical some excuse. The director has just arrived at Isla del Sol and greets the film crew, including Fonical, who is working as a cameraman and takes advantage of the opportunity to ask Patinuk about his manuscript.

"Patinuk, did you finally get to read the manuscript?" Fonical asks with incurable malice, perched on the fountain of the main patio of the ranch house where the film crew is staying.

"Yes, as a matter of fact, I did take a look at it," lies Patinuk, without blinking an eye, the first lie he's told in fifty years. "You've surprised me, and pleasantly so."

"If you think it needs any changes, please just come right out and say it," says Fonical, his confidence boosted by the first remark. "Anything in life can be remedied, except death, of course. Do you really think it's good?"

Fonical looks over at the group of friends and suddenly decides to put Patinuk to the test. "So you thought it was good, eh . . ."

Patinuk, an inexperienced liar, becomes an expert prevaricator overnight. There isn't a quiver in his voice, and he isn't the least bit shaken.

"Well, truthfully, the beginning was a little weak," he says casually, "but then it gets better. The plot takes on a more spontaneous flow and starts to carry the reader along. At least that's the impression I have."

Fonical isn't convinced that any novice deserves such high praise.

"So what did you think about the dwarfs, the part when they're going down the stairs?" asks Fonical.

"That's one of the best scenes in the whole book, if not the best," replies Patinuk, not realizing the fatal error he's just committed.

"You lying bastard!" Fonical exclaims. "My novel doesn't have any dwarfs."

Patinuk, who was fifty years old then, enjoyed the joke as much as anyone. He didn't care what Fonical thought, because he, Patinuk, the soul of goodness but no longer the soul of sincerity, is never fazed by criticism. ■

On two different occasions he ran across a Chaco Indian by the name of Fortunato Gallardo.

In 1957, he rode with a truck driver to the Pilcomayo border to deliver a load of the most diverse merchandise: sugar, kerosene, sweet potatoes, corn, nails, sugar cane, cooking oil, bread, mirrors, thread, shovels, and machetes. The driver had gone there on numerous occasions, and each time, after unloading the truck, had driven back to town, some two hundred kilometers west of the plain, his truck loaded up with fish and jaguar hides. It wasn't always an even trade, and his credits and debits rarely balanced.

It was then that he first met Fortunato Gallardo, a smiling man from the forest.

(Here we might remind ourselves of the fact that the Chaco Indians still follow the custom of taking anyone's name who impresses them with some unusual accomplishment, and also that Fortunato Gallardo, the original one, is the best violin player in Gran Chaco Province as well as a good composer. From his parents and grandparents he inherited a talent for praising his homeland and could discover natural beauty in the most austere landscape that he would then celebrate with a song, which is as it should be.)

In less than fifteen minutes of conversation, Fortunato had let him know that few things in life pleased him, and what did please him, in a nutshell, was traveling, lovemaking, and working, as long as his work didn't get in the way of his pleasure or his pleasure in the way of his earning a living.

The sun was so hot it was scorching the earth. But Fortunato was content on that blistering afternoon because the truck driver—whom he'd provided with an abundant supply of fish—had finally brought him two kegs of nails. Fortunato Gallardo, the nomadic version of the original musician, was with another Chaco Indian, his loyal friend Abundio.

Six months later he made the same trip on the same truck with the same driver. When they got to Palo Marcado, they took the road to Canto del Monte, but decided to stop to rest at Porvenir, a place near Esmeralda. Porvenir is a poor ranching district where Fortunato would stop off from time to time. They saw him there that afternoon, propped against a carob tree with a broad smile on his face. His loyal friend Abundio was squatting on the hot ground next to him.

After they'd shaken hands, the truck driver told him that he'd come to collect for the nails.

"I can't pay you right now, *che*," Fortunato told him.

"Why?" asked the truck driver, irritated.

"Because I can't. You know you brought me the nails, but what you don't know is that Abundio stole them from me," Fortunato explained.

The truck driver looked over at Fortunato's expressionless friend. "Abundio, is that true?"

"It's true, *che*," Abundio replied, still squatting on the hot soil of the Bolivian Chaco.

The two men from the forest began to smile at each other, but not maliciously, and the truck driver, who wasn't smiling at anyone, began to look over his accounts to see if he'd received enough fish to cover the cost of the nails. ■

The first time he got drunk he was thirteen, which was the same age he was when he first slept with a woman. He got drunk accidently, as often happens when minors go to adult parties and come away with their heads spinning and sick as dogs.

Two cocktails were enough to put him and his sidekick over their limits. He looked up at the night sky of Villamontes and, feeling rather giddy, asked his friend, "Where are Jupiter and Saturn?"

He still remembers the general jubilation, the murmur of voices through the orange grove near the church of St. Francis.

That was the first time but not the last, though he never developed much of a taste for that kind of drink. As he lived his life, he walked the hard ground and discovered as he went that his organism contained an infinite number of beings, a multitude of personalities that over the years were trained, hushed, and reduced to three, sometimes two, and eventually to a premonition of unity.

One of those beings—now called Jursafú—read Hermann Hesse's *Demian* some twenty years ago, a novel recommended by one of his friends when he was at the University of La Paz. During that period he called himself Fielkho, and Fielkho would never forget the passage when Sinclair, the novel's protagonist, becomes friends with the church organist. Everything was going along fine, until one day the spiritual guide of that sensitive soul ran into his disciple staggering down a back alley. "Drinking's going to be your ruin," said Sinclair and Fielkho in unison. But the Other didn't put in his two cents' worth. It was different, joining his drinking buddies for a couple of rounds and then stumbling through the back streets of the world. He'd look at them and chuckle, not that he was laughing at them, or with them either, but because it was funny watching them try so hard to walk upright and keep their balance.

With the same good humor, he accepts the fact that Fielkho is now Jursafú and will take on other names in the future, considering the many miles he's left to go on the broad earth. The Other, on the other hand, has suppressed such alterations, since that day when he was walking home from school and in the middle of a patch of sandy ground asked himself, "Who am I?" Not only was he unable to answer the question, he forgot his own name. He was content to live the rest of his life not knowing who he was or what his name was, like a rock on a rock pile, like a grain of sand on the enormous sandy plains of the world—not knowing how large that might be—hardly suspecting that he embodied something certain and invariable, and believing in change as a given, while disbelieving in any particular instance of change.

He never cried again after that and instead made silence his means of expression. He can't help but smile when he remembers that Jursafú—before he became Jursafú—had been Fielkho, Ktnixio, Goter, and many others, as was the Chaco way. The Other's childhood was full of Chacos,

Guaranis, Tobas, Tapietes, Chulupis, Chorotis, and Chiriguanos. Of the primitive tribes he knew, the Chacos were not the liveliest; neither were they the cleverest. They would sit like birds in a tree and all of a sudden take off running as if the devil himself were after them. All the strength in the world couldn't stop them then. And if Chacos ever had a little problem that turned into a big problem, they would take the tiger by the tail and do what had to be done: if necessary, they would burn their belongings and leave the malign place behind, calmed by the peace and brotherhood that comes with such a sacrifice. Chacos not only run faster than the devil, they often change their names. For example, the Other had a friend who was called Ifsa. A few months later he changed his name to Pedro and then Fermín and later on Estanislao. He didn't see the man anymore after that so he doesn't know what name he goes by now. But if he should see him again, he'd recognize him in an instant but wouldn't be able to call to him unless he whistled. For a long time the Other didn't know the significance of a whistle, which he'd rarely heard among "civilized" people. But then he found out that Chacos often change their names for religious, ethical, and aesthetic reasons. "I'm not idealizing them; that's how they are," said the Other to someone who'd asked if he wasn't exaggerating. But what he'd said was true: whenever Chacos come across someone who is uncommonly talented or virtuous—kind, strong, courageous, just, or whatever—they don't hesitate to take the name of the venerated individual. Without stopping to ask anyone's permission, they do this in order to pay homage to special people and to prove their admiration by spreading their names to the corners of the earth. And since it's a custom which Chacos take seriously, it isn't to be discussed or joked about.

And this is what happened to the man who now calls himself Jursafú, though the Other knows nothing about the many people who have been the objects of his veneration, either of their moral fiber or mental capabilities. And though the names of human beings are their secret codes, their actions become the written language of these codes. The Other remembers the time when Fielkho admired Sinclair and his friend Demian and hasn't forgotten his displeasure when he thought of the demonic presence of the organist. Over time he became a better person and learned not to judge anyone. And now he dreams of very little except "to become a rock" and to laugh at his own problems but feel concern for others who have problems—which are actually the same aspiration.

Fielkho dissolved over time, making room for Jursafú, a man who at some point had been formidable, though now he staggered along a back street in La Paz, trying to get to his room and stop feeling like a rooster in another rooster's barnyard. He was alone, without his wife and children, without commotion or affection. So he sat down, opened a bottle of *singani,* and went on drinking, while the Other, who was given to profane language, started to curse a blue streak, cursing his luck at being stuck for life with a degenerate.

Jursafú didn't agree. Actually he didn't have an opinion. Orana had become Laura, but before he could turn around, Constanza had appeared. He'd escaped from a serious relationship, blessed by their native province, and had fallen into the abyss of a love marked by the city. He'd destroyed his own home and someone else's as well. He was headed toward destruction and was dragging others along with him. In the middle of one of his drunken episodes, he realized that he was completely alone in the world. He was born alone and was meant to live alone because the universe he carried in his soul had disappeared, leaving him as its peculiar survivor. It was quite a shock to him to realize that he was walking along the edge of a precipice. He'd done it all his life, but he'd been protected before by an innocence which shielded him from the difficulty of his mission. One mistake and it could be all over. If he slipped, death would know it. His informants, beings hypnotized by shimmering lights that normal people couldn't see, would keep him abreast of any change. For months he timorously watched the skyline of the city at night and gradually learned to tolerate his feelings of alienation. What else could he do? And finally one night he wrote: "People who know a great deal are wise, and wise people know that nothing is worth the trouble but anything deserves your best effort." Exhausted, he fell asleep, not expecting to wake up alive.

But he woke up alive and happy. "You really put your foot in it, but you managed to get off cheap," said the Other, finding him healthy and refreshed, seeing that he'd come through a light rain and not a downpour. But Jursafú didn't agree. Something had touched his most sensitive nerve and maybe for a reason. Perhaps now he would write a work that had been germinating inside of him for a long time. "People don't come into the world for nothing," he thought to himself, "and excuse me, life, if I don't waste any more time being sorry for the past or trying to change what can't be changed."

"Jursafú has just shut the corral gate, but the donkey's already gone," said the Other in a loud voice.

"You're supposed to shut the gate after the donkey goes out. You always learn after it's too late. There's no such thing as learning a thing in time," Jursafú replied.

"Praise a dunce and watch him go to work," said the Other, with his habitual sarcasm.

Jursafú quietly served himself a maté, and tasting the warm tea through a straw, he felt as though he'd been talking for hours with a close friend. But the friend had gone away without leaving a sign, and he knew that he was alone. He knew it when he looked at the world and found it rejuvenated by a recent absence. ∎

He had just turned fifteen a few days before, and after having made plans to go hunting with the men of the forest, he knew he didn't want to go. His enthusiasm for hunting was surpassed by a strange eagerness, a desire to be among the trees and search his own soul for a feeling that had sunk deep inside of him. That morning the rustic woodsmen went out toward the middle of the forest, and the next day, when the last stars were fading from the sky, they returned bringing wild turkeys, parrots, doves, a pair of *urinas,* and the babies of a dead monkey. During that same period, when he was fifteen, he allowed his feet to follow the path to the Laguna Verde; and there, in that vast, green setting, he would sit quietly, leaning against a tree, staring sadly at the gentle movements of nature, where animals could be brutal without losing their innocence. Sitting among the dead leaves and new buds, he felt as if a baby bird, nestled in the center of his chest, were begging for food. Many years later he discovered that the bird was called melancholy, but he didn't have to wait so long to find out that he was in love with someone who came to him with a smile on her face and her hair plaited into moist braids. The following night and all the nights that followed, the head of that goddess would appear to him with her distant, human smile, her lovely eyes full of painful contradictions, a mark of pleasure and vexation, and a fragrance of earthly smells with a hint of something lunar.

Protected by the pious shadow of selflessness, the boy of fifteen disappeared from the terrestrial globe while a stranger in Rome with a large mustache and the soul of a foreigner boldly watched a woman with soft, white skin—a deforceor of nocturnal weapons—become rejuvenated by a constant flapping of the wings of desire. Like all untranslatable things, this woman, a product of many masculine dreams, either didn't have a name or politely accepted any name assigned to her. Between one strange woman and the other—if they were, in fact, strangers—there was an important nexus that instead of uniting them seemed to push them apart: the vagina, uterus, crater, the abyss that attracts like an icy wind or repels like the warm message of distant springs.

The boy who had once been fifteen fell again and again into the same trap, and he remained there for an unknown length of time, a believer extolled by the hymns of night, a prisoner who could have been freed had he known the password. And when at last he was able to scale the prison walls, the world he saw hadn't changed. With a breath of fresh air, he was revived; but he remembered, with some pain, having sunk into the depths where a friendly, voiceless animal encouraged him to sink even further.

The knowledge that access to human mysteries requires a person to risk everything frightens him still. He vaguely suspects that he has lowered a bridge for the two strange women to greet each other or fuse into an indivisible mass. Standing on the bridge rather placidly, he allows himself to watch the infinite flow of waters with their terrible forebodings, with their masks of pleasure, honest pleasure, held aside. He doesn't attempt to rationalize or to lie; he continues staring at the immortal head, the contradictory smile of a solitude without mysteries, the mysterious emanations of her feminine universe, thighs grown weary with time or with insatiable desire; and the wind, always the icy wind of the sacred transmutations. ∎

The man is alone at the top of a hill. The afternoon winds blow through the trees in the valley of Irpa Irpa, bringing thoughts of times passed.

A reddish moon rises in the night sky.

It's August of 1970, and the man has suddenly learned that he will die on a particular day, August 14, 1977. Just the thought of leaving the world he loves shakes him to the core, but he is grateful for a chance that Time has given him to peer into the future.

Time with a capital *T* is hard and translucent, has no cardinal points, and isn't ruled by time. "A luxury that doesn't glitter. The only thing that is victorious in its domains is the memory and perhaps the lightning of premonitions," conjectures the man who is now lying beside a dark-skinned woman. They are alone in a room in La Paz with shadows flickering across the walls.

"What is sensuality? Maybe it's the body's voice, exhausted by its ephemeral condition."

The woman was born twenty-two years ago in the highest zone of the country, not amid the melodies of the barley fields but in the low dales where the multitude defends itself against the dry Andean plain. Any intruder who sees her knows that she is beautiful, silent, and given to meditation.

The man gives the impression of either being at the top of a hill or of finding himself in an ocean of rock and transparency. He slowly blinks his eyes and looks at her body, "a sleeping memory where nostalgia for life's beauty explodes." Scurrying like a happy animal through memories and fields of tall grass, he looks at the countryside—it's August 14, 1970— and feels the warm skin of his companion. His body moves in all directions, surveying the entire landscape and listening for a voice that comes out of the woods at Irpa Irpa.

"Reality is irreversible and anterior, like a dream. But I can touch you and day-to-day existence begins to glow like holy ground."

He holds tight to a willow twig, a habit carried over from his rural past.

The woman whispers something in his ear. A prisoner of presentiment, she's asking him to comfort her.

The man is holding a book in his hand, as if the habit of reading were an indelible mark even in moments of greatest animal innocence. He has been coughing off and on. He stops and takes the woman in his arms, gently opens her up, setting her brown skin on fire.

"Are these hills the only place I can find your memory? Maybe I'm dreaming that I have a body, and you're dreaming that you are with me."

The figure, suspended in twilight, looks at the distant hill, the profile of the living glory of the universe, and feels insignificant in the face of the mysterious love that surrounds her.

"We are the parts of a landscape yet to merge: tall trees, damp soil, rocks carried by silence during an eternity, birds obedient to an overwhelming instinct, nameless objects bathed in a light that sanctifies and transfigures them; perhaps palm trees in the distance, shading the rising sun of an immemorial summer."

The man isn't satisfied. He takes her in his arms. She slips out of herself, abandoning herself to love.

"We're getting ahead of the memory. There wasn't any light, except the light that sustained the memory."

Bathed in the soft light of the hills, with a willow twig in his hand, he is shaken by a strong conviction.

"Dust to dust . . . Tomorrow we'll be the dust of other travelers and perhaps the accent of other voices lost on the broad plain of nostalgia. We'll go back to the comfortable life of often traveled roads, to the humility of a wildflower returned to life as something different, perhaps as a hardworking bee. We'll have won our victory when we become who we've always been, sometimes the cruel hangman, sometimes the defenseless victim. Will other eyes let us see what we've never grasped? Maybe then we'll know that true power doesn't have to be offensive."

He holds the woman by her thighs and runs his fingers along her tense skin, probing it and stopping at some little hill, discovering that her body is able to accommodate the necessities of his anatomy made of love and death. Her feminine movements don't recoil at his first charge, jubilant and full of life.

The figure crowns the darkened hill with her melancholy. The visitor from Irpa Irpa feels that his anatomy is partly hers, and he isn't wrong: she's come from many centuries prior to the imagination, the curd of distant battles, crossed by luminous signs.

The man hovers over the sensitive neck of his companion, conquering her under the shadow of her black hair, running along her skin, illuminating her, convincing her, and she sinks into the deepest part of her soul, clutching with complete familiarity a body that she has just known.

The man stays inside of her, changed into an enduring similitude of things past, a fair copy of the uncertain future.

Their bodies are unexpectedly docile.

The woman's fragrance is captivating, like the smell of trees in Irpa Irpa, which the man who knew he would die on August 14, 1977 had seen—or continues seeing.

Returning to the reality of La Paz, the woman of uncommon mystery dresses herself in a disguise of ordinary clothing. And the man disappears without promising to return, passing into the once impenetrable glass of Time. ■

During the year of secret inaugurations, he experienced torrential rains. Streams of warm water ran through the open countryside, while the winds drew melodies that he would never forget from the trees. The world remained silent, interrupted by the light of something recently come to life and by the water spilling intermittently from the leaves of trees. People were damp, happy, and conversant with their *alpargatas* covered in mud and the tendons of their souls fortified by solitude and poverty.

It rained as was necessary. The next season the moon came out and projected the shadows of trees onto large tracts of ground where crickets and other contented insects gave vent to songs which credited them as living creatures.

From that zone of the earth, he received such a bounty of melancholy and happiness that he never felt anything other than supreme gratitude for the gift of such a life. Though he never thought they were talking about him, he heeded the words of the men who traveled the treacherous climbs: "If you aren't careful, you could become a liar; if you aren't careful, you could flunk out of school." ■

"If you aren't careful . . . What do you mean, if you aren't careful?"

"I don't know exactly, but you have to be careful with words, especially words that refer to people," explains Constanza, running down the steps of an establishment on Landaeta Street.

They have just attended a lecture on literature. The speaker began his talk with some comments on poetry, distinguishing it from the other genres and designating it as the best instrument for obtaining important revelations. Then, after a detailed description of the goals of philosophy, he went on to discuss narration, the domain of the novel. But a question led him away from the novel onto the topic of "eternity." He said that poetry was the most enduring of all substances and that a whole universe could be reconstructed with words ordered according to the rigors of the poem.

"What do you mean by 'eternity'?" some confused person asked.

The professor replied with a dictionary in his hand, "Something that has neither a beginning nor an end, a concept that presupposes the presence of time, total and infinite."

Suspecting that his words hadn't met the expectations of the disoriented listener, he decided to illustrate his definition with an example from literature. He chose a passage from an Argentine author. Preoccupied with "the eternal" as a philosopical concept, the Buenos Aires author leaves home and travels toward the humbler zones of the national capital, which he has never before seen. One night in February 1955, he goes out for a stroll and, lost in thought, stumbles into a low wall with a fig tree stretching up above the terrace and other details that can be made out in the moonlight. The speaker recalled the words of the Argentine on that occasion, "I'm living in eighteen hundred and something."

"It's the fish's mouth that gets it into trouble; everything born of man is sinful," says the man who at one time had experienced torrential rains. "Have you ever noticed that wisdom literature never tells us how to attain happiness but how to avoid unhappiness? It's proof enough that happy people don't even have a shirt on their backs. The word 'eternity' . . ."

"What the speaker was saying," interrupts Constanza, "is that poetry allows us to catch a glimpse of the eternal. Because what the Argentine writer has created is poetry," she adds convincingly, "to illustrate his personal experience of time. Or do you see it differently?"

"I agree that the concept of 'eternity' presupposes the presence of time," he affirms, "which according to the dictionary doesn't have a beginning or an end. But it runs the risk of becoming a lopsided argument because space hasn't been brought into the picture, and in my estimation, space must be included before we can arrive at an accurate perspective."

"Give me an example," says Constanza smiling. "The professor chose one that he considered valid, but I can see you're not convinced."

"I'm not a *suppressor*," he says, making fun of the professor, "and I have no intention of behaving as one. What I'm trying to say is that any object or idea can be viewed from different angles, some of which may prove astonishing; in other words, there's nothing in the universe that isn't subject to diverse interpretations. But what I'm saying is that sooner or later, no matter what the interpretation may be, it must be subjected to reason. Tonight's subject, for example, might be viewed from a materialist perspective . . ."

"Reduce time to something material? Really, that seems impossible."

"No," corrects the man, trying to be a good student. "What I'm suggesting, and I think I can prove it, would go like this: Abstract concepts like time, spirit, soul, infinity, possibly because they are inaccessible, require some material receptacle, not so they can become 'objects' but so they can be understood by human beings. Like in your case, for example."

"What do you mean, 'in my case'?"

"I mean that your name illuminates your actual existence," explains the man, "but the only thing that gives meaning to your name is your presence. It's the same way with 'eternity.' If we accept the idea of time as something infinite, that's the end of it; but if we give it a practical application, that's another matter, because then we've given it a spatial dimension."

Constanza is walking along a street of her native city with her eyes fixed on the distant, shadowy mountains.

"For example, what comes into your mind if I say that those mountains are 'eternal'?"

"That there're going to be there forever, which is the way I'd like it to be, because they're beautiful."

"And their form is never going to change in all that time," the man adds. "If we say that they're eternal, then we must think that they're going to maintain the same form they have now, which is a strange thought because time also strives to be eternal; its greatest achievements are found in the earth's petrified chronicle, but the changes that occur escape us in our search for chronicles of a more trivial nature. The desire for 'eternity' has resulted in deep holes in the earth as well as great mounds, sometimes because the Incas wanted it that way or, more often, because of the whims of men. It isn't easy for us to believe that time must come to an end or that we must simply wait and watch, like prudent virgins."

"All right, Jursafú," says Constanza, naming him, "what does the shape of the mountains have to do with what the Argentine said?"

"You said that our words reveal us. It's true. I would say that when we make poetry with our words they disclose our inner being, the world of our beliefs and desires. And tell me, *vos,*" he said, imitating the speech of *porteños,* "why did the author leave Buenos Aires and go looking for inspiration in some out-of-the-way place? Isn't it curious that a thought that never occurred to him at home, in his grand residence, occurred to him in some run-down neighborhood where the people live who make his lifestyle possible?"

"Well, maybe he found authenticity there," Constanza replies.

"If that was the case, he should have spent some time there instead of strolling through. But remember, that isn't what he did. People often mistake their good intentions for reality, regardless of the situation. The Argentine, like many who think they understand, went there as a stranger and thought he perceived something immutable in the humble lives of the dispossessed. His veiled desire for things to remain unchanged prompted his oration to 'eternity' in that austere setting, where the many work so that the few can continue living their idle lives."

"But you're suggesting that the author was wearing a mask. If that's so, what was behind it?"

"Maybe lots of faces or none, because a lie outlives the one who tells it, but speaking the truth extends a person's life. And besides, a text has many interpretations, especially if the author, like the Argentine, is rich and prolific in his inventions and connotations, and even more so if we consider that words never confine themselves to one meaning. The word is the person, but the conceptual world that it presides over is as vast as the world of all people."

They walk along Landaeta, transforming the shadows of the night as they go. And the man thinks of Caryl Chessman and of his Bolivian advocate who defended him to the end, two solitary beings who without knowing each other experienced a split-second encounter—deeply human yet unreal—on that same street. They go on down the street, Contanza in front, Jursafú behind, looking at her long braids dampened by the earth. ■

He forgot the woman's name but not her black hair and green eyes. Married, with two children, she seemed to be standing on the sidelines of her husband's life. He earned a living as a professional photographer, but the remainder of his life was a mystery. They lived together in a pension in Salta. He, too, had lived in Salta for a year, when he was sixteen, and had crossed paths with the couple at the pension. He'd felt a special warmth toward them, especially the woman—with her long hair and almond-shaped eyes—though he had never spoken more than two words to either of them. That same year, 1958, he also met Leoncio Suárez, a young man from Cochabamba whose family had encouraged him to leave his native valley in order to become an engineer in the city, never suspecting that every weekday the boy would sleep till noon instead of going to class. The residents of the pension would gather around the tables in the large dining room, telling jokes and hoping to be the first to spy Leoncio crossing the living room with a towel over his shoulder, half awake or still a prisoner of his libidinous dreams. The most merciless of the group was a loudmouthed referee who'd grown rotund over the years and who always reached the dining room before his wife. A carbon copy of Tita Merello, the wife would follow shortly, wearing a tight-fitting, see-through dress and with her long hair draped over one eye; in other words, she seemed ready to dance a tango.

Several Bolivians lived at Alvarado 931, but they were greatly outnumbered by the large gaucho clientele. One Saturday night, Leoncio Suárez, a soccer player named Jorge Quinteros, Pipo Canterini, and some others, whom the boy of sixteen allowed to slip from his memory, went out to make the rounds. After they'd drunk a few beers, which the boy of sixteen passed up, they wandered toward a darker, seamier side of town and ended up on the doorstep of a house illuminated by a red light. Inside, to the great surprise of the young boy who wanted to become a lathe worker, sat the woman in the tight-fitting, see-through dress, clearly willing to dance a tango, as she probably did every night, since she was charged with satisfying the sexual and sensual needs of the clients. The prostitute, used to working nights, decided to ignore the fact that this curious and casual encounter with the residents of the pension would seal her husband's lips for a long while. The next day was a glorious one for the young man from Cochabamba who at last won the respect he was due because, unlike the others, he kept his mouth shut when he saw the referee and never uttered a word about the behavior of his wife, a referee in her own right when it came to games of love.

That night—which was Independence Day in his country—the young Bolivian exile dreamed that he was copying a long poem into an Argentine notebook, with blue lines spaced far apart and wide margins. The next morning he could remember only a few verses of the poem, which he copied on some paper from a real notebook, which was later stuffed in a bottle and thrown into the stream at Quarisuty in his native village. Time, which encapsulates all things, saved very little of it from oblivion: "Forgotten empires" and the figure of a woman with eyes that changed colors like the dawn, her infant son, a feminine torso, a beautiful bosom, and an air that suggested readiness for blind passion on the battlefields of love, buried and unburied in the infinite countries of the world by the constancy of masculine dreams. Submerged, eternally submerged in an embrace that time can never touch. ■

The *urundel,* a wild and hardy tree, would seem to be American in origin, though it is commonly found on other continents, disguised under different names, hidden beneath strange and unintelligible signs, just as the seven cardinal virtues reappear mysteriously or stigmatically in the most unlikely dialects.

The cortex, a certain challenge to the axe, is protected by a rough bark that has an abominable tendency to injure anyone who unwittingly comes near it. Therefore, termites and similar creatures stay away from this tree, left to abide, involuntarily, in total solitude.

The *urundel*'s flowers are shrouded in secrecy, if, in fact, it produces flowers at all when human beings are around. But this isn't why it can't be seen in parks, squares, or along avenues. Besides being a rough looking tree of a beauty not readily perceived, its branches are rather sparse, unlike the many varieties of trees that offer abundant shade. It's as though its desire to grow tall made it deaf to earthly considerations. But that isn't the way it is when you dream of a great *urundel* from the distant past, swaying in the fresh, morning breeze.

The *urundel* doesn't grow on the banks of lagoons, ponds, or streams, and therefore, its presence—far from announcing that those who've gotten lost have found their way—is proof enough that their struggle must go on. It's superfluous to mention, then, how diligently it strives to draw moisture from the earth and thereby tolerate the burning heat at midday.

In spite of its heroism in sterile ground, its beauty isn't striking or enviable. Used for firewood, it puts out smoke until it's sickened and driven away those who suffer from the cold; then, alone, it begins to burn. But it would be a mistake to consider it inserviceable—if it were, it wouldn't be thrown on the fire. It's just that it requires more patience than people generally have.

The *urundel*'s death is equally strange. Its roughness and lack of luster are deceiving, and often it's taken for dead when it's still alive—alive after a fashion. Or the other way around, it sometimes creates an illusion of vitality when it has long since gone to rest.

The forest dwellers long to dream of the *urundel,* though its meaning remains impenetrable for curiosity seekers and other strangers; notwithstanding, it is known that the word *"urundel,"* when spoken by a woman, can be fatal, because it can congregate poisons or make a person fall in love. But sleeping or awake, one should always approach the *urundel* with devotion and caution. ■

Thereabout the year 1964, the current Jursafú gave the Other one of the worst scares of his life. Until that time, and maybe ever since, their relationship had been like that of a horse and rider—not knowing for sure which was which, though at times they would take turns carrying each other.

In the above-mentioned year, Jursafú was in La Paz, unemployed and rolling around like a bowling ball—which is how his friend the Other liked to put it—feeling as if he were materially hanging by a thread but all the while confident of his own worth. In this contradictory state of affairs, and calling himself Fielkho, he wrote a singular text that revealed not only what Fielkho was, but what might occur as far as his relationship with other people was concerned.

Each time the Other read it, he could not help feeling that something catastrophic was about to happen; he was at the mercy of a man he didn't understand, without knowing for sure which of them was the horse and which the rider. The text, titled "The Possibility of Fielkho's Being Arrested and Sentenced to Death," is as follows:

One of these days the world may wake up on the wrong side of the bed, haul you in, and sentence you with the following words:

"You use the best means of transportation our country has to offer, and you travel anywhere you want, usually to a place that is prosperous and happy, and you decide to spend some time there basking in the sun, without contributing anything at all to its maintenance. In addition, you do strange things for which you haven't been punished because of slight errors on our part, but now you're being judged because of a small error on your part.

"So travel wherever you want, buy our newspapers, read them, inform yourself about the things that happen to us, but we don't want to hear anything more about you, no matter how insignificant it might be. You don't tell us anything about yourself; you go into a movie studio, come out again, and disappear into some dark alley, and nothing happens to you, as if you were some privileged character.

"But you aren't interested in what goes on here. Many have taken time from their work to watch you and report that your reaction to events of great consequence has been total indifference. But when spring comes around, you're the first one up and out to enjoy the day, and you've been seen jumping up and down under the trees.

"How could we help but regard you with reservation; and if you were to explain yourself, you would prove us right. We're convinced of it, but we're also sure that you'll never talk. You lie around for long periods of time with your eyes closed and not emitting a sound.

"Since you've been noted to have a certain tendency not to react to anything, some take you for a peaceful man. Fortunately, we haven't given credence to that opinion, and make no mistake: we aren't smiling. And if we were before, don't take it as a sign of our affection but as involuntary proof of a virtue that we have never exercised and have no need to exercise in the future.

"You must die. We should add that you have no right to be surprised at our decision. We would never have become suspicious of you, or at least any suspicion we might have had would have disappeared, if it hadn't been for a slight error, so atypical of us and so typical of you, which is that of speaking a language that no one can understand but all fear." ■

Héctor Alvarez's pseudonym is the name of a mysterious fish that lives in the Plate River. The author's works include some twenty volumes on theater, poetry, and essay, as well as a trilogy. Someone has described his work as "strange," meaning that it attracts and repels at the same time and that his unusual prose and overly traditional thought serve only to conceal visions that are unsettling and potentially dangerous.

At noon on January 8, 1969—in a restaurant in Buenos Aires—Héctor is talking to a young man who says he's recognized his voice. It may remind him of a voice that disappeared from his life during the shadowy days of childhood; or maybe it's like the voice of the deceased Héctor, who taught him to pick up his feet when he walked, to keep the mud off them. At any rate, it's someone's voice who passed from life, his vision steadily fixed on November's paradises and the breezy springs of a country of beautiful movements.

The young man is surprised that he is able to talk to him comfortably when the mysteries of literature are all they have in common. Héctor, on the other hand, is amazed at a marginal person's ability to carry on the ciphered, transparent language of his American ancestors. They talk with fervor and moderation, and neither man knows who the other is, which is how it is when the memory contains music that can form unlikely bonds or restore distant friendships. Though they've never faced a common enemy, it's as if they'd survived a shipwreck that for others had been mortal.

Suddenly Héctor begins to discuss subjects that concern him but that only much later will preoccupy his interlocutor.

"Be honest and accept the consequences; be creative and accept the consequences; allow one's conscience to take control and accept the consequences. And above all, if you choose the path of the artist, understand that life is a risk. Imagine that a person who's well versed in social etiquette goes to an ordinary gathering—with grandparents, aunts, uncles, and cousins—without any clothes on. His intentions may not be bad, but can you imagine what the host would say? To put it mildly, 'What the hell's wrong with him, coming here in his birthday suit?'"

Both laugh out loud.

The trees shine forth with a greenness typical of summers in the federal capital, a city which Roberto Arlt, Ezequiel Martínez Estrada, and Horacio Quiroga experienced with varied fortune.

This recent arrival to the circle of writers is twenty-seven and very frightened. A decade ago in the city of Salta, he met Leoncio Suárez, a lazy but charming youth from Cochabamba. Nine years later in La Paz, he began writing a book and halfway through decided to make Leoncio the main character of a subplot. The fictional Suárez was no different from the real one: as good as gold and missing some of his lower molars. Except in the novel he would be hit by a train. It never occurred to him that his friend might feel the sting of such a plot. But he did, as the author's relatives—accompanying him as far as Tartagal—have just told him: Leoncio Suárez was killed at a railway station near Salta. And the author calculates that it happened the same night he concocted the story.

"This really frightens me," he confesses to his friend. "How can a person smile when he discovers so abruptly and so early in his career that words have the power to influence and reveal?"

Héctor isn't a snob, and he's not impertinent. He's like others from Buenos Aires but without their excesses. He listens attentively to what the younger man has to say but by his silence implies that perhaps his friend is making too much of the incident. Perhaps Hector does this to avoid going off on a tangent, because at his apartment—where they continue their conversation over a cup of coffee—he asks him to take a look at an ordinary piece of furniture.

"Look at this. It's an ordinary table, but ordinary life is precisely the scene of strange occurrences. Sometimes I get up in the morning and to my displeasure find a water mark on the surface. As you know, water isn't a propitious sign; to the contrary, it stands for hell and darkness. The sages claimed it stood for the feminine part of the universe, symbolizing the descent to amorphous depths, a test no child of God can avoid, since all of us come equipped with our own particular hell which we must learn to decipher. When I see the water mark, I conjure up its message, just as the alchemists did, because it's part of the mischief—who would say it isn't?—and you have to pass through it to reach the secrets of life. And besides, it shows us what we're made of, tells us who we are, and forces us to perform a thankless task, which is to learn to laugh at the person we want to become. This is where the false lose heart, go astray, or end up throwing themselves off a cliff. It seems so simple, doesn't it? But it takes years to understand the simplest things in the world. Just as it takes an eternity for complex subjects to attain the transparency of a parable. This is the door that is closed to the imprudent, but the law of those who aren't afraid of anything as long as they can hear their own resonances in the darkness of the sacred world. What can you do? When the light of the universe grows pale, you need to say, 'Our Father who art in heaven,' and when the light acquires a splendor that invites you to drunkenness, you must ask that it 'lead us not into temptation.'"

In the days that followed, Héctor Alvarez's friends began to gather, and later on, his friends' friends. One day the visitor, in the company of some of these friends, nearly drowned in the River Plate. And his last night in Buenos Aires, he got to see the little road that time has not erased; and also, at a local night spot, he saw a famous boxer, an innocent clay idol toying with his popularity and not suspecting that a year later someone—who was already lying in wait in a North American city—would stab him to death. ∎

At least three times it occurred to Jursafú that literary texts, no matter how arcane, require questions; in other words, ambitious works as well as more modest texts are the product of an unending series of questions.

"It doesn't matter who does the asking; the important thing is to find the answers," he thought, scratching his head, "because if the questions are answered, this means that there's an interlocutor and that literature can be defined as a dialogue, as a conscientious attempt to communicate."

"With an interlocutor on the other side of the table," he added, content with himself, "it's a horse of a different color. People don't write for themselves. They write for others . . . because others push them to do it."

He was happy with his sudden realization. However, the most difficult part was left to do: to prove that his theory had application in real life. ∎

A person who calls himself Paco could just as easily call himself Pancho. But if that person is an agent for a Spanish firm, he probably goes by Paco. He has never stated a clear preference for the former; he just scrunches up his nose whenever anyone calls him Pancho.

Pleasant and polite, as soon as he arrives at the office—where another foreigner is sitting—he takes a short literary break, usually with the same foreigner, a somewhat antiquated individual, as innocents often are. Preliminaries out of the way, their conversation turns to a book that the dark-skinned man suggested he read two weeks before and that Paco, born to take orders, purchased immediately. The title of the book is *Pedro Páramo*. Juan Rulfo published it about the time the dark-skinned man went to live in La Paz, and the man began to read it one sad, gray afternoon when he was without money or a future. His stomach was empty, and a friend who'd long since gone away had suggested that he explore the universe of a man called Pedro Páramo, as well as the rustic world of Miguel Hernández, and the sad, flowering rushes of César Vallejo, a Peruvian mestizo who frightened an intruder in Paris only because he suddenly felt like laughing, though he'd rarely laughed in his life.

"If you're not used to it and you suddenly let loose with a big laugh, you could hurt yourself permanently," someone had warned.

The dark-skinned man is remembering that individual (who thought it a virtue to remain in one piece, when life plainly shows us that you don't have to be unbeaten to be a winner). But he changes his train of thought, because Paco, as it turns out, doesn't like Rulfo's novel, "so morose and full of dead people, so complex and void of any meaning."

"No, my friend," says Paco, loudly, "it's absurd for dead people to converse with the living, without stammering or anything. I like for things to be clear and to have some substance. Look, the book may be good, as I've heard said, but I don't like it."

The dark-skinned man tries to absorb the shock, as if he's gone up to an old friend and the friend has knocked him down with one blow.

But Paco changes the subject when some people come into the office. This day everyone is talking about Melquíades Suxo, an Aymara Indian who received the death sentence for raping a minor, though they failed to prove that he actually did it, which some considered unimportant. The announcement is brief, laconic.

"He was shot at dawn. It seems that Suxo had been drinking and was talking off the top of his head. He kept on saying what he'd said from the beginning: that he didn't know anything about anything, and that after he was dead they ought to let him visit his family, at least every Friday night."

"What a crazy Indian! If there were any doubt, that ought to prove that he was demented," laughs Paco.

"But some people are saying that there wasn't any rape, that the dictator had to try out the death penalty on someone, and as usual, the victim was an Aymara."

"And how can that be? They couldn't get a word of Castilian out of him," says Paco seriously. "His nephew's the one who made his final request. The Indian never opened his mouth."

The dark-skinned man feels as if he is looking at a mask and not Paco's shining face. Without knowing how, he manages to see through the mask and finds nothing on the other side. A cold shudder runs down his spine, and he remembers something a dead friend said: "All times are beautiful, but be cautious about your own. You're living at a time when derisiveness is acceptable, and the cultivation of forms is taken as a sign of intelligence. Be careful, because the content that gives value to form is already in decay."

A scene from the past suddenly flashes through his mind. He can see a forest and in that forest, some untamed Chaco Indians. As if in a dream, he is reminded of their custom of using various names to pay homage to the most significant moments in life.

"Paco, you're far from being Pancho Francisco," he chides his friend, laughing.

With a very slight scrunch of his nose, Paco asks him, "Why do you say that, my friend?"

"Because, obviously, Paco suits you better." ∎

St. John's Eve didn't go so well, though it had started out nicely. He was with one of his younger brothers with whom he could usually talk without long pauses or problems of any kind. The next morning it seemed like a nightmare, it had been so strange and unsettling. But he got out of bed, got ready for work, and put it behind him. At the office, he ran into someone who had just arrived from Mexico and who could converse easily on any topic as long as he didn't have to remain silent.

He had first seen the man several years before. Now someone had just introduced him. Five minutes later, or maybe less, the man who had just come from Mexico directed the conversation toward a particular topic, the devil.

"The devil doesn't exist. It's just energy, usually human energy, and it hasn't been proven scientifically," babbled the man. "They've been doing experiments in Germany . . ."

"Which Germany?"

"West Germany. Well," he continued, after the interruption, "the experiments have proven that a person can move a pot or even a bookcase just by looking at it."

"You're right, the devil doesn't exist," said the man who'd had the nightmare. "And as you say, it could be just energy," he added. "But if I'm ever out in the woods and I see a man with boots on and a frock coat with a tail sticking out from under it, and if besides that he makes fun of everyone, with an intolerable irony typical of some people I've seen in dreams, I probably won't have time to think that he's just energy but will probably take off running, losing my *alpargatas* in the process. Or I may freeze, waiting for the worst to happen, even for the world to end before my very eyes." ■

"I've never wanted to be rich," says Marcos Salazar. "Money always causes problems."

It's the only answer that this Callawaya Indian, born more than forty-five years ago in Curva, gives without hesitation. Everything else is neither here nor there, except he does express, out of sheer kindness, a preference for the raising of certain animals: chickens, rabbits, and sheep.

Short but hard as a rock, Salazar invariably pays homage to the sun on Saturdays. Though it's his only devotion, it is nonetheless sincere. The rest of the week he's a trickster and even something of an adventurer.

With a bit of a swagger, he says that if the Inca wanted a monolith, all he had to do was to crack his whip; and as far as he's concerned, the Inca is the only sovereign and made the hills and the valleys as well.

The Callawaya, Marcos Salazar, is a builder, carpenter, tapestry maker, a genius with flowers and fabrics, a tinsmith, locksmith, and, of course, an expert in herbal medicine. On rare occasions, as if he were handing them a piece of his heart, he passes on to his closest friends a wise saying that came down from his ancient ancestors and shouldn't for any reason be considered alien to these enlightened times: "In life, just be as you are, no more, no less."

In 1971, Marcos again proved his friendship for the dark-skinned man, who at the time was doing poorly and hadn't a *real* in his pocket. Working together on a piece of laurel, they decided to become blood brothers and to seal their pact with a word: both agreed to call themselves Zapopeta.

They didn't break the pact and were serious at keeping their word. But every time they said "Zapopeta," they'd laugh their heads off for a good five minutes.

Two weeks ago the dark-skinned Zapopeta was walking down a street in Villa Fátima, home of Salazar the Callaway, just as Zapopeta Marcos, wearing bright-colored clothing—which was typical of him—and a cloth hat cocked to one side, was coming down the street in the opposite direction. He was on foot and you could see him a mile away, coming from El Alto de La Paz. It was like a dream or a daydream, and also it was the last time that the two Zapopetas ever shook hands in this ephemeral dream we call life.

That night or early in the morning, the dark-skinned Zapopeta dreamed that he was cutting an Aymara's hair with enormous scissors. He was doing a fine job, and the Aymara wheeled around and said to him, "You're a fine worker."

"Yes, I am a good worker. I try to be. And I hope it does me some good when I'm crossing the rivers and the hills," said Zapopeta the barber.

"You don't have much time left," said the Aymara.

"A few years at least, I suppose. Or do you disagree?"

"No! Not a year, not even a week. You're going to die today."

With a jerk, the dark-skinned Zapopeta woke up and walked around in a daze for the rest of the day, astounded at all the random stupidity there was in the world. It was a perilous day. He talked to Marcos Salazar that evening; they ate a dish of potato starch and celery, and drank a beer together. His daughter, Teresa, and wife, Peta, were also there. The dark-skinned Zapopeta left his host with a smile on his face, and he died that way, without letting anyone know that the beating they'd given him at El Alto de La Paz had sealed his fate. ∎

He was just a child when he first met the mute. This occludent individual was called Pancho Francisco, and since he wasn't deaf, he could hear perfectly well if anyone ever chose to speak to him. Pancho hadn't yet reached an agreement with destiny, but one day, suddenly and without complaint, he suggested the following compromise: as long as he was on the earth he wouldn't sin, but he would suffer all the maladies that human beings usually suffer as well as enjoying the pure hilarity of life. In other words, he would subject himself to a regular change of seasons, of being either happy or horrified.

Besides being mute, Pancho Francisco seemed to be living in a storm, and he appeared intolerably dense to everyone who tried to decipher the faint smiles that crossed his lips from time to time, for no apparent reason. He was often seen with Guarani Indians and occasionally with mestizos and whites. He himself was a mestizo with a Guarani mother and a Chaco father. And though he didn't use words at all, the fluidness of his silence implied that at some point he had spoken both the musical language of the former and the invisible language of the latter.

He wore a narrow-brimmed hat and either sandals or boots, though for long periods of time, when he felt a special attachment to the earth, he wore no shoes at all. He wasn't a slovenly type, but on occasion his misery achieved the dignity of nakedness; and whenever that was his lot, he accepted it without complaint. Every now and then he would sit down next to a wild mulberry near the door of a shack built in the woods, and he would roll up one of his pants legs, revealing an incurable sore on his shin that he displayed like a great reward. For a long time he stayed at the shack—which the child could never forget—and then one day, when it might have been stormy or not threatening in any sense, he disappeared without a trace, to resume a life that only he could understand or appreciate.

He was gone for so many years—or at least his absence made it seem like a long time—that everyone believed that Pancho Francisco had said good-bye to the earth forever. But that wasn't the way it happened. One night, when least expected, he returned in pitch darkness but by an illuminated path, carrying a green bottle filled with lightning bugs that he ate one at a time, smiling, as though he were eating grains of toasted corn.

He communicated to the others, using sign language, that he had just returned from a distant province. He must have been full of gratitude and admiration for their customs because he often threatened to return there.

The child, after a long haul, became a man, but Pancho Francisco probably hasn't aged a day—wherever he is, swallowed up by the heavens or sheltered by the people of that distant province, which will surely be the final resting place for his nostalgia. Because Pancho Francisco left again without saying a word. But the other man, the one who saw the wound on the mute's shin, is still around and carries the images of many people, the mute included, floating blindly in his dark soul. When he looks at them, it's at a great cost to himself because the world, which takes on a special beauty and coherence, also acquires the power to annihilate its observer. The prototype of a madman, but with a number of saintly traits, Pancho Francisco came to symbolize the stranger in the conscious minds of the people, the foreigner whose stay on earth manifests a kind of exquisiteness proper to those who never offend other people, who don't disturb the silent stars with constant sobbing, who never ponder, who prescind from the official orientation of human beings, and who, fundamentally, through their own resources, reach a peacefulness they haven't asked for but which inside them grows larger and more noble.

When the time for testimonials finally arrived, someone was able to read what someone else had written of Pancho Francisco: "A disturbing example for the classic philosopher, except that the enlightened sage is more likely to be acclaimed for the tragedy of his failure than for the victory of his success. . . Also a model for adults who think they can read and understand things they can't write and who, for good or bad, are neither mutes nor parrots, and, therefore, need language to attain primordial silence." ■

More than two decades ago, he dreamed that he was walking among the beautiful trees of his arid homeland. He saw a tree. It wasn't a *lapacho*, a hardwood member of the begonia family, or a sumac, or a *quebracho*, famous for its medicinal bark. As soon as he'd laid eyes on it, he knew it was an old, hardy *urundel*, with its rough bark and proverbial tall branches.

In the dream he was able to do what he couldn't have done in real life. He peeled back the bark with his hands and entered the rose-colored cortex, which suddenly began to grow. The inside of the tree was covered with hieroglyphics; he couldn't read them but knew nonetheless that their meaning was sacred, just as when a person meets up with a snake, looks it in the eye, and feels the impact of its curse.

The man who was having the dream was just an ordinary muleteer who'd gone to high school for a couple of years; and the universe, in his mind, was still his native province: Don Nicomedes' farm, his neighbor's parrot, Don Deterlino's yoke of oxen, and so on. True, he liked to watch the stars but wasn't aware that they were ruled by precise laws or that the mystery of their origin had consumed the lives of many prophets, scientists, astrologers, and soothsayers. In the innocence of his isolation, he was content to see a star fall, to witness the fleeting splendor of even the smallest star. He had never breached the limits of his own superstitions, which, time and again, stopped him from becoming petulant. In time he learned that real humility is practiced privately and rests on an obvious and enduring maxim: you can fool other people but you can't fool yourself. But the time for that discovery hadn't arrived; in other words, he was still dreaming, his eyes riveted on the massive cortex of the *urundel,* whose form began to blur until it no longer looked like a tree but resembled the enormous doors of a cathedral, and he could tell they weren't ordinary doors, even though he was dreaming. Something about them— something he would remember after he awoke—made them different from other doors. He was amazed by their tremendous size, which distracted him from the main point of the vision. But a strange voice—maybe the dreamer's voice—came from somewhere, the beginning or the end— wherever we have been and will be One—to tell him that the hieroglyphics "were the language of the birds." He was confused when he woke up but knew that a bird's language is its trill. Having grown up in the forest, surrounded by birds, he could easily recognize the trills of many birds, as well as the variations of a particular trill, indicative of a bird's melancholy at twilight or its nostalgia for a lost mate.

For two weeks he thought quietly about what he'd learned and then set about reading books and traveling from town to town, like a bird hopping from one branch to the next. One night, when he'd gone on to other things or become another person—an apprentice to tedious reading—he found something that perhaps he'd been aware of all along: an old legend that had been passed on in its rustic form. It revealed that the language of the birds was a remnant of the first language, a light from Paradise that had been left and that not only allowed for a full, happy harmony between man and nature but was, in fact, that harmony. With its power weakened, scarcely a memory of its archaic splendor, this word had reached us by way of poetry. And for salvaged fragments of that ancient language, poets would have to pay with their lives. He could feel a distant breeze of lost purity. The humdrum of contemporary existence was actually the sleeping face of an eternally powerful world, and it was poetry's role to wake up the animal that lay so close to the fable. What else could it be, to create from common words the splendor of the poetic miracle? A woman had imagined the clouded faces of the magic medallion: giving up one's life to redeem poetry, the poet's death in exchange for the brilliant silence of the restored word. Wasn't that what Alejandra Pizarnik foresaw when she encapsulated the paradox with her dying words: "Death has restored to silence its magic spell"? ■

He can't remember when he first felt it his duty to write a book; but he never forgot that writing it had carried him not along the winding paths of mental calculation but over the rough roads of life and living. He was impressed by writers who could elaborate a text logically but realized that the only dialogue that suited him was born of a search of his own soul and a subsequent comparison with nature; or it could happen inversely or simultaneously. A bird, for example, a summary of memories amid the blind voices of the trees, the chant of the unalterable present . . . were all parts of a larger map that was difficult to read, because the observer, the impenitent, smiling expert on objectivity, had also been included. And then the dreams; the intricate light that fell on every vanity, especially the conviction that man is master of his actions. And the vast lacunae in his knowledge to which he reacted sensibly, staying out of unfamiliar terrains and keeping to the paths where he wasn't thought an intruder. He was happy when he finished his first book, learning in the process that rigorous preparation was the counterbalance to ease in writing. "It could be different for others," he said with due respect, "but what do others have to do with my experience? Nothing, as far as I can tell." He did what he was able to do and for a brief time experienced the joy of writing, which in the course of time and space was from February 23 to June 13, 1967. More than a decade later—December 31, 1980—after a time of silence and a serious physical challenge, he started another book, and though he hasn't finished it, the ending must be set, just as life concludes with death. One night when he was working late, he suddenly became frightened. "It takes intelligence and courage to finish what was finished from the start, for what does such a task have to offer if not an invitation to insanity. And no one can guarantee me that I have the virtues to resist such a fall." Knowing that something is finished—a half-written book—yet not being able to intuit its final meaning creates an arduous chore for the memory. He glanced down, slipping away from the world and absorbing himself in writing, hoping to avoid the first without totally renouncing the second. A difficult problem with numerous ramifications, but he has managed to solve it in his own way: by confining his writing to writing and his life to life, in other words, by connecting the present with the past and life with death. He is certain that as each word is pronounced it immediately becomes a minuscule but essential part of a larger text, broader and more detailed and called "complete work." Paradoxically, the complete work constantly requires words, voice, concepts, and accents that are still absent, just as death requires every organism to perform trivial gestures and boring promenades, to make hard decisions and continue living—even though one's actions may be derisive—in order to reach the last objective: a gunshot at dawn, a cease-fire, a truce of absence, resplendent silence amid the darkness.

Jursafú and the Dead Man as the Other Sees Them

God speaks to human beings by way of silence. Humans speak to God through the broad foreboding of death. A vast, cordial dialogue is appropriate to human beings. Also anger, which is common to beings that move from one place to another. It is impossible to imagine anger between immobile things such as trees and rocks. Could this be why people adore inanimate things even before God? Drawn by nostalgia for a world without hate, they sacrifice the White Llama of their tribe to obtain the hero, a god made to their own size and with whom they can communicate through mindful reverence.

Monday, December 31, 1980, Jursafú wakes up at seven o'clock in the morning, as usual; and after drinking a maté and remaining silent for a couple of hours—also as usual—he leaves for the offices of the newspaper located on the second floor of a tall building on Pompilio Daza Avenue in La Paz. During the morning, while he does the things that he has to do, he hears a rumor that doesn't bode well for the crew of editors, including the director, messenger boys, and everyone else who is around there.

He skips lunch this day, which he's done twice a week for a long time, trying to cure himself of a stomach ailment that has resulted from constant worry. Though he isn't at all wealthy, he hopes by way of these small deprivations to help correct the much greater, constant deprivations of his dispossessed countrymen; in other words, he is ingenuous and presumptuous, as are many intellectuals. But he has never understood why his solidaric soul has chosen to manifest itself by means of sharp pains in the lower part of his abdomen or in his back around the area of his kidneys, which is sensitive and requires protection.

Faithful to a rhythm that isn't mere routine, after the noon hour he goes punctually to the editing room to lay out the material for the next day's edition. And as soon as he's finished his work, at five-thirty, he decides to spend some time working on the end-of-the-year summary that the writers offer their readers in their special competencies.

A threat of reprisals against the newspaper seems imminently real, though no one actually expects violence. It doesn't make any sense. But the editors of the newspaper have forgotten that *common sense* isn't taught at military schools or universities. The problem originated with an article about the illegal promotion of several military officers. The newspaper then inadvertently added fuel to the fire by publishing a "story" in its literary supplement which certain residents of an eastern province considered offensive to its women. Groups that opposed democracy have been encouraging the "injured" parties, and this literary "slip" is said to have been aimed at the military officials who have already taken revenge for the "affront" committed against them by setting fire to the offices of the newspaper in Santa Cruz.

Since July 17, 1980, the country has been operating outside the law. The government had then tightened its grip by creating paramilitary forces. The populace, who have remained passive, are living in abject terror. An "accident" might happen at any time, and no one is immune. From one day to next, everyone has become a suspect, and not even priests or military personnel, usually protected from such attacks, can consider themselves safe.

Jursafú is reflecting on the situation when the director of the literary supplement comes in. He is an old and distinguished gentleman to whom the country is greatly indebted, culturally speaking. Calm and in a fine mood, he asks Jursafú to make him a copy of an article in which he's tried to explain the "story" to their eastern readers. Parenthetically, he tells him, or begins to tell him, that Bolivian men suffer from three maladies— instead of two, as an author of the past century claimed. And taking a look around, he adds that what really drives him to distraction is the provincial attitude of the Bolivian people. Jursafú replies that they might be provincial but that it doesn't make them any less dangerous.

Suddenly, things begin to happen quickly, and he doesn't get a chance to ask which malady the nineteenth-century author overlooked. Jursafú has reached the third paragraph of the clarification when he hears someone tell the editor that he'd better get out if he wants to avoid further torture and interrogation. He is about to go on with his writing, but it is too late; armed guards start coming into the office, first one and then another, until they are too numerous to count. Their leader and guide is a young, dark-skinned man who stomps around the room with such conviction that no one dares to challenge his authority. He carries a machine gun, which he is ready to fire at the slightest provocation, and shouts instructions to his men who are as short tempered as he and apt to respond in like fashion. Their images remain fixed in Jursafú's memory. but they are holding clubs instead of automatic weapons, a transformation he can't account for.

The temporary editor has thought many times about the cryptic meaning of the story of Cain and Abel and about the thieves who were present at Christ's agony on the cross. Not that these are the only paradoxes that life has to offer, but they are good examples of instances where logic truly fails. He can think of other examples, such as Job's inscrutable adventure with God and the devil, the story of Faust, and the mysterious parable about Jesus cursing the fig tree for not bearing fruit out of season. These incongruities, which a true believer wouldn't question or make light of, have made him wonder if man doesn't use an extreme form of rationalism to give meaning to his precarious existence on earth. Such hardheaded individuals, to avoid polemics with the faith that soothes them, would also have to accept the luminous "incoherences" of divine conduct toward human beings. Jursafú decided early on that the saying "no one understands God's plan" was a rational person's reaction to the first divine paradox.

But these theological musings have nothing to do with what Jursafú feels when the armed guards come marching into the editing room. His train of thought suddenly switches to another subject. From childhood he's always believed that people, though apparently diverse, can be divided into two groups: those who think and those who act, with neither band taking precedence over the other. Some remote god has planned it that way for the precise purpose of making them need each other—like the two sides of the magic medallion. Jursafú can think of no other reason why thinking types should become so attached to the visions of practical types, who have a gift for ordering people around and without "sheep" wouldn't be able to exercise their leadership abilities or express their authoritarian spirits. And to illustrate his point, he cites the case of Ezra Pound's humiliating submission to Benito Mussolini. In turn, these happy practical types, with their steady nerves, will never overcome their sense of inadequacy at not being able to ascend to the universe of pure thought, to which they attribute many virtues that probably exist only in their imaginations. He mentions here the example of Hitler's fondness for painting and his passion for music. When the two types are mixed, the product is usually mediocre, though Malraux, Hernández, and Bolívar can be cited as exceptions. He also mentions that the smallest misunderstanding between the two groups can lead to violence, as if anger were their usual state of mind.

He now focuses on the fury of the first armed man and remembers that "it's silly to waste your energy on something that's not going to last. For example, why get angry if the next minute you may be laughing your head off?" But this man isn't just angry, he's carrying a machine gun; though for some strange reason, it looks to Jursafú like a club, a dangerous one, no doubt, since the man holding it has taken complete control of all the editors. Where could he have seen him? Where has he seen this army of dummies, living models of authoritarianism, exact replicas of the original despot? Maybe when human life was just beginning? And now, here they are again, resuscitated in the editing room of the newspaper, flooding it with ignorance, slamming a door on the future, forcing him to recall the images described by a geology student who often dreamed of himself in pitched battle.

His name was Adrián, and he spoke with a derisive tone: "When the forerunners of human beings, who drifted like tiny sailors in a very large ocean, finally managed to get out of the water and plant their feet on firm ground, they began to imagine a tough individual whom they raised up as a depository of their greatest hopes. They created him out of their rough indolence but promised to do whatever was needed to keep him alive and thriving.

"But what happened when these primitive individuals, used to grabbing their food with their own hands, discovered that apples grew beyond their reach? The *practical man*, still in the initial stages, had a long way to go to get to the phrase 'be realistic, ask the impossible.' So he gave up, forgot about the apples, and lay down in the weeds. But someone else was with him, a type that goes around with his head in the clouds. His friend, the practical man, had lost interest in the apples, so he suggested that he might extend his reach by using a club. With this artificial extension of the arm, the practical man knocked the apples out of the tree and satisfied his hunger.

"His fuzzy-headed friend didn't want to spoil his party, so he didn't bother telling him that man can get along quite well without artificial arms. A tree can be told by its fruit; fruit-bearing trees, when their fruit is ripe, abandon their loftiness and extend their branches toward Mother Earth, as if to offer her the visible results of what they've extracted from her by invisible means. 'So, you don't need a club, my friend,' cried the fuzzy-headed man, dodging the first ungrateful blow." ∎

"You're off your rocker," says another fuzzy-headed man to his modern friend. "You ask me why intellectuals are opposed to weapons? Well, I'll bet you one thing, it isn't out of the kindness of their hearts. It's probably just a precautionary measure. When you think, you liberate all the demons in your head. You become disillusioned because you start to see things as they really are. Thinking is learning to put up with your own demons. And when you don't think, you send them packing."

The angry guards have stormed back into the editing room with another group of invaders who have joined them. Together they undertake their mission. Jursafú suddenly sees the designer in the "literary" office, the brother of the regular designer who was shot during the November 1979 massacre and then, for safety's sake, took off for Ecuador. The situation is looking bad for his replacement, who becomes terrified as two guards approach.

"Is this the one?" asks one of the guards, pointing with feigned calmness to the elderly director.

"Yes, that's the one," answers a tall man with fury in his eyes, identifying his victim.

They're ordered out of the room, and Jursafú joins the others who march out with their hands behind their heads. The tall man about fifty years old is wearing short boots, earns a living as an architect, and appears to be in charge of the guards. He's said to have killed two people—and it is true, he killed two Indians in Chuquisaca—and for a time was committed to a sanitarium. At one time he'd been an officer and a gentleman, and though he's given up his uniform he hasn't been able to give up the power it implied.

"You bastard," he thunders, hitting the man for the first time. "I'll give you reason to offend the women of Santa Cruz."

He shouts a string of obscenities. Jursafú looks for the director, but he can only see the man in boots who is totally out of control. Jursafú's a skeptic when it comes to faces, though he admits that a lot can be seen in a face and that the eyes are the door to the soul. But "faces" as such? He thinks there aren't many different kinds of faces. There're a few archetypes and complexions, but they don't suggest any substantial differences in a person's development. But faces seem to conform to these patterns— some call them archetypes—probably to facilitate a convivial existence. A man with an eye in the middle of his forehead will always be considered a mythological creature because people can tolerate things that are either "close by" or "at a great distance," neither of which requires them to behave in a responsible manner. People don't give a hoot about things that are far away from them; and as for things close by, people threaten them as if they were similar to themselves, and project their own needs onto them. But things that occupy a middle ground, these are the things that can be alienating. And perhaps for this reason, man finds it very difficult to accept a possible kinship to the ape, regardless of what scientists say. It's not that he minds occupying a place in the animal kingdom, but what really sticks in his craw is the idea of accepting the ape as a blood relative. Why? Because it undermines his divine status on earth.

Despite its likeness to other men's faces, the face of the man in charge reminds him of something in particular: a man shooting a Guarani in the back of the head. He can also envision a vast plain in the background, a child standing next to other children, and the execution taking place in a field of tall weeds. This man, like the other, thought he was protecting his family's honor, and like him, was impugned for a heinous crime.

A whole lifetime of images boil up inside him. A wilderness of images with no rhyme or reason. He's always suspected that "to think" is to pick and choose and then direct every aspect of one's existence. "In order to achieve this artificial course, one must learn to profit from external elements without losing a drop of oneself. On the other hand," advises the speaker, "when you aren't meditating, you will observe the blind potentiality of repose."Trembling with fear, he looks at his friends standing with their hands pressed against the wall. The guards are kicking them.

Everything seems to be leading toward a fatal trap, and nothing suggests that it's a practical joke. He feels fear overtaking him but convinces himself that the only way out is to stay in control. During his already long life, he's experienced all kinds of frightening situations but never such a suffocating collective nightmare, which, paradoxically, he seems to be confronting alone. Though death hovers near, he doesn't consider taking his own life; such desolate thoughts have never seduced him. That anomaly belongs to people who have time to think but rarely affects the working class, who wouldn't kill themselves even if they were starving to death. They fight for their lives like caged animals and would turn to crime before harming themselves physically. Of course, there are exceptions to every rule in this universe of ours, and such a case is the llama, the "sober companion to the Aymara," a beautiful animal who is likely to commit suicide if some ignorant foreigner loads it down and forces it to walk faster than its normal pace. It walks along for a time as if nothing were wrong, but at the proper moment butts its brains out against a large rock. Workers have committed "suicide" many times by picking up the gun. Intellectuals have appealed on many occasions—not all of them laudable—to "drastic" means in order to carry out their protests.

"I'm not going to kill myself, and I'm not going to behave like a wild animal," says Jursafú. "That's not what's happening here. The hangman has pointed us down another road while he recuperates and amuses himself, hidden in the dark explosion of neighbor against neighbor."Things could get out of hand, but that doesn't happen. We walk along in silence, staying clear of the door to tragedy, muzzled by disgrace, and perhaps embodying an ancient hope: to decide how we shall die, to live so that when the end comes, death will be a testimony to our existence on the earth.

Decide how we shall die. Had he heard that or read it somewhere?

The adventure seems to be reaching an end, he thinks, as he shuffles along the corridor with his friends. He walks along slowly, with images from the past flashing through his brain.

He remembers an author who was popular during Jursafú's youth saying that "people are glad to give their lives for an ideal," but they think it's foolish to live for one. But this continent is so different. It doesn't matter whether you're a person or an animal, because violence affects everyone, whether you control your instincts or allow them to control you. Decide how we shall die? Of course. Live life to the limit so that death will come as a proper end to the human experience.

When they get to the reception room, he sees the chief executives of the newspaper with their hands up and standing against a white wall. He escapes from that reality to slip into one that is even more terrifying: Latin America holds the chilling record for the largest number of suicides among intellectuals. He'd learned that fact over a decade ago from an intellectual who later put an end to his own life. How could life become so intolerable in a place called the continent of hope?

He becomes distracted, staring at the back of a fellow worker's neck, who, in turn, has become distracted staring at the necks of other workers. He looks at his ears and his modest clothing, not remembering his fine sense of humor or his taste in music. He can still remember him at the last office party, sad and reserved, drinking beer and tapping out the rhythm of a Paraguayan polka playing on the radio. ■

"You like radio music, eh?" Jursafú commented.

"Aha!" his co-worker replied after a long pause, without raising his head.

A couple of hours later at the home of one of the photographers, the editors, animated by the boleros of Pedro Vargas, the Panchos, and some other groups from the past, put away several bottles of *singani*. At that time people were talking about a possible Paraguayan invasion, which wasn't such a wild idea, given the strange visit of the mayor of Asunción to Villamontes. He'd come to the city of broad avenues without an invitation from the authorities in La Paz and had gone away content.

"And I suppose you'll go to war," said Jursafú, "if the occasion should arise, as people say it will. After all, Paraguay is in the hands of a dictator."

"Similar to the one we have here, which nobody bothers to mention, in spite of what he's doing to everyone," his co-worker answered and went back to listening to the unconvincing melancholy of a bolero.

"Well put," chimed in a man from Chuquisaca. "But things change when it's a matter of national pride. We're not going to let internal conflicts get in the way of protecting the petroleum fields that General Bernardino Bilbao Rioja so fiercely defended in Villamontes. We lost fifty thousand people there, but we saved a part of the national wealth."

"I don't know if I'd fight in another war like that one. I like what Marshal Félix Estigarribia said in Brazil: 'Wars only prove that they're useless.'"

"Of course, after he said it, they threw him out of his plane. Better not bring up Estigarribia, but tell us which war 'like that one' you fought in, if you wouldn't mind saying. If I'm not mistaken, you weren't even born yet when bullets were whizzing in the Chaco. You were just a gleam in your father's eye."

Everybody laughed, but the eastern Bolivian answered, undisturbed, "Actually, my father was killed in the capture of Villamontes."

"You mean in the defense of Villamontes," said a man who was a stickler for historical details.

"No, my friends, I mean the capture of Villamontes," he responded stubbornly. "What fault is it of mine if my father was Paraguayan and my mother a pretty Bolivian girl?" He punctuated his statement with a long pause, staring all the while at the floor.

"So, that explains why you're not a regionalist," said the man from Chuquisaca, offering him another glass of beer. "You have enemy blood in your veins, or maybe I'm wrong. Maybe you are a regionalist after all."

"No, you aren't wrong. I have nothing to do with that disease that came here from the Iberian peninsula. I'm not that stupid."

"Fine, but let's leave the Iberians out of it," said the man from the lovely white city, trying to be conciliatory. "Recently a historian—who just happens to be one of your fellow countrymen—said that Bolivian regionalism actually started a long time ago. During the early years of the Republic, it wasn't only isolated, as the *collas* say, but completely invertebrate, as the *cambas* say. If you lived in Santa Cruz and wanted to get to Europe, you had to cross the Atlantic Ocean; but it was easier for the *collas* to go by way of the Pacific. Therefore, the *collas* and the *cambas* rarely crossed paths, and this mutual ignorance gave birth to regionalism. If you lived in Cochabamba, it didn't matter which route you took, because you were the same distance from both ports. In other words, geography is what creates a particular point of view, which can be good or bad for a community. In our case, it didn't work out so well because we don't understand each other."

"I'm not sure I follow everything you say, but what a hell of an interpretation," the man replied, rather peeved. "I suppose if you believe that, not a damn thing happened here and everything's just fine. But, let me tell you something. Those *collas* and *cambas* who never laid eyes on each other here saw plenty of each other in the Old World, passed their regionalism on to us, and now we're stuck with it, all of us—Aymaras, Quechuas, mestizos, and whites. Not to mention the wild Ayoreos."

"Yeah, the Ayoreos. They're so different from the Aymaras," said a man who was incapable of sticking to the subject.

"Ha! They're plenty alike, ever since they got screwed by the white man," replied the *camba*. "An Aymara friend of mine, who knew a lot about the Ayoreos, said that in the ancient Andean language *ayoreo* meant 'the one who went away.'"

"Fine, so what does it mean?"

"There's nothing mysterious about it. It just refers to the fact that the Ayoreos were Aymaras who took off for the eastern plains to keep from being enslaved by the Spaniards."

"That's interesting, *che*," said the half-drunk man from Chuquisaca, yawning and slowly strumming a guitar.

Jursafú looked at the guitarist whom he'd met that evening. He'd just come back to Bolivia after spending a number of years in Spain. After getting mixed up in the guerrilla activities at Ñancahuazú, he'd gone to Europe and started a career as a journalist. The *camba*, on the other hand, he'd known since 1961, a year he'd gotten to know a number of people, close up or at a distance, who sooner or later would have an impact on his life. These friendships had formed at the university dining hall where many a provincial student came for meals. When they sat at the same table, they would talk, but many of the people he saw there he only knew in passing.

The *camba* was a friend of some of Jursafú's friends—or maybe it was the other way around—many of them members of the newly formed Left who were very enthusiastic but at the same time knew that life sooner or later would return them to their original destinies, which weren't exactly revolutionary. They got deeply involved in the Nationalist Revolutionary Movement—a regime that had given up its chance to unearth the real face of Bolivia and was now teetering on the edge of disintegration. But Jursafú was excited to be in La Paz nonetheless, in part because of the novelty, in part because of the fear. He was still carrying the scent of the trees of his homeland when he participated in his first demonstration, along with his friend Argel, and knocked heads with Andean reality. They both smelled the gunpowder and the tear gas and were terrified to see dead people who had just been alive; and the following day, they were shocked to find out that a talented artist, a member of the Communist party, had been assassinated. Calixto Choquehuanca had left for the other world under circumstances that remained a mystery. It was a difficult time, but limpid and innocent. Then Julián Tuercas and Adrián appeared on the horizon; the first was a painter and architecture student, and the second, a budding geologist who was responsible for getting many of his friends money for going to the Islas Afortunadas. Everybody who was able to go, went, except him, who'd been so eager to experience that country's magic.

Some years later his *camba* colleague had given up medicine and started attending the union meetings on Pompilio Daza Avenue. Jursafú gave up geology, also, never suspecting that a decade later he would see his friend again, transformed into an excellent journalist who made him feel like an amateur by comparison. Jursafú was still uneasy about writing articles that thousands of people would read. But as soon as he'd written his first news story, he ceased to be what he was—a careful reader who, like everyone else, thought that what he read in the newspapers was true. It also came as a shock to him that he was able to write in a roomful of strangers, since he'd never been able to write a line with people milling around him. He overcame that in no time, and between one interruption and another, had soon solved his hunger problem. What was much more difficult to learn was what no university ever teaches: the buddy system, the language of one's peers, their tricks and skills, their fears and desires, their vanities veiled as modesty, their pedantries . . . and the hangman's constant vigil, the artful manipulations of this judge of human conduct.

Journalism, in one sense, seemed like a noble service; but in another, it seemed like mere gossip, respected by the public because it was performed by professionals. *Communication* was a magical word with all sorts of connotations, and in a country like Bolivia, its destiny was a mystery. But he didn't think it was an accident that the mass media in a poor country where many languages were spoken was in the hands of the elite. And it wasn't coincidental that many people suspected of authentic communication had found it necessary to pay with their lives.

Such insolence can't be tolerated. And the experienced *camba*— standing against the wall with his hands in the air—is sure of it. All the others, including Jursafú, are in the same position, trapped in their invisible thoughts while time drifts away, leaving time for everything. Time is real—Jursafú had come to that conclusion long before—the proof being that if we concentrate on its passing, we grow old. But time is also unreal. External time, which is often theoretical, becomes vital when it is forced to move at a rate determined by our psychic universe. True, a day has a certain number of hours, but sometimes a second is enough to foresee an entire eternity, a phenomenon that presupposes the totality of time. "I'm not a number or an inert object," says Jursafú. "I'm a conscious mind in a fiction called life. And now I feel strange because I'm trapped by a phenomenon called time. I don't have the tools to understand it, but I could use it to destroy myself." His arms, suspended in air, begin to ache, but an innocuous melody encrusted in his memory comforts him, "Life only reveals its secrets in death." The certainty of reaching the end of his adventure on earth has been molded into a pleasant phrase. He says sadly, "Man, pushed to the limit, turns into a phrase, maybe a golden one. So the wise sayings we learn have a purpose after all. And when we choose them— because they mean something in our universe—it's as though we were promising to live or to die for them."

"Die for a simple phrase." A strange sort of communion is taking place between these trapped, silent beings, who are there to atone not for a human error but for the shortcomings of those who don't understand that a world without truth is a dark, desolate place. Here they are, long eared, fat or skinny, with hair that's straight or curly, but always good humored and with a devilish look in their eyes. The whole country is represented in the editing room of this Andean newspaper, which makes the people who've come there to defend the honor of the women of one province seem even more ridiculous. But the grotesque thing about it is that the man responsible for the "story" or the "insult" was born in the same province as the people he's offended, but, of course, he hasn't been arrested. The whole room is suddenly silent. Maybe no one has spoken the entire time. "If you don't love your country, you're worthless." "When you leave your country, you abandon your own gods." "If you can't understand a foreigner's silence, how can you expect to understand his language." With sayings of Bolivians, Romanians, and Poles buzzing through his mind, Jursafú becomes increasingly bored watching the silent breathing of the long-eared, short-haired man standing by his side. ■

"My name's Miguel Tintaya," said the long-eared man, laughing. From time to time they'd greeted each other and, thus, miraculously, had formed a bond of friendship. Tintaya worked hard from sunset to dawn in the circulation division of the newspaper. By the time the sun came up, he was so tired that he would sleep till noon. A personal calamity had probably brought him to the main office of the newspaper and now has placed him in a position to share an even greater calamity of a collective nature.

I think that Miguel Tintaya is a good man. Jursafú also thinks he's a good man. Maybe everybody does. I heard one of the reporters say that a good person symbolizes holiness on the earth and looks out for outcasts and untouchables. It's the same in nature, which includes trees and birds of a sacred character, creatures that never come to harm. Jursafú discovered this when he began to roam the world, in other words, at the age of six, when he learned that men like to hunt. But they didn't hunt all the time, just at certain times, when it seemed as though they were being forced by some inescapable need. Like all children, he wanted to do what the adults did, so he made himself a sling, like the ones the Guaranis carry around their necks, and he went to the woods, vowing to bring back pigeons, ringdoves, *ulinchas*, and parrots. He heard a bird chirping in a thicket, inviting him to join the celebration of nature. He followed the sound until he came upon a tiny, cinnamon-colored bird singing with all its might. He didn't know that it was an ovenbird whose mission it is to sing. But he discovered this when he loaded his sling with a rock, determined to put an end to the bird's unending joy. The ovenbird stared back at him with its small, round eyes and went right on singing, knowing that it was safe. He couldn't kill it, just as he could never take an axe to a myrtle, a beautiful little tree whose aroma suggests the vastness of the universe: tenderness and sensuality, light and darkness, melancholy and wantonness, the power of silence and the hope of activity. When he would approach the supple branches of the tree to harvest the delicious fruit, he always laid his axe on the ground. But he didn't mind hacking away at a *clavelillo* or a *sacharosa,* shrubs that employed a cowardly means of defense and were as likely to cause harm—without reason or forethought—as some were to produce benefit.

"A member of the myrtle family. A direct descendant of the ovenbird. It's as though the songs of fraternal men were looking for the light by way of his throat."

"He's a real Aymara," one man said, "and a good man besides."

"Being Aymara isn't necessarily a guarantee of virtue," said the man who was standing on the other side of that man. "But Miguel Tintaya is a good man. And if we're going to talk about race, he's Aymara through and through."

The *camba* colleague was at the other end of the table with the correspondents, messengers, administrative assistants, and columnists who could zero in on a situation in the blink of an eye. At the democratic gathering organized by the directors of the newspaper, no one was more anonymous than Miguel Tintaya, with his bushy hair and big, hazel eyes. The large number of participants, at least a third of whom were special guests, parsimoniously devoured the appetizers, listened to a couple of speeches, drank a discreet quantity of beer, made a few toasts, and began to drift out, having left the place a shambles. Tintaya stood for a while in one place, then another, until he eventually came face to face with Jursafú, to whom he offered a drink.

"You know," he said, mysteriously.

"I don't know anything, Miguel. What is it I'm supposed to know?" he asked, somewhat disoriented by Tintaya's affirmation.

"You know I want to study."

Jursafú didn't understand what the man was getting at, and his first verbal contact with the Aymara left him in a state of confusion. But only a few minutes later, everything became clear. Though his friend had only completed his primary education, his greatest goal was to study journalism. He ingenuously believed that it was only a matter of going to the university and registering. Plucking up his courage, Jursafú laid it all out on the table, explaining to Miguel what some considered the prerequisites for entering the university: first, earning a diploma—in his case, through adult education, since he was over thirty—and then getting accepted, with the understanding that the university was private and he would have to pay tuition.

"Sometimes I don't think I can do it," he replied with resignation. "I work at night, and it would be hard to get up in the morning."

Jursafú toasted him for his courage; Tintaya belched and changed the subject.

"You know," he began again, passing his tongue over his lips to wipe the foam away.

"I don't know anything," Jursafú replied with a smile, fearing he was about to destroy another of the man's illusions.

"I'm telling you, you know," Miguel added, his lips stretched by an enormous smile that was blossoming on his brown face.

"Well," answered his interlocutor, amused upon realizing that Tintaya was guided by another logic that deserved respect despite the fact that it had been mangled in translation to the Castilian language. "You're stubborn as a mule if you insist that I *know*."

"I always knew from the beginning that you knew," said Miguel, laughing and clicking his glass against his friend's. He reminded Jursafú of their gray, silent homeland.

The doors of intimacy were standing wide open. The slow beginning ended with several rounds of beer. Tintaya was the middle child of a large family. They had left their community at Caracato without breaking their ties. He was responsible for taking care of his younger brothers and sisters and also his aging parents, who were nearly blind and living at Chuquiago in Nuestra Señora de La Paz. That was why he was working at night and why he wanted to study during the day.

"He wanted to die, he was so sad and ailing."

"Who wanted to die?"

"My papa."

"You've taken him to a doctor, haven't you?"

"Well, not always to a doctor, *che*," Tintaya answered, alluding to his lack of money. "But I dream about him."

"What are you talking about?" asked Jursafú, focusing his full attention on Miguel.

"Well, I had a dream. A pretty yellow snake bit me on the ankle. It was a big snake on the patio of my house. Well, I was scared, *che*, and I woke up and dug a hole in the spot where the snake had been, and I found a small pot with bones in it. The *yatiri* said to break the pot, and Papa broke it and now he's fine."

"You dream all the time. I know."

"Yes, all the time. You know," answered Miguel, smiling again.

But he doesn't feel like laughing. It's just a conjecture, because Jursafú can only see the back of his friend's neck, and Miguel Tintaya is looking at the backs of the necks of the men who've just arrived, some older men who have been kicked and shoved from the room where they were analyzing the current status of the newspaper. Miguel is lost, just as Tupac Katari must have felt lost among gold-crazed individuals navigating through the symbols of his own blood, crossing the continent as a premonition, appropriating the collective memory. The scene of his quartering could be seen in every school in Bolivia, perhaps as a homage or perhaps as proof of the carnage. Jursafú had seen it at the Rufino Salazar School among images, now vague, of the country's history. He remembers the strong croups of the horses and the riders who took off like lightning in four directions.

Moved by the tragedy, he remembers spending an entire night trying to imagine what the Andean martyr must have felt. He couldn't do it. He decided that a person's authentic place in the world can't be understood. He also discovered that people are capable of sublime action, but this doesn't prevent them from doing truly evil things. This was pure reality transformed into an often repeated thought: Katari's remains, scattered throughout the broad American land, can't be found in any specific place and yet are everywhere. His body is the perfect center of a circle so vast that it allows the sacrificed man to be omnipresent. And hadn't the same thing happened to another man who'd met his destiny at Ñancahuazú, a man who'd managed to express the dilemma of the social revolution in a few words: "It's easy to stick your foot in it; what's hard is getting a toehold."

A rural scream, an act of total wisdom. A voice crying out in the wilderness.

Shouts are coming from the hall. Threats are heard amid furious cursing. Jursafú is sinking into a bottomless pit of insults, and after the shadows have moved away, the insults can still be heard. But he isn't there with Tintaya and his *camba* colleague. He's kneeling with his face to the wall at the house where he lived when he was eleven years old, afraid that the officials who tried to run down the people of El Palmar are now going to murder their children. It occurred on a moonlit night in 1952, about midyear. The whole town was suddenly shaken by a volley of bullets. But the next day everything seemed fine, and since no one mentioned the events of the previous night, Jursafú wondered if the whole terrible incident hadn't been destined for him alone. It happened the same year that people started telling him he'd have to study if he didn't want to be treated like a pack animal. But he was slow to leave the village because he'd already figured out that the ones who went away to study somehow ended up exploiting others rather than helping them to overcome their exploitation. And who were the "others"? They were the ones who'd decided to stick to plowing the land of their ancient ancestors. Violence and ingratitude. His mind had been in a state of turmoil for several years, ever since he'd learned that Simón Bolívar, a week before his death in Santa Marta, had shrunk to a weight of less than fifty pounds, beyond the reach of his friends' indifference, blind to the loyalty of men who, defying danger, brought boards and nails for his coffin.

His memory begins to fail him. He has stared at a spot on the wall until he's become that unreal spot. The same thing happened to him as a child: he would stare at a tree in the forest until he became that tree; he would love a road so much that he could feel the comings and goings of a solitary life flowing over him; he would watch the horizon until he himself became the anxiety it signified for human destiny. Then a figure would suddenly appear who would distract him from this pure, meditative state, when, like now, his body would turn into a mass of human flesh kneaded by thoughts from the past and by a fear of death. From a very young age he'd made a distinction between "death" and "fear of death," the second of which he considered a private matter not to be intruded upon by anyone. As far as other people were concerned, they could use any number of formulae to distinguish between "knowledge" and "mere information," but his formula was irrevocably tied to his "fear of death," as if his body were a springboard to enlightenment. "People who can situate their egos in the proper place can eliminate unnecessary fear," he'd often said in the past, never suspecting that some time later he would be forced against a wall by people he didn't know and who would hold him there, suspended between two worlds: the one he could touch and the one that pulsed through his veins.

"They can fill you full of bullets," says a voice from the shadows, a familiar voice, always ready to help.

"I've never doubted it, especially now."

"You've gotten yourself mixed up in something, haven't you?"

"I'm worried about my children. I've learned a lot, wandering through the world—like everyone else. But I'm a father, and I'm supposed to go on protecting my children. Before I leave the earth, I want to remember every being I've known—human, animal, or otherwise—so I can embrace them before I die."

"I didn't ask what you wanted," says the voice in a neutral tone.

He's so sad that subtleties of language escape him. As time rushes by, his mind fills with images from the past. He can now understand the urgency of the smiling Chaco Indian who was on his way from La Paz to Tarija, and having finished the first part of his journey, sat in the restaurant at Patacamaya at eight o'clock at night, waiting for someone to decide to serve him a meal. After Jursafú had drunk a cup of coffee to combat the intense cold, he followed the road heavily traveled by trucks, and he raised his eyes to the sky, clear and full of stars, and the world of men felt cold to him. The dark, impartial sky reminded him of a line that Gustav Mahler had made into music: "I looked up at the heavens and not a single star smiled back at me." He was in love with Constanza, and the night seemed possessed by loneliness. He was on his way to Tarija, traveling alone except for the moon, to a valley where an anonymous, rural heart had dared to give its own version of what it's like to long for a loved one: "The stars in the sky, I count them and some are missing, yours and mine, the most important ones." He went back to the restaurant and saw that everyone had finished eating except the old Chaco Indian, who wasn't smiling any more because finally his anger had gotten the best of him, "Hey, boy, couldn't I get at least a bowl of soup? Time is passing. It flys by when one is traveling."

Jursafú is amused, thinking about what had happened to the old man. Something similar is happening to him right now, but he can't manage a smile. He is trapped in bitter silence and can't say a word.

"If you die today, will you fade from life with no regrets?" asks the voice.

"You should know. The rule of those who seek a higher knowledge is to do as much as they can every day, so that when they go to bed at night they can sleep peacefully."

"But when I wake up and see that I haven't died, I immediately give thanks for the mystery of being alive. 'To me every day is sacred,' a crazy man affirmed. I think it's a good motto."

"And I can't believe that I'm going to die here, as you suggest, at the hands of these pathetic fools. I'm a true believer in something a Bolivian writer said in the heat of battle during the Chaco War: 'I know that at birth people receive a certain number of words, and they can't die until they've used them all up because, otherwise, they won't have lived.' Augusto Céspedes wrote that, maybe when he was near Platanillos, at the side of a road where the weeds grew tall."

"Truth doesn't belong to one person, it belongs to everyone. How can you have forgotten?" says the shadow, who seems to be scolding him.

The presence of his executioners is beginning to make him sick to his stomach. And the guards are just as sick of them—mere "armchair revolutionaries." One of the guards suddenly shouts, "Let's be done with them!"

The editors don't wait for a second invitation and try to squeeze out through the small door that stands between them and the big door. The guards begin to jab at them with the butts of their guns, and in the chaos, the clock on the wall of the waiting room is knocked over and breaks as the people rush out under a shower of blows and insults.

The editing rooms are on the third floor of the fifteen-story building. The business office is on the ground floor, the printing presses, on the second, and the other floors are occupied by embassies and various divisions of the government's information services. As the members of the newspaper staff pour out with their hands above their heads, Pompilio Daza Avenue looks especially sad and haggard with crowds of people leaving their offices in search of the precarious safety of their homes. Only a few of them are going to movies or other diversions of doubtful merit. A watchful eye is about to detect the crowd's reaction to the presence of armed guards who are climbing into ambulances because, suddenly, hundreds of staring eyes are focused on a spectacle they can do nothing about. Nevertheless, the Andean populace wants to be in some sense what it has always been, even in the midst of terror: while a few journalists are being beaten, in a dark, distant room someone is being tortured, and in a nearby bed a couple is fornicating, and further on a man is climbing down from a train and looking at the city for the first time, and maybe some solitary man is discovering the inscrutable metaphor of the bee and the flower.

Jursafú sees the clock fall and receives the first blow across his back. But he feels a pain of another kind, even more painful than that caused by the butt of the gun: "What kind of person would hit a defenseless man? There isn't any answer, at least for those who believe in a higher justice, above the laws of men, a justice that all must seek if they wish to do what is right." He understands the difficulty of such a mandate because he knows that men's laws are a mere reduction of life's higher obligations. Society uses human law to reward or punish its constituents. And the law corrects itself when individuals challenge it and fight to change whatever is out of step with the times. But sometimes those who attack the status quo must pay with their lives, and we have history to prove it. The community, with the law in its hand, creates its own martyrs, thus winning the respect of future generations and proffering a luminous, coherent tradition. Despite its vacillations, the law can be deadly for specific individuals because it never allows its victims to fully confront their enemies.

He feels a blow to the back of his neck as he goes through the doorway. They're stepping on one another trying to get out onto the street. Without thinking, the guards continue to jab and kick at their victims, but Jursafú manages to get past the door and down the steps. He pauses in front of the main door where more guards are standing ready to jab him with their guns. ■

"What kind of country is this?" he shouts in desperation. "Its citizens are immortal and ubiquitous. I've seen them everywhere, since my childhood, well dressed and idle, on the streets of towns and villages, at the head of patriotic parades, sponsors of every civic organization. If they suspect the slightest challenge to their privileged status, they become enraged. Because to protect their lifestyle, which depends not on their own merit but on the oppression of others, they'd do anything. They've proved it time and again. They aren't happy; they never were. But their injustices are so far-reaching that they are responsible for the unhappiness of people they don't even know. I'm still a young man, but I'm already fed up with their cock-and-bull stories. Why, for example, would any professional allow his fellow workers to be treated like slaves? The answer is always the same: it's taken him a lot of hard work and sacrifice to get where he is and now he intends to stay there. I once wanted to be a geologist, but I saw that a lot of people were getting left out in the cold so that I could realize my dream. How could I ever complain to them about the sacrifices I had made? People aren't equal: there are many different kinds of people. But money shouldn't have anything to do with it. It should depend solely on talent. And the curious thing is that the people whom society chooses as models are the most humble people imaginable. Maybe Albert Einstein was a little cracked as some have said, but who would ever think of him as disloyal, arrogant, or cheap? And maybe Plato's world of ideas was somewhat strange; and maybe he was wrong to expel poets from his Republic, as any intelligent person would say. But who would ever suspect him of being a rogue? No one. The wind blows where it wills and reveals the power of the soul. Who could hate them? Who could hold a grudge against Feodor Dostoevski? Who could hate him for taking a loaf of bread or stealing a kiss from a surly maid? No one, not even a madman. 'I hate people who manage to do what I can't do,' says the person who hasn't begun to understand the simple maxim, 'Know yourself.'

"They told me not to hate anything except the things that lead to injustice, suffering, and grief. They said to me: 'We aren't big, small, or even medium sized. We're the same as always, faithful friends of poverty, outcasts from only God knows where. And now we've come to this valley, knowing one thing for sure: a clear conscience is better than a feast at another man's expense. When we lie down at night, my son, there's nothing to disturb our sleep, no memories of terrible acts against defenseless people. So here we stay, from the sheer light of dawn to the last rays of the sun when our work is complete and we can watch the happy flights of birds returning tired to their nests. Where could we possibly go to be valued more or cause less regret?'"

"It's a good thing that Don Jorge Arce left when he did," he says to himself.

"Nobody leaves at the wrong time, Jursafú," Jorge Arce replies. "And don't forget what I said."

"Which thing do you mean?"

"You told me one time that I was a good man. But you still thought it was funny when I stuck my tongue out before or after I laughed. You were always waiting for me to do it."

"I'm sorry about that, but we have to laugh at something. And even though you aren't around here anymore, I still remember you as a good man."

"Thank you. You'll always have a big soul, and you won't ever be a businessman or care too much about money. If you had money in your pocket, you could have anything you wanted, except access to the higher realms of knowledge. If you want to avoid unpleasant surprises, forget about power. Not only women but everything in life is like your shadow: if you try to take hold of it, it slips away; if you try to run away from it, it trots along behind you. If you want your shadow to stay out of your way, then live in the noonday of your soul."

"I'll try my best not to forget that," says Jursafú.

"You're smart to do it. Life is beautiful because it's full of surprises," says the voice of Jorge Arce, getting louder and hoarser. "I died less than a week ago, so it's still hard for me to believe I'm dead. Last Wednesday I said to myself, 'I'm going to retire and take a rest from my chores.' And look what happened. I retired and dropped dead and never got to take my rest. You can't imagine what it's like to rest on the other side of time, far from the feverish dreams of mankind."

"I dreamed about you right before I woke up, and I thought about the dream on my way to the office."

"Yes, I could tell you were dreaming about me."

"You were with the director of the newspaper, and it was raining. Both of you were trying to keep dry and you were standing under the eaves of a beautiful mansion, the kind you see in dreams, and it was made out of whatever dreams are made of."

"Rain doesn't get me wet anymore, no matter how hard it falls," says Jorge Arce, smiling from the shadows. "Nobody around here asks why water makes you wet. They wonder how it is that water continues to be water yet doesn't wet the dead."

"And I guess that's how it is," Jursafú thinks to himself, trying to protect himself from the guards as he moves down the steps. As the guards goad them along the street toward Plaza Villarroel, he smiles remembering that his friend had said that people should change their way of thinking if they found a better argument but not because someone beat the stew out of them.

"Don Jorge, you know, if something isn't close enough for me to sniff it, I'd rather not be involved. But you must have run into a truck driver who years ago dedicated me to God. He probably knew at the time that my loyalty wasn't worth much."

"Don't worry, sooner or later I'll get to know him. It's different here. Memories belong to everyone and no one can pretend to be anything they're not."

"Good God, how I love life!" shouts Jursafú, suddenly changing the subject.

"It's really that you don't want to die," Jorge Arce calmly says.

"I don't want to die like this. I'll have to die someday, but not like this because this isn't the way I've lived. Do you see what I'm saying?"

"Yes, I think I have an idea of what you mean."

"You're making fun of me. Do they let you make fun of people and play jokes around there?"

"You have the nerve to ask me that? You, of all people. My memory isn't so short."

"Which memory are you talking about: the one that lights the way or the one that pushes you to the brink?"

"I can promise you that your subtle jibes would be appreciated around here. Jursafú," he says, becoming more serious, "as far as memory is concerned, I heard a very wise saying once: 'To avoid a mistake, think about it.' And may I humbly add my own maxim: A little joke can spare you a mean trick."

"And what does that make you think of?"

"Something trivial, of course. What ever happened to your friend you used to steal cigarettes from and then give them to me?"

"Don Jorge, that was nothing, and besides, you were the one who benefited."

"I'm not criticizing. I just asked a question. Put your mind at ease. I don't think any of us has ever acted precipitously, though I'd have to admit, some of us may have wanted to. I worked at the newspaper for ten years and never saw anyone become violent. My first year there, a friend asked me, 'Jorge, where do you work?' And my answer was something I'd heard said at the office, 'I work at a place where no one is indispensable.' My friend, wanting to console me, said, 'For a Bolivian, you're lucky. You have a job at a decent place.' That's what he said to me. Anyway, what became of the man who supplied me with cigarettes?"

"He left. He managed to get to safety. He had a premonition that bad things were going to happen in Bolivia. So he decided to go to some place where nothing was going to happen; that's the route he took."

"Well, tell him hello for me when he comes back."

"How do you know he's coming back? He packed everything he owned and took off like a streak of lightning."

"Don't be a fool, Jursafú. Everybody comes back. Every now and again, I'd want a cigarette, and one day, instead of sending somebody else to get me one, I asked for it myself. I'd just come back from Plaza San Francisco, where the largest political party was trying to have a rally and a huge crowd of protesters had gathered. 'Can I have a cigarette?' I asked, but he ignored me. I don't know where he wanted to take you, but with his boyish enthusiasm he was saying, 'Come on, *hermanito*, let's go.' Then you said to him . . ."

"No, *licenciado*. I don't like to stand for a long time in one place, clapping my hands when I don't even understand what they're saying."

"That's why we're going, *hermanito*. We're going to hear what the candidates have to say."

"Why don't we wait till after they've finished their speeches?"

"Why? So we can watch everybody leave?"

"Yes, I can tell you exactly where they'll be heading. Some will go to Sopocachi, and some to Miraflores, Villa Victoria, or Achachicala. Truth is a reality shared only in the realm of theory. Remember the famous statement by Albert Camus?" Jursafú asked.

"Which one, *hermanito?* There're so many," replied the man who supplied the cigarettes.

"Well, I'm not referring to what he said about women being our only memory of Paradise. I was thinking about when he said that 'an artist's solitude brings together those whom society has separated,'" said Jursafú, filled with a strange melancholy.

"Well, that's fine for art, but this is politics. Politics, *hermano*, pure and simple." But then the man with the cigarettes was no longer listening. "Hello, Dynamite," he said.

Dynamite—that was the nickname of one of the photographers—had just come into the office, after having a bottle thrown at him while passing near the Naval. He was carrying some photographs that he'd taken at various cultural events around the city.

"Hello, chief, and little chiefs."

"What's going on out there?"

"I think the army's pretty upset. Here are some pictures. There's a good one from the art exhibit, just as I was walking into the room; and look, there's an artillery man. This one, look . . ."

Only a portion of the exhibition room was visible in the photograph but enough to show that a large number of people had attended. There was a close-up of the "artillery man," as the photographer had called him, staring at an oil painting that had caught his attention—why, it was impossible to say. There he was, an outcast, a bum, a person who might even have been considered a juvenile delinquent by some members of the community. He had a sparse, black beard that was entwined in his dirty clothing.

His whole appearance indicated that he'd been through the worst of times. Doubtless, no one had invited him to the affair, and he wasn't so brazen as to ask for a drink: despite his poverty, he was capable of a certain dignity and wasn't about to ask for help of any kind. There was only one explanation: some ancient demon must have guided him there to stare with amazing interest at a painting by a Bolivian artist, a particular painting which depicted people like him, "panhandlers," in other words. As it turned out, he hung around the exhibition room longer than the protectors of the nation's culture could tolerate.

Might Albert Camus have been thinking of this artillery man when he summed up his luminous vision of existence in one lucid sentence? Or if not the French novelist, there were others who had adopted a brotherly stance in such circumstances, such as the author of a beautiful story that the one who is now closed up in a building on Pompilio Daza Avenue read in passing in a French newspaper. In a few words, a poor wanderer who was very wise—or maybe poor because he was wise—arrived at a village where he was already known by reputation. The wealthiest man in town wanted to offer the pilgrim his hospitality, if only for an hour. The pilgrim, shabbily dressed and wearing the dirt of the road, accepted the invitation to the gleaming mansion. While he was there, he got an urge to spit but didn't want to soil the floor. After resisting as long as he could, he finally spit in the owner's face, which was the only dirty spot in the entire house.

Reading the story, titled "Thinking Doesn't Stop," Jursafú was able to detect the author's convictions: The truly great ideas, ideas of tremendous depth, can only be extracted by the most generous people, who travel the world over without a shirt on their backs. Paradoxically, the "possession" of vital knowledge demands an absence of material interests as a counter-balance. If thinking doesn't stop, then it must be man who has sat down to take a rest. And even an earthquake couldn't budge him from the spot. You can talk to people about anything as long as the conversation doesn't involve delicate or offensive topics. And if you don't believe it, think back to the biblical parable of the rich young man. A perfect example of a good man with limitations, he wanted to give to the poor but not an amount so great as to endanger his paternalism. ■

Trimming his fingernails to curtail his temptation to steal, Jursafú put the kettle on for maté. While he was waiting for the water to boil, he began to mutter to himself, "How can you discuss property with a person who uses material wealth to prop up his spirit? It can't be done, no matter how hard you try. But why can't it? Because as soon as you mention the word *property*, they get the idea that you want to destroy the entire system, pull it up by the roots. And the person wasn't far from wrong who said that *thinking* and *walking* were acts that spontaneously run counter to property, which isn't of noble origin—though it presumes to generate nobility—because in some sense it signifies *usurpation*."

Jursafú could always think of some example involving the Chaco Indians to support his ideas. These *primitive* people never give in to the temptation to fence off their possessions, precisely because their nomadic existence has led them to a more noble idea of what it means to *possess* the earth. "All of us have seen the small valleys of the earth," Jursafú thought, holding the *poro* between his hands, "and we've seen the beautiful trees, the rivers and streams of clear water, the barren hills where we were born. But only a degenerate could think that all of that, created without his lifting a finger, could belong to him and could be his to sell whenever he wants. Where did he get the idea to say, 'This is mine; therefore, I can bargain with it.' Especially when one of the sacred texts warns from the start that man came to the earth on the last day of Creation when everything was made and in its place?"

While pondering these questions, Jursafú reached the conclusion that art represents one of the few generous spheres, perhaps because it inherited from the first people—who now consider themselves proprietors and sell their souls and bargain with the devil—the need to name things in order to get by in a world of shadows. "Art demands constant attention and great sacrifice," thought Jursafú, "all in the name of pure, useless creation. It doesn't allow for such foolish things as vanity, which doesn't mean that there aren't any predators lurking around, only that such creatures, used to deceiving others, let their masks slip in a second when nudity comes into play."

"Unhappy are those who wish to be enslaved but allow themselves to go astray in the wilderness of freedom," proclaimed a shadow, transformed into an echo.

"But it's strange, nonetheless," Jursafú replied, "that art is so attractive to 'practical people.' First, they want to dominate it, seduce it, grab it by its weakest part. And then, if they fail, they trample it with their boots."

"Art has a bulletproof vest," whispered the echo. "Remember that people don't outlive anything, precisely because they carry the mark of immortality. To the contrary, these ephemeral beings can only perpetuate themselves through *creation*. Every last one of them is taken in by the seductive song of the *creative act*. Do you remember 1964, when you were rolling around La Paz like a bowling ball? I wanted to tell you a thing or two, but you wouldn't listen to anything I had to say."

"I can't remember a single day of 1964. Sorry, but I'm in a hurry."

There's one night I remember. Jursafú was walking along Juan de la Riva Street with his friend Julián Tuercas. An automobile suddenly pulled up next to them and stopped. Two men in the car motioned to Julián to get in. He leaned against the car door and talked to the men, who were friends of his, about something—what, I don't know. But a few seconds later, he and Jursafú piled in with the others and drove off toward the stately home of a powerful individual, a high official of the ruling Nationalist Revolutionary Movement. Their host, who was graying at the temples, greeted Sanguinetti, Jocollo, Tuercas, and even Jursafú—who'd come along for the ride—with solemn cordiality.

It was obvious that the house was luxurious, but the owners found it necessary to emphasize the fact: this crystal came from Bohemia, these excellent pieces of pottery from Mexico, this small black piece, whose use is unknown, from India. What a pity they couldn't show them their first mansion, which they'd been forced to sell because of financial problems. Then they all sat down at a table set with china, silver, and crystal and began to carry on a polite conversation, mentioning in passing—as if discreetly stuffing a potato into their mouths—Bolivia's agrarian reform and several other bloody battles that the people had fought and won. But after a few drinks, the young artists forgot about their hosts and began to discuss things that interested them, like the color one should use to achieve a particular effect, the Impressionists' approach to light, the importance of Cézanne, Surrealism and dreams, Arturo Borda and Cecilio Guzmán de Rojas, the stony transparency of the Altiplano, the mysterious Aymaras who are accustomed to looking at great distances and for that reason are easily lost in the forest. The painters' conversation became more and more esoteric, and the owners of the luxurious mansion were finding it difficult to follow what their guests were saying. Jursafú, who knew little about painting, was as quiet as a mouse during the first course, but gradually began to put in a word here and there. The host, who'd made it known that he was a great lover of art, also wished to express an opinion at a particular moment in the conversation. He thought the time was right and said what he had to say, but when no one seemed to hear him, he repeated himself in a louder voice, trusting in the efficacy of his political power if not in the persuasiveness of his words.

Sanguinetti, who by then was behaving like a monkey, cut him short, "No, Doctor, you aren't allowed to speak."

The doctor was confused, thought he'd misunderstood, and tried to pass it off.

"You'd best keep your mouth shut, Doctor," Sanguinetti threatened. "You shouldn't speak. Shall I tell you why?"

"The evolution of the mural has nothing to do with the historic moment or the superstructure. As part of the infrastructure, it's related to the revolutionary process. Therefore," the doctor of agrarian reform declared impatiently, "massive action leads to . . ."

"Doctor, please keep your opinions to yourself . . ."

"Why can't I speak, my distinguished Sanguinetti?"

"Because you're a mule, a complete and total mule," said Sanguinetti, ignorant of the great truth he was speaking.

The doctor decided then and there that he was a mule and that he was going to kick them all out if they didn't leave his home immediately. And he would have done it if he'd had his cohorts with him, who when necessary could beat the straw out of anyone. Instead, he turned the conversation into a violent assault, and the artists soon found themselves in the street, breathing the cold morning air, like roosters in some remote corral . . .

The first of the armed guards who line the steps kicks him in the rear. He doesn't feel a thing, but he does recognize the aggressor. This is the third time he's seen him. He met him when he was accompanying a young woman who'd gotten into a scrape with a lawyer concerning the mortgage of a plot of land. The woman had mortgaged the land to borrow money to bury a friend of hers who'd died in Santa Cruz. The pettifogger, who was this same armed guard, had threatened to turn Jursafú over to his son, an official at the House of Government. The second time he'd seen him was the day after the coup that took place on July 17, 1980, when he'd run into Constanza and the two were walking slowly along Landaeta, which like all the other streets was empty, traversed from time to time by an ambulance or official vehicle and disturbed now and again by the gunfire of snipers. They got to the Plaza del Cóndor just as an ambulance, transformed into a vehicle of repression, had pulled up at the corner. Several armed men got out, and this man was one of them. He was dressed in the black garb of a solemn Bolivian minister and with a machine gun in his hand raced up a flight of stairs as if the devil were chasing him. He was pursuing a leftist whom he obviously hadn't found because he returned, walked into a shop, and emerged angrier than before. And where had he seen him a third time? He'd seen him in a store downtown where he'd gone to buy cheese and other items. The man—always dressed in mourning—waited on him politely but had a look of resentment on his face. And now he was seeing him again, in black, having been on the earth for more than fifty years, not having done what he might have done, but, yes, preventing other people from realizing their dreams. ■

"*Hermano*, you're exaggerating," one of his friends said to him. "Generalizations aren't going to get us anywhere. It's a mistake to throw everyone into the same basket."

"I'm just telling you about something I saw a long time ago and something I saw today. Comparing and exaggerating aren't the same thing. It's dangerous to generalize but it's also dangerous to think it's all a matter of isolated incidents."

"I don't know why you get so upset over some poor sucker, some idiot with authority, I mean power," said his friend Argel.

"You and I see things differently. There are a lot of people running around this civilized world of ours, people who've been around for a long time but who do a lot of outrageous things. And they're snobs about it to boot."

"Anybody can make a mistake."

"Argel, what I'm trying to say is that 'education' is no guarantee of honesty or loyalty. The educated and the ignorant, as soon as they get a little power, start doing terrible things. And as soon as they get a chance, they'll carry off the saint and the poor box with him. It's always the same. It's like a rabbit; it pops up when you least expect it."

The voices came from November 1979, sometime after the bloody military coup that put an end to the brief democratic government. In November of that year, more than four hundred people were massacred in the outlying areas of the city. Bullets fell from the sky, and wherever the people went, day or night, they collided with gunfire. The ones who managed to live through it would never forget the surprise attack on the Day of the Dead, when many died—adults and children, wives, nephews, and grandmothers. Some were on their way to the cemetery carrying flowers for the graves of their dead relatives; others were on their way home. But the results were the same for all. The photographs that came out in the newspapers were similar to images created more than a decade before by Arciles, a famous and often censored Bolivian director. Precisely because Arciles' films had been prohibited in Bolivia, the real images now seemed to prove that censoring films or works of art that supposedly attack people or institutions wasn't the solution; the solution was to stop killing defenseless people, unless you wanted the daring "intellectuals" to feel obligated to concoct more atrocities with the single goal of putting an end to the first atrocities.

"Fine, but that colonel, as you well know, was put into power by the Russians," said Argel, speaking confidentially.

"I doubt it. And I have my reasons," said Jursafú calmly. "And for the record, I don't think the Russians are saints either."

"Listen, they're planning something pretty awful," Argel added after a pause. "I know what I'm talking about. Why do you think the gringos are taking their time in recognizing the government? On the surface, the government looks like it's right wing, but the Americans haven't recognized it and everybody's just waiting around. And some people are saying that the order for the massacre didn't come from the Burned Palace. It came from the American embassy! What do you think of that?"

"Must be some sort of revenge, because that particular colonel likes to butt heads with the gringos," said Jursafú maliciously.

"They haven't come to blows, but he's asking for it, and nobody seems to understand what the hell he's doing," the engineer observed. "The Left isn't supporting him either."

"They're taking their time, maybe too much time. We won't find out the details until later when the 'predators' scribble something down in a book. Wait and see. Martyrs will be popping up everywhere, not to mention members of the 'resistance' who are in it up to their eyeballs. But I was thinking about another fight."

Argel raised his glass, toasted his friend, and then ordered another round of beer. "Which fight do you mean?"

"The colonel who's now in charge was let go when the Nationalist Revolutionary Movement was at its peak. Despite the fact that he's kin to a Chaco War hero, he ended up in El Palmar just the same. He drove a truck between El Palmar and Yacuiba four times a day, carrying passengers to the Argentine border and then back again, a total of sixty kilometers in four trips. As you well know, there wasn't anything to buy here, and a lot of Bolivians went to Argentina to get the essentials, leaving all their money in the hands of the gauchos."

"I didn't know that, *che*. I mean the part about the colonel's job."

"He was skinnier than a Chaco dog but was polite as could be to the passengers. He was the only driver who didn't have an assistant, somebody to help the women with their bags, open and close the door, and then sit there with his mouth shut. The driver had to get up early like everyone else and so the people of the area grew to respect him. They liked him even better when they found out that he was the nephew of a Chaco War hero. But no matter. The colonel never opened up. He was as silent as a mule, though he did get drunk twice a week at the brothel in Yacuiba, where he first met up with the gringos from the oil companies who were looking for the black gold that Standard Oil had tucked away somewhere on the plains of the Gran Chaco. The place wasn't the same then, and the people started to change their ways because all of a sudden they had money in their pockets and got used to some things that weren't going to last . . ."

"When did all of that happen?" asked the engineer, still amazed at what his friend was telling him.

Ignoring the question, Jursafú went on with his story. "The thing is that this colonel made such a fuss in the brothel that even the whores ran away, leaving him to slug it out with the gringos."

"It's hard to believe, *che*, that the colonel was a driver in El Palmar," Argel said, this time convinced that his friend was telling him the truth.

"What's hard to believe is that this same man was once a decent human being with all the good qualities you expect an honorable person to have. That's what's hard to swallow," said Jursafú, lifting his glass to Argel.

"It's true, *che*. Power corrupts."

"Or money."

"It's the same thing. You need money to get power, or vice versa. It's better not to open that can of worms," advised the engineer. "Because there's no going back. Good-bye conscience. It's true, *hermano*, we're the devil in disguise with a layer of false melancholy to fool the innocent. We're sad when it suits us, mean when the occasion arises. And where were you during the November massacre?"

"I wasn't there. I was at the newspaper. It was the first night I'd had to stay at the office. I wasn't by myself. All of us were there. That morning we saw the tanks pass, which woke the people up to their impotence. We watched, petrified, the way we always do when history is in the making. When the sun came up, we all went our own way. 'Every pigeon to its own nook' was our password. It was like any other day. There wasn't anything unusual. The sky was dark, gray, and indifferent to human suffering. I left alone and walked for a couple of blocks until I came to a corner. I'll never forget that corner. Before I left the building, I'd already seen a group of women in the distance. They were dressed in black and huddled together in a circle. Their terrible sadness had wiped away any trace of anger, as they stood staring at two huge puddles of blood, one next to them and another a short distance away. It looked like somebody had been slaughtering pigs right in the street . . ."

Jursafú mechanically holds on to the banister and runs down the steps as fast as his feet will carry him. The blows from the guards' weapons manage to keep up with him, but he can't stop or turn around. There are people in front of him and behind him, hoping to break through the door that leads to Pompilio Daza Avenue. "Why am I running like an idiot?" Jursafú asks himself. "It's not going to do any good." There's a lot of space to cover, even before he can reach the corner where the women in black had been silently standing, their anger wiped away, their spirit destroyed, consumed by the loss of loved ones. Jursafú can still see them, their silhouettes clearly defined against the opaque sky of an abandoned city. Enigmatic participants in a horrible event that appears to have brought suffering only to them, they stand huddled together, wrapped tight in their own convictions. "That's the pain of honest living," says the temporary editor, imagining them in the small coves of life, their dark faces creased by suffering, imperturbable, without rancor, as though an incorruptible spirit, caressed by an invisible tenderness, lived inside of them and turned them into dwelling places for the repressed sobs of men. "May the dead and God forgive you if you ever make any one of them suffer."

"Any woman would bury her dead, so what's new about that?" says a skeptical voice.

"Haven't you ever seen them buying sugar on the street corner, looking at things that no one else sees? Maybe you haven't seen them. Some are feisty, some polite. It depends. But if you ever intuit what they're thinking, you'll go with them and bear the mourning that no one wants to see. They're the creators and keepers of the affectionate diminutives of a violent language, ready to lift up whatever falls . . ." ∎

" ' . . . and from that time on he found the help he needed.' Would you agree, sir, that it's a good story? Or rather, couldn't it be made into a good story?"

"I also used to think of it as a story until life showed me that the greatest realities are often part fiction. During the week I spent in Huanuni, I saw them again—the women in mourning. It was a barren place without a single tree, but I stayed on for seven days to shoot a film. We needed to take pictures of the mine, inside and out. For seven days the sirens blared constantly. Sirens, in a desert of rock and transparency. Ambulances came and went with the wounded and the dead, though there was little difference between them in that godless place, where hope rests with the devil. As the ambulances drove away, they always carried the dark silhouette of a mourner sitting quietly by the side of someone en route to his final resting place. It isn't easy taking pictures of a mine; I can guarantee you that. Barren rock, sand pits, strong wind, orphaned children quickly fluent in the language of necessity. It was the first time I'd seen the mines of Bolivia, and though my dreams never ceased while I was in that stony land, I discovered the meaning of 'hardship.' You've probably guessed that I went there to learn about motion pictures, but I left humble and ignorant."

"Making movies in Bolivia isn't so hard since you don't have to create an illusion. And it's even easier to do if the story is set in the country," said Sanguinetti, comfortably situated in his workshop in Cota-Cota. "Point the camera where you may, the results are going to be original, especially for anyone who hasn't lived here."

"And even for Bolivians," added his neighbor, a strange combination of a boxer and a sculptor.

It was a gathering of civilized men. And their conversation contained as many subtleties and strategies as any discussion among refined individuals. The only difference was that these intellectuals were from the Andes.

"Of course," agreed Sanguinetti. "Our reality is so rich and diverse that it can't help but seem original. In other words, you don't need a lot of talent to turn it into art. Arciles knows this, and that's why he's given us so many Indian films. It's easy to sell a product that's guaranteed to be good. But nobody has been able to convince him to shoot a film in the city. Why is that?"

"Maybe he doesn't find La Paz interesting as a city. I suppose you're talking about Andean cities," observed a tall woman with light blue eyes.

"That may be," said Sanguinetti, assuming a somewhat affected style. I, on the other hand, think there are lots of ways of covering up one's shortcomings, and one of them is to go to the country. Besides, many directors have taken the folkloric approach. You can go up to any Indian in a mine and say, 'Get over there,' and, of course, he does it. And you can say, 'Act like your life is unbearable,' and he does that too, because that is exactly how life treats him every day. Set up your camera, and you've got yourself a movie, illusion and all. And when the Europeans who feel guilty about the Third World give you a prize, then it's official. Arciles knows, however, that if you make a film in the city, you have to 'direct.' You have to work with inept actors who don't have the vaguest notion of what it means to act. Arciles knows how to trick us, plain and simple. I go about it differently. To me the world's a challenge, and I could never call a person an artist who takes such a cowardly approach."

"What you're talking about is theater, or maybe you've turned Fellinian on us, which I personally consider a mistake," refuted Mauricio Santillán, who was quick as an eagle. "If an actor wants to be creative in his work, then he must make a choice, either to play the role objectively, knowing that he is not the role he is playing because in reality his personality is quite different, or to become the character, heart and soul, and during the entire production, act as though he were that person. Critics can't seem to agree about which method is preferable. And as is often the case, they have accepted both alternatives. As far as what you're saying is concerned, I think it all boils down to a matter of preference, artistic preference. Each person can do as he chooses."

"Yes, and to hell with everyone else. Isn't that what you mean?" retorted Sanguinetti, scratching his head with such art that he seemed to be caressing himself. "Everything you've said has to do with theatrical technique and the role of the actor. But, Mauricio, what is acting anyway?"

"Well, it's a way of showing others the best you have to offer," he responded dryly. "To embody an ideal is a common human aspiration. It's more or less the same with acting, if we accept the idea that acting is an attempt to cover up the unattractive parts of our personalities. We're always trying to eliminate any sign of that vain, hidden self. I suspect that only extremely evolved creatures can get along without it. They don't need to act. They've made adjustments in their personalities so they can behave just as they are, in public or in private."

"Mauricio, I think we were talking about Bolivian films," said Sanguinetti, running his fingers through his curly hair.

"Yes, and what I've been saying pertains to Bolivian films," he replied, defending his point of view. "At any rate, Sanguinetti, it doesn't matter because your question is what confused the issue. What difference does it make how a director proceeds? Something more important needs to be addressed: which type of acting suits our country, the kind that requires actors to be objective, or the kind that allows them to throw themselves into a role? If Arciles has opted for the second, I don't see anything wrong with it. He has the right to do what he thinks best, and I would disagree with any judgment that claims his work is aesthetically deficient because it deals with social problems."

In 1969, Mauricio developed quite a reputation as an author, no doubt because of his lucid objectivity, but also because he'd written an exemplary novel that went unnoticed for quite a time, because it lacked a simple ingredient: the Bolivian landscape. Jursafú, for one, was glad that a Bolivian author had at last decided to give up *costumbrismo*. Here was something new, something that had nothing to do with the landscape, exploited for so many years by people who had no desire to improve Bolivia's anemic society. About that time a famous author of Chaco War novels said something that not only revealed an important personal truth but was also applicable to many Bolivian intellectuals: "I've been a bad politician instead of a good writer." As for Mauricio Santillán, who was a member of the bourgeoisie, he wisely chose to follow his historical instincts. In other words, instead of becoming a spokesman of an unproductive class, he became an advocate of the dispossessed, and involved himself in Andean politics by way of the illusory French salons of Marcel Proust, by no means an easy route.

To many young people it seemed curious that, though many Bolivian politicians had used the novel, the epic, or the short story to address the social concerns of their country, none had managed to produce anything but apocryphal versions of that country's reality, which was hard to pin down even for realists. Many odes had been written to the Mamoré River and to Illimani, so many, in fact, that one was led to suspect that sensuality was off-limits for Bolivians. (It wasn't funny that poems often began, "A handsome maid of swollen breasts . . .") One night Jursafú got up the courage to pose a question, one that had been waiting in the wings since time immemorial: "Why is it that so many people who first take the arduous road of fiction then follow the slippery path of the politician?" A young representative of the Nationalist Revolutionary Movement was able to give him half the answer: "We're all cut to the size of our country." But Jursafú then posed two additional questions: "Can you tell me which set of dimensions causes a nation's best people to begin as writers and then embroil themselves in politics? What kind of geographical entity is it that instead of putting its writers in control of their works turns them into grandiose works of fiction?"

Eventually he got his answers. Arciles had problems with the authorities. His first full-length movie, which was filmed in Isla del Sol, was about a rape but also treated the oppression of Indians. The next few films, equally controversial, paved the way for the most powerful one of all, one portraying a massacre at a mine. When Jursafú saw the photographs in the newspaper, pictures of women in mourning, he recognized them as the ones Arciles had taken more than a decade before, during the Day of the Dead Massacre. There was nothing fictitious about them, and Mauricio Santillán had been right when he spoke of a second approach to acting. To complete the paradox, the same people who had perpetrated the massacre had also suppressed Arciles' films.

"How can it be?" someone asked. "How can they suppress a fictional version of something that is allowed to happen in real life?" ■

"Good God, how can it be?" asked a woman in black who had spent the entire night alone standing next to a pool of dried blood, watching a city besieged by unequal forces go up in flames.

"All of the great battles, the ones that create heroes, are always unequal. Don't forget it," whispered a sleepwalker on that November morning of 1979 as he looked for the dried blood, well accustomed to the loss of loved ones.

"I dreamed that an earthquake destroyed the city," sobbed a neighbor who lived a simple life. "I woke up with a start, opened my eyes, and saw the walls of the city in ruins. I rubbed my eyes, drank some black coffee, and saw the same thing all over again. That's all I could see. So I went back to sleep and, protected by my dream, gathered up my children and headed for Villa Fátima, and when I got there I saw the buildings going up in flames. I didn't want to leave Villa Fátima, and I hid in a dark street so I wouldn't have to see what was happening. But it was in vain because I saw a big crowd of men trying to bury a human figure that had light brown hair and was wrapped in beautiful white cloth. The figure was struggling and it stretched out its hand, begging for my help. I tried to offer it my left hand but the nightmare was so frightening that I woke up, hoping it was a dream. In the comfort of the rising sun, I felt a terrible pain in my back about the area where the kidneys were wisely placed."

Jursafú, who had also suffered with his kidneys, got to the newspaper just in time to hear the muffled cry of one of the typists, "My God, how can it be?" The radio had just reported that the body of a priest, Bolivian but Spanish by birth, had been found. He had recently participated along with men, women, and children in a hunger strike against the seven-year-old dictatorship. He had been kidnapped and later killed. He wouldn't be the only victim, though the fatal day, July 17, 1980, hadn't yet arrived.

That horrific day began disguised in a clear light. At noon, Jursafú left the newspaper and could see dust rising up along Pompilio Daza Avenue. He could hear machine-gun fire and realized that the streets were empty. After the attack on the Bolivian Workers Union headquarters, fighting broke out in various sections of the city. The news spread rapidly: several miners had been killed and Mauricio Santillán had suffered the same fate. These were the final touches of a military coup that had begun in Trinidad, the capital of the Beni region. He went back to the newspaper and looked at the last photograph of Santillán, inviolable in his sadness, suspended in the air of his premonitions, surrounded for the last time by those who made every day into a day of sacred effort, the miners. Beside the photograph, the photographer had laid six empty cartridges on the news editor's desk. ∎

"These are the shells from the shootout at the headquarters of the Bolivian Workers Union," he said, showing Constanza the relics of an unequal battle.

They were standing on the corner of Landaeta and October Twentieth and began to walk silently up the steep slope of Landaeta, a street that Constanza's provincial companion had often climbed. When he first came to live in the Andean capital, he had always taken that route to the university, and had taken it again in the evening to get to Argel's room where he would stop for a rest. He was an engineering student like Argel, and though both felt disoriented in the city, they were happy. During that time, the chairman of civil engineering was trying to break the students from using certain geographical names, not that anyone should be afraid to mention them, but they weren't to be used anymore. "Students, this isn't choir practice or a sewing class. In case you're interested, the law school is on the eleventh floor. And if you don't know anything about the binomial theorem, well, the military academy is over at Irpavi."

He didn't choose law, and he didn't go to Irpavi, and geology wasn't worth the effort either. And besides that, he'd felt all alone in the world ever since he'd asked himself the first question one day when he was walking through the forest: "Who am I?" He hadn't retained the vaguest memory of what he'd been before he got to the earth, and the universe for him was bound by his own existence. "I'm grateful for the objective spirits," he affirmed serenely. "But as for me, I wouldn't be offended if they classified me with the small number of creatures who believe in a humble, subjective realm. It seems to me that the universe is unending, which leaves me like a parrot tied to a stake. Life holds a lot of terrible possibilities—and I'm not thinking necessarily of a nuclear war, which the people who didn't want to die alone thought up. The real disaster is of a personal nature, and nobody is going to escape. I often think of that metaphor, luminous and real like the final paradox, 'the springboard to darkness and dissolution.'"

"What were you like back then when you didn't pay any attention to anything but trees," asked an invisible shadow.

"I was so close to nature that I knew nothing about the things that men have done since the beginning of human life. Everything was a mystery and a miracle, and even now my beliefs haven't changed, except, in place of my innocence, I now have a number of allegories, half a dozen riddles, and a few bad jokes, all wisely mixed together with world history."

"And words," added the shadow, like a light.

"Yes, words. I don't know why, but since I was a child I've always been intrigued by how easy it is for children to learn the language of their elders, and also by the fact that children seem to have a special sense for what is acceptable and what isn't. And speaking fluently means knowing how to use words that are acceptable and ones that aren't. When you speak a language fluently, you open up a door to knowledge . . ."

"Name another one, Jursafú."

"You know as well as I do, silence. To me, the mute will always be a lasting emblem."

"Don't pay too much attention to that saying about keeping your mouth shut and flies not being able to get in it. For every proverb, there's another one to contradict it. 'There's many a slip between the cup and the lip.'

Because being a mute is one thing and learning to keep your mouth shut is another. In other words, there's an enormous distance between a natural state of being and something you learn. And for the rest, both words and actions can be used to communicate. But communion is different and only comes with silence that must be learned."

"I think I used to know that with my entire body. I was staring up at a star and could feel my whole being shaken by something that I later realized was happiness. And suddenly I knew that nature wasn't man's worst enemy, like the people who get rich from it often say. It's man himself."

"That was when you started saying 'Don't trust a man any further than you can throw him.'"

"Yes, I said that to cover up my great affection for human beings. I open my eyes wide and put my soul on alert and repeat a very wise saying: 'We are the only examples of the impossible, and this is why love delights in torturing us.' It's true, I've always felt at home in nature, but my basic instinct was also to be with people like myself. So I was always waiting for a friend. And that's when the problem started."

"Why would you call something that's completely natural a 'problem'?"

"It's simple. Until I reached a certain age, I always thought that people were what they pretended to be."

"And aren't they, Jursafú? Some reveal exactly who they are and others could stand to reveal a little more. So what? Most masks could easily be tossed aside because what they're trying to hide died a long time ago. That's all there is to it."

"Well, I doubt that's all there is to it. I have respect for memories. In fact, I was just listening to one: 'I'm the protagonist of an action. How much time has to pass before I become the protagonist of the memory of that action?'"

"You've managed to dredge up one of the better masks," said the shadow.

"Not I. I hate the kind of writing that a mask requires. It's an atrocity."

"There's nothing atrocious about it. It's not the same as trying to read what you haven't learned to write. Like most mortals, you think that something's 'good' if you like it and 'bad' if you don't."

"Yes, I know what you mean. I've fallen into that trap a number of times," he sadly confessed. "But now I'm too old to be making that mistake. I know that we're all part of a system and I'm as much a part of it as anyone."

"Such an excellent answer deserves a question," said the shadow by way of introduction, and then it suddenly asked, "What's your greatest vanity?"

"I don't have to answer that, you know. You can't force me to say what's in my heart. We all have the right to our own privacy."

"You're an open book to me. There's nothing you can tell me that I don't already know. I was just testing you, to see if you could stand to tell the truth."

"I know that you know everything. But you want me to say it out loud, write it down. Well, there's no such thing as writing out loud. Paradoxically, the signs that record the voice are silent. I wrote it down when I first saw a tree: 'My greatest vanity is knowing that everything in life is useless. You're born, you live, and you die. You disappear. Though curiously, *uselessness* needs life to become visible and demonstrate its great value.'"

"The term *uselessness* is easily misunderstood. I'm saying something, Jursafú, that you thought more than twenty years ago."

"But as you might have guessed, I don't think that now. By trial and error, I managed to figure out what it means to be useless. Of course, it still worries me that the people who control the wealth get to decide what every individual in the community is worth. It worries me so much, in fact, that I've taken a completely different approach: things that are truly valuable, or, in other words, things that are least offensive are totally useless in a utilitarian sense. Nonetheless, the same things are absolutely necessary for *love* and *knowledge,* without which one can never reach the hermetic meaning of human life on earth."

"But it's crazy to mix love and knowledge and to make one entity out of them both. One of them is enough to make you lose your senses. And if you do . . ."

"You may think it's crazy, but I don't. When I was with Constanza, I learned about the power of uselessness. I don't have to tell you this, but when you love someone the process of learning goes on and on. And thanks to Constanza . . ."

The light of the Andean afternoon filtered through the closed curtains of the memory. The cigarette that Constanza was holding in her left hand had burned out, and the gray ash was about to drop on the tablecloth. It was a miracle that it hadn't fallen yet. The brilliance of the shadows was contained in two ashtrays that rested on top of a rustic bookcase packed with books. Jursafú handed the girl one of the ashtrays, the one that looked like a precious Mayan object. She casually refused the offer, "That's too pretty to use. I'd rather use that plain aluminum one . . ."

"Saved by intuition!" cried the shadow. "When something is beautiful it often seems untouchable. And if Satan tempts you and you touch it, you die."

"Though they're just words, there are many antidotes for such threats. Anyone who dies from contact with beauty should find consolation in the words of a wayfarer from Sils-María: 'If there aren't any tombs in a place, there aren't any resurrections.' I've never seen the solitary hills of the Old World, but I've learned a few things on these scrubby plains. For example, I've learned that love is a springboard to profound truths. The force of Constanza's love made me see that the greatest instrument of knowledge, love, manifests itself in nakedness."

"*Nakedness, uselessness, knowledge*—these are very weighty things, Jursafú," said the shadow skeptically. "What is nakedness?"

"The opposite of possession. Lofty thoughts and feelings are diametrically opposed to ownership, which, paradoxically, lies in the vicinity of surrender. I've seen it born out in a number of relationships. All else seems a permanent, demonic temptation. Being tempted isn't the worst thing. It's being tempted all the time that's bad. Christ only gave Satan forty days."

"That's the way it had to be. It was impossible for Christ to be tempted by the devil. Gold represents the most precious thing to man, maybe because it disturbs him that it can only be purified with fire, the destroyer par excellence. The Son of Man is like pure gold, a material that can't be corrupted, but he's also a spirit that won't give in to any earthly temptation. How could Satan tempt him if he didn't need anything?"

"Sanguinetti said something similar to me once," Jursafú added.

"Your friend Sanguinetti is nothing more than a divulger of other people's knowledge. That dry, simple piece of logic was elaborated by the alchemists, whose glory has been reduced to mere hermetic triviality."

"I think you're talking about the ones who knew how to turn lead into gold and coal into diamonds. I have my reservations."

"My dear Jursafú, I'm not talking about a lot of tricksters. Here we pay homage to alchemists."

"Say what you may, my rule of thumb is if you can't do it, don't brag about it. In other words, I don't believe anybody can turn lead into gold. If it were possible, people would have made themselves a stash as big as all outdoors. I know people."

"Yes, but maybe I know them better. I don't look at them as if they were stationary pieces on a chess board, which is an advantage," the shadow sadly affirmed.

"I'm glad to know it," said Jursafú, cautiously. "The body offers a great range of possibilities as far as knowledge is concerned, yet its physical limitations must be respected. Despite its porosity, a human organism can't surpass its limits. A fully evolved body knows when it's getting too big for its britches. It knows what suits it and what doesn't. But people like to amuse themselves and sometimes their worldly games get the best of them. We know that some would kill for a grain of mustard, but despite their wild ambitions and vanities, they can be as happy as you please."

"But why do you say 'people'? Why do you exclude yourself?" asked the shadow.

"It's not that I exclude myself; it's just that I have my own world, without stars that are beyond my reach. I used to go to bed tired and wake up anxious. But now I've stopped trying to do what can't be done."

"But your exaggerated fear of death isn't exactly a sign of good health," argued the shadow.

"Yes, death . . . that's another matter," said Jursafú, by way of justification. "I hate to think of my destiny as being in the hands of a bunch of impudent fools."

"Jursafú," said the shadow compassionately, "the fundamental problem of existence is the impossibility of embodying the 'self' in an efficient manner. The flesh is terrified at having to accept a phenomenon that rules out its continuance—death. And paradoxically, the very knowledge that is needed for survival on earth arises from the primordial fear of not existing."

"I don't like hearing my body referred to as flesh. I'd rather say 'my body,'" said Jursafú, visibly frightened.

"It's the same thing," the shadow answered. "Your body must learn to accept the fact that it's going to die. That's the only way. On the other hand, when you lose a child, your soul accepts it. If you say 'I feel it in my soul,' you still haven't exhausted the vast universe of emotion. That's only a beginning. You, who often speak of the outrageous importance given to material possessions, use denial when it comes to your own body."

"It's not the same," said Jursafú, unable to overcome his fear. "My body is my only dwelling. It devours only what it must and tries not to hurt anyone. Besides, I don't own it; it's my 'self.' My body is like a stomach that will eventually devour itself, and thanks to the body, I can tell the difference between what is volatile and what is corporeal. But if you take my body away, I have no guarantee that I'll be able to sense corporeal things. I know what you're thinking, but what do these turkeys with machine guns know about doubt and certainty?"

"The body becomes accustomed to itself precisely because it doesn't see itself. That's why it resists its own demise. On the other hand, the so-called real and external aren't as weighty as we think. We can remember them or forget them. They are peripheral to the body. And we don't ever think about this because we never forget it."

"This conversation had to occur sooner or later. I suspected it from the beginning. But who are you anyway? There were times when I couldn't sleep for feeling your presence. You don't have a body, but even the roughest, most rudimentary universe couldn't exist without you."

"It's natural for it to be that way. And you got off course when you tried to remember what existed before you, what existed before you ever appeared amid the trees. You will perceive your true memory when you have gone and can say fittingly, but without words, 'I have been.'"

"I've caught you now, my dear shadow," Jursafú exclaimed. "Who's to say that I've never been a lizard, a tree, a flower, a bee, or the solid radiance of inanimateness?" ∎

The world suddenly bursts forth in unbroken silence. Jursafú doesn't know where he is. He imagines the soft hairs on Constanza's arms in the light of an afternoon, and he is overcome with gratitude, remembering the aroma of a darkened room where the noises of life entered like gentle doves taking flight from the hills of a city that is fearful, worn down, humiliated. Tormented by the interminable violence of the moment, he recalls the taste of her lips and manages to whisper, "All was written and all has come to pass. The man who never understands soon enough— since, for him, timely understanding seems impossible—is the only straggler; and now he's turning vinegar into wine."

He runs down the steps at full speed and reaching the ground floor he thinks he only has a short distance to go to reach the street. He's right. As soon as gets to the street, the nightmare will be over. It won't happen. Those who were ahead of him have stopped dead in their tracks before guards who are blocking the main door. Guards have stormed the advertising offices and have closed off the restaurant full of frightened customers. Jursafú's group has come to a violent halt. Some are standing near the elevators; others are peering into the restaurant. Just then, one of his co-workers, a fat, jolly prankster, lets out an absurd yell of combined fright and surprise, "But Wipo, *hermano,* what is going on!"

He has recognized one of the guards. But the guard, busy beating people with the butt of his machine gun, hasn't time to remember anyone, much less a jolly fat man whom he played cards with the night before. The prankster is completely taken aback, unable to believe that his friend of the night before, though only a casual acquaintance, is now holding him under aim with a machine gun. But that's what he gets for listening to the advice of so many so-and-sos: "Anything can happen in Bolivia. Poor country, five million inhabitants, four million of them illiterate but not stupid by any means. Of the remaining million—who've had some kind of schooling—a fraction are professionals. And out of that group, only a few ever read. Which makes it easy for the elite who run the country because they're always the same. The old conservatives have allowed their descendants to become leftists. No matter what the proclamation, revolutionary or otherwise, what really matters is staying in power. And if need be, the same people who governed as leftists can become moderates, moderate conservatives, or even fascists, as the Spanish say. The only bad part is that the process can rarely be reversed. It takes a miracle for a right-winger to evolve toward the Left. They don't come and go. Except Mauricio Santillán, who was such a miracle."

These people, on the other hand, whom the guards are threatening, are coming and going. Gripped by terror, he's also coming and going. The danger of violent death is so overwhelming that eventually he calms down and waits for the worst to happen. An electrical shock runs from his head down to his feet. This adventure called life is about to end, in front of a restaurant of all places, where people eat to live. "It's like dying of thirst at the edge of a watering hole," he once said to Policarpio Paucara in this same locale. Arciles must have introduced them, but they'd become friends on their own, and now the whole thing was just a blurred memory: he could see him with his cup of coffee, looking like a hardworking rural man, devoted to his origins.

Maybe Jursafú was being unjust, but he wasn't at all sure about politicians who had nothing in common with the people they represented, other than an "ideal." But in Policarpio's case it was different. He was from another time. The clothing he wore labeled him as a bearer of other landscapes, and he didn't dress that way just to show off on May Day. What looked natural on him, on others was a mere disguise. To the extent that it was humanly possible, he'd broken the barrier between the country and the city, which is especially hard to do in Bolivia. In other words, he was repeating the adventure of Federico Escóbar, the deceased leader of the mine workers' union who refused to speak the language of the city and as punishment was ostracized. He was more interested in the *ends* than the *means,* convinced as he was that between the means and the mediator there was a short step, and that between the mediator and the impostor there was only half a step. ■

"In my opinion, the historians haven't done right by Pedrito Perchin," said a man with glasses and a long beard. "He's managed to last for decades as the leader of the mine workers, but he's never been studied seriously. He's played an important role and it shouldn't be overlooked."

"Yes, amazing, isn't it?" affirmed another man with glasses and a beard. "Of course, there are other cases like his. Since the Chaco War the leaders really haven't changed; the ones who have been replaced died of natural causes and not because of the demands of conflict."

"Yes, you're right," added another, also with glasses and a beard. "The leadership hasn't changed and probably won't. Fortunately, it all goes to prove that certain of our colleagues have been right about social change in Latin America."

"Absurd, isn't it? If it weren't such an interesting place to live, frankly, I probably would have stayed in Lovaina," added a bearded man with glasses.

"Most of the leaders," affirmed a bearded man with glasses, "are sufficiently talented to see how things are developing in the modern world. When they've been in exile, they've made contact with scholars and other thinkers. I've met and talked with a lot of them personally, in Europe, and I'm convinced that, if the occasion should arise, they would support social change. But lamentably, they come back from exile and act like they never set foot out of the country."

"Why is that, do you think?" asked one of them curiously.

"I haven't the foggiest idea why it's impossible for these men to pass their own native Rubicon," one of them replied lighting up a Gauloise. "You, being a college graduate, would know that trends can't be predicted from purely circumstantial phenomena. However, in these particular circumstances, we may find some comfort in statistics. How many overthrown Bolivian presidents have gone to Europe and died because they couldn't live in the Old World? Not long ago I saw a picture of an Andean leader, an excellent photograph. The ex-leader had breathed his last breath in a small hotel in Florence. I doubt he hadn't enough money to come back to Bolivia. It's more likely that the current dictator decided he ought to die in exile."

"That's just an anecdote and doesn't help us solve the problem," complained a bearded man with glasses. "It's true that many Bolivian leaders have gone to Europe, but it's also true that many European leaders have come here and have adopted us as their second home and have died here."

"But there're some subtle differences," said a bearded man with glasses, requesting a drink from Helga, the owner of the house. "Don't forget about European racism. We've been victims of it ourselves. They, on the other hand, come here as if they were traveling to their colonies, with total confidence, because what they find here is a rough copy of the original they've left behind in their homeland. And what may seem culturally foreign to them, their fondness for folklore allows them to assimilate. Actually, there's no reason why it should affect them since even the country's inhabitants tend to overlook it. Paradoxically, the Bolivian elite, purveyors of the European or North American model, are like squatters in these parts, though they never forget to foment an outrageous nationalism. But when the bullet comes out the wrong end of the gun, they always go running off to the Old World. It's amusing, reading the letters exchanged by military and civil leaders, each taking their turn in exile, overwhelmed by the country's woes."

"But a lot of time has elapsed between the last century, to which you must be referring, and this one," said one of the bearded men with glasses, putting out his Gauloise. "It would be a mistake to judge the present by the values of the past, which have nothing to do with today."

"To the contrary, *licenciado*," said the bearded man with glasses. "It wouldn't be a mistake because basically nothing has changed. In their dealings in the capital, our leaders mimic the submissive conduct of their subordinates in the provinces; but in the provinces, they imitate the authoritarian conduct so typical in the nation's capital. Pedrito Perchin's success—viewed from this perspective—wasn't due so much to his loyalty to the miners' cause as to that sector's lack of ties with the city and, therefore, its need for a mediator, which just happened to be Perchin."

"Then you must think of Perchin as totally bilingual, or am I assuming too much?"

"No, not at all," replied the other. "Perchin can speak the miners' language just as well as he speaks the language of city folk. He's fluent and articulate in both, which is admirable and also makes it hard to tell which is his native language."

"No doubt, it must be hard to figure him out. I remember," added the bearded man with glasses, "that the tabloids tried to make him look ridiculous with a photograph of him walking his Pekingese, and they weren't exactly in Villa Victoria. Can you imagine Perchin behaving like an 'insensitive bourgeois'?"

"It's all relative, my friend," argued the other. "I guarantee you the miners must have been moved when Perchin, several decades ago, was willing to exchange his bourgeois lifestyle for a pair of overalls. In other words, a translator is a scoundrel if he doesn't say for whom he's translating. Or in biblical terms, wherever your treasure is, there also is your heart—or your native language."

"Of course, all that happened a long time ago," the bearded man with glasses reminded them, "when Perchin was one of the strong men in the Nationalist Revolutionary Movement."

"Or maybe you've got it backwards," corrected the bearded man with glasses. "The Movement was the ruling party and Pedrito Perchin was the strong man from the opposition."

"Was that when the government offered Perchin an ambassadorship in Europe?" asked the bearded man with glasses.

"Exactly," his friend replied, blowing a long stream of smoke and adding, "they tried to tempt him with an ambassadorship so he'd stop giving them hell about the miners' wages. And what's curious is that he accepted and packed his bags, leaving everyone who'd said he wouldn't do it standing there with their mouths open. From the door of the airplane, he shouted back to the reporters that he was very concerned about the economic difficulties facing the miners."

"What a jackass! The very least they should have given him was the firing squad," said the bearded man with glasses, crestfallen.

"Well, he didn't get the firing squad or anything else. As soon as he got back, the miners lifted him up on their shoulders and paraded him around. I wonder if they're as strong as Andean novelists make them out to be?"

"Yes, I wonder," said the bearded man with glasses, laughing. "The miners know what's going on, but they've learned to make concessions in their dealings with city people, just as the Bolivian elite has learned to be submissive in its dealings with people from the capital. But the results aren't the same."

"An interesting interpretation, my dear *licenciado,*" said the bearded man with glasses, emptying his goblet. "The truth is that nothing has changed, absolutely nothing. If you want proof, look at the photograph that came out in last week's *Publicidad.*"

"The one of the general slipping down in front of the cathedral? Some reporter set that up," claimed the bearded man with glasses.

"I'm not talking about that one, but it probably got a lot of laughs. The one that caught my eye was less spectacular but more revealing. The colonel who's the prefect of Cochabamba made the American ambassador an 'honored guest' of Bolivia; but that wasn't enough, so he presented him with an Aymaran scepter, which seemed to make him happy, though I doubt he realized that he'd been made a spiritual leader of the Aymaras."

"Bolivian presidents get the same treatment."

"But don't forget," the bearded man with glasses clarified, "that the Indians first look at all the foreigners in their country and then choose one of them for a patron, and that way they avoid problems with all the dangerous intermediators of power. A good way to get the system to work for you. I wish I could say the same for the prefect of Cochabamba."

"The colonel's gift to the ambassador implies a lack of imagination," replied the bearded man with glasses. "If you don't have any imagination you have to imitate and in this case what we've got is a poor imitation of Aymaran astuteness. In the name of Western democracy, the Bolivian commander has asked the gringo's permission to oppress his own people. And, of course, the request has been duly received, in the name of Western culture."

"Why does this surprise you?" asked the bearded man with glasses. "Why are you so perplexed? Since the fall of the Nationalist Revolutionary Movement, the military has been doing exactly as it did before. Except that it inherited some of the defects of the failed 1952 revolutionaries without picking up a single one of their virtues. Correct me if I'm wrong."

A bearded man with glasses came running into the room, and after catching his breath, said, "They've just arrested Policarpio Paucara."

Silence reigned over the entire city. A manifesto signed by the arrested leader had appeared in the deserted streets. Either no one had seen it or they were afraid to repeat its message: "We don't need to borrow heroes. We should be proud of who we are. Our ideology and our leaders should come from our own struggle. Tupac Katari isn't just a rural martyr. He is a sacred example of the people's resistance to domination. This country has been built with the blood and bones of the people. But the people . . ."

"That's the bad part," mumbled one of the bearded men with glasses. "After Pedrito Perchin gave in to the Ministry of Interior, things pretty much came to a standstill."

"How did it come about?" asked a bearded man with glasses.

"They shot him in the back," said the bearded man with glasses. "His backbone is full of holes. And besides that," he added, "he's implicated some other people. There was a scuffle on Buenos Aires Avenue and while he was fighting with the police, his address book fell out of his pocket, but as luck would have it, some little kid went running up to him saying, 'Hey, mister, you dropped this . . .'"

"It's not hard to imagine what's going to happen next," said a bearded man with glasses. "Book or no book, we've had it. We're trapped. The Interior Minister has already said it, 'Bolivians, write your wills.'"

"What would my will be?" Jursafú asks himself, looking half dazed at the men who've blocked off Pompilio Daza Avenue.

"It's curious, but the state of siege they've declared for the entire country isn't going to be noticed anywhere except in the cities," said the bearded man with glasses. "If you think about it, at this hour the Indians are peacefully making their way across the arid plains, and I'd like to see the man who could keep up with them much less catch one of them."

Jursafú's co-workers go tumbling down the steps. One stands up; one falls down. His *camba* colleague standing in front of an open elevator is tempted to jump in.

"We pay by leaving the country," said the bearded man with glasses, "while those who are to blame for our struggle move right along, happy as can be without a flicker of remorse."

The workers from the newspaper are flying in every direction. Some are coming; others are going, like bats out of hell. They catch their breaths and take off again as fast as they can.

"We're sticking our necks out, trying to resolve our country's problems," said the bearded man with glasses, "but not a damn thing happens."

Suddenly Jursafú hears a howl, not animal, not human, but the long-awaited release of someone discharging his terror in a way unfamiliar to most Bolivians—pure silence and resignation before the avatars of existence.

"What do you mean, nothing happens? In the country, people are dying for lack of a simple bottle of pills. And that's the truth of the matter, though you may not want to hear it."

"And something else that's true. You people are a little remiss, to avoid saying lazy. I don't mean to offend anyone, but every now and then we ought to face the truth."

"We aren't afraid of the truth. And we're not lazy either. Do you really know what's happening in the country, or is it just hearsay? Have you ever seen misery, even at a distance? Do you know what it's like to live and breathe poverty? To have nothing to put in your stomach and dream that you're eating? Have you ever pretended, even for an hour, that everything was hopeless? With all due respect, let me tell you something: rural people don't pretend to be fatalists; they're fatalists by experience. And experience has taught them not to depend on anyone, because if they do, they may fall flat on their faces. There's no two ways about it. They don't trust anyone and for good reason. I'm sure you know why, comrade. So you'd have to be a scoundrel to expect them to be calm and trusting. They live in constant fear, and they don't trust anyone except other ravaged people like themselves."

"Why do you say 'ravaged,' my friend?"

"Comrade, if you keep calling me your friend, I may get angry. But instead of getting angry, I'd rather lay out a couple of arguments. By 'ravaged' I mean people who haven't anything except their own strength. Do you ever wonder what they do on an afternoon while well-intentioned people like yourself are sitting by their windows watching the wind caress the begonias, araucarias, and bougainvilleas?"

"It's hard to imagine the two at once. No, I can't say that I do."

"That's what I thought. We're worlds apart. We don't even feel the same winds. I don't know why I even bother to ask you such a question, but at least don't lie to me. If a rural man gets sick and goes to a doctor, who knows what might happen to him? They might end up killing him for nothing. And since the doctor can't understand him, he doesn't know what hurts and what doesn't. But the man takes a chance and knocks on some quack's door. Then if he borrows money to pay the bills, they kill him with mortgages and interests; and they can always track him down. If he goes to school, there's always some teacher around to tell him he's retarded. And if he should ever hire a lawyer to defend himself against so much abuse, in a flash the whole thing can easily be turned against him."

293

"If you're talking about yourself, I'll be glad to help you if I can. I could talk to the prefect or the colonel. Not that we share the same ideas, but he owes my family so much that even I reap the benefits. I'm sorry, but that's the best that I can do."

"And why the hell do I need *your* recommendation. I'm Bolivian too. And I'm sick and tired of watching and waiting. But I keep on nibbling at my misery, trying to keep my fingernails clean."

"Maybe I haven't explained myself clearly."

"Maybe you haven't, but I'm tired of listening."

"Don't be that way. Misunderstandings can happen, even in the best of families. Why shouldn't they occur between people who are fighting for the same cause?"

"Yes, but if we continue, you may catch me off my guard and ask the impossible. Your friendship could end up costing me a mule and its foal."

"Let's forget about personal things and get back to the original topic. The problems of the rural people have nothing to do with the system, and the solution is obvious: make them part of the country's progress, the progress of all Latin America, by force if necessary. Science has its use; and technology, no matter how sophisticated, has only one goal—to benefit society. We can't go on living like animals, and we may have to take drastic measures . . ."

"And you, comrade, what are you if not an animal sitting behind the wheel of an automobile? But that aside, nothing, I mean nothing, is going to be done by force. Would you like me to force a can of rotten sardines down your throat? It would make you sick to your stomach, wouldn't it? So why don't you understand that it would make others sick too? And last, I'd like for you to know that your ideas aren't new. You're ignorant, you've allowed yourself to be deceived, and you need to realize that. Rural people are used to lies and misery. That's all they've ever had. And that applies to every aspect of life, comrade. A rural family is happy if three out of eight children survive. They love deeply but never get too attached to people or things. But to understand that paradox, you have to know what it's like to live in a washed-up world, to live on the edge of an abyss, holding onto the weeds to keep from sliding in. Have you ever heard the expression, 'A poor man's joy is the end of his sorrow'?"

"Comrade, please . . . stop exaggerating. The rural people, as you call them, are moving to the city to test their luck, and that's fine; but they're abandoning the land . . ."

"So there's no one to raise the potatoes that you eat, of course. I've heard that argument a thousand times. The truth of the matter is that they have to give up everything in an effort to make a better life for their children. You'd have to walk in their shoes to know as much as they do. The intellectuals and the politicians say one thing, and the rurals, knowing another, follow their advice, with only their faith to sustain them."

"And what is that faith, comrade?" ■

Jursafú said to himself, "This scoundrel is trying to pull my leg, but he's not going to get away with it."

At the international exhibition in Kassel, he found himself surrounded by gringos. The celebrities of the modern art world had gathered there, including the best critics, of world renown. But no one was more curious than Jursafú, and he, a mere layman, had come to this German industrial town and was now on one of the lighted patios of the exhibition hall eyeing a large chunk of twisted iron that had diagonal saw marks running through it. The artist's purpose was clear enough, but his work elicited no aesthetic response. So Jursafú smiled and muttered an opinion to himself, "This scoundrel is trying to pull my leg."

Suddenly a Norwegian, of about sixty years, was standing by his side with a tape recorder in his hand, the typical leather bag over his shoulder, and the required note pad sticking out of the inside pocket of his jacket. Jursafú looked again at the large iron figure and then walked from hall to hall until he came to one of the smaller rooms where again he encountered the Norwegian, absorbed in the dated brush strokes and blots of paint of a large, white canvas. Breaking through the linguistic barrier, he asked the Norwegian what he thought about modern painting.

The sixty-year-old man responded, "Compared with the experiments of the modern spirit, the blood transmitted by rural people is a guarantee of certainty." He calmly noted something on his pad and then added, speaking slowly and serenely: "I'm an art critic; it's my job, and that's why I'm here. What I'm saying is that I can't ignore these artistic trends, I must familiarize myself with them. But as for what I feel, I can't say that they inspire any sort of aesthetic feeling, and it's not because of a lack of sensitivity on my part. Their failure to interest me has another cause. For centuries my relatives have plowed the earth, and my family are still farmers, except for me, of course. But that experience must affect me; otherwise, how can I explain my refusal to accept as art experiments and objects that I understand with absolute clarity?" Someone was motioning to him from another room. "Art that isn't felt doesn't last. Good-bye, my friend."

He hurriedly walked away, speaking rapidly in another language to his friends, a language that was incomprehensible to Jursafú, who also passes into another dimension as he receives the last blows to his ribs. He runs across Pompilio Daza Avenue as fast as his legs can carry him. Some of his friends run in one direction and some in another. He decides to join the crowd on the other side of the street. Though he doesn't know it, his friend Guillermo Soliz, a messenger at the newspaper, is right beside him. Now they're among the crowd and can relax. They walk for a stretch without opening their mouths. Since Guillermo is bound by promises that a businessman could never understand, they walk along for another stretch without saying anything.

Seeing him, he remembers; or remembering, he sees him. He first noticed him one afternoon a long time ago. It was a pleasant time for everyone except Guillermo Soliz, who had such a terrible pain in his stomach that he fell down writhing on the floor in the editing room. They immediately carried him to a hospital. Some months later, when the two of them were talking about illnesses and sudden death, Guillermo told him that after his attack he fainted, and he woke up in the operating room, surprised to find himself wearing a white gown. But he was even more surprised to see shiny surgical instruments on the table beside him, which removed all doubt concerning where he was and what was going to be done to him. They were going to split him open like a lizard. Not at all pleased at the prospect, he jumped up and ran out of the hospital without stopping to put on his pants.

He never had another stomachache, which is a blessing, considering how fond he is of parties. He earns a pittance but manages to save enough so he can dance like a fool at the festival of Nuestro Señor Jesús del Gran

Poder. On a somewhat different scale, he was repeating the experience of the camel: he drank once a year in order to sustain himself for twelve long months in the desert.

"This year the parade is going all the way to 16 Julio Avenue," Guillermo Soliz had told him.

But there wasn't any parade this year, only a river of fear washed into the deserted city. On more propitious occasions, an unending stream of multicolored dancers, viewed by a wide array of tourists, had moved down the street toward the government center. The back and forth movement of diverse elements was like the process that preceded the acceptance of new terms—which originated from contact with Aymara and other indigenous languages—into the official language.

From time to time, the government authorities tried to revitalize the city's traditions by allowing more ancient rites to be performed, such as the *ch'alla,* a yearly tribute to the Mother Earth, who on occasion had spilled blood in order to establish her preeminence in the deserts of rock and transparency. The experts on such simple matters have complicated the natural processes by using inflated terms like "ethnofolklore" and "transculturalization." Guillermo doesn't know the jargon and prefers to use an example, demonstrating the comfort he feels among his own traditions. He's a real Andean, and at the festival of Jesús del Gran Poder he dances like a wild man in the traditional parade of folkloric groups.

"Where could you go to be valued more and despised less?" asks Jursafú in a playful tone.

"Yes, *don,* you're exactly right, *don.* There's no where to go," replies Guillermo Soliz. ■

"This is our country. Where could we possibly go to be valued more and despised less?" wonders Jursafú reaching his own door. He looks at the rough objects that are his only possessions, elementary in their modesty but of singular worth to him. They are furnishings he made when he was sad, trappings of a past life spent in the warmth of family and friends. A lovely light enters the room as if to announce that the peacefulness of the afternoon is still possible in distant worlds. He becomes sad and feels alone amid the small number of objects which speak to him of a universe where the joy of life has dwelled. He puts out the light of his hope, better to see the course of his ideas. He meditates on the mysterious power of actions, knowing that each one of them conceals the enigma of the protagonist's not knowing under what circumstances the action will be remembered. He made the rough chairs in Villa Fátima, without a care, not realizing that he was building them to see them later in their true dimension, illuminated by the passing of time and by the exemplary light of love and misunderstanding. He suddenly realizes that what he has just lived he will later remember, though he can't say where that might be, ignorant of the power of his nostalgia. This house isn't his, just as none of the places he's lived in since childhood are his; and sometimes he occupied them illegally, though always with respect, as one who lives and dies within their walls. In this house, or in any other, he might relive the nightmare of seeing the city destroyed and then running with his children toward a safe, barren land. "Everything seems foreign to me except the shelter of my own body," he thinks, running his fingers over his skin. He is a little sore where they hit him, and this is the third, perhaps the fourth time that he's experienced such a thing. And as in the past, it occurs to him to change vinegar into wine by performing some ordinary task or by writing.

"The first paragraph of a story should contain a summary of what you want to communicate to the reader," the editor-in-chief had told him. "Journalists are supposed to be truthful, objective, and concise."

"Concise."

The editor-in-chief had smiled, "Yes, don't run on forever. You'll wear out your reader. Nobody's got the time."

He'd accepted the recommendation, not taking into account so-called objectivity, which he considers an illusion. "Any day they could kill me or I could die. The objective world will continue undisturbed, but my subjective world will have come to an end, unable to speak about the deserts of rock and transparency. In summary," Jursafú conjectures, "objectivity belongs to immortals, or it may flicker through the brains of those who watch a game of chess. Here, objectivity is synonymous with impartiality, which can be a virtue or a symptom of apathy. No. I prefer the serious saying of a dead friend: 'The only important news, the news of our own death, we'll never read in the newspaper.'" ∎

He got out of bed, unsure what day it was. He could only perceive the music of a universe paused on the brink of destruction. As impossible as it seemed, he'd managed to escape the nightmare, but now he missed it, just as survivors of an accident miss their last glimpse of the wreckage. He washed his face, drank a couple of matés, and abandoned his dark room. Out on the street, he began to walk as if in a dream. He followed his usual route, and by the light of the street lamps could see the usual couples, sheltered by the world's shadows, assailed by the illusion that they were participating in something primordial.

"People in love are likely to get themselves run over by a truck. They're put off guard by an energy that binds them together and separates them from the rest of the world," Jursafú said to himself, examining his own indolence and sensuality, which were always on alert, from an infinite perspective. Pushing his memories to one side, he fixed his eyes on a point on the other side of the city, a place high on a mountaintop that for him held special meaning. He stopped for a second to look for the exact spot, and though it was far away, he began to walk in that direction, quickly, knowing that sooner or later he would have to reach his destination.

He followed a path that he had traveled on many occasions, accompanied by a poet who was rumored to be insane. But there was no basis to it. To the contrary, he had shown himself to be sensible when many had lost their wits, and to act normal in situations in which his cohorts had bared their teeth and flashed their knives. Jursafú knew that his friend was a member of the Bolivian Communist Party, but they had spent some pleasant times together, talking about anything, perceiving the sacredness of human emotion and detecting the costly illusions of some they knew who'd suffered the repressive hand of the Nationalist Revolutionary Movement. His friend's insanity was nothing more than an escape, a respite. ■

"When you think you work, and when you work you rest," said the crazy poet Tarairí de los Montes, without a pause.

Jursafú was astounded by this lively creature who, by some secret method, had learned to content himself with little but to love life as if he had a lot. He approached life guardedly, as Jursafú discovered one Monday in 1965 when invisible strings guided him toward Tarairí's neighborhood, a miserable corner of of La Paz, a sunny spot where people had crowded together to enjoy a free recitation by Tarairí de los Montes; and the poet was happy too, because his books were selling like hotcakes.

"Comrade! How are you? What's new?" inquired the poet, who was standing in a doorway near the Bolivian controller's office.

"The only thing that's new," lied Jursafú, "is that the country's most important critic has finally taken note of your work."

Tarairí didn't respond. There was no way to know if he was simply credulous or had long ago taken leave of the world of praise and adulation.

"He says that at the very least your poetry is a sincere and original contribution to Bolivian literature," Jursafú added, "referring, of course, to the poetry of the last few decades."

"Now I know you're lying," said Tarairí de los Montes, smiling. "It's a fish's mouth that gets it into trouble, comrade. If you'd closed yours sooner, I might have believed part of what you were saying. But you went too far. It's absurd to think that anyone would pretend to understand my poetry, much less praise it. Comrade, let me tell you something I've known for a long time. Nobody is going to understand what I've written for at least five hundred years. Then people will study it and understand it. But no one's going to understand it now."

Then Tarairí de los Montes burst out laughing, as did Jursafú. They were old friends and joked with each other about everything. When Jursafú first knew the poet, he thought that he said the word "comrade" with a warmth that welled up from the greatest depths of human sincerity. He could find no rational explanation, but his friend's throat became somehow nobler when he pronounced the word, and perhaps for that reason he repeated it often. It was a habit, nonetheless, that eventually got him into trouble. Some man heard him say "comrade" and, wheeling around with a scowl on his face, asked him if he was a communist; and Tarairí, unable to lie, said he was, and besides, had no qualms about screaming to the rafters, "I'm a communist, by damn, and proud of it." So they beat the stew out of him, but he wouldn't take it back. However, as they say, the soul resists but not the body. He got out of jail with a terrible case of whooping cough and by the time he reached Vallegrande, his lungs were very inflamed. After a few rough months, he returned to the City of Illimani.

Jursafú ran into him one winter morning at the Camacho market, apparently in good health and with a big smile on his face, except that the smile emerged from a face that was so white it caused alarm.

"You're a sight for sore eyes! I see you've managed to recover."

"Of course, I recovered just as everyone recovers, but the cause of socialism is immortal," he affirmed with an optimism tinged with suffering.

"But regardless, Tarairí, there are laws. What they did wasn't right, but no one has been punished."

De los Montes became serious. "Comrade, you're either an incorrigible idealist or a fool. How can you put stock in bourgeois laws? We're fighting for the dictatorship of the proletariat, and it would hardly do for us to appeal for protection to a system we're trying to destroy. I could get kicked out of the party just for mentioning such a thing. I'm not that big of a fool!"

Tarairí de los Montes repeated the party slogans like a parrot. It was obvious that he was trying to put up a stiff front and above all to prove his loyalty to the ideology of Marx and Lenin. But his imagination was way ahead of his method and eventually made a shambles of what his militant spirit had so eagerly ordered and classified.

"Of course, Tarairí," Jursafú replied, "but torture is a violation of human dignity. And besides, you should have stayed in La Paz instead of running off to Vallegrande, without a word to anyone."

"I can accept what you say about torture, but the rest, comrade, no. According to my way of thinking as a militant socialist, making oneself the victim is like feeling nostalgia for the brutal power of the oppressor. So, comrade, you won't catch me complaining. I'm being totally frank: you'll never hear a word of complaint out of me. You've just been a witness to my conviction. Now, comrade, ask me how I feel. Ask me if Tarairí de los Montes is in perfect health and ready to make important decisions. As you might guess, my answer will always be the same. No matter who asks, I must respond quickly and automatically, 'Yes, comrade, I'm fine.' And do you know why?"

"Well, of course. Because you're fine and it would never occur to you to tell a lie."

Tarairí's interlocutor was captivated not only by the dialogue but also by the fact that while he employed the familiar *tú* with the poet, Tarairí addressed him as *usted,* and strangely enough, it didn't seem the least bit incongruous.

"No, comrade, that isn't the reason. The reason is that I have to be okay because no one else can be okay for me," Tarairí replied and then burst out laughing. "Comrade, there are extreme situations when no one can take our places. And misery and happiness are two of them."

"I'm glad you feel that way," said Jursafú. "If I understand what you're saying, none of us are necessary but none of us can be replaced, and therefore it's important to be okay. Of course, there are probably conceptual differences that only a socialist would understand."

"Yes, I think you're right, comrade," Tarairí replied and then asked his friend another question, "And do you know what the key is to always being okay? Anyone who wants to become a socialist ought to know this by heart . . ."

"Well, I want to be a socialist, but I can't say that I know," replied Jursafú, realizing that between one thing and another, he was falling prey to his interlocutor's implacable logic. He remained silent, walking along next to the poet and admiring him for his stamina. He looked at the sky and saw that it was bathed in a light that reconciled him with former illusions. He perceived the splendor of the earth and the beauty of life.

"I'll tell you what it is," Tarairí finally said, "and I hope I'm not wrong in thinking you're one of the ones who's been picked to perform a difficult revolutionary task. The key, comrade, is very simple, which doesn't make it any less powerful. Don't forget that it's a *truth* and like any truth it took a long time for it to evolve into a proverb, or a parable if you prefer. 'Don't ever make a habit out of anything, not even a whore.' That's the key. Because for a revolutionary, habit is more important than life itself." ∎

Jursafú's temples ached from thinking so long about a world that had long since disappeared. Busy listening to voices from the past, he didn't notice that he had already reached Plaza Gualberto Villarroel. His eyes surveyed the large green space that bore the name of the martyred president, a late homage, no doubt, to the green-eyed individual who had deserved political and human consideration from the deceased Jorge Arce. In the large square that sloped toward Miraflores, children continued playing under the diffuse light of an indifferent sky, ignorant of the history of a country that in some sense protected them, with its diverse climates and adverse course of tragedies. One of the children was running after a ball that rolled down the hill into the darkness.

In those days past, he too was a child, enraptured by the aromas of the forest, disoriented by the voices of his elders.

"Did you know the colonel?"

"I knew him when I saw him, nothing more. I was the best marksman in the regiment at Ibibobo, which had the best marksmen in the whole region. I'm not lying, though I had a hard time believing it myself. The colonel said he wanted me to go to La Paz and join the presidential guard. I didn't much like the idea of being sent to the palace, because once you're there, my son, you never get out alive. You either end up stiff as a lizard; or you might end up filling somebody else full of holes. It all depends on who shoots first. But not even animals should be killed in cold blood and people even less, no matter how mean they are. So I said no, I wouldn't join the guard."

"But they say he was a good man."

The old woman responded, "Yes, we always remember the dead as being good. You know why, don't you?"

"Don't tell me you actually knew the colonel with the green eyes!"

"Well of course I did!" the old woman exclaimed, annoyed by her interlocutor's doubt.

She was a happy old woman with beautiful green eyes and distinguished features that must have been handsome in her youth. She'd had too much to drink and was becoming hysterical.

"I come from the Yungas," she said, lost in reverie. "They brought me here when I was just a girl, and I never left my aunts' house because I didn't know the city. It was a big house about three blocks from Plaza Murillo, though I've forgotten exactly where it was. I'd been in La Paz only a week before the fighting broke out. That was the twenty-first of July, 1946. One of my aunts said to me, 'Vicky, don't go out, child, don't go out of the house.' But I slipped out that evening and walked through the dark, abandoned streets. I was frightened, wandering around like a lost soul, not knowing where I was going . . ."

"So what was he like, the colonel with the green eyes?"

"As I was saying, the streets were empty. I only saw one soldier, at least I thought he was a soldier. I thought I could see people running in the distance, being swallowed up by the darkness. Then a shadow came creeping along like a cat and passed close by my side. Dear God, I was scared! I heard it say, 'What are you doing here, little girl? Run along home.' Then it continued along the street. But I didn't pay it any mind and just kept on walking . . ."

"According to what I've read, that was a terrible ordeal. What do you think, Doña Vicky Rada?"

"It was just the same as it is today. A lot of gunfire and a lot of dead people. Just the way it is now. I managed to get to the square. I'm not sure how. He was hanging there naked. That's how I got to know Colonel Gualberto Villarroel. Dear God, how I took off running! I'm from the Yungas, you know . . ." ■

Jursafú leaves Plaza Villarroel and enters the section called Villa Fátima. It's been a long time since he was there, and he finds the many changes disconcerting: paved streets, a steady stream of vehicles, some small, some large. The smaller trucks are from the city; the larger ones have come from the Yungas, bringing people as well as tropical fruit. This is a "favored" zone of the city; in other words, it has provisions of all kinds, whereas before there was nothing, and the people had to walk to the top of the hill. Jursafú climbs the steep slope that he used to climb, and far from being tired, he suddenly catches his second wind. An unexpected peace comes over him.

"Villa Fátima has changed, Zapopeta," says Marcos Salazar. "You'd get lost, Zapopeta. You always got lost."

"There isn't time, Zapopeta."

"Time, time, there's time to spare, Zapopeta." Marcos Salazar's laughter, full of goodness and an incurable irony, is the same as always.

Jursafú walks over to the window and looks out as though he were seeing the city for the first time, the great illuminated city, paralyzed in the dreams of unknown beings. It's ten o'clock at night, more or less. Midnight hasn't arrived. The blood beats to the rhythm of a neutral moment. Something washes over the images of the past and restores them to a jubilant present which is different and yet identical for inorganic life. At dawn, this sky, this light, and the purring of existence take on a different tonality. It is a setting shared by people who exhaust their energy—though not their happiness—in the toil of daily life.

"You remember that Aymara word? What does it mean, Zapopeta?"

"Which word do you mean, Zapopeta?"

"Aruskipasipxañanakasakipunirakispawa."

"Don't ask me that, Zapopeta, or I'll have to whip you."

Jursafú sits slowly eating the *ocas*, devouring the *chuño*, and drinking a beer, feeding off his hope that someday he will put his experiences into words, with all the vim and vigor he can muster.

A thought as cutting as reality pops into his mind: "La Paz is a city controlled by terror," and then the images of men being shot against enormous walls, the back of a Guarani's neck waiting for the bullet, and the incommensurable Latin American night. It's a long time before the beginning of another day, and he knows that he cannot sleep. He prepares himself to stay awake.

The Other and the Dead Man
as Jursafú Sees Them

My head is a broad, stony ground; those who go away do not return,
and those who are due to come do not arrive. That is why I am leaving:
I do not pray to saints who perform no miracles.

In 1961, when I first arrived in La Paz, I had no place to spend the night, which is why two or three times a week I would climb Landaeta Street to visit my friend Argel. I would go in hopes of getting a good night's sleep, but in order to get there, I had to make friends with a ferocious dog that acted as if it owned the entire neighborhood. It's the honest truth. The dog waited for me every night, blocking the winding path that I usually followed, and as you might guess, there were many times when I was forced to sleep on the street.

If I was able to get past the dog, then I would sit silently in my friend's room until he returned, the reason being that the room didn't belong to Argel. He was a temporary guest of the house's owner, just as I was his temporary guest.

One night as I sat waiting for my friend's return, I was frightened out of my wits by an unexpected visitor; though in the long run, it was to my good, taking into account that I hadn't a single *real* to my name. Because the visitor was none other than Ciscar Zenteno, a man from Tarija, who'd left his native valley to find work toasting coffee for the owner of the mansion; and it was he who provided me with a way to disguise my poverty. But I should say from the beginning that though Ciscar Zenteno was undeniably smart, his intelligence was totally blocked by his inability to read or write.

While my friend Argel roamed the streets till the late hours of the night and then entered the house by the front door, I became close friends with Ciscar, the proof being that by the third visit, he stole a bottle of milk from the kitchen and presented it to me like a trophy. Such a gesture of friendship required a sacrifice on my part, so I drank the entire bottle without blinking an eye, though the sight of milk could give me diarrhea.

Ciscar Zenteno liked to talk about farming more than anything else, and once we'd found our topic, which he discussed with great emotion, the rest was easy. Even stone sober, he could sing all the tunes of his district, which is a lot to say for someone who isn't a songster by trade. One night, as a joke, I asked him to sing. And he sang. I felt a little uncomfortable at first because I thought he'd turn me down. In my experience, singing without the benefit of wine, no matter how good the person's voice, had always seemed a little unnatural. Fidgeting in my seat, I sat waiting for him to finish, and as he was coming to the end of a song, I promised myself never again to make such a request.

Like a good rural man, Ciscar maintained a lively correspondence with natural phenomena. In other words, he always knew exactly when a storm was brewing, or when the rains would be light, which was the best time for planting lettuce and carrots. If the rivers began to swell, he became anxious, but thanks to his expert predictions, he was always able to save his crops. On starlit nights, he would look at the shadows of the moon and know what kind of year to expect. And like a good *valluno*, which was what we called the people who lived in the valleys, he would limit his predictions to his own barren hills without venturing to guess what might happen in regions that held no special interest for him.

He'd never left his native valley, not even to take a look at the other farmers' sheep. When he decided to come here, he made his plans in a very determined way and with a specific goal in mind, but the high Andean plains eventually put him off course; and at present, more than anything else, he was just homesick. His salary was larger than usual, which was some compensation, but the leisure it afforded him was useless for a man all alone. Yet Ciscar wasn't the kind to become discouraged at the first sign of trouble. And he wasn't especially impressed when I told him that in my district we had thirteen different knots for tying up a pig so as not to damage its legs. He admitted knowing only twelve and began to demonstrate with a piece of houseline, calmly and patiently, and with an assurance common to people who never make a mistake. After he'd proved his skill as a muleteer, he waited around for a few minutes so I could show him the missing knot. Then he went for bread and coffee.

As the evenings passed, Ciscar Zenteno became more and more friendly, and we began to share supper and the items that his family sent from Tarija. And though our trust in each other seemed to grow, the conversation never strayed from the strict course set by the *valluno;* in other words, we never talked about anything except farming. Nonetheless, the day of enlightenment finally arrived for both of us. After drinking some red wine, Zenteno took a letter out of his pocket that cast serious doubt on his marketability in the world of credits and debits. "I want you to read it to me," he said dryly. And, of course, I read it to him just as if it had been addressed to me. According to his parents, they were in need of extra hands to prepare the soil, and they'd gotten less rain that year than the year before. Everyone was in good health, thank goodness, and the spotted cow had given birth to a pretty calf. In the postscript they said that his gear and clothing were in the hands of his friend Eulogio Gálvez. They didn't mention the lovely Florinda, which was perplexing, but he accepted it nonetheless.

Over the next two months, I read several letters for him, knowing that sooner or later I would become Zenteno's scribe. And I did become his scribe and performed my duties to the best of my ability. But realizing that a dependency should never become a vicious habit, one night I suggested that he begin to educate himself. "Well, since you don't know how to write, you might at least learn how to read." This wasn't an especially logical proposition, as any first grade teacher might know, because reading and writing are like twin animals that drink from the same trough. Ciscar was prepared to challenge my implacable logic because, pointing to a line in a letter he'd just received from his parents, he replied boldly, "Read, of course, I can read. I just can't say the words out loud." Those were the last words I ever heard spoken by that sincere human being. I hope I was a good friend to Ciscar Zenteno, as he was to me. I wrote a lot of letters for him, transcribing his invariable concern for parsley and chicory; and I read every letter that arrived from his beautiful but untranslatable universe, nostalgic, full of certainty, and illuminated by his memory of a girl with long braids who was called Florinda Gálvez.

I don't know what happened to Ciscar Zenteno, but what happened between the two of us was kept secret to prevent the details of a faithful friendship from circulating freely, like mere gossip. In his district nothing was considered trivial. To the contrary, everyone was thought to have a destiny which must be seized arduously, the proof being that my friend took his leave in a noble fashion, without making a sound; and maybe that is why his image still glistens in my memory like a leaf drenched in the darkness of a tropical storm. I understand that this freshly printed image is an inferior product of my imagination. But if I'm not allowed the privilege of invention, then I will point out that the empty spot in my life, produced by my friend's departure, was filled by the Other, whose story I can relate only if I'm allowed to tell it "bit by bit"—which is what he used to say when he was trying to order his life without denouncing the madness of spending it recklessly in the streets of the world.

Okay, we'll take it bit by bit.

Last week I was searching for a particular passage among the books of my very reduced library, and just as I was tiring of such a tedious endeavor, I ran across some annotations that, thanks to this insolent scribe, were beginning to make some sense:

> The dogs get the best meat.
> It's easier for dead things to exist.
> Where could you go to be valued more and despised less.
> Not just fire but trees and sleeping dogs. All the things that exist without causing any trouble to anyone, burn and give more pain than fire itself, once a person has left the road.
> Where there are mares, there are colts—some better than others.
> While you're turning on the light, you must accept the darkness.
> There's no sacrifice in remaining silent provided the silence knows your name.
> What's the rich man going to sing about if he has no troubles to bemoan?
> Remain silent, keep each thing in its place, and maintain a healthy respect for disorder.

Let the dogs bark and the roosters crow so I can tell where I am.

When the dark light is singing, I decipher nothing, so I allow you to be my guide. The music of the unknown I know quite well, which should explain my terrible excitement.

Let us be on our way, for there are many more to come; and they must receive hugs and kisses as have we.

He remembered his family again with great tenderness. He knew the time had come for him to go. He sat quietly in thought until the clock tower struck three. He watched the world grow light. Then his head dropped to his chest and weakly he drew his last breath.

It's a dog's life.

Doubtless, the Other had never heard the story of Akakiy Akakievich and his adventure in the city, "which got along perfectly well without him, just as if he hadn't existed at all." And even if he'd heard it, I doubt he would have included it in the above text which, with the exception of the paragraph by Franz Kafka, is a collection of things I jotted down when I was in Paris—under a variety of circumstances—as well as some popular sayings that were common in Gran Chaco Province. A wild combination and not without humor, as suited the author who was affectionately called the Other.

This sketchy introduction is little more than a springboard to my last meeting with the Other, which took place on December 31, 1980, the day he said good-bye to the Callawaya, Marcos Salazar, and walked down the steep slope from Villa Fátima thinking about the awful thing that had happened to him at his office.

I'm surprised that I find it necessary to include such minute details.

He reached his room and for several hours did some work. Then he went out, thinking he'd spend the rest of the day with Laura and the children. But as he was locking the door, he had the strange sensation of having seen his cherished possessions for the last time: the container of maté, a few books, and five pieces of bark that he kept as a reminder of the trees in his province. Maybe he felt that way because of a need to rest at the end of a year that had been busy but lonely, or because of the formal embrace he had to suffer before beginning a new solar cycle.

"An inconvenience that others might call happiness," he thought, walking away in the dim light. He was expecting something out of the ordinary to happen and found the serenity and indifference of the light somewhat disarming. He looked across at the trees on the next hill and the sad lights of the houses whose shabbiness became apparent with the light of day.

He felt in touch with the world of shadows and paused mechanically for a moment before starting up the interminable row of steps, which were easier on the legs than on the heart.

Modest, melancholy, and with his usual nobility of spirit, he blended into the darkness and began preparing himself for the long-rehearsed question: "Who am I?"

It was a laughable question and a complete waste of time because the Other knew exactly who he was, but, paradoxically, he was always surprising himself. To put it briefly, everything that went on inside his body was a variation on a central action that in the last few years had been repeated with such devotion that his senses had become very perceptive. And though he was well prepared to weather any storm, he became quite docile when confronting the sensual offerings of life.

Before reaching the flat ground, which offered a lovely view, he was overwhelmed by a terrible certainty: never again would he embrace Orana. His dreams suddenly fled from his mind, and he began to feel like someone was holding a knife at his throat. That special light settled in his eyes which caused him to view life with a feverish gratitude for all that was distant and eternal. The present couldn't hold back the immensity, but he, who could grasp it in an instant, was no longer any use in the present. He remained at the lookout, perhaps disturbed at the notion of looking down on the hills from an even greater altitude. He didn't realize that he'd have to stay there forever on that spot, at first respectfully breathing in the air, hoping to blend it with the warm breeze of his native plain. He was surprised at wanting nothing, absolutely nothing, not even his modest memories, which is what he usually wanted, certain that they could offend no one or deprive anyone of anything. He didn't feel lost or feel that he would ever again need the kind of orientation that people usually require. He tried to pronounce a word to see if he was still alive, but all that came out was an aroma of vegetable silence; life's hallucination had been spoiled by the definitive good-bye. ∎

The actual exchange of gunfire was brief; though isolated shots were often heard during that night of violence. Shadows slipped into the darkness, and others seemed to emerge behind the steps of the executioners. The street corner was suddenly populated with dead people and ghosts. There was nothing except an ominous, unending silence ready to growl at any moment, like a caged animal. And then the soft, friendly sound of the river, the inconstant image of immutable time, the channel by which dreams slip away.

At that moment I remembered that "writing, with its silence, can rescue the human voice," an impoverished version of the saying, "the stomach eventually devours itself," which the Other was particularly fond of. And at the same time I realized that I would never hear the Other's voice again, though on occasion I said to myself, with his rural innocence, that "I could hold on to his voice but not his word."

According to an ancient belief, the universe is *real*, but its geography is so vast that we actually think of it as something fictional. *Reality* is the opposite of what we call *fiction;* and between these two extremes lies a lovely spectrum that allows for an infinite number of variations. The land of gold exists, but it lies at the most distant point, depending on the illusions of the beholder—individuals, of course, who are the most faithful conveyors of reality, and also palpable samples of fiction, the flesh and bones of shadows, as many poets have said. Because as soon as they become aware of their ephemeral condition, they disappear. But this kind of *consciousness* only develops in situations of crisis, when we stop to ask ourselves, for example, "What should we call the things around us?"

At this point, my Bolivian experience advises me to list about half a dozen examples of so-called situations of crisis: love, death, travel, work, God, and the devil. These are the materials that ordinary people use to weave their lives, and on numerous occasions, they have turned them into myths or used them as toeholds to keep themselves from plummeting into the abyss. I've omitted landscape from the list since it is implicit in the subject who creates or suffers through situations of crisis, in their varied forms and combinations.

The country where you're born is always visible in your face. And the fact that nowadays, at the end of the twentieth century, people tend to appear anonymous doesn't alter the basic truth of what I've said. To the contrary, it proves it by exception. Maybe Danes, Norwegians, or Germans say very little with their faces, but people born in the Third World, in Latin America, for example, are living maps, faithful, magical replicas of their geographic surroundings.

All this is explained by the fact that the "first people" of the world, Third World citizens par excellence, have nearly lost touch with nature, while the "second people," bored with their "marginality," still haven't freed themselves from the yoke of the landscape; in other words, they haven't been able to transform it into words. The populace of any region of this continent of hope might offer compelling evidence. In Bolivia there's proof to spare, a bounty of living examples of man's relationship to nature. Take the *tarijeño,* for example, whose voice and walk echo in the valleys and dales of Tarija, with their wide variety of trees, their deep rivers, and aromatic twilights. The same could be said of *paceños*—people from La Paz—and *cruceños*—people from Santa Cruz. Or, wandering toward the shores of Sagrado Lake or the Mamoré River, one might say the same of the inhabitants of those regions.

Bolivia is a tribute to brevity and synthesis; and in that sense—as the junk pile of the continent—its vast and varied territory brings together all the nationalities of Latin America. But "every person is cut to the size of his country." In other words, as Bolivians we possess the mystery of all authentic creations, that is, instead of floundering in ambiguity, as those who can't see beyond their own noses think we do, we reject and destroy, and are reborn and rebuilt from our own ruins. And to conclude the paradox, our growth has occurred in a reverse manner: the population hasn't increased so much, yet we feel more and more cramped. The changes have been substantial and often painful and have given us a special outlook, one that allows us to survive disaster as well as fashion—the greatest disaster of all.

We must realize that the period prior to our country's birth wasn't a happy time; to the contrary, the most important men of the War of Independence, Simón Bolívar and Antonio José de Sucre, wrangled endlessly over the destiny of the peoples who would build the nation in which we now live. In spite of everything, the youngest man got his way and founded a nation that would bear the name of the man who refused to be its father. That's where the entanglements and premonitions began, because the symbols that appear along the course of human events are a great deal more significant than the events themselves; the latter occur only to open the way for allegories that illuminate our wanderings on earth.

Think about how strange it seems, yet also how typical, that the son, Antonio José de Sucre, rebelled against the father and founded a country which he then named after the father. This didn't happen by chance; it was a practical joke typical of sterile men, because, as everyone knows, neither of them sired any children. Maybe they compensated for their short-comings by creating an offspring that existed in a fantasy world, a world of pure fiction. And maybe this is why the lights and shadows that populate the nation's history are more apt to conjure up legends than to convey simple, everyday events. We should remember, however, that Sucre, in founding Bolivia, was trying to stabilize the continent. If Upper Peru had been included in Argentina, a great imbalance would have occurred, just as if it had been annexed by Peru. Sucre, the author of the plan, got blasted from where he least expected, from the country's own inhabitants.

The founding of our country is a topic for lengthy discussion, yet very little has been said on the subject, and what little has been said has been ignored. At any rate, we read what we're required to read and memorize what we must; and the rest, no matter how useful it may be, goes unnoticed. I'm speaking from experience, because over twenty years ago I read an article in a newspaper about psychiatry in Latin America. And the author, a psychiatrist who was considered a nut, pointed out a number of factors which had hampered his branch of medicine in Bolivia. Since the article was written in a very technical language, I can't reproduce it exactly. But I can remember what the author said about the first man who lost his mind on Latin American soil. He wasn't just any ordinary neurotic, but someone who went crazy over love. I have no idea what this curious hero was like, but according to the doctor, he was a Spaniard who'd only recently arrived in the New World. Unfortunately, he didn't fall in love with one of his kind but was seduced by the exotic language of an Aymara maiden, who squatted down to urinate behind a rock just as darkness settled upon the hills and solitude spread across the vast Altiplano.

It may be difficult to accept, but that episode is the cornerstone of our romantic history. Though it isn't the worst thing that ever happened, and besides, it adds a certain flavor to our collective history. Every president reveals something about his country, but only three of ours have been truly archetypal: Melgarejo, rebuffed by his lover Juanacha; Belzu, deceived by his own wife; and Ballivián, who slept with every *pollera* that crossed his path. This trio turned into a curious quartet when the first woman was elected president.

As far as God (the founder par excellence) is concerned, we needn't discuss his luminosity here. But we do need to mention the colonists' misuse of God to reinforce the oppression of the native peoples; their churches attest to their sordidness, their craving for gold. These Baroque churches with their emphasis on form reveal the absence of a true spiritual content. Anyone who travels the endless Altiplano is soon to encounter one of these ruined temples, which paradoxically prove the inability of Spanish architecture to seriously alter the arid landscape, magnificent in its solitude. The religion that arrived from the peninsula didn't prosper in the desert. To the contrary, the desert swallowed up the scaffolding of this religion, alien to the rhythms of the American continent. And anyone who researches the architectonic manifestations of the Aymara religion will discover a synthesis of the two cultures, for the native ceremonies continued to thrive alongside the Catholic rites and to voice the irony and vengeance of the conquered religion. Anthropologists can still observe a peculiar dance performed by the Aymaras of Achacachi, who during the mass shout "Christ, you old donkey face" and other such phrases, which no one has ever considered insults, but symbols of a great clash between cultures that deformed the Spanish rites and destroyed part of the native memory.

I would like to describe an event related to what I've just said. In 1965, in Miraflores, twelve youths were playing a game that consisted of writing questions and answers on identical pieces of paper and then separating them into piles. As each question was read, an answer would be chosen at random. One night the question came up, "Who is God?"; and after a few moments of doubt, the shadow gave its answer, "Be careful with the answer." And maybe we should ask ourselves, "Have we been careful with our answer?" In other words, when we talk, do we know how to construct a dialogue? Four years later I was in Paris, living among the most superstitious and rational people on earth. While the French seemed to be doing quite well with both questions and answers, I discovered something I'd been searching for since the beginning of my days. To the question "Who is God?" someone answered, "He's who he is when the devil's sleeping."

In Bolivia, the devil isn't the one who's been sleeping; it's the other one, the one who bears the luminous face of the universe. Collectively, we've been acting out the stories of Job and Faust. But if God is asleep, what's the reason for our sacrifice? This question isn't silly. We've suffered as much as we can without knowing the object of our suffering, and we've weathered all the storms without losing our faith or wasting time on absurd lamentations. To the contrary, we've held tight to the pure language of premonitions and innocently offered a prayer to the heavens.

I wish to illuminate these pages with a memory. Many years ago, a man was traveling to Tarija; and when he got to Oruro, he still had a smile on his face. Toward evening, he and some other travelers reached a place where the road split into three. From the top of a hill, he could see deep into a valley that was already draped in shadows, and in an isolated spot, he saw something that plunged him into thought, maybe because the surroundings invited meditation or because night was falling upon the world. As darkness covered the land, a large number of dancers formed a circle on the lonely desert. He could see them dancing rhythmically in the distance, without any music other than what nature provided. It wasn't a local festival or a fair because there wasn't anyone in the surrounding area; only the human circle broke the immense silence. Was this simple, powerful dance an expression of sacred joy? A jubilee of Quechuas and Aymaras on the border of an adverse world? What divinity were they toasting with their bodies in the open air? Ambiguity hovered over the dancers; they might have been harbingers of the devil, who, by virtue of the lateness of the hour and the gravity of the place, had been changed into messengers of a more benign universe. An incantation, a dance of sacrificial victims, a rite directed to the blind eyes of the gods. The traveler looked at the dark sky and the few timid stars, and watched the dancers lost in the deep valley. He tried to imagine the ancient people from whom they had inherited blood and memory. And then, not trying to understand, he uttered words from his soul in praise of that silence, "The writing of the circle is mortal for the tribesman."

This anecdote is just a story about a man traveling through the province. But metaphors are nearly always springboards to topics of a higher caliber that can be debated but not denied. Aren't we creating a kind of metaphor when we trace the roads we've traveled on a map of a country or the world? Members of my generation often did this, from which I inferred their inclination toward travel, or maybe it was the pleasure they took from gazing at clouds and barren hills, never losing their balance as they walked the rugged Bolivian landscape. "A map is as revealing as the palm of a person's hand. All that is needed is someone qualified to read this kind of writing"—the judgement of that generation.

But we Bolivians, though we may be magi of great imaginary maps, are not travelers. We've produced only a few explorers, which confirms the truth that if one person is to travel, then another must remain at home. So we stay in our villages watching the Cochabambans, who think of themselves as world travelers; but they would hardly qualify if compared with travelers from other countries. Though the ones who really stick their necks out for us are the Callawayas, the authentic wayfarers of these lands. They roam the Bolivian countryside with ease and travel even to remote lands. They travel out of necessity or in search of impossible things, for which we salute them. They are always enriched by their travels and never perverted. What more could we expect of a traveler? Callawayas pass into foreign lands as easily as they penetrate the barriers of other languages while never renouncing their own, because like the "savage" Chaco Indian, they use a secret tongue. And for this reason they are able to forgive those who live off the sweat of another's brow, and to heal them with a variety of colored herbs.

That is our history. But whether we look to the present or the past, we feel ashamed. Old photographs taken at opening ceremonies of public squares always portray the Indian as a beast of burden. And revolutions haven't changed this. It's still a common sight to see an Aymara with a wardrobe on his back, following behind the owner. But if we are shamed by such spectacles, then we can seek comfort in popular literature, in *kaluyos, huayños,* and *bailecitos.* But this can produce further embarrassment, for what are we to think when we hear lyrics like the following: "I'll snitch me a pig from the boss's pen, make stew with the fat and a vest with the skin"? The situation is the same everywhere, so there's no point looking around. And the causes are obvious, so there's no sense in getting a lawyer to figure them out. In other words, we might as well get to the heart of the matter: What is work? A mad poet once hit a sensitive nerve when he said, "When I think, I work; when I work, I rest." And a big eater once confessed that he'd never eaten a better stew than the day he worked like a mule, planting cassava. Resting and eating, seemingly disparate ideas . . . But work, whose creative, solidaric spirit redeems us, can bring them together. And it's a short step from what I've just said to the stark reality: "We work so we can eat." If people eat, it's because they want to live, and just as we live, we die. For reasons we're all aware of, a Bolivian's life expectancy isn't that great if compared with the indices of the industrialized nations. But some would claim—undisturbed by the expression "misery loves company"—it's not how long you live but how intensely.

We watch a bee buzzing around a geranium, and we're amazed or perhaps moved. Then we look at the hills spotted with eucalyptus groves, and we convince ourselves that death is part of our heritage, inscribed in the landscape and on the faces of all Bolivians. Cause and effect seem so powerful that even those who have no aptitude for premonitions can predict their own futures and those of their neighbors. Che Guevara's appointment with death in a humble place like La Higuera, after leading a spectacular life, transfigured him and revealed his destiny as well as the destinies of his executioners. Those who live here must confront a terrible paradox and also a frightening metaphor; for in Bolivia it's the willingness to live, not to die, that signals courage, and it can't be done halfway: you either find the path or fall headlong off a cliff.

I'm what's called a "writer," which I say with a certain petulance and irony, but I still haven't described the circumstances that led to my becoming a newspaper reporter. And I would like to do that now by means of a fable I'll call "The Other's Encounter with Death."

The Other, like most people, was a product of human love. He didn't know the time or the place of his conception, but remembered clearly the nights he spent with his parents under the vegetable wagon, listening to the earth's sacred breathing.

Ten years later he would meet Laura Medinaceli, who was the dream of his youth as well his adulthood. They took off their clothes and made love for the first time in September 1966, on the first day of spring, in a room with light blue walls which the Other had just rented in Miraflores, a section of the Andean capital. He married Laura and tried to live with Orana, a sensuous woman from a primitive world, with long, flowing hair and a quiet soul. Orana had lived in the Other's hometown for part of her childhood and also for a brief period during adolescence. They saw each other on rare occasions, usually during the Christmas season. One December, now lost in a maze of memories, the Other led Orana along the edge of the damp vegetation until they reached a bridge where a freight train usually passed at night and at five o'clock in the afternoon. With their arms around each other, they walked down to the stream and stood in wonderment amid the tall spurges. They then walked across the hard-packed sand and sat down to rest on a large, black trunk, which contrasted with the clarity of the day, though the day itself was cloudy, and a light rain was falling. Hidden among the trees, they caressed each other until their carnal inclinations began to surface, and as they looked into each other's eyes, their modesty gave way to intimacy. But despite their having carried out the preamble that separates people from animals, the Other didn't penetrate Orana nor did she offer herself to him on that warm, cloudy day.

A great deal of water passed under the bridge, and late one night, when the sky was overcast and a warm breeze was blowing, the Other led a girl with long, wavy hair back along the path that time hadn't erased. In the shadow of the trees, they removed their clothes and made love on the sand. It wasn't raining, but it looked as though it might, in spite of the diffuse moonlight, the stillness of the air, and the primitive hospitality of the forest. This wasn't the first time they'd embraced, but it was the first time that Constanza had lain down on the Other's native soil and had allowed herself to be mounted with great tenderness by a man from Bolivia's most remote province. When they returned to the world of reality, they found it illuminated by stars, and life seemed beautiful and attainable.

And after that experience, notwithstanding the limitations of his rudimentary soul, he knew that access to knowledge of a higher value for human beings was only possible through the uncontrollable energy of love.

319

"Love is risky," he said, before entangling himself in the apparent contradictions of love and jealousy. His body now contained the six elements and they had begun to express themselves with clear signals. The amount of each element differed and could vary according to the circumstances. The only thing that seemed to interest them in particular was to maintain a harmonious balance among themselves. The body was a destiny in itself, and moved along like a wagon tilting toward the side that carried the greatest weight. During times of affliction, the soul became silent, but the body was always disposed to read its destiny, saying "yes" when appropriate and just as ready to say "no" when it wasn't.

"You're as stubborn as a mule," a friend once told him. But he wasn't stubborn; it was just that he couldn't lie.

"Are you Catholic?" asked a tactless person whom he didn't know.

"No, but I believe in God."

"Then you must be a Marxist," someone added in desperation.

"I'd like to be because I hate injustice, and there are plenty of people around who can't defend themselves."

"Then you don't like to work," accused a managerial type.

"Yes, as a matter of fact I do, but not enough to saddle myself with a job like yours."

"Then you can't work with us," said a fat man with glasses.

Some years later, between one mistake and another, he realized that what had saved him was his instinct. In the first place, there were some people—the dangerous minority—who lived off the immense, innocent majority, without feeling any pangs of conscience. And besides that, those who were in "authority"—the highest form of laziness—had sunk to such depths that "authority" was nothing more than "power." Human history had its sensitive spots, times that were especially cruel. True enough, physical slavery was a thing of the past, but it had opened the way to an even more terrible form of oppression because not only was it invisible, it destroyed people at their center, at their souls, where they seek repose and make decisions.

"So," he thought to himself, "here I am studying to be a professional like so many others, living off others and thinking it's okay because it's hard work becoming an engineer. In nothing flat I'll cease to even think about it, and the whole thing will seem natural. And though I may look more like the bad guys than the good guys, I'll just be one more victim in the great machine that gobbles up human beings in the name of progress. So . . . the best thing for me to do is to stop studying."

"I'm quitting school too," one of his best friends told him.

"Why?"

"*Hermano*, I'm sick of studying. The whole thing seems stupid."

"No, you'd better stick to your studies," he told his friend, though he wouldn't have minded having him for a traveling companion.

But he resisted the temptation of dragging his friend along on a wild goose chase and maybe watching him go over the edge of a cliff. Pausing to take a sip of maté, the Other told him: "Knock on the door. If nobody answers, then why open it? But if you knock, and you're really listening, and you hear something, no matter what it is, then be courageous and walk right in, even if every person or thing in the room looks strange to you. Then, only then, can you be sure you're in the right place."

More than a decade later, his friend, who'd become a wealthy industrialist, dropped by his house. They talked like good friends; and though their points of view were very different, they could understand each other. In many respects, Argel was more skillful that the Other. He had developed his talents and was energetic and bright. And according to the Other's way of thinking, he had done exactly what he needed to do. Over twenty years had passed since they'd come to La Paz, and each one had managed to lay out a very personal path for himself.

But the Other felt that he was going to die soon, though death would mean opening the door to a much vaster and more lucid world where the mind and heart would erase the shadows of his affliction.

"I'm building a house where I never hope to live, but someone else will fill it with his words. This is my destiny, and it will be accomplished shortly. I sense it at night as if someone from another world were speaking to me."

"I've felt the same thing and thought it was my age, this business of feeling like you're one step ahead of death," said Argel, who wasn't talking any more about the usual topics: politics, business, and women he'd gone to bed with recently.

"Oh, I didn't mean to imply that I was *running* from death. Anyway, it can't be done. Remember the Persian legend that Jean Cocteau put into French? But I'm not afraid anymore, the way I used to be. To the contrary, it's something real, something I feel inside. I feel it in my breathing, in my whole body."

"Maybe we're feeling the same thing. I just express it differently, emphasizing the fearful aspect."

"Well, it doesn't matter because I'm glad you said what you did. I might find it beneficial, for several reasons."

The Other was especially interested in the turns that life could take. One of those turns was being able to talk to Argel about things that people normally didn't discuss. And while he was talking to his old friend, he became exceedingly happy.

"Beneficial . . . if you say so, but what I don't find at all beneficial is that other people don't seem to know anything about it, and you have to live with 'other people.'" Then Argel confessed that he was able to find some relief in his work, a very practical kind of job, but things didn't always turn out the way he wished.

After a pause, the Other said, "Knowing that death is near may not be such a bad thing. Do you know why?" Without waiting for his friend to answer, he replied: "Because that's the only way we can really be conscious of our own existence. And having this kind of consciousness means understanding other people, probing the depths of their souls, and finally, realizing that we are the only impossible thing; and maybe that's why love delights in torturing us. We all hide from death as best we can; but when people return from the wilderness, not only have they learned to live on their own, they can see through a false mask in an instant."

"Okay. But awareness of death forces us to live more intensely. What's to be gained from that?"

"Just that. Living intensely. Which is no small thing. Or maybe you don't see it that way."

"*Hermano*, I'm sorry to have to tell you, but that's no way to live. Look at all you miss. Trivial things, maybe. But at least they add some spark to your life. There are all kinds of people in the world. Good and bad, ordinary and complex. And a lot of them never worry about death."

"That's relative, Argel. If you live your life intensely, then you meet the people you're supposed to meet, the ones who find you attractive. There's a secret force that allows us to attract some and repel others without offending them with our indifference. And if someone else rejects you, there's no reason to feel badly about it. As we live our lives, we learn that we're good for some things and not so good for others. So it makes sense for us to be with the people who appreciate our talents. Doesn't it seem strange to you when somebody says 'He's so much in love with Eulalia, it's killing him'? I've always heard that love was one of life's great joys, maybe the greatest. But the closer one gets to death, the more love one feels. My dear Argel, if you want to live intensely, you must be conscious of death. And, as you well know, you must have love also."

"Yes, it's all very logical, but death is hard for me to accept," Argel replied, ready to talk about something less serious.

"Sometimes our lives seem to be in a mess," continued the Other, "and this causes us pain. We suffer. Nonetheless, there's a kind of coherence to human actions, even if we can't see it. And since we're on the subject, I'd like to mention an excellent essay by someone we know. He says that when you're in a state of crisis, the everyday things become important. In other words, there's a commonality in human nature, and our most subtle spiritual experiences push us in that direction. For example, he says that when a person loses his mental and physical faculties—his ability to speak, walk, feel, and so on—life still goes on as long as the person can breathe. And life doesn't stop till the breathing stops. As you can guess, what brings life to a close is life itself. And that's, more or less, what the essay says. But keeping true to tradition, which means accepting an idea, correcting it, purifying it, and transmitting it, also means it's all right to add something of our own.

"When a person is about to die, someone holds a mirror to his mouth to see if he's still breathing, which is like saying he's still alive. The mirror, which reflects our faces and also reality, or perhaps reality is our face and therefore difficult for us to see . . . Anyway, the mirror will become hazy if the person is still breathing, in other words, alive. Breathing perpetuates the system, which consists of bringing something into the body, transforming it, and returning it to the external world. But if the mirror reflects reality in all its glory, then the person is no longer alive. For me, the mirror is a valuable symbol because it teaches us the advantages of living close to death. Because when we live at the edge of our own lives, knowing that we may die at any moment, then we don't obscure the mirror of reality; to the contrary, we see things as they really are and not as they seem or as we want them to be. Death, as I see it, is able to bring the self to its greatest potency, and it does this, paradoxically, by threatening it with extinction."

The Other's dialogue with Argel led them toward unsuspected topics, which is often the case with long conversations. In other words, the discussion became less and less intense until eventually they got around to talking about old times. Argel reminded the Other about Rosario Pantaleón, one of their classmates whom he hadn't thought about in a long time. They also mentioned Ciscar Zenteno, who'd become a prosperous farmer in Calamuchita where he lived happily with his wife and numerous children. They also recalled some funny scenes between Sanguinetti and Adrián, the former, a famous painter and the latter, a promising geologist who was now six feet under but spoke to them from time to time in dreams.

Then Argel told him all about the bad business deals that the government was involved in, which constantly came to his attention because of his dealings with company executives. His condemnation was unequivocal, "I used to admire them, *hermano*, because I thought they knew what they were doing. But they let me down. They're just as they always were, a bunch of worthless bums." Finally, they got around to the same set of stories that ended every conversation, without noticing their wives' knowing smiles or realizing that what they were doing was a sign of growing old.

Despite their familiarity, neither the Other nor Argel knew much about each other's life. They were unaware of many things that had happened since their long lost youth. They'd lived different lives; but guided by prudence and respect, they allowed the boundaries that divided them to remain unaltered.

Only on one occasion were they able to understand that life has its costs and that the universe is charged with indecipherable energies. On that occasion, they experienced the same "accident" but drew diverse conclusions.

In 1977, about midyear, Argel suddenly showed up at the Other's office. He'd been drinking, and the effects of the alcohol were beginning to show. Aggressive and enthusiastic, he told the Other he wanted to talk to his old friend, so without further ado, they took off for the Other's house, carrying with them several bottles of *singani*. The two friends drank and laughed late into the night, remembering funny things that had happened.

Then Argel began to look at the books that the Other had piled against the wall. And the more he looked, the more serious he became.

"We're not alone," said Argel.

He repeated the phrase several times, and the Other understood him to mean that people weren't alone in the world. In other words, that human beings, though they may act as if they were alone, are never truly alone.

"What kind of people do you go around with, anyway?" asked Argel.

Then he picked up his glass and threw it against the wall, dispelling the imaginary figure that frowned at him from across the room. He felt a little better, and after giving the Other a detailed explanation of what had just occurred, he was totally calm. Meantime, the Other, despite the alcohol he'd imbibed and the temperature of the room, remained silent in fifteen languages. Argel swore he'd seen the devil, but the Other decided not to mention what had happened on St. John's Eve, when, in the company of his brother Demosthenes, he'd tolerated the presence of an unwelcome guest. So he rested his head on the table and said nothing, waiting for his friend's fear to pass.

"Well, I guess you're not going to answer me. You're not going to tell me about your friends."

With his head still on the table, the Other listened to his friend's voice and found it strangely melodic. His accent was somehow different. Then something happened that made the Other raise his head. He felt a cold chill run from his scalp down to his toes. His whole body was cold. Something was happening that he'd hoped would never happen, because, before his very eyes, Argel became the man with the wide-brimmed hat, wavy, white hair, and an ironic smile. In other words, it was the same man whom he'd seen on St. John's Eve, except that this time it was very dark and there was no one else around. The Other could hear a rooster crowing in the night and was vaguely aware of the other noises of the city: a car coming down the street, a whistle, the meowing of an alley cat.

During that time, he had premonitory dreams that accompanied him in his daring attempt to learn about death through love. He was thinking in similar terms in 1965, when he wrote a short piece titled "Letter to a Stillborn Child." From his childhood, when life was full of vitality, the Other had sensed the presence of death, and now he was going to know it first hand, which cost him dearly and required him to travel in the company of the devil for quite a length of time. Unsettled but without hesitation, he traveled that path, tolerating a terrible coldness. But he couldn't tell anyone, not even his good friend Argel. He had to carry it in his soul, knowing that he would be a springboard for other beings. But since he was stubborn, he was ready to die if he had to, but with his soul at peace. He'd reached the boundary and had passed over into an unknown territory, without signposts, where one had to rely on one's own sense of direction. He got his fingers burned but was able to escape and was sure that he hadn't been saved by accident.

His rural common sense told him that his road was about to end, that people like him didn't have a future or any hope in a world that demanded all kinds of concessions. On the other hand, he could stay by himself for a week, drink his maté without blinking an eye, and repeat without moving his lips, "This is my enlightenment; my heart beats to its own rhythm, and why should I try to change it?" Out of stubbornness, he slept with his eyes open, and when it was dawn he got up feeling that he had one less hope and was happy for the loss, which didn't alter his humor or disturb a hair on his head.

Maybe I should say here that because of my emotional involvement, I'm probably not the best person to talk about the Other's life. My affection for him goes so deep that even when he told me that my ideas were wild and impractical, I couldn't say a word in my defense.

"You're incapable of living alone," he told me. "You're always trying to regain something that was lost by someone else. That's your hope—to retrieve your life through art. I, on the other hand, belong to that class of individuals who are nothing but pure loss. Unlike you, I'm unable to compensate with words, though my scattered memories can make me feel a little weak. I know you've been seduced by the metaphor, that mechanism that allows you to intuit the depths of dreams, the enigma of life. And though I like you very much, I doubt your aptitude for such things. For example, what do you know about the relationship between the flower and the bee? Since I was a child I've known that I was the very essence of nostalgia, which is true for life in all its forms. Nostalgia for things that were but are no more; it's simple to grasp the form but not the content. The flower contains a memory of the bee, just as the bee contains a memory of the flower. They recognize each other in a perpetual present, and their attraction for one another is irresistible.

"People are the same. If something is sour we want to make it sweet. But in this miraculous process, habit never takes over because just as things become routine, along comes death and transforms us. I know from my rural origins that this is a real metaphor, a variation on God's sacred metaphor, though not the only one. How can you be asleep and dream that you're laughing? And which of these is real, the sleeping you or the laughing you? Remember the two-headed dog? Well, it's the same principle but in scientific terms. A melancholy animal acts as a dummy for another animal that is momentarily happy. Now, how does this work for you and me, since we seem to be taking turns performing different tasks in this human scenario? Have you loved Constanza as much as I? And Orana, that feminine miracle, so tender and innocent, has she loved me more than you? Could you die for her, or would you leave that job to me?"

As you might guess, I never responded to these questions, which sounded more like accusations; the first reason being that while he was speaking from his heart, I could only respond with my lucid mind. And second, I knew how stubborn he was and that he would go to great lengths to obtain his objective. His logic was actually quite dangerous because he believed that the energy spent in proving a point could transfigure it and place it in a glorious light. For example, he thought of the city as a woman and, as such, thought it ought to be conquered. For him, this wasn't mere speculation. But when he went to Paris, his conviction suffered a severe setback, for there he encountered a culture based on a language he couldn't understand; and wandering around like a lost dog, he was able to smell the aromas of that captivating universe but could never call it his own. He was terribly attracted to French women; and while he was waiting for the right one to turn up, he passed the time in medieval churches or in bookstores, with an imperturbable air, until finally he gave up, tired of the whole business.

He purchased a ticket back to America and went to say good-bye to that unapproachable *woman* named Paris. It was his last night in the City of Light, the last night of autumn. A soft breeze was blowing, and the lights of the city were beautiful. He walked for hours along Boulevard Sebastopol, looked at Tour de Saint Jacques, and then turned down Boulevard Saint Michel. In the Latin Quarter, he mechanically entered a record shop he usually visited and looked through the suites by Handel, carefully selecting a few as souvenirs to carry back to his rustic world. He chose suites 5, 10, 13, and 14, for the clavichord, while a pair of unknown eyes were staring at his hands. Again he found himself on the threshold of that strange language. Barbara and the Other walked back together. She was a young woman, Arabic or perhaps Jewish, who knew a lot about psychoanalysis, which he later discovered in the room on Maire Street where an amorous nude poured out a soulful story of a cabalistic tradition she no longer wished to continue. The Other sold his ticket and stayed with the girl; and later, when he finally decided to go back to his continent, he stood looking out of a window in Barcelona and said to Francine, "Not only do we live for our ideals, we must be willing to die for them." He felt sad speaking Spanish to a woman who understood only half of what he said. And sadly he thought of his future and all that related to that diffuse scenario.

A short time later, aboard a ship, he began to think of what could happen to him if he didn't find work in his country. Finding a job would be the toughest job of all and one he couldn't escape. On the high seas near the equator he suddenly felt the ship floundering from side to side and feared that some ancient sin had risen up from the mysterious sea. But "original sin" had nothing to do with it; it was his fear, fear of not finding work. He needed to earn a living by the sweat of his own brow so that his conscience would remain clear. And like the ship, he later floundered from one place to another in his country; and in the city of La Paz, when he was about to go under, he found himself completely alone. But he stayed on, without knowing what it was he was anxiously awaiting, despite the fact that his search for a job had given way to an even greater challenge, one in which his life would be at stake.

In the evening, in a part of the city called Villa Fátima, he poured rice into boiling water from a half-empty bag, the last of his rations; and as prayer time settled upon the hills, he watched the geraniums in the garden blown by a wind that chilled his soul. He remained in La Paz as long as he could and then bought a ticket for his native province.

Some years later, sitting in a rustic, yellow chair, drinking maté and rubbing his nose, he said, "He who seeks finds, but you don't always get what you're looking for." He'd found work, but thanks to Constanza, his family was falling apart.

Shortly before midnight, on December 31, 1980, he sat rubbing his nose; he'd been forty years on the earth, had been better off at some times than others, and had often thought that it was a miracle he was still alive. He wasn't one to settle for crumbs, but he could get by on very little; and he was grateful to be that way because it allowed him to enjoy the beauties of life, which to him were the real blessings. For example, he'd gotten to know the city by means of an illicit relationship with a woman who had also put him in touch with the real heart of his country; but in getting there, he had innocently cast aside many conventions. "What's coming in isn't going out," he thought, appealing to the clarity of his soul and knowing that he'd done all he had to do, both in the city and in life. He thought about what he'd said. It sounded to him like a distorted version of something Christ had said, "Everything that comes out of your mouth is unclean," or a subtle variation of "It's a fish's mouth that gets it into trouble," or a darker version of the quaint expression, "Keep your mouth shut if you want to keep the flies out."

But in spite of it all, he wasn't going anywhere because no matter where he went it would always be the same. Though his sadness clouded the horizon, he remembered that "we embark upon a journey as we are, and the journey can't change us; it only enriches or perverts us." Moreover, he still remembered what Danilo Romero had often said: "*Pibe*, time wasted is time to spare." In other words, he was lost again in his memories. He got up, opened the door, and looked up at the sky full of stars. He enjoyed the freshness of the air on the outskirts of the city. A river flowed along the eastern boundary, a river he held in his memory with the softness of its sound intact. He could never have imagined a noiseless river, except maybe in dreams or in his writing. This river was very beautiful and flowed into the realm of dreams without relinquishing its music.

He went back into his room and closed the door. He was standing between four walls; and though there were no silk curtains, there were prints of Renaissance art, and crafts by medieval artisans, together with photographs of a great personal value: pictures of Guaranis, Quechuas, and Aymaras. As he looked at them, he was distracted by more important matters, like the approaching armed rebellion, but decided there was still time for him to embrace Orana.

Suddenly he began talking to himself: "Soon I'll be able to embrace Orana just as I have embraced Constanza. I'll say what I've always said to women. But have women ever told men what they mean to them? Men have composed endless songs, some awful and some like heavenly hymns, to convince women or to seduce them, maybe because they know they wouldn't be what they are without women. But women, who don't seem especially concerned about men, go on being their own mysterious selves. And they defend their mystery like lionesses protecting their cubs. Because if a woman loses her mystery, then she stops being a woman, and the man goes off chasing some artificial firefly. Man says that woman is a road to wisdom, not the only road but maybe the most magical one. However, in my case, woman was the only road. Even Satan has appeared to me in a feminine form. Anyone who takes the wrong path is in danger of falling into the abyss. And women do deal in unreality: it's their lack of reality that calls to us with a scream or a melody. There's nothing alarming about things that are good and kind; we can find those things by the side of the road. And it's strange that only a few women, usually the less feminine ones, have become artists; but if you really think about it, it's natural. Motherhood redeems them from all evil and excuses them from the search that man is condemned to for life, trapped in an inconclusive destiny. Because man, despite his virile member that marks him as a creator, is without a doubt a castrated metaphysician, a melancholy eunuch pacing back and forth in front of a work of alleged spiritual value but that somehow lacks that miraculous spark, the aroma of the expectant woman."

Disturbed by grave thoughts, the Other stood up again. Something was telling him that he was reaching the limit, and he knew that he had managed to do the impossible: with the strength of his own soul, he had managed to summon a dead person so that he could speak to him while he was still alive. According to his dangerous way of thinking, being in touch with things around us is the same as communing with something that was once alive; and the best communion with the universe is achieved by communicating with the dead.

He looked up at the incredibly clear sky filled with stars that perhaps didn't exist any longer but that had existed in such a way that their light still reached the earth with the power of an inordinate love. His rural soul became tremulous, seeing that the world was still innocent. For some reason he remembered two dreams of the many he'd had since he arrived in La Paz in 1961. The first one places him in a Tiwanacota village with deserted streets swept by the wind. He walks looking for the center of the town, which seemed lost in a remote past, and eventually he comes to a square where people are silently waiting in line to speak to a master of ceremonies. The Other takes his place in line and waits his turn to approach the bonfire. But then he realizes that he, too, will be sacrificed in the purifying flames. The dream ends and he tosses and turns in the bed, without intuiting the dream's message.

In the second dream, he's soaring through the heavens, amazed at his ability to fly. He looks for a place to go and decides to head for his province, but instead of arriving at his destination, he comes to a lovely circle of earth with very tall vegetation. In the middle of the circle, a beautiful young woman—no one he's ever seen—is standing still as a statue and smiling up at him. There are many people around but none of them go near the river of light blue waters. The Other enters the magic circle, and suddenly black horses come running out of the forest, wade into the river, and come out white and shining. He takes off again, filled with a strange gladness, but once he's in the air, he thinks he must have done something wrong because he can't seem to find his way home. This was about the time that the Other was finishing up *Tirinea*.

And then, propped against the doorway to his room, he was glad to have found the secret center of his country, not in the slippery world of dreams but in the austere geography of the earth. ■

He traveled for a full day in the direction of Cochabamba, and after a brief stop, he and a group of investigators traveled on toward the ruins of Incallajta, a bastion built by the Inca Indians to stave off the Portuguese, who had incited the Guaranis to conquer the entire region. When they got to the ruins, the experts explained to the others that the neighboring Indians never visited the ruins and were scornful of anyone who dared to anger their gods. Among the ruins was an unusually large temple without a roof, as if such torpid structures had ever been needed for communication with the heavens. The Other had come face to face with the presence of an incomprehensible past, a form of writing that was illegible to the unstudied.

After spending the night at Incallajta, the delegation left for a town that wasn't mentioned in the itinerary, and arrived before midday. The Other perceived the silence that reigned in the lovely village and the aroma of its distant vegetation. The streets were clean, and the architecture of the houses obeyed an Indian style; the walls and roofs were made entirely of American clay. No more than thirty families lived in the village; and when the strangers arrived, the women and old people began to appear in the doorways. The Other sat down in the sunny square to eat some bread and soon noticed that the only church was out of sync with the spirit of the place, not only because its tower was decorated with calamine but also because it was an artificial addition to a community that could get along without it.

About midday some sheep started coming out of a building on the square. They moved without a sound as if emerging from a dream and moved along to a rhythm that wasn't animal or human. After the last sheep, a young girl came out wearing a skirt and blouse, leather sandals, and a dainty hat; her long braids framed a face of untouched earth. He watched as she walked along divulging her incipient femininity, still untouched by suffering. The Other was seeing her for the first time but recognized her as the girl he'd been searching for all his life, waiting for the blossoming of the *urundel,* picturing her as Ipapecuana, and tremulous, begging her to show him the inviolable center of his country. ∎

He stopped looking at the stars and went back into his room. He went over to the shelves piled high with books and picked up some volumes bound by an Argentine who had been living in exile in Bolivia. He thought of the light blue shirt and the locks of blond hair of that Jewish socialist, whose name was Atilio Levy. The Other picked out one of the books. There was nothing engraved on the binding or printed on the blue division pages. But on the second page of the text, the full title appeared, *The Invisible Face: The Last Human Dreams.*

Carrying the book in his right hand, he walked over to the yellow chair that he'd built out of some old wooden crates when he was living in Villa Fátima. He sat down in the chair as if to rest himself after a very difficult chore and leaned back in total comfort.

According to the experts, the print was "Univers 67," and its size was ten point. The faded blue pages reminded him of the subtle passing of time. He flipped back several pages until he found a particular sentence. He read along willingly but without hope, as if waiting for a miracle:

> For a long time, a man with a withered face has been sitting on the terrace of a cafe, with a glass of beer on the round, metal table in front of him. Before him lies the main square of this city near the sea, with its many street musicians and tourists, like him. It's seven o'clock, and the sky has a reddish or perhaps pinkish tint; however, this tranquil color fades into an horizon painted in harsh, threatening shades. It's not that it's going to rain; a terrible storm is about to hit. Off to one side, close to the sandy beach, the sea is very choppy; and rumors of an approaching cyclone have begun to spread among the crowd of tourists.
>
> A large number of visitors as well as residents are leaving the city; long lines of cars have formed on the highways. Some people have left on planes. The sky isn't neutral, but, to the contrary, suggests that something terrible is about to happen. The man with the weathered face watches the artists working on their paintings as the sun sets. They work busily like bees, mesmerized by the mysteries of their easels. He hears the muffled sounds of an unfamiliar band passing along the street. His glass of beer still in front of him, he continues watching the sky, waiting for something definite and discovers ominous signs hovering above the city. But despite the danger, the city has a magical glow. The man lifts his right arm as if to wave to someone, and with his left hand he toasts with his glass.
>
> A Jewish woman is sitting next to him, an ageless beauty escaped from a worn out world; she is slender and pretty. Her suffering, now in the past, has embellished her, marked her with the silent

sign of triumph. Something makes her stand out in the anonymous light of the afternoon, and amid the rumors of danger, she remains calm, an invulnerable being in a magical city. She was born in some city in Europe destroyed by the Germans during the Second World War. Her glass of beer reflects the strange light of a shared world. The air is warm and damp, and at times, becomes turbulent; it gives the strange impression of depositing the soot and bad air of the abandoned factories.

"Tomorrow you're leaving, and who knows if I'll ever see you again. That's reason enough to tell you my secret."

Her pale blue eyes fill with tears. The man says nothing.

"My husband committed suicide, publicly. Where? In Sweden, far away from here. He preferred dying over selling out to the enemy."

"That's terrible," replies the man with the weathered face. "It's questionable if a person should take his own life for personal reasons, but if a whole community is at stake . . ."

"It turned out just as you might have imagined. I'm living in a country that's an enemy to my husband's country. I'm a trapped victim. I'm not a citizen of his country or the country where I live. I work but not for the enemy. No one can know about my husband. My life depends on it."

"What's it like knowing that you will never tell the secrets of your homeland, no matter what?"

"Like anything worthwhile, it isn't easy. Tell me. What's it like knowing a fugitive's secret?"

He breathes deeply to relax himself, inhaling the turbulent air. His eyes fill with tears, not from the present but from an unearthed past.

"If you'd like, we can go back to the hotel," the woman tells him. "It's getting late, and I'm cold."

They walk arm in arm for eight blocks, illuminated by the light of a darkened world. A natural disaster is hovering over the city and threatening to destroy the precarious human order. By the end of the first few blocks, the woman has recovered her serenity and with clear eyes, like a wash of light blue, she begins to appreciate the things around her. A smile is sketched upon her face. She doesn't feel walled in any longer but comforted, as by a lullaby.

"Tomorrow you're leaving on the *Michelangelo,* and the weather reports aren't encouraging. The cyclone's already done a lot of damage on the eastern shore of your continent."

"And you?"

"I'm leaving at the same time but on another ship. We've shared a place on land but with different time schedules. Tomorrow it'll be just the opposite."

The man nods his head. His weathered face bears a smile of gratitude.

"I'm also beginning to believe that I may never see you again," says the woman with the blue eyes. There's a coldness in her eyes, of feelings blotted out by memories or by their own transparency; a deep emotion suddenly surfaces like a drowning woman. "I never write letters; I don't stay in touch with anyone. It's crazy, but I live like a complete unknown in a country that isn't mine."

Both are standing at the reception desk of the hotel. They've picked up their keys, but the man, as if hearing his name called unexpectedly, suddenly turns around.

"Barbara, I'm going back outside for a minute. I want to take a last look around, say good-bye to the city," he says staring into the lovely face of Francine.

A couple comes out of the same hotel, also wishing to take a walk around. The woman, a middle-aged mulatto, is accompanied by a white man, who gently touches her arm. They amble along slowly as if walking toward the end of their lives, trying not to muss the fragile carpet of their memories.

The man with the weathered face, after regarding the couple with a mixture of warmth and admiration, walks hurriedly down the street and loses himself in the crowd. Everyone seems to be outdoors. At the first corner, which is shaded by an overhanging terrace, he stops to listen to a talented group of musicians who have attracted a large crowd with their jazz improvisations. The melodies are recognizable and stir up hidden stories of black men and women. The man with the weathered face feels superfluous among that audience. The leader of the group is an older man with thinning hair and a long, white beard. He plays a few light tunes to prepare the listeners for the arduous session of improvisations. Everyone is out on the street, and life is a dream come true. The scene becomes a din of blaring music and loud applause. A young drummer, about fifteen years of age, begins to play. His rhythms are frenetic, smooth, and terribly sincere. His movements are furious and spontaneous. He plays on and on, and the older man applauds and smiles, perhaps remembering that he, too, had been young. He seems to be saying to him in some secret code "Suffering isn't enough; frenzy isn't enough. They wear you out and for no reason. If you want magic and conviction and you want it to last, you must stick to tradition. Pain isn't enough. You have to live as though you were dead."

Everyone is out on the street. The man with the weathered face meets other groups as he passes along. The sky is still dark, if not to say threatening, and the air is like a warm wave pushed along by some unintelligible being. But life goes on. The man with the weathered face knows this and brushes past the people making his way into the night, heading toward some undefined goal. His life force moves him along toward the end of the road.

In other zones of the threatened city, identical to ones he has just seen, life is still controlled by the unforeseen. Peering into windows and doors, he is amazed to see numerous dancers, naked men and women, excited by the intimacy of night, far removed from a confused, anxious audience. They dance and fornicate before the viewers drawn in by the night. Life goes on. On the next corner, he encounters smiling faces that invite him in, to come into a place where life goes on. The man with the weathered face looks closely at the faces but finds nothing more that the gaping grin of a horrid, broken universe. The panes are transparent, but clients and performers are veiled by the intimacy of the night.

The man with the weathered face thinks about stopping for a beer at one of the terraces along the route that appears to be straight but is actually circular. He feels rejuvenated, and terribly interested in the life that goes on, always beyond his reach. He looks up at the stars, and a sky that isn't his, before spotting a feminine figure on the street that belongs to nobody and to everybody. At first he thinks that she's with someone, but then he sees that she's alone. The man who appeared to be with her was just another pedestrian lost in dreams. The man with the weathered face can only see her from behind. She is wearing a thin dress, proper attire for a warm evening. She has a shapely figure defined by some hidden, sensual power. Every stride reveals the precise form of her legs; her steps obey a rhythm attained through practice but designed to lend spontaneity to her movements. The neck of the unknown woman, her silky hair, her bare arms corroborate the power of her thighs, appropriate to a life of intimacy. The man still hasn't seen the woman's silent face, and seeming not to want to confront her reality, he follows her docilely, intrigued by the feline quality of those movements, tolerant of tenderness, warmth, and masculine dreams.

After walking for many blocks, the incredibly beautiful woman goes into an establishment. The man with the weathered face stops and looks at the luminous signs next to the door she has chosen. But it's as though he hasn't looked because he doesn't understand any language except his own. At any rate, he knows his fate and enters the building as if it had all been arranged beforehand; except that a rustic staircase throws him off guard, and he smiles, wondering if he hasn't entered the wrong building. But pushing that thought aside, he ascends the wooden staircase.

Meanwhile, he realizes that life goes on, perhaps in the street outside, perhaps in the rooms of this vast house where the woman with the powerful body is hidden. Additional luminous signs confirm his ignorance of foreign languages. It doesn't matter, he doesn't care. He has been liberated from messages that his soul can't understand. Finally he comes to a counter. The brothel is being run by women who speak the mysterious language, and they hand him a book to write down his name and address. He pays the necessary fee to enter the world of the unknown woman who has brought him this far without an exchange of words in any language. In the darkness he makes his way to a patio, bumping into things he can't see, and then knocks three times at a wide door. Inside he sees the woman, as if through a distant, open window; and she signals for him to enter the room reserved for them. She leaves him standing in the middle of the room and goes out, promising to return quickly.

He's astonished by his surroundings: a broken down cot, draped mirrors, some depressing pieces of furniture. He silently ponders the horror of poverty, a painful test for the human soul. Without a doubt, ugliness is a punishment. He knows that he's not used to this, and for that reason he doesn't flinch. He wants to reach the limit. That limit is the woman, and she has returned. She isn't beautiful; she was beautiful. Her change had been so abrupt that her suffering hadn't marked her in a human way but instead turned her into something infernal. Her body doesn't inspire pleasurable thoughts. It bears the marks of many beatings, of violence carried out by people that she would surely be unable to recognize. But they are still around, in a world where life goes on. They are there.

The man with the weathered face takes off his clothes and bares his soul, knowing that he has no desire to fornicate. He wants to talk. He's forgotten his inability to speak to people who express themselves in a language foreign to love. She furiously tries to hold him back when he indicates a readiness to leave. But the man with the weathered face has decided to go back to the street and heads in that direction, where life goes on. From the street he'll think back to the room he's just left; life goes on.

He descends the stairs, leaving them all behind, one by one, and at last finds himself on the wide avenue. He spots the same musicians and the old black man with the young drummer, now calm, at the height of his conviction. The sky is still threatening, and in some areas of the city it's begun to rain. The warm winds have brought in puffs of cold air. The man with the weathered face detects the odor of dirty water, the abandonment of interior patios, the last mystery of a besieged city.

He makes his way back along the street. He can't forget what his eyes saw an hour before. Or was it an eternity? Feeling a little tired, he passes by the windows where the performers were fornicating or pretending to fornicate in front of their usual audience. On the return trip, the bright lights rob them of the beauty which the intimacy of night had artificially imposed.

The man reaches the corner where he first saw the woman with the powerful body. Life does go on, he thinks to himself, looking again at the stars that seem to have distanced themselves from humanity. Then, an indefinable force causes him to lower his eyes, and he sees a woman chasing a girl, a lovely adolescent escaped from a dream. He thinks they're playing a game despite the barricade formed by the curious onlookers. The crowd doesn't allow her to escape from the furious woman. There isn't the slightest sign of a smile, of friendly complicity, on anyone's face. Suddenly the woman catches up with the girl and knocks her down; the girl falls and the woman kicks her in the face. The man with the weathered face doesn't know if the scene is real or a terrible vision. The older woman takes the girl's head in her hands and beats it against the pavement.

The man with the weathered face begins to accept the bloody scene acted out before his eyes. The girl, bruised and battered, begins to defend herself, as people usually do. The onlookers stand motionless and silent as if in a dream. The whole scene is a terrible nightmare. Some policemen watch petrified by the intensity of the spectacle. The woman decides that she's punished the girl enough and starts to leave in the company of the police. Momentarily, the roles change, and several men become the protagonists; they rush by pursued by other men who are seemingly better runners. The young girl sits naked on the pavement with her head down; her only privacy is the shelter of her crying. She cries as though wishing she hadn't survived the beating. Then suddenly her sincere soul finds the right words, and her body quickly dispatches them; she opens her mouth and gives vent to a ghastly tirade, cutting and cold, superior to human desperation.

The Other, who hadn't moved a muscle when he first heard the screams, laid his book aside because the screams weren't coming from the blurred pages of a book. He stood up, opened the door, and looked at the sky. There was nothing except the usual things, which moved along but never went away, sustained by the splendor of constant re-creation. He put on a jacket and left the room to look for the screams that were bursting the tympanum of his soul.

Notebook Number 5

The Dead Man

The circle is mortal for the profane. But I march in, eyes closed and facing life.

I know perfectly well who I am. Different from before when I hardly knew what I wasn't, I'm now filled with certainty and am completely at home with myself, like a person who's survived a terrible disaster. As you might guess, I still have a touch of the fever that left me prostrate, looking at my beloved country on bended knees.

It's natural that it happened that way; and that's why I have to be careful when I get the desire to smile as I once did, trusting in the animal good health of my youth. Now I need to regain the former vigor of my body without making myself a victim of superfluous, irresponsible enthusiasm. A convalescent must act prudently. I learned that lesson twenty years ago in the middle of a public thoroughfare, looking at my friend Rosario Pantaleón, who was a member of my graduating class and perhaps the first student of rural origin at the Colegio Nacional San Luis in Tarija.

In 1960, I received my diploma from that school and said good-bye to Rosario and my other classmates. A year later I ran into that same industrious student on one of the main streets of downtown La Paz, and in less than two blocks learned that my companion had been unsuccessful in Córdoba and was now back in La Paz seeking his fortune. The only problem was that he had only a fifty-*centavo* piece with which to seduce fortune, and the one who is writing this had about the same. At a street corner, beneath an indifferent sky and in the midst of a smiling multitude, we combined our resources and bought an ice-cream cone.

The ice cream was for my friend, who looked pale to me though he didn't care to discuss it. We walked for a couple of blocks in the same direction, not knowing exactly where to go and finally found our way to a part of the street where a number of large commercial firms were located. We were just about to enter the plaza where Colonel Gualberto Villarroel was hanged. But my friend took one look at a clump of trees, saw the shade of their branches, and then fell face down on the pavement with the ice cream at his side. I suppose that Pantaleón was having an epileptic fit. While a crowd gathered around, I had the good sense to take off one of his shoes; I located his big toe and pressed it back to make him recover consciousness since, as most would know, the infallible remedy for reviving a person who has fainted is what I did to my esteemed classmate.

Whether the pain which I inflicted on him was stronger than his infirmity or his attack was just a passing thing, the result was that Rosario Pantaleón opened his eyes and tried to get his bearings amid a crowd of curious spectators. I managed to stretch him out so that his head was propped against the white wall of a shirt store. And after a few minutes, which seemed to me like an eternity, he recognized me in that sea of faces, and then he realized that he'd lost his ice cream, which by that time was past recovery. Shaken as I was, I unwisely tried to buck him up in my rough manner: I looked into his face and catching his attention, winked at him. Pantaleón, who understood this language quite well, tried to wink back and in fact was able to wink at me with his right eye, but the gesture caused him to faint again.

Eventually both of us ended up in a nearby café. A man whom I knew by name took pity on us and before asking us where we were from and what we were doing in the city, ordered three cups of tea. This "what's his name" was a well-known politician who for a quarter of a century had been letting everyone know that nothing that occurred in Bolivia deserved his approval.

After spending a couple of days in a hospital, Rosario Pantaleón disappeared from La Paz without a word. And this is one of many similar stories, though not an especially tragic or spectacular one, that occur every day in La Paz. My story is actually quite like his, simple, void of important deeds but, nonetheless, in need of a spotlight to illuminate the common events that weigh upon my heart.

I have just left the park and my eyes renounce the melancholy lights of the neighboring hills. Something has been destroyed in my being, a fracture that far from condemning me to dissolution, seems only to have been the price of rebirth. Like someone raised from the dead, I have turned my head toward the vast, well-known street. My feet choose that route traversed by the usual strangers. My steps are lost among an infinite number of steps. The street belongs to everyone. We, those who have come back, have said that "knowing a person" is more than recognizing a face and giving the common salute. We strangers have exhausted the trivial meanings of words to rescue their powerful essences. We have attained solidaric silence, distance, and respect in order to access the mystery of the many lives around us.

The pedestrians hurry by, which is typical for New Year's Eve. There is urgency and emotion in these inhabitants of a concentration camp once called a free country. The precarious economy of the country is a shambles; this has brought together two things to form a common martyrdom: having nothing to eat and being deprived of the right to protest. Every friend and neighbor has been cast to the wind if not imprisoned, exiled, or dead. The forms of death which a dictatorship selects are not equivocal; and we are here to prove it. And though it may be difficult to accept or to admit, there are many around who've changed their ideology, and others who've turned informant. The human being is a mysterious creature who presumes to be clear and constant. The masses of people are even more frightening, thinking what they don't feel or feeling whole-heartedly what they've never thought. An obscure face, indeed, so different from the children in masquerade who run through the streets carrying drums and other instruments with the single purpose of singing Christmas songs, orphaned, broken lives that come down from the hills to the indifferent, democratic streets.

A wave of strange souls has taken possession of the streets. The myth of communication is alive and well and is becoming immortal in the arteries of the city, precisely now that the country finds itself on the brink of catastrophe. I can see the prayers on the faces of every passerby, prayers to their gods against the half dozen rogues and tricksters who have the nation's future in their power. Only danger unites us, and the real poets keep a reign on their nostalgia when communion is the subject. We think that we communicate with our neighbors, when what we actually do—amid errors and suppositions—is confirm our own illusions. If the word "table" has an infinite number of meanings, what must happen in the case of abstract concepts, so dear to those who seek liberty, though they may never have been disposed to sharing it. The Word comes from the distant past and dwells in the blood and is divulged by means of the mouth of the disoriented man—a fallen god, ephemeral and perverse, as though he'd been bound and gagged as a child, but likely to redeem himself on some limpid day, transparent as his dreams.

But life is beautiful, populated by everyday beings like Patinuk and the man who is speaking. My dear friend Patinuk, now that I am well and able to walk the streets, I'd like to think about some of the things you've seen in your quarter of the city. Maybe you've forgotten, but I, on the other hand, can remember everything. A man with a pale face was going to the Valley of the Moon and another man, an Aymara, was coming from the Abajo River. They met, and without preamble, talked about a variety of topics, but you couldn't hear what they were saying because you were standing too far off, which was your downfall or perhaps your virtue. The pale man then went to a nearby store and returned with a bottle of refreshment. The Aymara lifted his head as if to look at the blue sky at midday and opened his mouth so that the pale man could pour half a bottle of *mocochinche* down his throat. Then it was the other man's turn, and he opened his mouth so that the stranger could do the same for him. When they'd finished, they both had a good laugh and went on their way as if nothing had happened.

Patinuk, you didn't realize it but you provided me with a wonderful example of real human communication; and at this stage of the game it doesn't concern me that your story doesn't live up to rigorous scientific standards or that it lacks the revolutionary pretensions that often are nothing more than a varnish of paternalism. Patinuk, you're about fifty years old now, and thirty of those years you've dedicated to motion pictures with the enthusiasm of a true scriptwriter. However, when I look at you close up, I see that your life has suffered in the process. But come to think of it, in our country who hasn't suffered? Walking along the street, I think about all the different destinies and my own destiny, a voice without an outlet. I've known Patinuk for a long time, and thanks to him, I managed to survive a job that was a mystery to me inside and out. I'm referring to images that move (like life), the images of motion pictures, which without a voice never come to life.

I wasn't confident enough to play a joke on him since he was a man and I was just a boy, but one night, on a street corner near the university, I decided to listen one last time to his gibberish about fighting to liberate the Indians. I'm sure that he meant what he was saying, but I wasn't convinced by his good intentions. So I screwed up my courage and asked him a question, "Patinuk, what are you going to do when there aren't any Indians and only human beings?" Strangely enough, the question didn't offend him.

Neither was I offended by what happened to me in the park when I secretly observed the illuminated shadows and listened to the weary voice of the deep: "My adventitious readings haven't stayed in my blood nearly so long as the events marked by millenary disasters and triumphs. This is how I learned respect for humility. The countryside is populated by enigmas of the wilderness, despite my elevation—by the grace of the works of the eternal teachers—to universal brotherhood, to the hidden sobs of those who seek the light. When I was nine years old, I hadn't become bad yet; I was at an age when memories don't send up any smoke because the future still hasn't become a horrible, raging fire. It was peace which nature had achieved in my astonished body, in the animal that moos, in the tree that flames up like a faithful emblem of the dawn. But now, distant and alone, I look at the earth and all the unattainable things that hold me here in the presence of the music, love, and death. In some ways I conduct myself like the best members of my race: I observe the horizon and stick my foot into the abyss and descend toward a reality that a girl made possible for me to see."

In spite of the many things I wasn't allowed to read, I've known since childhood that a person has to live to understand the meaning of what is written in the blood; live the way everyone lives, with few complaints and renewed strength. And now I'm here among the crowd, remembering the decisive events of my destiny, conjuring them up. Someone died inside of me to transform me into another being. Someone was the seed of the tree that I've become; that person submitted himself to destruction to favor the happiness that I now contain. I don't know which seed I was, I only know that when I was made of decay and possessed nothing of the diurnal world, I had to succumb to a process of renovation required by the earth. I'm the result of that seed, with happiness on one side and the threat of danger on the other. Being pure *form,* I run the risk of behaving irresponsibly, as do the paternalists. "May the gods free me from such a temptation," I once said. And they saved me, because I'm a father of several children and a child of life, in as much as I'm a child to myself: a reborn father and a child of what was destroyed.

And this is how I travel, alone, remembering my children and recalling other lights and shadows—life carried out in the warmth of amazement and inexhaustible paths. This is how it was, how it had to be. In 1960, I was out walking, just as I am now, with a classmate through the green fields of Tarija, with my notebooks under my arm. It was the last week in November, when a Brazilian poet, who wasn't as famous then as he is now, arrived in the City of the Guadalquivir. He thought of himself as an affiliate of a movement that promised brotherhood, justice, and the destruction of restrictive molds and other banalities. He couldn't have been any other way because when a person is daring enough to seek a happy verbal order—and this is the only thing that choosing poetry as a means of expression can signify—logically his blood will be stirred to anger when he discovers a troublesome external disorder made up of inverted hierarchies and an unbalanced distribution of the earth's wealth.

The Brazilian poet gave two talks for a well-fed, silent audience in one of the most prestigious centers of the provincial capital; I remember the titles well: "Charles Baudelaire and Edgar Allan Poe, Parricide" and "*Martín Fierro* in the Prose of Ezequiel Martínez Estrada and Jorge Luis Borges." As retribution for all his style and subtlety, the well-fed, silent audience offered the speaker a barbecue under an arbor in the beautiful valley. We weren't present as invited guests at the folkloric feast that took place in one of the loveliest gardens along the shore of the Guadalquivir; but thanks to the musical entertainment offered by the locale, we were able to take part in the activities of real intellectuals instead of the trivial events of budding scholars.

While everyone was dancing the *cueca,* the smiling Brazilian poet noticed that an old man was trying to make it up a hill with a bundle of wood that was too heavy for a man of his age to be carrying. The man and the bundle weren't going to make it up the slope, and that was clear. So the good-natured intellectual left his partner on the dance floor, walked over to where the old man was struggling with the bundle, threw it over his shoulder, and carried it up to a level place on the road. No one asked him to perform such a favor, but he did it anyway, and his conscience was clear. Everyone applauded except for the old man, who went on his way without stopping to thank the man who had helped him. An hour later, between the warmth of the wine and the noise of the guitars, no one realized that the old man was back, this time with two bundles of wood. And this time he pronounced loudly what no one had heard when he'd said it softly, "Where's that young man who carried the wood up the hill for me? Now I need him to help me with two bundles."

This anecdote reveals the natural intelligence of people who break their backs along life's roads. It's a kind of lucidity that respects itself and doesn't disdain reality. And there are many examples of this in Bolivia. It's easy to talk about but difficult to achieve, at least for anyone who's trapped in the arrogant molds of modernity, in other words, what one ought to say, ought to do, ought to think. Here's another example, and I didn't make it up. Everybody knows that Che Guevara had asthma when he came to Bolivia, though no one but a rural person would have made the following statement about the disturbance caused by the uniformed defenders of the nation's integrity, put at risk by this "odious stranger" with a beard: "Knowing Che was sick, I could have caught him easy as pie."

These and some of my other examples are flowers that have blossomed from the seed of the *urundel,* the straightest, most robust tree that grows in the forest. A seed falls to the ground and thrives in a perpetual present. No one sees it except those who understand the humble language of everyday existence.

On New Year's Eve, strolling along the street at my normal pace and looking at the dampened lights of the city, I happily sense the power of the seed of the *urundel,* just as the "savage" is happy when he sees that life doesn't change and that everything becomes apparent when a person is in tune with the hymn of silence.

Of course, I'm not a savage because I don't believe in savages, as do minds that entertain themselves with illusions. It's a known fact that the word "savage" is used when someone wants to denounce an indecency, as though roguery were common to the primitive people who roam naked through the forests. In my brief but fundamental escapades through the forests and streams, I've never seen any kind of indecency, much less any sign of the so-called savages' destruction of the land they've inhabited for centuries. To the contrary, they leave it as it was when it was given to them at the beginning of time, covered with flowers, full of rivers and lagoons, and populated by numerous animals fast as lightning. They take from nature what they need to live, without making great piles of things that they aren't going to use. The savage is proud, prudent, and careful as a cat, and with that, he has enough. The same can't be said of the city dweller. One week without running water or deodorant and the entire shining city would become a quagmire, a garbage dump that would chase away any primitive person, who lives, loves, reproduces, and ends the radiant cycle of his life with a prayer, without damaging the landscape for those who follow.

That's how it is with cities, and the Andean city is no exception. Sometimes I see it as though I were dreaming or dead and looking at it from far away. The city is warm and friendly like will-o'-the-wisp, like a sacred fire where souls are purified or lost forever. It contains beautiful things as well as ugly things; I realized this as soon as I saw it. But I decided to stay, just as others decided to leave, and they left. On this very corner— from where I can see the liberator Simón Bolívar on his stone horse—in 1963, I met a couple of Chacobos who had come from the Beni region to find out if they wanted to live in this city they'd heard so much about. They hadn't come of their own volition but because they'd been sent by their tribe. They had crossed sweeping rivers and green, inexhaustible plains, determined to discover the truth and to draw their own conclusions. I joined the group of people who had surrounded the Chacobos, and heard that one of them could read Castilian but was unable to speak the white man's language. His friend, on the other hand, could speak Castilian but couldn't read, and therefore they formed an inseparable pair. They calculated the size of the city and then headed off toward the land where there's no room for nostalgia.

But I am here, nearing the crossroads of a new year, surrounded by anonymous beings. I've been here for twenty years, thinking about what my elders taught me: "They'll kick you when you're down. But if they can't level you with one blow, then they'll say to you, 'How do you do, sir?'" After my first downfall, my soul became stronger than before; and now it says to me, "We'll do what we have to do." I look at the faces in the crowd and go on my way. I walk along submerged in unending time until suddenly I catch sight of Constanza, lost in the tide of existence. I don't know if she's alone or with someone. When a person is part of a crowd it's impossible to tell. It astonishes me that in the city we can cross one another on the street like perfect strangers, each headed in a fixed, unalterable direction. She is on foot, as I am. But people don't make love standing up, except in unusual circumstances; they make love lying down, which is also the most comfortable position for sleeping or dying. We aren't in bed any longer but are making our way through life, walking along not seeing each other, dispersed among the human crowd.

I believe I see Arciles far in the distance, but it can't be he; it's only my desire to see my old friends. But Arciles disappeared off the face of the earth after the military coup of July 17, 1980. They've all disappeared, leaving only their shadows behind in the streets where I now wander like a ghost. Corruption grips the city, and the best thing a man can do is keep his mouth shut while continuing to think. Those of us who've studied every angle of a flea's nose, besides pondering the idea of working in order to eat, discovered a long time ago that the only miraculous thing about thinking is the freedom it imparts. People will use any method to win their freedom: logic, the gun, or tremendous indifference. And they are more noble than their abusers might ever imagine, and also happier.

Walking through the city looking at the buildings and the people, I'm making more turns that a dog before it lies down. Let's start with that expression, "making more turns than a dog before it lies down." Then comes the question: "After which turn does the dog lie down?" And the answer: "After the last one, of course." The next question might be more serious: "Why does it lie down after the last turn?" Or: "Why does a dog go around and around before it lies down?" Because it uses its paws to make sure that nothing is there. It could hurt itself by just plopping down on the ground. Bayonets are all around us and until recently a clandestine government proclaimed from exile that the law of the jungle had taken root in our country—which showed how little they know about the jungle!

Adrián, who knew his plot of land like the back of his hand, made up a story that a sloppy author put into writing under the title "The King of the Jungle," which goes like this:

> Once upon a time a young goat decided he would sit down in the middle of the jungle. A donkey that was passing by saw him there and, after the preliminary greeting, asked him about his work. The kid, who wasn't feeling at all lazy on that luminous morning, told him that now he, the kid, was the king of the jungle and would behave as such. The astonished donkey replied that the lion was the king of the jungle, as everyone knew. The kid then corrected the pleasant, bushy-haired animal, spitting out a string of improprieties. And the donkey, who was totally unprepared to rise up against anything he considered absurd, and knowing that being in control of one's actions doesn't mean controlling their consequences, went on his way spreading the news among his companions of the clear forest. But to confirm the news, all the noisy animals left their jobs and went to the middle of the jungle. The kid, feeling quite confident at that hour of the morning, told each one of his visitors that he was in fact the most important individual in that hierarchical universe. By noon the disagreeable message had reached the ears of the lion, who took off immediately for the middle of the jungle where he said to the alleged monarch, "Hello, kid. Will you please tell me what you think you're doing here in the middle of the jungle?" The kid, enlightened for the first time in his life, said to the furious, maned animal, "Hello, lion, I'm just sitting here telling lies."

This version of the story doesn't belong to Horacio Quiroga, Latin America's best fabulist, but to the crow, which according to Julian Huxley is the only animal with a malicious sense of humor.

A story reveals the personality of the writer, who may choose to praise life or to denounce injustice, usually by the indirect route of the metaphor. Because intellectuals have no appetite for killing or inciting others to kill, their stratagem is different. The masses, on the other hand, may prefer the fox's tactics. The people won't allow imposters to speak on their behalf

just as a fox won't put up with worrisome fleas. He expels them personally from his hide by first finding a watering hole and then making use of
a straw that he carries in his mouth. He begins to wade slowly into the
water, and the alarmed fleas seek refuge on his back. But unfortunately
for the fleas, the water level continues to rise as the fox sinks lower and
lower into the pool, so the fleas have no choice but to climb up on his
head. And there they remain until the water begins to wet their delicate
feet. When they're about to lose hope, their tiny eyes spy the straw, and
the whole gang—heads of households, grandparents, grandchildren,
sweethearts, in-laws, and lovers—rush for this last bit of dry space. There
they sit, contemplating their fate and awaiting the arrival of the last
stragglers; and when all of them, rogues and innocents, have lined up on
the straw, then the fox heaves the whole lot into a vast ocean, into the
middle of the small lagoon, and walks away unashamed and without any
tracks of arrogance, having freed himself of an absurd burden and having
done what was necessary for his well-being, as is natural to those who
follow the dictates of their intelligence.

My nose sniffs the air and likes it in spite of everything. I'm approaching the house where Sanguinetti once lived, one that this notable Bolivian
painter used as a studio. The window illuminates the figures of unknown
persons who have nothing to do with the intellectuals who once got into
a terrible argument about free will. Of course, nothing happened except
that they all got drunk and the problem remained unsolved, defying logic
and augmenting its enigma. The dialogue on free will went into the grab
bag of memories, but what had to happen did happen and to the letter,
though we may think that we have been victims of bad luck or that fortune has given us a light whack across the back.

Tonight, on the eve of a new solar year, my steps resound with determination, maybe because my soul has perceived a former home, a place I
rented when Orana and I lived together. We were newlyweds living in a
place filled with geraniums, and kindly neighbors, where the landlady was
a disgruntled old woman who suffered from the hardships of an extended
maidenhood. For a long while we were visited by many friends, some who
came alone, others who came in groups: Argel, Adrián, Arciles, Patinuk,
Fonical, Santillán, Sanguinetti, Cranach, and many other unnamed

353

acquaintances who made it possible for us to have a civilized social life, because the crisis that would change all of us, forcing each one to look out for his own interests, still hadn't arrived. But many months have passed since we all went our own way—like all Bolivians. We've been torn apart, exiled, murdered, and none too few have been reshaped by that classic moderation that the coward and the traitor use to disguise themselves as friends. We will return to that "civilized social life" because the time of tragedy will be short-lived. But I'd rather see us blown up, torn apart at the seams, if that's what it takes to make us show our true faces. We only become honest in critical situations; we show our teeth and flash our knives. But once the waters have subsided, everything goes back to normal and nothing's changed except that some died and others didn't. And the proof is in the fact that yesterday's irreconcilable enemies have become friends, if not allies, in the circus ring of life.

I don't own a house, so the room filled with geraniums is one of many I've rented in La Paz. I walk through the nocturnal streets remembering a passage from a Latin American author:

> When we imagine the world, nature and all that surrounds us, we think respectfully of mankind's ability to take a desert and make it into a happy home. Thanks to man's desire to create, the most distant places bear the human accent and footprints that restore our faith in ourselves. Amid so much explored and surveyed geography, we must make an enormous effort in order to return to the initial hour. In that unnamed place, dawn wasn't dawn but absolute uncertainty; night, the worst kind of affliction; the mind and heart, a sack of surprises. We've turned the world into a home, say those who have no home and at the end of the day make a precarious roof for their heads, a place to rest their tired bodies. In the morning they're up and searching for new territories. These are the lucid guardians of the initial fear, and they have returned to their nomadic existence to distance themselves from the cowardly minorities who have abandoned the magic route of the traveler.

And as far as I'm concerned: "When a person discovers that consumerism is at the basis of our economy and our everyday conduct as well; and we have reached the extreme, so common today, of acquiring things that only serve to enslave us; and when to justify such a deficiency, considered success in modern terms, we resort to the most bizarre arguments; when all of that has happened, then the body reaches its limit and shouts, 'For the long journey, we must free ourselves of excess baggage.'"

I've always had to be on the move. And especially tonight when my loved ones are waiting for me. So the old adage is fulfilled: When one person travels, another must stay at home. World travelers need to tell their tales to a group waiting around the fire or next to a sophisticated chimney. The narrator must amaze; the listener must be perplexed. But in life, each must have his turn. For many years I stayed at home waiting for someone to return. And now I'm looking at a street in Bolivia's largest city, and I look at all the unfamiliar faces. An insoluble bond unites us, and I walk along opening up a passage for myself into their mysterious dreams; they, too, are sad and pass quickly along toward the other shore, the start of a new year. What I like to do on this day is shout, "Happy New Year, fellow citizens!"

I first came to La Paz at midnight on December 31, and entered the city on January 1, 1961, confused about my future and without a friend in sight. I'd been traveling all night on a train full of drunks. Despite the alcohol I'd imbibed, I wasn't drunk, possibly because I was so anxious to see the famous City of Illimani, "cradle of liberty and tomb of tyrants." On the train car it was pure bedlam; some sang while others sobbed uncontrollably. Tears don't require translation; they're the same anywhere on earth. Songs, on the other hand, vary from place to place; and though the ones the happy drunks were singing weren't unknown to me, the accent of the songsters was strange, unlike any I'd heard on the plains. At the station a fight broke out between an Indian man and woman, more violent than any fight I'd ever seen; so violent, in fact, that a man hit the Indian man on the chin and the Indian woman immediately kicked the defender of the weaker sex and knocked him off his feet.

The next day I left the hotel and began to walk down the first wide avenue I came to, not knowing how to reach the downtown area of this organism that served as the seat of Bolivia's government. But I was in luck and happened to run into a friend who was a kicker for Chaco Oil Club. Bruno Audivert let me stay at the club house, and everything went along smoothly until he got kicked in the ankle, lost his position on the team, and had to go back to the province; and then I had to deal with a ferocious dog and become a scribe to Ciscar Zenteno so I could spend the night in the room of a budding engineer, Argel.

Now I'm paused on the brink of a new year, 1981. And I'm walking open-eyed down a street that I used to walk down with a head full of dreams. I walk along as sure-footed as a trained animal, never hesitating. I come to the fence of the only zoological park in the city. Not even a shadow remains of the establishment where I got drunk along with numerous university students who sang the "Internationale." "Don't be a reactionary! Sing!" they told me. But I didn't sing, not because I was a reactionary or a wet blanket but because I didn't know the words to the famous hymn. That December of 1961, I took a good look at the hard-headed young man who was trying to get me to sing and to become a revolutionary. Five years later, he was always taking off or coming back, and on one of his return trips, he brought some medicine for the asthmatic Che Guevara but was never able to deliver it to him. Eventually he ended up in the United States where he became an anthropologist and one of the most unbending Indian scholars on Latin America. Notwithstanding the meanderings and misdeeds of this singer of the "Internationale," his friend Che Guevara was even more of a blockhead because the whole time he was in Ñancahuazú he was tramping on weeds that provide excellent relief for the asthma sufferer.

I'm speaking of a time when I had many friendships, though Adrián still wasn't among them, despite the fact that both of us were from the south. About that time I was staying at an inn that offered two entrances to its guests. I remember a tree next to one of the exit doors. But now I'm near the real inn, not the one in my memory. And I see that the new owners have erased even the shadows of the former occupants. I look at the tree and see that it's old but strong, fortified by the hardships of the past, now a friend to oblivion. I've never forgotten that tree, maybe because of a rainy Sunday, a gray afternoon whipped by winds that brought torrents of icy water. I'd been studying all day and decided to stick my nose out, and there was a dog standing in front of the inn; he wasn't pissing and he wasn't going on his way. He was just standing there, as if the rains had left him addled. I called to him and he came, sad and obedient. And he stayed with us a week until we took in another dog that was skinnier than he was, and he got offended and left. The years have gone by, and here I am again, in front of one of my former dwellings, feeling overwhelmed by events but strengthened by a desire to move on.

The girl who later became my sweetheart was no more than seven then, but I am in a pensive mood on account of a tall, pale, slender, beautiful young woman from the Beni, who was a little like Orana but was different when she laughed or when she sat quietly with her long, loose hair flowing into the mysteries of womanhood. She was slightly melancholy and lived at Plaza Villarroel, until one day she took off and was never heard from again.

And I ask myself what good it does remembering my former lodgings or placing the shadow of a memory over the image of a lovely girl who isn't one any longer. I'll remember her one last time, before confessing that I really don't enjoy recalling all the places that I lived but that weren't my home; though my prodigal heart was never damaged by it. But yes, I would like to remember the first room I rented with my own money, which I earned working as an office boy. True, my first night there, some scary individual tried to steal everything I owned, but that didn't stop me from being happy, because in that room I began to collect my first personal possessions which allowed me to know, not proudly but with certainty, that I had the minimum that was needed to reside any place on earth.

But my happiness was short-lived because as soon as I began to look at people and things, I noticed the face of an indigent child, doubtless the son of parents who'd come from the provinces. It didn't help to think that sooner or later a life hacked out with a machete would win out over one built on trickery and oppression. God only knows who is more affected by the contradictions in life, the people who suffer or the people who make others suffer without realizing it. At any rate, only maturity allows us to assess correctly what occurs in this valley of tears. I'm reminded of something that happened to a rural man who was terribly poor and had numerous children. He was very happy when he had managed to save a hundred *pesos,* with which he hoped to overcome any calamity that might befall him. So he was walking along the road feeling happy and thinking of his uncertain future, until he came to the usual fork in the road where he ran into his best friend, a great practical joker who had just lost a son. "*Hermano,*" said the sad joker, "you have to lend me some money to bury my boy." The man with the hundred *pesos* thought for a second and then handed his friend the money, not knowing or ever finding out which was more important in life, putting food on the table or burying the dead.

Of course, this kind of anecdote doesn't suit the people who are interested in cultivating the intellect or developing society's analytical powers to the maximum. That kind of person doesn't have time to waste on minor things; they're too busy trying to change the structure and the infrastructure of an unjust social order. But I'm talking to the people on the street, because when they talk among themselves—when we talk among ourselves—they (we) can talk about anything and everything. For example, I've just seen a man who needs to get something off his chest. He's the same man who said to me a decade ago, "Stubbornness leads to chaos." And it's true, obstinacy supposes an abyss; but it's just as true that obstinacy produces a resplendent apparition of images that give meaning to the world. Such respectable and opposing points of view require a decision, if not to say a choice.

I'm inclined to go the second route, professed by an old Aymara who sits wrapped in the solitude of the night, removed from the hustle and bustle of the city. I greet this ancient man, and he remains seated, asking nothing of anyone. His silence voices what his grandparents, also very poor, often said: "To be no better off, why bother? And we can do no better." He's been sitting there for thousands of years, and that is why he knows what we want and what disturbs us. Maybe he's a Callawaya and has the wisdom of those who perform the rites of life, heart, and spirit, in darkness; or maybe he's a medicine man who knows not only the plants and herbs of the earth like an open book, but has also traveled barefoot over the rough and roadless places of the human soul. The city, desirous of this man's blessing, acknowledges in private what it refuses to recognize in public—his spiritual authority. Maybe he isn't a Callawaya but some simple human being who has stopped to rest at the side of the road, at a distance from the opulent multitude. His eyes are sunk back in his head, and he seems to be staring from the depths of his past, not at the present but into the future. He is the *present*, his own springboard to a state of peacefulness that he hasn't asked for but in him becomes grander and more noble.

He is the unalterable *here and now*. Adrián knew this well, which is why he wandered off from the group of geology students who were on a field trip in the Altiplano. When night came to that arid plain of silence, Adrián had no choice but to seek refuge in a shack that was only a dot on the broad, unfamiliar landscape and talk with an old Aymara, exactly like the man I'm casually observing on the wide avenue of the city. This situation is quite similar to that one because my friend didn't know the Aymara language and the Indian didn't know Castilian. But they could communicate through signs, pauses, and amicable silences, with a dish of *ocas y chuños* for the engineering student and some straw and ponchos to protect him from the bitter cold of night. At midnight, next to the fire, the old Aymara untied a bundle of secrets knot by knot, singling out mementos and articles of clothing until he reached the final bundle containing a publication which Adrián knew well. *The Second Declaration of Havana* wasn't translated to Aymara, but the man from the Bolivian Andes somehow knew that this document pertained to him. I look into this Aymara's eyes and say *adiós* and he responds with a slight movement of his head and continues chewing with such discretion that no one would suspect that he has coca leaves in his mouth.

What does this man have to do with the fate of the nation? A great deal and nothing. Like everyone, I have to be inside by nine o'clock at night, and like everyone, I hear the permanent droning of the military convoys. The trucks come and go with their cargo of coca leaves, delivering them to some unknown place where a drug that's destroyed the illusions of the nation's capital is being made. Some consider it tragic, others, laughable. Coca, the most important ritual plant of Andean culture, has been converted into something demoniacal for Western civilization; it has become history's subterranean vengeance. How else might we explain the fact that a path to religion has been turned into a bottomless pit for the men who through centuries performed the role of executioner among the marginal communities of the continent? What must the Aymara be made of to meet life head-on every day and rub elbows with the devil—which he does when he chews coca—and then rise up buoyantly from such a deep miry place? Any person from this region is careful when he travels because he knows that the pit isn't there for you to fall into but to help you appreciate the right road as you ought to. American, after all, he makes use of the coca leaf, but not to keep from facing harsh reality or to propel himself into a world of fiction. Far away, in silent, unending solitude, he accepts the fact that life is like the land, full of high hills and deep valleys that lead to vast plains; and therefore, we must walk it at a rhythm that our bodies can adjust to and according to the capacity of our lungs. Reaching the top of the hill can be a reward, but anyone who continuously seeks the heights is risking addiction to the precipice. A real traveler by definition stays clear of harmful habits.

While I walk through the city which has been liberated for a single night, I imagine the feelings of those who celebrate the arrival of another year and the hope of those whose feet are touching the earth. My heart is with the second group, with those who grab hold of life with their hands, without the protection and the deception of transparent wrappings, and provide an illusion of "realism" to console those who've never known what it's like to be down and out.

It never occurred to me to look for "realism" in "fiction," maybe because I've encountered demons of every size and shape, and in circumstances that discretion forbids me to mention. So I laugh and start to tremble. One time there was no work for my body, and my soul became very weary. Then I went to visit a friend, not so he would find me a job but just to talk. And who would have thought it, but he saw through me in an instant and did something he'd never dared to do before; he tried to convert me to a religious sect. On another occasion I went over to Cranach's house during a time when he was involved in cocaine trafficking; and to keep up with the times, I decided to take a sniff of the white powder, which probably remained trapped in the hairs of my nostrils because I didn't travel to any paradise except the one that my dreams forged every day.

Finally, in 1970, when I returned to La Paz to try my luck—after breaking my back looking for work in other places—I decided one day to go for lunch at a place where I hadn't been invited. It was the end of December, and I was alone, as I am now, waiting to see what God would ask of me. I didn't have a *real* to my name, and I ate with great relish in the home of a woman with lovely green eyes. As I was leaving, she slipped a manuscript under my jacket. When I got to Villa Fátima and while I was pissing, I remembered the folder, which I untied and placed on top of a pile of papers. Then I turned around to observe the loneliness of the world and felt very sad, seeing how the wind of the Andean evening was whipping the leaves of the red geraniums. I looked at the calamine roofs and felt lonely at my heart, and my body shuddered as it inhaled the solitude. That wasn't the first time I'd felt alone in the world, nor will it be the last. But it didn't matter. I discovered this when I first realized that I was born drugged but had come to exalt life. My body, drunk by nature, has always been a primitive yet heavenly hymn. So how am I to understand people who take drugs only to turn their backs on life?

And now that an Aymara Indian wearing a cap has been made the demon of the community, I'm more convinced than ever of the brutality of such a pretense and the need for revenge. The old Aymara continues chewing the coca, as if he were oblivious to it all. But Satan can't deceive me, much less this living symbol of other ages. History's subterranean vengeance. The fallen angel is venting his fury on us and on others, with modern weapons and subtlety to disguise his roguery. The punishment falls on our souls because our heads don't know how to free themselves from an exclusively Western way of thinking. Poor heads, they've replaced the heart, and to cry with joy or sing with anguish they use a confusing language unlike the voice of the hills or the silence of the desert. The silence may be the same as the one that whispers an irrefutable truth in my ear, "the people have only two fates: to transform the world into words or to change it at the point of a gun." I think anxiously and tenderly of Jursafú and the Other, who have engaged in painful periods of searching. While the first, who has used various names, spent a lifetime preparing himself for the word, the second began to suspect that his patience was running out and that dying with dignity would be better than allowing his silence to put an honest face on the injustices of the scoundrels who'd taken over the country.

My steps ring with conviction through the endless streets of the city. And I greet all the kind, unfamiliar faces that surround me on this last day of the year. I could just as well be in the countryside, but I'm walking through the city, comparing the two lifestyles and seeing things for what they are. I live in another world which has become pure nostalgia for an apparently lost universe. I have nothing but a certain knowledge of heeding the silent axis of my being. As an heir to the experience of anonymous muleteers, I know that when they can't knock a man down with one blow, they make him a gift of perpetual presence, where there's no room for remembering things that are lost or for gathering harmless courage for the future. I intuit that perpetual presence in my body; and I allow it to flow, observing the living and the dead, with my soul in the vast river of nature. And if nothing seems to matter to me, it's because my inner workings are involved in fundamental things. What's important is for people not to be blind to what is fundamental for their neighbors or end up speaking for everyone and giving nothing to anyone.

Sometimes, lost in the leaf pile of a blind universe, I've heard it said that "man is good until society perverts him." But I say that if a man is good, why would he stop being good when he becomes part of a community? Could anyone be considered good if he's good only when he's alone? To the contrary, I think that people are good, noble, and valiant. And they aren't perverted since they continue to build communities to their own measure. Truths haven't changed; the only thing that's changed is the language used to express them. And it's changed because nothing that was proclaimed has been fulfilled. The first people lived their truths without the benefit of tradition as a reference. Today people support their truths with history but live in fear of admonition, thinking their work may be useless.

But the alphabet isn't an adornment; it's for writing and reading, which means tearing up the original and plunging into the foliage of powerful language. And we're happy tossing the originals away and entering open-eyed into lucid memory, which saves language from petrification. I'm now a prisoner of many inept forms of expression, like "disgraceful sinecure," "unjust calumny," "condemnable theft," and other such phrases. But aren't all sinecures disgraceful by definition, as are thefts condemnable? Which implies that we are swimming in a sea of unnecessary adjectives.

Behold the great city, which Alberto once told me about with such innocence, a city made of dreams, washed by time, submitted to the transparency of the Andean heights, "luxury of the dawn of day," according to one La Paz poet. I respect his opinion though my heart disagrees, because for me it's been a purifying flame that's singed everything, even my memories; and the gods have left me as I am, relieved of all excess baggage. I'm not the Other, who probably died, weary of the pace of a world he didn't want to be part of, a victim of violence; though he himself took on the violence of lucid existence. I'm not Jursafú, who put up with a hurly-burly and a half and took many a violent fall, only because he hoped to put the Other's life into words. On this New Year's Eve, I'm allowing myself the luxury of walking around without a single document identifying me as one of the damned in this world of credits and debits, without anything that tells the authorities who I am or what entraps me in the humility of a routine. I'm just walking along in search of the sacred shadows where the diverse, contradictory elements of life jump and play. Endless life, resplendent and new, obtuse and opaque, small in its complexity and grandiose in its simplicity.

The debits have changed me into a being without a name, and I direct my steps toward a party for friends and relatives. I've decided to walk down every street of this city where history rushes past and life goes on. On every corner I see that life continues, blends with an ancient past changed into air of passive freshness. I have no name and nonetheless I perceive the goodness of a universe, powerful because it's human. I am crossing the ambit of history amid the living and the dead, on the way to my destiny, as if I were reaching the last page of a book that was shifting and quaking. My steps sound like the last words of a text that overtakes me. I will no longer write letters to the other world, or about the other universe, because the people whom I loved and who were emblems of nostalgia begin to breathe happily in my redeemed blood. And in homage to the seed of the *urundel,* I have recovered those loved ones.

The will to live in foreign lands condemned me to a long silence, to the redemption of other universes. I'm coming to a lovely home where my loved ones are waiting for me. From this high point of the city, I can see all of La Paz, illuminated. My eyes behold the light, dampened by a vague emotion. I haven't stopped; I continue walking. My ears have just heard the first fire crackers typical of midnight on New Year's Eve. In a few seconds, Bolivians will put aside ill will, meanness, and the love of money, and embrace one another with brotherly love. But tomorrow they will get out of bed wanting to make up for lost time and immune to the spectacle of misery. The festivities heighten just as I reach the house where my loved ones have gathered. The sounds of the rockets become increasingly violent, escape from the ambit of dreams and penetrate reality.

I'm reminded of the last sequence of a Bolivian movie, maybe the first important movie made in our country. Who would have believed that twelve minutes of film could denounce the hatred of some and the poverty of others. And the reaction, unexpected by the minority: striking workers and now soldiers in tall boots marching and armed to the teeth. And the next take, with the anemic, thread-bare people positioned with rocks and rifles along the modest fences of their marginal territory, definitively entrenched in fatigue that became rebellion. Nothing violent has happened yet, but it's in the air, like an ambiguous longing. And now the shooting begins, from those who've come to destroy a common but unshared world. They don't have to wait for an answer. Volleys of gunfire announce the battle, pitiless and to the death.

The spectator can no longer see the actors. He only sees the images of malnourished children, barefoot and homeless, standing at the top of a hill, listening to the machine guns. The language of need has made them strong before their time, and now they feel that they are being defended by those who courageously have taken responsibility for their lives. There's no respite in this unequal battle, perhaps as now, when life has become pure fiction. The rockets aren't innocent fire-crackers but the start of a luminous day full of unexpected promises we're willing to die for. A revolution. The people up in arms against infamy and shame, at last the voice of rebellion, because as the Other said, "Offenses have their limit and silence can talk." But the great store of repressed emotion now gives energy to the supreme act. The long-awaited liberation has exploded into deaf thunder, and those who held back because of fear have embraced one another in the solidaric struggle. The rattle of the machine guns and isolated shots have changed the city into a thundering voice.

I approach the fence of the residence whose value isn't contained in the materials used for its construction. The entire house is made of a transparent substance, like the substance of dreams, and I have managed to arrive at the supreme hour, in love with the truth. As I draw near the large windows, I can appreciate the joy of the people who have gathered there: unfamiliar men with beards, glasses, mustaches, and long locks of hair, and lovely women, young and old, and children radiant with hope for a better world of wisdom and frivolity. They all seem to have escaped from a bonfire, somewhat singed but still able to represent Bolivian intellectuals. Doubtless, they are good people, as one would expect of those who have ennobled their hearts in the bonfire of suffering. I feel sure that the majority have suffered long and repeated periods of exile, and many are relatives of the martyrs who have recently reclaimed the country. It's the kind of brotherhood or secret sect that prospers in life's scenario, dispelling the idea that to understand life you must abolish all its sacraments.

After walking for so long, I ask myself if I really wanted to come here, if there ever was a time when I could have been their friend. I haven't an answer. But I continue standing at the door of this temple of the initiated. My eyes are still fairly good, and I can see Orana inside the house. I am surprised by her tenderness and her transfigured face; she looks vaguely like Constanza. Or maybe it's Constanza who looks like Orana. Like me, she wanted to live according to the dictates of her heart, and her body reflects her suffering. Like everyone, she has a history that no one knows and that the profane's curiosity will never discover. Like everyone, she can only converse with her soul when she's in the privacy of her own unceremonious world. She is talking to the artist Sanguinetti, cordial but reserved, full of Aymaran sobriety and silent to a fault.

Things are happening with incredible speed, but my memory—which is my recompense—traps every detail. There's Patinuk with his seal-like temperament and his bulletproof goodness, surrounded by friends who are also my friends. Everyone I've known in the City of Illimani is there, except the dead whom I carry toward the purified territory of nostalgia. It's midnight, and they all embrace amid the confusion, like the survivors of a shipwreck.

The great cycle has been fulfilled. Many have picked up the gun to guarantee this small happiness, and some have remained with their hands stretched out toward the unknown with the nobility of extinction on their faces. My mind wanders toward the valleys, plains, and the hills of this country called Bolivia. My eyes encompass the entire land where many struggle from dawn to dusk to make their way. But its light escapes me. I must cry long and hard in the lap of death to recapture that image, transparent and retouched for our dreams, an everyday occurrence for the muleteer. There's a certain dignity in the brotherly embrace of our country, magical from beginning to end. And the diverse tongues of its inhabitants are nothing more than an attempt to translate the primordial silence that shelters us into human languages.

It's midnight, and my solidaric soul lifts its eyes toward a neutral sky filled with indifferent stars. A great moment illuminates us all, those who are powerful and those who come from distant plains, those who've returned home bearing the sign of illumination and those who never strayed afar, those who are mute and those who involved themselves with words, those who sought love but met up with the devil, those who have died and those yet to be born; a great moment illuminates us all, even those who never lift their eyes. I lower my eyes, overwhelmed by the inexplicable weight of solitude, and I ring the bell three times, as I usually do. But my habits and superstitions seem to go unnoticed amid the uproar and confusion of voices, until finally a stranger comes to the door. He welcomes me cordially but with some misgiving I say hello and try to enter the place where all my friends are gathered. But he politely and cautiously stops my advance.

"Your name, sir," he inquires, protected by transparent lenses.

It wasn't then that I discovered I had no profane name but much earlier when I overcame inertia and burst into life and began walking until I stumbled upon an uneven landscape at the edge of a blindly flowing river that was soft and friendly like a dream. Pointlessly, the man repeats his question. Through the crowd, I see Constanza with her honest smile and at her side the smiling Jursafú and all his smiling friends. I remember the two-headed dog and make my way back to a universe of blind certainties, looking for my true body, gliding slowly among the festering shadows that melt definitively into the city of combatants, into the thundering noise of solitude.